L'il Darlin'

Peril, Loss *and* Love
in the Convict Lake Backcountry
of the High Sierras

November 2020

SANDY STACEY

Dear Verna,
I hope you enjoy my story!
So much love,
Sandy
aka
Kims Mom

ISBN: 978-1-09830-632-8

Acknowledgments

This book is dedicated to my mother and father who gave me life and education.

To Donald Freed, master teacher, comrade, trusty friend, and his wife, Patty, for encouraging and guiding me in their weekly tutorials as I brought the ones I love back to life through my story. To Marvin, the force that brought me to the house of Patty and Donald and all my writing classmates who patiently listened and encouraged me chapter after chapter, after chapter. And to classmate and editor Lisa Haviland, who patiently, efficiently and successfully brought my work to completion.

To Cowboy Bobby who holds the memories in his heart with me and helped me to keep the courage to write this story. To Chub for his encouragement and support in the darkest of times and Floyd for his loyal and tireless support on the trail; lastly to Will Robertson the youngest of the cowboys.

To my amazing daughter, Kim, and her husband, John, who cheered me on with love and support in bringing the book together. To my son, Steve, and his wife, Judy, for their love and support during my writing. To my beautiful daughter Lori who kept the printer paper and ink flowing while writing; and to her loving family. To my cousins, Richard Wasserman and David Wilk, for their lifelong guidance and support. To all the Fogelsong family who gave me my start in life and never let me go, especially Aunt Gen, Pop, Nino, Shelley Theresa and Cathy.

To my many friends who have stood by me, held my hand and encouraged me from start to finish, especially Lucienne and Oscar, Bill and Judy, neighbors Hal and Cecily, and lifelong friend Eva Rodick and daughter 'Becka. To our many Colorado friends for their encouragement and for bringing my story to life with help of the Loveland Harrington Arts Alliance.

To all at the Elk's Lodge #2389 in Yucaipa who encouraged, loved, laughed, sang with me and never let me lose faith in my efforts over these past years. Johnny and Deanna's Karaoke at the Lodge makes Saturday nights so beautiful and special for Cowboy Bobby and me.

Special thanks to my support team- Dr. Srikureja who saved my life a few months before Marvin introduced me to the Freeds and to Paul Richards, craniosacral specialist and his amazing side-kick therapy dog, Manny, who freed me from 50 years of debilitating memories.

And extra special thanks to Tom Sparks, hair stylist who has kept me coiffed through storm, chaos, trials, tribulations and the angst that goes with life, writing and publishing.

To my eight grandchildren and four great-grands who will pass this on long after me.

To cover artist Jack Olson, Severence, Colorado, who brought Suzy horse, the mule Midnight and me to life at Convict Lake.

And very, very special thanks to all of you readers who enjoy my story.

"The Last Day"

May 20, 1980

"Over! All gone! Over! All gone! But is it?
Could it just be the beginning?"

~ Sandy Stacey

L'il Darlin's last day on the trail shines bright and glittering with blue skies and fluffy pillows of white clouds, their crests glorious in the sunlight, but L'il Darlin' could not see the glory; the dust from the hooves of the horses ahead blinded the beauty. She pulled her kerchief over her nose – too late. The dust seeped into her mind, turned into dust devils, galloping, mocking, echoing the clicking sounds of the horses' hooves on the slate rock trail, and turned into a frenzied song stuck in her mind like a broken carousel. "Over! All gone!" The dust devils mocked and sang, "Over! All gone!"

L'il Darlin' shivered and her legs shook so hard against the sides of her horse Suzy, that Suzy turned to look back at her, ears alert, eyes questioning. She must stop shaking, but failed because her body remembered what her mind was desperate to forget.

She could not let the dust devils get to her. She had a job to do and she was the only one who could do that job. Chub, his dog Poco, Bobby and Floyd were 3,000 feet below, back at the barn waiting. L'il Darlin' was high above on the 30-inch wide trail up the mountain taking a young couple to the meadow below Lake Mildred, a perfect place to spend the last day of their honeymoon.

She looked down at the lake below her and words refused to be erased from her mind, instead they spilled onto her tongue, words she spoke daily to the tourists as their guide: "*You are looking at Convict Lake, 7,580 feet elevation, one of the deepest in the Eastern High Sierras – a depth of 140 feet of sparkling, brilliant, turquoise blue water, so clear you can follow the rays of the sun to depth of 30 feet or more.*"

But today, the last day of her mountain life, her words were not spoken; they were stored in her mind. Today, she used her eyes to see, to save, collect her last mental photographs of the lake's astounding, magical reflections of the mountains and surrounding trees, beautiful trees draped in dappled leaves of green, celebrated the coming of spring, the rebirth of the earth – but L'il Darlin' will have no mountain rebirth. She will leave the mountains tomorrow. She has a job to do today.

The young honeymoon couple had turned down the road this morning on a whim. Ordinarily, Chub wouldn't have booked their ride today, but this wasn't an ordinary day, so L'il Darlin' took them to see the meadow they had heard about, the bride rode ahead of her, the groom in the lead. She needed to give all her attention to them, their horses, her job, her commitment to Chub.

The sun's rays warmed her cheeks and shoulders. She slid the zipper of her jacket open, slipped her arms out of the sleeves to let the sun shine warm on her shoulders, but ice inside her body chilled and burned. How unfair, this last ride of her mountain life was being spent behind a couple full of firsts, but L'il Darlin' mustn't think about that now. She must keep her attention on the couple ahead, the bride riding her daughter's horse, Bridger, a mustang born on the open range, a bay with a black mane and tail, red tinged in the sunlight, white snip and blaze down his nose, and the groom riding Cotton, Cowboy Bobby's "helluva" cow horse, a sorrel with three white socks, a reddish mane and tail, a long strip of white down his face.

L'il Darlin is heartbroken that this is all coming to an end, but she can't change the circumstances. She must do the only thing she can do: collect and imprint on her mind the sight of the mountains, trail, sun, sky, clouds, moon, stars; save the scent of the trees and the clean, clear, fresh air; the pungency of mules, horses, trail dog Poco; the aroma of Chub's sun-warmed leather vest, the smell of his Bull Durham tobacco. She must collect the sound of the lapping waves of the lake, of the tumbling stream, the screaming of the wind and, above all, the sound of Chub's soft, southern voice telling the tourists the story of how Convict Lake got its name.

L'il Darlin's mind plays back Chub's voice telling the legend a little way up the trail, before the tourists reach the noisy stream. Chub stops his big horse, Greydog, turns back to the tourists and their horses, points his big hand to the mountains, gives a little cough into his fist to clear his throat and – *"Look there, folks, we're gonna ride the trail the convicts rode in these mountains. It was September 17, year 1871, six convicts totin' two Henry Rifles, the best repeatin' rifle a' that time, hid out after they'd escaped the prison in Carson City, Nevada. They hid out fer days with nothin' ta eat but rose hip berries."*

The tourists would lean over their saddles to look at the fleshy, bright colored fruit of the roses right under their horses' feet, then Chub would give another little cough into his big hand and start up again: *"A local posse caught up with three of the convicts on September 27, 1871, Black, Morton, and J. Bedford Roberts. Black killed posse member Robert Morrison, a 34-year-old Wells Fargo agent, merchant and groom-to-be. Walked up behind 'em, pointed his gun at the back of Morrison's head an' fired. Killed 'im instantly. The Paiute Indian guide, Mono Jim, was also killed."*

The tourist's eyes would follow Chub's big finger as he pointed up the trail. Mt. Morrison, 12,241 feet over there, is named after Robert Morrison, an' the smaller mountain, 10,669 feet, is named after Mono Jim."

The tourist's wide eyes go back and forth in their heads as Chub points out the sights. *"The lake an' stream got re-named from 'Diablo Lake' to 'Convict Lake' an' the stream got re-named from 'Monte Diablo Creek' to "Convict Creek" 'cause a' that ambush."* Then Chub would turn Greydog around, wave his big hand to the tourists to follow him and head for Convict Creek.

The climb was steeper; the wind picked up. L'il Darlin's attention locked on the honeymooners, their safety, their dreams delivered. The trail was at its narrowest, 25 inches wide, the drop on the left side, "a long way down" as the cowboys say, maybe about 1,000 feet. Suddenly, the bride stopped Bridger, shifted her weight in the saddle, turned her head over her shoulder, cupped her hand to the side of her mouth and hollered, "Hello!"

What's she doing? "Are you all right?" This isn't a good place to stop for conversation. The husband stopped Cotton and turned in his saddle to look at them.

The bride called out again. "Yes, I'm fine. I want to tell you, I've gotten strong feelings from you that you're a writer!"

"A rider?" The wind whipped their voices around. L'il Darlin' stood in her stirrups, grabbed her saddle horn, leaned forward as far as she could to hear the bride better.

"No, a writer!" The bride enunciated the word with a bite. Her words carried back on the wind. "I'm a psychic! Your destiny is in your writing."

L'il Darlin' could not believe it! The bride ahead of her on the trail suddenly identified herself as a psychic, tells L'il Darlin' that she is a writer and her destiny is in her writing? L'il Darlin' sat back down in her saddle with a thud. This wasn't the time or place to make sense out of the psychic bride's words. The sun was high; Cotton, Bridger and Suzy were restless, moving their feet in a little dance on the slate rock. They were about an hour before the meadow. They moved forward. The psychic bride's words kept repeating in L'il Darlin's mind: a "writer," a "destiny"? She had never thought about writing, yet thoughts began to take shape, thoughts of writing about these past years in the mountains.

She shut her eyes to remember the first time Suzy swam her across Lake Mildred, the brilliant blue lake above them, the first in a chain of lakes that made her picture a broken sapphire necklace clinging to the necks of the mountains. Memories tumbled through her brain like a kaleidoscope: the canyon where the morning sun turned the orange and pink layers of rock into flaming ruby and gold candles; the canyon where huge expanses of glittering granite and rock astound your eyes, the sun playing along mountain peaks of purple, brown, black against a sky full of clouds, huge and white, sharp-edged against the blue, gold-edged near the sun, as if someone had run a pen around them in gold ink.

And Chub, he fell in love with these mountains years ago, like a man falls in love with a woman, "'til death do us part."

The groom called out to L'il Darlin' after she had safely brought him and his psychic bride to their destination; the meadow was beautiful, beyond their wildest dreams. L'il Darlin' turned Suzy back toward the trail as the psychic bride called out, "Remember your destiny."

L'il Darlin' turned to the psychic bride and groom, nodded and smiled to them. Floyd would come up later in the day to return them to the barn. She looked at the psychic bride and blinked as the bride's image turned into a distorted, puzzling reflection in what appeared to be an ancient, polished, broken, mirror. She grabbed herself, squeezed, trying to keep her spirit from draining out through the soles of her boots, as the psychic bride's smiling, waving reflection turned into herself so many summers ago, so happy, so blissfully ignorant of the future.

L'il Darlin' and Suzy began their descent down the trail, Suzy's back legs slid over the shale, her front legs walked, one two three, one two three, one two three, a wayward waltz dropping from the clouds taking the form of their two shadows against the mountain wall, and whispering as soft as spiders' legs on silk into her ears: "Remember your destiny; remember your destiny."

PART I

THE EARLY YEARS
1937-1970

"Examination of our past is never time-wasting.
Reverberations from the past provide learning rubrics
for living today."

~ Kilroy J. Oldster

CHAPTER 1

42 years earlier

September 1938
Monticello School for Girls
Los Angeles, California
4 years old

"The farther back you can look, the farther forward you will see."

~ Winston Churchill

Mama's sad; I'm happy. She's shaking; I'm excited. Look at my pretty school! The school is so big, so many pretty stairs and trees and flowers and a big, pretty door. Mama says if I like the school, I can stay. I like it! I want to stay here. I don't want to go back to the apartment. I don't want to hide anymore.

Mama rings the pretty doorbell. It makes a big sound, ding, dong, ding, dong! A little lady in a long white apron opens the door. We go inside to a big room. It's so pretty! All the walls are white and the floors are shiny grey. A big glass table is in the middle with lots of tall, pretty pink roses in a pretty white vase and a big round mirror with a gold frame is on the wall. I can see Mama in it, but I can't see me. Where am I? I'm not hiding. I don't have to hide here like at the apartment. Why can't I see myself in the pretty gold mirror? I hold Mama's hand tighter.

The little apron lady takes us into another big, pretty room with lots and lots of books from the floor way up to the ceiling and there's a big tall ladder with wheels. I could climb up the ladder to the very top and hide behind those books, but I don't have to hide here. This place is for children. This is a school for children. Mama and Daddy would have to hide here, but not me.

I don't want Mama to go, but she can't stay. She gives me a big hug and kiss. I want to cry, but Mama shakes her head; she'll "come back tomorrow." Mrs. McBride smiles at me and takes my hand. The stairs are too big for me to climb, but Mrs. McBride helps me. She smells good, and there's a white lace hanky in her sleeve that smells like sweet flowers when it gets close to my nose.

We go upstairs and go into a big, pretty pink and white room with lots of windows and pink ruffly beds. They look funny. I like Mama's big bed at the apartment. It comes out of the wall with a big thunk when the bed hits the floor. Mama lifts me to the middle and I sit there and wait for her to get in so I can snuggle against her. I use her arm for my pillow and she holds me and sings to me so I can go to sleep. I can't go to sleep without my pretty Mama's song.

It's time for bed. The little apron lady helps me get into soft, pretty pink pajamas. I close my eyes and hear Mama's voice singing. I can feel her arms around me. I smell her perfume. Daddy doesn't like her perfume, but Mama and I do. I'm so sleepy. My eyes close and the scary dream comes back again.

There's a big, dark, noisy street with big buildings. We go into one of the tall dark buildings and step into an elevator. A man asks Mama what floor we want. She tells him to go to the top. He pulls a big iron gate across the elevator. The elevator is slow and noisy. We go to the top and the elevator man pushes open the gate so we can get out. There's a hallway with lots of doors with names on them. Mama goes to one and pushes it open. There is a big room with a desk and light. It smells funny. A big, tall man with a long beard and funny little cap on his head gets up from the desk and starts looking at me. Mama talks to him and goes to the big, tall, dark window, puts her head against it and starts to cry. Her tears make lines on the glass. The man shouts at Mama. She turns around and pulls me behind her. He reaches out his hand and gives her something. Mama takes me down a long, long, cold, cold, dark hallway. She can't stop crying. My pretty Mama can't stop crying.

The sun hurts my eyes. Where am I? A tinkly bell rings. I rub my eyes. Where's Mama? Who are those girls? Where's Mama?

The little apron lady brings me a white blouse, blue skirt, white socks, and brown and white shoes. Everything's so nice and feels and smells so good. Ummmm — the little apron lady brushes my hair. I like this school! I want to stay here! The apron lady takes me to the top of the stairs with the other girls. Oh, no! They're all in line! They look like me! How will Mama find me! We all look the same. How will the golden mirror know I'm here? I can't stay here. How will Mama find me?

Mrs. McBride comes out of her door. She's so tall and pink and smells so good. She laughs, "Good morning, ladies!"

"Good morning, Mrs. McBride." They hold out their skirts, put one foot behind them and dip down. I don't know what they're doing.

"Did you sleep well?"

"Yes, Mrs. McBride"

"Then let's go down to breakfast."

She goes to the top of the stairs and the girls make a line behind her. She slides one pink toe off the top stair and puts it down carefully on the step below. Then she slides the other pink toe off the step and puts it down beside the first one. She talks as she moves. "Heads high, ladies, don't look down; back straight, eyes straight ahead! Fingertips lightly on the banister, other hand held gracefully at your side and smile, ladies, smile. You are making an entrance, a first impression. Look and act your best. Your future might depend upon the way you enter a room."

I don't know what she is doing or saying. I'm just going to hold tight to the little apron lady and smile my best smile.

We go into the dining room. It's so pretty and sunny. There are white tablecloths and napkins, pretty glasses and flowers on every table. The girls march straight to their tables and stand by their chairs. Mrs. McBride takes my hand and we go to the center of the room. "Ladies, before you sit down I want to present our newest and youngest student, Suzanne Van Dorn Stacey. Please welcome her by saying, "Hello."

"Hello, Suzanne," they all say together.

Who are they talking to? That's not my name. I'm Sandy. There's a funny feeling in my stomach. Where's Mama? She'd better come get me. I don't belong here. I'm the wrong little girl. I'd better go back upstairs and wait in my pink ruffly bed 'til Mama comes to get me, but breakfast smells so good, I think I'll wait until after I eat.

Mama didn't come today, but she'll come tomorrow and take me back to the apartment. We have to wait until dark so I can sneak in. Sometimes, when Daddy is with us he pushes me through the window. That's funny unless I scrape my knee against the windowsill — that hurts. It's better to run tippy-toe down the hallway as fast as I can so no one will see me but the little mouse that runs faster than me. I don't think he's supposed to be here either. If the mean lady sees us, she'll make me, the mouse, Mama and Daddy all go away. Oh — I'm so sleepy. I hope I won't have any dreams.

The great big bus closes its doors behind us with a big whoosh! The driver looks at Mama. "Keep your kid quiet or you'll have to get off the bus." Mama smiles and tells him I'm a very good and quiet little girl. He starts the bus with a lot of noise and awful, ugly smells. We stop for lunch. Everyone looks at Mama because she's so pretty. We drive for a long time. I lean against Mama and fall asleep. When I wake up, the window is dark; time for bed. Mama stands up and reaches way up high to pull the little curtain away from our high bed. She screams! People jump up. Mama screams some more. There's a man hiding in our bed. The driver stops the bus and comes back. I'm scared he will make Mama get off the bus because she's making so much noise. He'll take her away from me. I'm so scared! Mama! Mama!

"Wake up, Suzanne! You're having a bad dream. You're here with me in school. Tomorrow, you'll meet your French teacher, Mademoiselle Lenhart, in the lovely sunroom. Go back to sleep now and have pretty dreams." Mrs. McBride pats my hand.

I close my eyes again and try to sleep, but I have another dream. *Mama, Daddy and I are standing in the apartment with a big, round mean lady. She is telling Mama and Daddy we can't stay here because the apartment doesn't allow children or pets. Daddy reaches his hand out to the mean lady. She grabs something from his hand. "All right", she says, "but if anyone sees or hears the kid, you will have to move."* I'm so scared; it will be my fault if we can't stay. I can't breathe.

I start to cry again. I want to go home to Mama and sleep with her in her big bed with her arms around me. I want to smell her perfume and hear her sing. I cry harder and Mrs. McBride comes in again.

"Suzanne, don't cry. I'm going to get that chair over there and bring it right by your bed and stay with you until you fall asleep."

"But I can't fall sleep without my pretty Mama. She always sings me a song."

"Well, I can't sing you a song, but I can tell you a story, or I can tell you a poem that I tell my grandchildren. Hold my hand and close your eyes and I'll tell it to you: *I saw a little birdie going hop, hop, hop, and I said, 'Little birdie, won't you stop, stop, stop?' I was going to the window to say, 'How do you do,' but he shook his little head at me and far away he flew."*

Mrs. McBride pats my hand and smiles. "Do you feel better?"

"Thank you, Mrs. McBride. It's a very nice poem, but it doesn't help. It doesn't make me sleepy. I can only sleep when my pretty Mama sings me 'Makin' Whoopee!'"

CHAPTER 2

World War II

1941-1945

"Sandy! Sandy! Come in right now!" I'm playing outside the apartment building as I always do when Daddy comes to visit."

~Sandy

I run inside, through the front door into the hall to our apartment, the second door on the right. Mama and Daddy are sitting on the couch hunched forward leaning toward the radio. I hurry to sit on Mama's lap to listen.

"At 7:55 a.m. Hawaii time, the Japanese bombed the U.S. Naval Base at Pearl Harbor. Five U.S. battleships, three destroyers, and seven other ships are sunk and severely damaged. At least 2,000 Americans are thought to be killed or wounded."

"Oh my God, Van, what's going on, what's going to happen?"
"Stop talking, Helen. I want to hear the radio."
Mama sounds so scared. I pull her arms around me, shut my eyes and hide my head against her...

The war has been going on for ten months. Aunt Gen's four oldest sons, Bob, Bill and Ed are fighting in Europe and Erny is fighting in Japan. The whole world is fighting.

Aunt Gen thinks her sons must tell all the soldiers, sailors and marines to go to her house at 2828 La Salle Ave. in Los Angeles, California before they ship out. They'll know the house because there is a white flag with blue stars on it in the front window and his Mom will have ham and beans every Saturday night for them until the war is over.

Tonight is Saturday night and I'm home from school this weekend so Mama and I are going next door to Aunt Gen's to help keep all the service-men company and cheer them up before they're shipped out Monday to somewhere unknown. Everything is a secret now that there is a war on. Enemies might be anywhere, but probably not here at Aunt Gen's because Aunt Gen's favorite priests, Father Conway and Father Bajagalupe, come to her house every Saturday night, too.

"Mama! There's so many soldiers and sailors here tonight! Mmmmm, what smells so good?"

"Ham and beans, Sandy, but don't eat any. Ham isn't good for you."

"But Mama, it smells so good!"

"Never mind, you've already had dinner. Come on, just squeeze through and go over to the piano. Gen will be there in a minute. I'm going to find her and then start getting the guys in line. Excuse us, boys, we're joining the party. Hi, Gen!"

"Stacey, I'm glad you're here! What a crowd!"

Aunt Gen calls Mama "Stacey" because Mama doesn't care for her given name, Helen Leona. Mama looks so pretty tonight no matter what she's called. She has her best black slacks on and sparkly white blouse and her best make-up. Mr. Ziegfeld showed her how to put on a "face" and she's walking her special silk underwear walk. Mr. Ziegfeld told the show girls they must always wear silk underwear because silk would make them walk prettier. Mama doesn't have her silk underwear anymore, but she still has the walk.

Oh, boy; the party's going to start! Mama has all the soldiers and sailors in line. Oh, oh, one of the soldiers is falling down, but his friends are catching him. They're pushing him back in line and they're holding him up. He must be tired, I think, but it's kind of early for him to be tired.

Aunt Gen's at the piano. The music's going to start! I'm going to stay right by Aunt Gen all night long and watch her play. She has such pretty long fingers and she's such a good player. She used to play for the silent movies before she married Pop.

Father Bajagalupe asks for quiet so he and Father Conway can say a prayer for the boys who will be going overseas. They will be going off to war in a few days so a prayer is very important. Everyone is quiet and bows their heads, even the falling down soldier sitting on the floor.

Father Bajagalupe faces the boys, raises his hands in the air, palms down toward the soldiers, sailors and Marines, and begins, "Holy Father, we ask for your hand of protection and guidance for these dear boys going off to serve our country. We send them off in your care. May they safely return to their families and loved ones. In the name of the Father, Son and Holy Spirit, Amen."

Father Conway, Father Bajagalupe and some of the boys make a cross on themselves. They touch their forehead, then their chest, then one side toward their shoulder, then the other side. I try to copy them, but I'm not sure if I'm supposed to, but nobody's looking at me. Everyone has their eyes closed, even Mama. Pop's in his favorite chair in the corner of the living room by the fireplace. He has a little old table beside the chair to hold his whiskey and alarm clock. He likes his corner and stays there all night while Aunt Gen plays and he likes to wave his arms like he's conducting.

Father Conway and Father Bajagalupe sit on the couch. Aunt Gen's ready to play! Mama's in front of the line of soldiers and sailors, one hand high in the air, the other on her hip waiting for Pop to give the signal. "Ok, Gen, hit it!"

Aunt Gen makes a big loud chord on the piano! Mama starts marching and singing with all the soldiers and sailors marching behind her singing a war song:

"Over there, over there, send the word,
send the word, over there,
that the Yanks are coming, the Yanks are coming,
there's drum, drum, drumming everywhere.
So beware, say a prayer, send the word,
send the word, over there!
We'll be over, we're coming over, and we won't
be back 'til it's over, over there!"

Mama marches all over the house. One soldier keeps falling down, but his friends are dragging him along. Father Conway and Father Bajagalupe are by Aunt Gen and me at the piano. They're singing and marching in place and waving their arms, almost hit Aunt Gen on the head! Oh, oh, here comes Mama out of the kitchen with all the soldiers and sailors behind her, her red hair flying!

There are so many soldiers and sailors here tonight. Aunt Gen says her sons must have told all their friends to say "Hi" to her and Pop if they ever get to Los Angeles and La Salle Avenue. I'm sure glad I'm home this weekend 'cause there's so much fun at Aunt Gen's now that there's a war on!

Aunt Gen has a little white flag hanging in the window with four blue stars on it: one is for Ed, one for Bill, one for Bob, and one for Erny. There should be five stars because Aunt Gen counts Erny's friend, Wayne, as one of her sons. He doesn't have a mom or dad and he's lived with Aunt Gen and Pop for a long time. He's a Marine. I think all the service men know how to find Aunt Gen's house because they see her little white flag with blue stars in the window.

Now, with Ed, Bill, Bob, Erny and Wayne overseas, Aunt Gen only has Harry John (he's my age) and Baby Mike and me at home. Aunt Gen counts me as hers because she prayed to God for a little girl and God sent me to her after Baby Mike was born. I love Aunt Gen and Pop and all their boys; I want to marry one of them when I grow up. I can't marry Bill, though, because he's already married to Ginny and they're going to have a baby. Ginny will live with Aunt Gen and Pop until she has the baby and the war is over and Bill comes home. She says I can help her with the baby after it's born — I'm so excited! Ginny's upstairs sleeping, too tired from working at the laundry all day to come to the parties.

Aunt Gen is trying to get everyone quiet so I can recite President Roosevelt's speech. "Quiet everybody! Sandy's going to recite President Roosevelt's speech." Father Conway, Father Bajagalupe and Pop are yelling for quiet, too. I'm afraid because there are so many soldiers and sailors here, but I've been practicing with Mrs. McBride all week and am trying to tell myself to take some deep breaths and be calm. I take three deep breaths and start. "Yesterday, December 7, 1941, a date that will live in infamy, the United States was suddenly and deliberately attacked by naval and air forces of the Empire of Japan —"

"Bastards!" Everyone starts to yell. Pop's cursing and shaking his fists in the air. Father Conway and Father Bajagalupe come and stand by me yelling, "Quiet! Let Sandy finish the speech!" Everyone gets quiet and Father Conway and Father Bajagulpe go back to the couch and sit down. Pop's fingers are shaking so hard he can hardly roll his Bull Durham! I take a few more deep breaths and start again. "As Commander and Chief of the Army and Navy, I have directed that all measures be taken for our defense. But always will our whole nation remember the character of the onslaught against us!"

"You're damned right we'll remember and we're going to do something about it!" The soldiers and sailors are on their feet shaking their fists and waving their arms, all except for the one who keeps falling down and two who are running for the bathroom. Mama was right. They shouldn't have eaten the ham!

Aunt Gen starts playing the piano again to get everyone singing and marching instead of shoving and yelling. Mama gets the soldiers and sailors in line, and from the chord Aunt Gen plays on the piano, I know the Army song is going to start:

"Over hill, over dale, we have hit the dusty trail,
And the caissons go rolling along.
In and out, hear the shout, counter march and round about,
And the caissons go rolling along.
Then it's 'hi hi he' in the field artillery,
Shout out your numbers loud and strong, One! Two!
For where e're you go, you will always know
That the caissons go rolling along."

Mama and the soldiers and sailors are marching round and round the living room and every so often Mama does her shimmy-shake! She's so good! One of the sailors starts shouting, "Hey, what about the Navy?" Aunt Gen breaks into —

"Anchors aweigh, my boys! Anchors aweigh!
Farewell to college joys, we sail at break of day-ay-ay-ay.
Through our last night on shore, drink to the foam,
Until we meet once more. Here's wishing you a happy voyage home!"

Then Aunt Gen follows with the Marine's song for Wayne. Mama and the soldiers and sailors march through the dining room and head for the kitchen:

"From the halls of Montezuma to the shores of Tripoli,
We will fight our country's battles on the land and on the sea.
First to fight for right and freedom, we're the finest ever seen,
And we're proud to claim the title of, the United States Marines."

Oh, my! Father Conway and Father Bajagalupe have joined the back of Mama's line. Watch out! Here they come out of the kitchen again! Oh, good! Mama tells all the soldiers and sailors to sit down on the floor. Father Conway and Father Bajagalupe are back on the couch. I know what's going to happen. Aunt Gen knows, too. Mama's going to do her Charleston dance! Mama gives a nod to Aunt Gen. Aunt Gen raises her hands and hits chords on the piano and Mama starts to dance. All the soldiers and sailors yell and applaud and whistle when she does her high kicks. She's so good! The soldiers and sailors yell, "Do it again, Stacey! Do it again!" "Yeah, Stacey! Yeah! Let's hear it for Stacey, guys!" They yell and whistle and Mama raises her hands: "Let me catch my breath, boys, and then I'll sing you a song."

"Yeah! Yeah! Stacey's going to sing a song!" Mama catches her breath, she looks at Aunt Gen and gives a nod. Everyone gets quiet and Aunt Gen raises her hands and hits some chords. Mama starts:

"Another bride, another groom, another funny honeymoon,
Another season, another reason for makin' whoopee!"

Everyone whistles and shouts!

"A lot of shoes, a lot of rice,
the groom is nervous, he answers twice.

It's really killin', that he's so willin',
for makin' whoopee."

More whistling and shouting and hand clapping!

"Picture a little love nest,
Down where the roses cling.
Picture the same sweet love nest,
Here's what a year can bring…"

"Tell us what's it gonna bring, Stacey!" Mama points at the boys with her finger.

"He's washin' dishes and baby clothes
He's so ambitious, he even sews.
But don't forget folks, that's what you get folks,
For makin' whoopee!"

Some of the soldiers pretend they're washing dishes. Everyone's laughing and the living room starts shaking with all the boys getting up on their feet, stomping and clapping their hands. Even the one who keeps falling down is holding on to one of his friends and whistling. This is so much fun! I love the way Mama sings and dances! She's so good! I wish Daddy would come to one of Aunt Gen's parties and see how good Mama is. I bet he would love her then.

Everyone who can crowds around Aunt Gen. I keep my place at her knee. She says she's going to teach me to play the piano after the war is over. Father Bajagalupe says he'll teach me Italian, too, so I can sing some of his favorite Italian songs. Aunt Gen tells Mama she should give me singing lessons because I have a pretty voice. Of course, she's the only one who can hear me.

Aunt Gen raises her hands and brings them back down on the keys, plays some loud chords to get everyone's attention and then plays a big, big chord! The soldiers and sailors are leaning over her shoulders trying to read the words on the music she has on the piano in front of her. I, of course, know all the words by heart. She starts —

"M is for the million things she gave me.
O is only that she's growing old.
T is for the tears she shed to save me.
H is for her heart as pure as gold.
E is for her eyes with lovelight shining.
R is right and right she'll always be.
Put them all together they spell MOTHER.
The word that means the world to me."

Everyone sings really loud at the end and stretches the last note really long. Aunt Gen makes her hands go up and down over the keys, up and down, up and down, up and down before she hits the last chord! Aunt Gen and Mama and the soldiers and sailors are all crying and Mama doesn't care if the teardrops spoil her make-up because this is the end of the party.

Father Conway starts saying prayers for all the boys overseas, the ones in the house, on the floor and in the bathroom. "Father, bless these boys here and overseas. Protect them and their families as they wait for their return. In the name of the Father and the Son and the Holy Spirit. Amen!"

Father Conway and Father Bajagalupe make the sign of the cross on themselves and then take small jars of holy water out of their bags. The boys start coming to them one by one and Father Conway and Father Bajagalupe sprinkle holy water on their heads. The Fathers go over to Aunt Gen and sprinkle holy water on her head. I wish they would put holy water on my head, but I'm not sure that would be all right.

Pop puts his arms on his chair and pushes himself up making a grunting sound. He takes the alarm clock off the table and starts winding, "Party's over. Good night, everybody," and heads upstairs, stepping over anyone who is sleeping on the floor. Mama and I kiss and hug Aunt Gen, and two of the soldiers who aren't too tired walk Mama and me back to the apartment. I don't want to go back to school! I want to live with Aunt Gen like Ginny does, but I'm too young to marry one of Aunt Gen's boys and have a baby. And if I don't go back to school, I can't sleep in my pink ruffly bed, or read in the library, or have tea with Mrs. McBride. I don't know what to do.

I think I'll ask Father Conway and Father Bajagalupe to pray for me and ask them to sprinkle holy water on my head. I know they keep extra holy water in their fountain pens for emergencies. Maybe they'll even let me be a Catholic.

CHAPTER 3

The Yearly Military Ball

June 12, 1942
8 years old

"Maybe there's a sign over the door: 'Stoughton bottles not allowed!'"

~ Sandy

I'm excited because the Military Ball is tonight and my dress is so pretty! The top of my dress is shiny green satin with little puffed sleeves and the skirt is green net all the way to the floor: I hope I don't trip on the net when I go down the stairs or walk in the promenade or at the dance!

Mama and Daddy are here early so Mama can fix my hair in Shirley Temple curls. I love Mama when she brushes my hair into curls. Mama and Daddy both have red hair and I do, too. The shiny emerald green over the top of my dress makes the red in my curls kind of shiny and pretty.

This is my first ball. I feel like Cinderella. I have a dance card! I hope the dance card doesn't fall off my wrist! I hope at least two of the boys from the Military Academy ask me to dance so I can have names on my dance card at the end of the ball so I can show the mirror tomorrow. I hope my curls don't fall out when I sleep so the mirror can see them.

I wish Aunt Gen were here so she could see how pretty I look and hear the string quartet. Mrs. Gallantine, our diction teacher, told us about "String

Quartets" — two violins, a viola and a violoncello. Maybe someday I'll play the violoncello in a string quartet, after the war is over, of course. I think Mrs. McBride would rather I learn to play the violoncello than learn to play the piano like Aunt Gen does at her parties. Mrs. McBride wouldn't approve of anything at Aunt Gen's parties. Mrs. McBride says, "It is not proper for people to smoke, drink, play and sing popular songs or dance around the house."

I don't understand exactly as to what being "proper" means. Mrs. McBride says, "Proper means being decent or correct in one's behavior." I think helping the service men is decent and correct behavior. Aunt Gen and Pop help them by having Father Conway and Father Bajagalupe pray for them at her parties before they go overseas to fight in the war. I think it is decent and correct for Mama to help them by singing and dancing for them and leading them around Aunt Gen's house in a conga line to make them laugh and help them if they are afraid to go overseas and fight in the war. I think Mrs. McBride is also decent and correct when she helps them by having the school mothers meet in the dining room here at school so they can roll bandages to send overseas. There are so many very different ways to be proper and that's what makes me confused. I don't know which "proper" is the best. It would be easier for me if there was just one way to be proper.

Mama wanted to be proper and came to school one Wednesday afternoon to help roll bandages. Mama doesn't look like the other mothers. Mama always has her pretty make-up on and her pretend silk underwear walk and now that Mama can't buy silk stockings anymore because of the war shortage, she paints a line down the back of her legs to pretend they are silk stockings. The pretend stockings really go nicely with her pretend silk underwear.

The other mothers are so plain; I don't think they like Mama. Maybe if they heard her sing "Makin' Whoopee!" or watched her dance the Charleston and oh, oh, do her Baby Snooks routine, they'd like her because she's so funny and she worked with Fanny Brice in the Ziegfeld Follies! Yes, maybe if she did all that for them, they'd like her, but maybe not. Daddy doesn't like her to do her routines, either. I wish he'd laugh and applaud for her the way the service men do at Aunt Gen's parties.

Aunt Gen gave me a rosary so I can pray that God will make Daddy laugh and applaud and love Mama. Aunt Gen taught me all the prayers so I can say the rosary properly. I love the rosary; the beads are so pretty and feel so good and smooth between my fingers. Aunt Gen says I should say the rosary before I go to sleep each night and that might help me sleep better and have prettier dreams. I hope so. I don't like my dreams, especially the one about — Oh! Mrs. McBride is here to see how we look. We don't all look alike tonight. We all have different colored dresses. I think we look like a rainbow.

The music has started! It's time for us to make our entrance down the stairs! The young men from the Military Academy are marching to the bottom of the staircase. They're in a line and we're in a line coming down the stairs. They're instructed to take our hand when we reach the last step down. They're in uniforms, a little like the uniforms the soldiers and sailors have on at Aunt Gen's, except the young men's uniforms are smaller and fancier and they have white gloves on and none of them are falling down. Maybe it's too early and they're not tired yet.

Oh, my goodness! My turn to go down the stairs! Butterflies are in my stomach, but I have to descend. I'm going to go down just the way Mrs. McBride taught us, one hand on the banister, fingers resting lightly on the top, one hand gracefully at my side, back straight, head high, eyes straight ahead and smile! I really smile my best smile now as I know my future might depend on the way I enter the room and because I'm pretending I have on silk underwear.

I wish the mirror could see me walking properly down the stairs with my dance card on my wrist. I'd like to wave and show her my dance card, but the dance card might fall off my wrist and maybe that wouldn't be proper.

There's that word again, "proper!" I'm sure the mirror knows everything that is proper because she lives here at the school, where everything is proper.

My military partner and I walk into the garden for the "The Promenade." We are instructed to walk leisurely and smile. The garden is beautiful with tiny white lights sparkling in all the trees and bushes. The arches over our red brick path are covered with tiny white lights, in between the roses, and they sparkle like sprinkled stars above us. Mrs. Gallantine told us our path of arches is "like Monet's painting of his rose arches in Giverny."

Our parents are sitting around the garden on pretty little stone garden benches. Mama and Daddy have the best bench right by the koi pond. You can hear the string quartet from the ballroom. Everything is so perfect and beautiful except for my military partner. He's staring straight ahead and not saying a word. His arm is stiff and when I accidentally touch his glove, the glove feels slimy, icy cold and wet.

Mrs. McBride says a lady's job is to "make her military escort feel good and comfortable." I'm not sure how to do this with my military escort tonight. He's as straight and stiff and mute as a Stoughton bottle. Mrs. McBride told us we must never be Stoughton bottles. They are without imagination or expression. They are blankly uninterested in whatever is being said or done. Some of the young men from the Military Academy tonight are definitely Stoughton bottles. None of the boys at Aunt Gen's parties are Stoughton bottles. None of them are straight and stiff and wordless. No, there aren't any Stoughton bottles at Aunt Gen's! Maybe she keeps them away from her house with a sign over her front door that says, "Stoughton Bottles not allowed!" Maybe that's why I have so much fun there!

CHAPTER 4

Letter Writing Day

September 1942, Sunday afternoon
8 years old

"Ladies have to be careful around men because ladies can
never tell when the men might turn back into animals."

~ Sandy

*D*ear Richard,

The next time I write to you, I'll be using an ink pen that you dip into an inkwell on the desk. You have to be very careful with the ink and not get too much on the tip of your pen or it will be messy on the paper and you can get ink on your fingers. I love dipping my pen in the inkwell and Mrs. McBride says I'm ready. My friend, Eva Lee, and I have been studying the Palmer method of writing. It's so much fun. You don't write with just your fingers. You have to put your whole arm on the desk and make your whole arm and hand go up and down or round and round. You have to practice these up and down and circular strokes every day to learn how to form your letters and numbers. You also have to learn to make all your letters the same size, except for the capitals, make your numbers very clear and all your lines straight. You can't cross out anything. Mrs. McBride says, "The purpose of communicating in writing is to make your communication clear and easy to read."

The weather here is nice. I get to take little Theresa for walks in Baby Mike's stroller when I come to the apartment on Fridays and Saturdays. Of course, Baby Mike isn't the baby anymore since Ginny had little Terry. Her husband, Bill, is in the army overseas so he hasn't seen little Terry yet, but he's coming home on a furlough soon. We don't know exactly when, so every afternoon when I'm at Aunt Gen's house, I dress baby Terry up in her prettiest dress and I take her up and down the street in the stroller in front of Aunt Gen's house. We stop at the corner and look way up the street to see if we can see Daddy Bill coming, then we turn around and come back to Aunt Gen's. We're going to do this every week until he comes home.

Mama and Daddy are fine except for a big argument last weekend when I was at the apartment. Daddy wants to enlist in the Marines. He was a machine gunner in World War I, but Mama told him he was too old for this war. He started to yell and bang on the wall. I was afraid the mean lady would think it's me banging on the wall, so I hid in the closet and said my rosary the way Aunt Gen taught me. She said I should ask God to make Daddy love Mama the way everyone else does, except for the other mothers at school, but it hasn't helped yet.

I don't know why Daddy doesn't love Mama. I wish Mama would be nicer to Daddy when he comes to visit. Mrs. McBride says a lady's job is to make the people around her feel comfortable and good about themselves. Mama doesn't make Daddy feel comfortable and good about himself when she tells him he is too old to enlist in the Marines. I'm not sure what she should tell him. She can't say he's too young, that's ridiculous, but she shouldn't say he's too old. That hurts his feelings and makes him mad.

When I grow up and have a husband, I won't hurt his feelings and make him mad. Sometimes I think I would be a better wife to Daddy than Mama. She ought to change places with me when he comes to visit. She should hide in the closet and I should be in the front room to talk to him. I would make him feel good and comfortable because I have had that training and Mama hasn't. Then, he would love me. He wouldn't be mad at me. What do you think?

Love,
Sandy

"Suzanne, let's go into my office for a bit. I'd like to talk to you."

"Yes, Mrs. McBride." Oh, dear, I hope I haven't done anything wrong.

"Please sit down, dear."

"Yes, Mrs. McBride."

"Suzanne, I've just read your letter to your cousin Richard in New Jersey and I think we should throw it away and write a happier one to him next Sunday afternoon. It isn't proper to tell anyone about your mother and father's private business. Do you understand?"

"Yes, Mrs. McBride." But I don't understand. My mind starts whirling. Why can't I tell Cousin Richard about Mama and Daddy? Cousin Richard is family. His Mama and my Mama are sisters. Shouldn't they know what is happening in each other's lives? I think his Mama, my Aunt Dorothy, should know what is happening with her sister. Maybe she could help fix things, but Richard tells me his Daddy is always angry at his Mama, too, so I guess she doesn't know what to do either. Maybe Daddy is always angry at Mama because Mama hasn't had Mrs. McBride's training in how to be a wife and make your husband feel good and comfortable. Mrs. McBride says that men also must be trained in how to act in the presence of ladies before they are even allowed in a house. I don't think Daddy has had that training either, so how can Mama and Daddy know how to love one another? I don't even know where grown-ups go to get that training.

When Mrs. McBride talks about training men, I think she means they have to be put in cages like lions and tigers and have a trainer who works with them every day with a whip and makes them "Sit" and "Jump" like they do with animals. I think they have to stay in training for at least a year and only then can be allowed in a house in the presence of ladies. I know that's silly, but it's what I think sometimes. And then I think that ladies have to be careful around men because ladies can never tell when the men might turn back into animals. A lady has to speak softly and smile at them so the men will stay comfortable and feel good. I'm not sure who is supposed to know when men have had enough training to be allowed to come into a house. I'll have to ask Mrs. McBride. I guess Mama and Aunt Dorothy don't know any of this. Maybe that's why their husbands don't love them. I wonder if I could ask Mrs. McBride to explain all this to Mama and then Mama could tell Aunt Dorothy. That might be more helpful than me praying on my rosary beads because so far, that hasn't helped.

"Suzanne, your mind seems to be wandering. Please give me your full attention."

"I'm sorry, Mrs. McBride." Oh, my goodness, I didn't realize I wasn't paying attention. I hope she doesn't think I was being rude.

"Suzanne, I want you to use your proper name when you sign your letters. Do not use your nickname, 'Sandy.' Ladies do not use nicknames, abbreviations or slang in place of words. That is not proper. Now, that will be all. Go to the library and take time to think through everything I have just told you."

"Yes, Mrs. McBride. Thank you for taking your time to speak to me. I will go to the library and think of all you have said." I stand up from my chair, curtsy, turn and leave Mrs. McBride's office. I'm glad that's over. I want to go to the entry to tell the mirror what has happened. Besides Cousin Richard, the mirror is the only one I can talk to, but she can't talk back like Cousin Richard; all she can do is listen. I wonder if she can see the thoughts in my head? I hope so because it might take too long to tell her all my thinking and Mrs. McBride has asked me to go to the library to do my thinking, so I'll just wave to the mirror and blow her a little kiss as I go by. I don't think she has any friends.

I love the library. I love the look and smell of the books and my chair feels so good and comfortable, no wonder I love it. I love the library so much, but there is a part of me today that is sad because Mrs. McBride says I can't write my thoughts to Cousin Richard anymore. Cousin Richard writes to me and tells me his thoughts. His mother and father are always fighting. He isn't sure why, but it must be something very bad. Of course, his mother and father haven't had any training, either, so how can they know how to act? Eva Lee and I and our classmates must be the only girls in the world who know the secret of how ladies and men have to be trained.

Aunt Gen and Pop fight, too, but I know why they had their fight when I was at the apartment last weekend. Pop hid his whiskey bottle in the tank of their broken toilet on their back porch and Aunt Gen found the whiskey and got so mad! I don't blame her. Pop shouldn't spend their money on whiskey. They need their money for groceries.

Let's see — there's Aunt Gen, Pop, Harry John, Mike, Ginny and baby Terry, and when Father Conway, Father Bajagalupe and all the soldiers and sailors come to their house, Aunt Gen has to keep adding more and more water to her ham and beans. Aunt Gen is always praying on her rosary beads for God to help out and sometimes God sends eggs and milk and Aunt Gen finds them on her front porch in the morning. One morning, she found a pineapple upside-down cake on the front porch. She must have prayed extra hard for that.

Aunt Gen has had a hard time the past few years. When she married Pop, he was an attorney and they lived in a real house, but when the Depression and more and more babies came, they had to move to the desert in Barstow and live behind Pop's uncle's gas station. They just had a tarp over their heads for shelter and Aunt Gen had to cook on a little camp stove.

Aunt Gen told me that one morning Pop was using his straight edge razor to shave — trying to see his face in a little broken piece of dusty mirror he had hung on one of the poles that was holding up the tarp, squinting into the mirror – when he saw a rattlesnake crawling toward Baby Mike, who was sleeping on his blanket. Pop got so scared he dropped the razor and the razor landed right on the snake's head and cut it off. Aunt Gen said that God saved Baby Mike because he had plans for him when he grew up. Aunt Gen thinks God will make Baby Mike become a priest.

I'm very sad I won't be able to write any more letters from school to Cousin Richard. Maybe I could write from home, but we don't have a pen at home and I want to use a pen. I love to stand at the French door to Mrs. McBride's office, look through the little panes of glass and watch her dip her pretty pink feather pen into the inkwell. The pen looks so pretty waving around as she makes her letters and I love the sound of the pen when it scratches on the paper. When she is finished, she puts her pen down in a special place on the desk and leans her head down to blow very softly over the words she has written, then she rocks the blotter back and forth over her words.

Mama doesn't have a pretty feather pen, or ink in an inkwell, or a blotter or pretty paper to write on, but Aunt Gen has V-mail paper at her house. I write once a month with a pencil to all her boys. I can't write to Wayne anymore, though, because Erny came to the apartment last week to tell Mama and me Wayne was killed.

I was sitting at our kitchen table with my hands folded, politely waiting for Mama to bring me a plate of spaghetti, when a knock came on the door.

Mama started shaking and almost dropped my plate. I love her spaghetti and her sauce! Such a treat for me for Mama to cook – I even dream about spaghetti at school. Mama put my spaghetti down in front of me on the table and went to the door. "Who's there?" Her voice was shaking.

"It's Erny. I need to talk to you." He came in and told us the Marines landed on Iwo Jima near the base of Mount Suribachi on February 19, 1945, the day before my 11th birthday. Wayne was killed. Mama and Erny hugged each other and cried. I started to cry, too, but I'm not sure whether I was crying over Wayne or because Mama had forgotten to put the sauce on my spaghetti.

I don't think the war is fun anymore and the parties aren't as much fun either because we all cry so hard when Aunt Gen plays the "Marine Hymn" for Wayne.

I want the war to be over and all of Aunt Gen's boys to come home so I can marry one of them and be a wife who knows how to make them love me. Of course, if something bad happens and they don't come home, I can always marry Harry John. He's my age, you know.

CHAPTER 5

Two Mamas

August 14, 1944
10 years old

"If we're on the sidewalk, bad men will jump out of
the bushes around the houses and kill us!"

~ Sandy

I hope Mama's in a good mood when I get to the apartment today. I hate when she's in a bad mood. Sometimes, I think there are two mamas, the good one and the bad one. I know! I'll pretend I have a headache so she'll feel sorry for me and then the good mama will come out. Sometimes, I pretend I'm the only one living at the school, and I'm the only one that rides in the chauffeur's car, so I can choose my seat. I like to sit right behind the chauffeur — I like to look at his hat and uniform. He sits so straight; I wonder if he wants to enlist in the Marines like Daddy? Maybe his wife won't let him, like Mama. I wonder if he fights with his wife like Daddy does? Probably not because he's kind of small, unless he has a small wife. Daddy's bigger than Mama and I bet Daddy's scarier, too. Daddy carries an axe in the trunk of his car. I wonder if the chauffeur has one in this car? Probably not. Mrs. McBride wouldn't approve. I definitely do not think an ax is proper.

I hate being driven to the apartment by the chauffeur. I'm embarrassed. The outside looks all right, but I'm afraid one day Mama won't be waiting outside to come to the car to get me, and he'll have to walk me inside the apartment house to our door. There is a musty smell and sometimes you can see a mouse in the hall. Sometimes, when Mama sees one, she screams and runs back into the apartment, into the bathroom, and gets sick. I wish someone would fix up the apartment, but this is war time and no one has any extra money. Any extra money has to go to support the war effort. War is very expensive.

Now, when I stay overnight at the apartment, I'm too big to sleep with Mama anymore. I have a couch that turns into a bed. Mama won the money to buy the sleeping couch when we went to the racetrack with Daddy one day and she bet on a horse named Pompkie. She won $20! So exciting, but Daddy wasn't that excited. He was annoyed that Mama had won, but Mama and I were so excited we were jumping up and down and up and down 'til Daddy grabbed Mama and said, "That's enough." I don't know why he doesn't like Mama to be happy. Anyway, I'm getting used to sleeping by myself, but I do miss sleeping with my head on Mama's arm and her singing me "Makin' Whoopee." Now we just call out to each other – "Good night, Mama," "Good night, Sandy, sweet dreams," "Sweet dreams, Mama" – and then I turn over and try to fall asleep, but I don't like the sheets on the bed. They aren't ironed and they don't have the pretty smell like the ones on my ruffly bed at school. Oh, well; I really don't live here. Oh, my; I really don't live at the school either. I really don't live anywhere.

I wish I had a house like Aunt Gen. I'd love to live with her and play the piano all day. She's teaching me how to play, even though the war's not over yet. She's teaching me "Smoke Gets In Your Eyes." It's so pretty and Pop likes to sit in his chair with his whiskey and Bull Durham and listen to me. After I play, he applauds and says, "Play it again, Sandy, this time with more feeling," and I try again. Aunt Gen tells me to sing while I play and that will help me with feeling, but I don't think I'll have the proper feeling until I understand the meaning of the words better. Aunt Gen says that will come in time.

We're almost at the apartment and I have to get ready to pretend my headache. I pretend about a lot of things. I pretend I don't care when none of the girls at school want to talk or play with me. I pretend I would rather go to the library and have tea with Mrs. McBride. I do love the library and tea time, but sometimes I would like to see what playing "movies" with the older girls feels like. I've only seen one movie so far, but I can't tell anyone. I have to pretend I've never seen one so no one at the school knows that Mama took me because Mama would get in trouble because Mrs. McBride says, "It isn't proper for young girls to go to a public cinema," but I still think I could catch on fast to the big girls' "movie" game the same way I do to schoolwork.

Oh, good; here comes Mama to the car so the chauffeur doesn't have to come inside and I can tell Mama I have a headache and the chauffeur won't hear me and know I am telling a fib, but maybe he tells fibs to his wife, if he has one, so she will be nice to him.

I'm going to tell Mama I'd like to lie down on the couch with the big pillow from her bed under my head. The pillow smells like her Tabu perfume. Mama and I love the smell, but Daddy "hates it!" She shouldn't wear Tabu when he comes to visit. She knows Tabu makes him mad. Maybe she likes to make him mad, but why? He always brings things to us and sometimes, he brings fancy groceries. Mama doesn't even have to pray for them like Aunt Gen. I don't think Mama prays. I never hear her, but maybe only Catholics pray out loud. I pray every night, but I pray to myself so no one will hear me. I don't think Mrs. McBride would like me to pray. I don't want to take a chance. I don't want the other girls to hear me either. If they hear me, they might tell on me and that might make Mrs. McBride mad and I would have to leave the school.

Even though I pray every night for God to make Mama and Daddy love each other, it isn't working. Maybe you have to be Catholic to make prayers work. But how can God tell if you're Catholic? Maybe it's something in your voice. I'll have to ask Father Conway and Father Bajagalupe the next time they come to visit Aunt Gen to pray for Bob, Bill, Ed and Erny, who are still in the midst of all the fighting overseas.

Harry John and I help the war effort by peeling the silver foil off gum wrappers and making big silver balls. Aunt Gen takes them and the newspapers that Harry John collects from the paper drives and brings them to the collection centers to convert into "materials for war." Mama and Aunt Gen trade green stamps with each other from the ration books so they have enough coffee and sugar. Aunt Gen and neighbor, Mrs. Kelly, wait for the mailman every day. Mrs. Kelly lives in a duplex next door to Aunt Gen. She has eight children. The three oldest are in the Army. She has a rosary, too, like Aunt Gen, and sometimes they say their rosaries together by the mailbox while they wait for the mailman. Looks to me as though the mailman knows God and they pray to the mailman to ask God if their sons are alive.

Once, Mrs. Kelly invited Mama and me to her half of the duplex for dinner. She was having a big pot of vegetable soup and Mama said it was all right for me to eat some because there wasn't any ham in the pot. The soup had a lot of potatoes, though. After dinner, Mama and I didn't know what to do because the Kelly children all started to get ready for bed, but there weren't any beds. They pushed chairs together and put blankets and pillows on each end of the couch and the leftover children took their blankets and pillows and got under the dining room table. Maybe Mr. and Mrs. Kelly get the one bedroom, but Mama and Aunt Gen say they have never seen a Mr. Kelly. Maybe he got into the Marines like Daddy wanted to and Mrs. Kelly let him go because there wasn't any place for him to sleep or maybe he doesn't even sleep there, like Daddy.

Sometimes, I think Daddy's a spy for our government because Mama once told me if I ever accidentally saw Daddy on the street I was never to call out "Daddy" to him or go to him. I should pretend like I didn't see him at all. I've been practicing pretending in case that ever happens, but there could be another reason Mama and I don't know where Daddy lives or sleeps. The strangest thing happened when Mama took me to my first movie. I was so excited, but I also felt a little nervous because I knew Mrs. McBride said I wasn't supposed to go. Mama and I bought some candy at the little candy store right next to the movie theatre. So much fun! We picked our seats and the lights went out and there was a cartoon, and then there was some good music that announced a newsreel which showed all about service men fighting the war overseas, and then the real movie started.

I yelled out, "Daddy!" The man on the screen looked exactly like Daddy! He even sounded like Daddy! Maybe that's why Mrs. McBride didn't want me to go to the movie theatre: I would find out Daddy's secret life! He's a movie star! Mama told me to be quiet or the usher would make us leave. Oh, no! I don't want to leave. I want to watch Daddy! Mama said I was wrong that the man on the screen's name was "Spencer Tracy," but that doesn't make any difference because I have two names and I have two different lives. That could be the same for Daddy. This is so confusing. I wish I could write Cousin Richard and ask him about this. He's very smart.

It's always so dark on the way back from the movies and I hate walking the two long, long blocks to the apartment. Mama says it is safer to walk down the middle of the street than on the sidewalk. She says if we're on the sidewalk, bad men will jump out of the bushes around the houses and kill us. Mama puts her apartment key between her fingers and makes a fist with the key sticking out so she can fight off any bad man. She's very brave, but I don't think she's strong enough. We need Daddy. He should come and stay at the apartment. Where is he?

CHAPTER 6

Cantor's Delicatessen

August 14, 1945
11 years old

"Never let 'em get the best of you, kid!
Leave 'em laughing, head high, do a little
dance step and wave good-bye."

~ Grandmother

I'm so excited, so happy: Daddy, Mama and I are going to meet Grandmother, Grandfather and Auntie Ann at Cantor's Delicatessen on Brooklyn Avenue in Boyle Heights for lunch. They're visiting us and I've never met them before. They live in Florida, but they decided to come see us! They said Auntie Ann wanted to have dinner at her favorite restaurant in New Orleans, Galatoire's on Bourbon Street, so they got on a train, stopped for dinner and decided as long as they were that far, they should come all the way to California to see us!

Mama's happy and excited; Daddy says they are "irresponsible." Mama says Daddy shouldn't be so hard on them, should know what they're like, how they've always been. They like trains, they like moving around; life in vaudeville makes you like that. Daddy doesn't care and doesn't want to talk about family, he just wants to get in the car and get the day over, but Mama is in such a happy mood she starts to click her fingers and swing her hips.

She's going to sing and dance something, I can tell! She grabs a banana off the kitchen table and puts it on her head. Oh, boy, she's going to do her Carmen Miranda song; here she goes! Click, click, click, swing, swing, swing.

> "We're on our way, pack up your pack,
> and if we stay, we won't come back,
> How can we go? We haven't got a dime,
> but we're goin', and we're gonna have a happy,
> happy, happy, happy, happy time."

Mama sings and dances around the living room. She pushes Daddy back toward the sofa, pushes him down, leans over him and shakes her shoulders.

> "Gotta get goin', where're we goin', what're we gonna do?
> We're on our way to somewhere, the three of us and you!
> Who will be there? What'll we see there?
> What'll be the big surprise?
> There may be caballeros with gay and dancing eyes!
> Pack up your pack—"

Daddy gets up and grabs Mama. "Helen, for God's sake, stop that!

There's going to be enough of that when we meet up with your family. Get in the car!"

I hate it when Daddy gets so mad. Mama really shouldn't sing and dance for him. He doesn't like her to do that. Maybe he did once, but not anymore. At least she didn't do her imitation of Baby Snooks in her Baby Snooks voice.

> "A tisket, a tasket, a green and yellow basket.
> I send a letter to my mommy
> On the way I dropped it.

I dropped it, I dropped it.

Yes, on the way I dropped it.

A little girlie picked it up and put it in her pocket.

She took it, she took it, she took my yellow basket

And if she doesn't bring it back,

I think that I would die."

Daddy hates that song and Mama's Baby Snooks imitation with her voice in her nose...

...Oh, look, there they are! Oh, my, Auntie Ann is so pretty, but she's not very tall and she's smoking! Oh, oh! That's not good, she's so young. And there's Grandmother and Grandfather. My goodness, they're not very tall and Mama doesn't look like them, but they have happy, smiling faces! Mama rushes over to kiss and hug them and they all cry. Mama pushes me into their arms. I don't like that. I don't know them and they kind of scare me. They're all talking at once and I can't understand what they're saying. The words don't sound like any language I've ever heard. The sounds are harsh and kind of ugly. Why would anyone want to sound like that?

Daddy stands to one side. I wish he'd hold my hand. He's never held my hand. Maybe it isn't proper or something. Grandmother is shouting. "Who's hungry? I bet the kid is hungry. Come on, everybody, let's eat!"

"Oy vey, you call this a delicatessen? Are you crazy? This isn't a delicatessen. Carnegie's in New York, that's a delicatessen! Look at these tables! You can't eat and schmooze at these tables. Carnegie's has tables! Carnegie's has a deli and the deli counter, OY! Everything you want to bring home and eat." Grandmother puts her fingers to her mouth and makes a kissing sound. She's such a loud talker. People turn around and look at us. Grandmother starts talking to the people. "You call this a deli counter! Nothing's in it and what's in it I wouldn't take home, much less eat! You can't get good Jewish food anywhere but in New York!"

Oh, good; Mama's finding us a table waaaaay in the back, but Grandmother doesn't like it. "I'm not sitting back there, Helen. Have you gone meshuga? What's the matter with you? We're sitting here in the front." Grandmother is such a loud talker the people at the next table stare at us and Grandmother and Grandfather smile and wave at them. The waitress comes over with the menus and tells us her name. Daddy looks up at her. "Your name sounds Russian."

"Yes, I'm from Odessa."

"Well," Grandmother says, "you'd better start *rushin'* with our food. I'm hungry!" She does a little rhythm beat with her hands on the table. Bump da da bump bump, bump, bump! She looks over at the next table to be sure they see her. They nod and smile.

"So, Van, what do you do?" Grandmother is still talking so loud. While she's talking, she doesn't even look at Daddy; she looks around at the people in the restaurant, especially at the people at the table next to us. "Helen doesn't tell us anything."

"I'm involved in classified work, Ada. I have nothing I can discuss with you."

"Oy vey, the goy's in 'classified work'! A real macher!" Grandmother talks in a loud kind of pretend whisper and rolls her eyes at the people at the next table. "Come on, Van, what do you really do?"

"What I really do is decide what to eat. I suggest we all do that so we can have lunch." Daddy is very annoyed. He's mad. I can tell because when he gets mad, he gets a little white around his eyes and in the corners of his mouth. Daddy's very handsome, but he doesn't look handsome right now. His bright blue eyes are starting to change color. The blue is getting pale — changing into light bluish-grey. Even his red wavy hair looks different, redder with sparks.

"Oy vey iz mir, he's mad! Look at him, look at the punim!" Grandmother throws up her hands like Daddy's going to shoot. "Don't shoot!" Grandfather throws up his. The people at the next table are laughing! Oh, good! The waitress is coming over to take our order. The minute she takes our orders and menus and leaves, Daddy picks up his fork, shows it around the table and asks if anyone knows the origin of eating utensils. Mama groans and rolls her eyes. Grandmother groans, puts her head in her hands, gives a look to Grandfather and the next table. They are looking down into their plates seriously eating. Oh, my! Daddy has on his lecture face and tone of voice.

"Are you kidding? Are you meshuga? Who cares about a delicatessen fork? All I care about is my food and that Russian ain't rushin' with it."

Grandmother is talking even louder! Daddy's really mad! His bright blue eyes are ice-grey steel now and the white is getting whiter around his temples and his lips are thin. I'm scared! I'd better tell him I want to listen.

"I want to hear about the origin of the fork. Tell me, Daddy, tell me!" Everyone groans, even the people at the next table. All of them give me an awful look, but Daddy turns to me and starts talking: "When human beings discovered fire and learned to cook their food, they faced an unprecedented problem. Before fire, they used their bare hands to put food in their mouths, but with fire discovered, their cooked food was too hot and burned their hands and mouths. It became necessary to fashion crude implements from sticks, the wood of trees and plants to form barely usable spears, spoon-like shapes, cups and plates. Today, we use implements made of metals and alloys to form utensils that are perfectly balanced in the hand, light and easy to hold."

Grandmother can't stand anymore: "Tell the one about the ship, George." Grandfather nods, makes a serious face and gives a little cough to get the next table's attention: "Did you hear the news this morning, Ada? A ship carrying a cargo of yo-yos went down in the Pacific. It sank 146 times!"

Grandmother does her bumpty bump, bump on the table again and laughs! Daddy's furious! Daddy's a big man, but he looks even bigger right now. He jumps up, grabs the man who's starting to mop the floor a little way from us, uses bad language and tells the man to take his "unsanitary, smelly pail and mop out of the restaurant!" Oh, no! The manager is coming over and telling Daddy we have to leave!

Mama and I are so embarrassed, but Grandmother and Grandfather stand up from the table, tell the manager they wouldn't eat in his farshtunken restaurant anyway and then announce to the other customers, who are now looking at us, especially the table beside us: "We've been asked to leave better places than this. Remember when we were at that place in Manhattan, George? Now that was a place and here's how we left there!" Grandmother and Grandfather take each other's arms and do a little dance step as they head for the door! They wave at the customers and start to sing!

"Pack up all our cares and woes, here we go,
singing low, bye bye, blackbird!
Where somebody waits for me, sugar's sweet, so is she,
bye bye, blackbird!
No one seems to love or understand me
And all the hard luck stories they all hand me.
Make my bed and light the light,
I'll be home late tonight!
Blackbird, good-bye!"

Everyone in the restaurant applauds and waves so they turn around to do another chorus, but Daddy grabs them and pushes them toward the door. Mama's crying, Auntie Ann is seriously smoking, Daddy's going for the car and I want to hide! Everything is ruined, but Grandmother and Grandfather keep singing and dancing on the street. They finish their chorus and then Grandmother leans down to me. "Never let them get the better of you, kid. Always leave them laughing, head up high, do a little dance step and a wave good-bye! Never forget that, kid!" Mrs. McBride taught me how to enter a room and now Grandmother's teaching me how to leave one.

Daddy's back with the car. We're going to take Grandmother, Grandfather and Auntie Ann back to the Harvey Hotel on Santa Monica Boulevard, where they're staying. I sit on Mama's lap in the front seat and Grandmother, Grandfather and Auntie Ann are squeezed in the back seat. Grandmother yells, "I'm still hungry! We haven't had lunch yet and it's getting close to dinner! Stop somewhere!"

Daddy's furious because cars are getting in our way and Grandmother keeps yelling. He turns the car radio on really loud so he can't hear her. The voice on the radio excitedly announces Japan has surrendered! Cars start pulling over to the curb and start blowing their horns. People come into the streets. Daddy pulls our car over to the curb and we all get out. Grandmother, Grandfather, Auntie Ann and Mama run into the street singing! Mama's getting people lined up in a conga line!

"You're a grand old flag; you're a high-flying flag,
And forever in peace may you wave!
You're the emblem of the land I love,
The home of the free and the brave!
Ev'ry heart beats true, under red, white and blue
Where there's never a boast or brag.
But should auld acquaintance be forgot,
Keep your eye on the Grand Old Flag!"

I've never seen Daddy so happy. He grabs my hand – the first time he's ever taken my hand! His pretty Masonic ring presses into my palm. His ring hurts, but feels so good. We're singing and following Mama's conga line down the street! It's so exciting! The war is over! Oh, Aunt Gen's boys will be coming home! Ed, Bob, Bill and Erny will be coming home!

Oh, my! Which one am I going to choose to marry?

CHAPTER 7

The Freak Kid

September 1945
11 years old

"He called me Sugar and I called him Jolie."

~ Grandmother

The war is over! Aunt Gen's four boys are coming home. They're all right, except for Erny, who has malaria from fighting in the Pacific, but Aunt Gen says he'll be all right, too. That's good, but I don't think I want to marry Erny if he has malaria. I'm not quite sure what that is, but I don't like the sound of it. I think I like Ed the best. He's the oldest, big and handsome, and kind of reminds me of Daddy, but Bob, he's handsome, too, and the most fun. He's got a great big smile and the happiest-sounding voice. Bill is a bit short and most of the time he seems angry, but I couldn't marry him anyway because he's already married to Ginny and they have baby Theresa.

Aunt Gen wants me to marry Harry John. He's my age, but he's kind of skinny and he doesn't like me anyway, so that wouldn't work. I think I'll marry Bob; he likes me and he makes me laugh. He's very good looking and wears glasses with black frames that make him look like a doctor or lawyer or someone very important. Yes, that's it, I'll marry Bob. I hope he asks me.

Let's see. He's 13 years older than me. I wonder if Aunt Gen and Mama will think that's all right. I'll ask them, of course.

Thank goodness Grandmother, Grandfather and Auntie Ann are going back to Florida. They've decided to only stay a couple more days and I am glad. I hate to say that because Mama loves them so much, but it has been an awful time for Daddy. He refuses to see them anymore, so when Mama wants to see them, we take the bus on Western Avenue to Santa Monica Boulevard and walk two blocks from the corner, where the bus lets us off to get to the Harvey Hotel on the south side of Santa Monica Boulevard.

We're going to see them today, Sunday, and I'm home from school this weekend. I really don't want to go, but Mama is so sad they are going back to Florida. We're going to meet them in the lobby of their hotel, where there is a big, black, grand piano. I hope Grandmother doesn't tell me to play it. I don't think anyone is supposed to, especially a child, but Grandmother and Grandfather like to sing their vaudeville songs and they know I take piano lessons at school.

Mama and I sit on the dark brown, musty-smelling couch in the lobby, waiting for Grandmother, Grandfather and Auntie Ann. Before we sit down, Mama takes her handkerchief out of her purse and tries to brush off the place where she told me to sit. My hands are sweating thinking about Grandmother coming in and telling me to go sit at the piano and play something. I've never played on any piano but the school's and Aunt Gen's and that is a big, tall, brown, upright grand with yellowish ivory keys. I'm used to it and the wind-up piano stool where Aunt Gen sits that she lets me wind up higher when I play. That's so much fun, but this big, black, dusty grand piano in the hotel lobby doesn't have a wind-up stool, only a dusty bench and I can see the piano keys are dusty and some of them are yellowish brown and chipped on the edges.

Oh, oh! Here comes Grandmother, Grandfather and Auntie Ann. Mama rushes up to them, her arms wide wanting to kiss them. Grandmother holds up her cheek to Mama, but Auntie Ann is busy smoking so it's kind of hard for Mama to give her a kiss, but Grandfather has his arms open wide for her and they give each other big hugs and kisses. Mama has tears in her eyes when she turns back to me. Oh, dear. I don't want to see Mama cry. It makes me too sad.

Grandmother looks at me and says, "For God's sakes, kid, why are you standing there? Sit down at the piano and play something, anything!"

I'm scared, but I'm more scared of Grandmother so I sit down, but I don't have any music. Aunt Gen has all the music at her house. I do know two songs by heart, "Smoke Gets in Your Eyes" and "Sleepy Lagoon," but I've never played them for anyone but Aunt Gen and Pop. I love to play "Sleepy Lagoon" because there is a place in the bridge where you cross your left hand over your right and I love to do that. Fancy and fun, but I can't do that today because my hands are shaking so hard I can't keep them on the piano keys.

"What's the matter, kid, that fancy-pants private school hasn't taught you anything?" Grandmother is talking to me, but she's pointing and talking to some people who have come into the lobby and are sitting on some old chairs scattered around the room. She's pointing and talking to the people the same way she did in the delicatessen. "Look at her, folks, the little genius from the fancy-pants school and she's got stage fright! She's no granddaughter of mine. At her age, I was singing on street corners in New York, bringing home the money I got to my mother." Now, she turns, points and looks at Mama. "What's this fancy, genius kid you're so proud of bringing home to you, Helen? Nothing! She's a freak! What kid stands and curtsies every time an adult walks into the room? That school has turned her into a freak."

I sit on the piano bench shaking and sick to my stomach watching the people hurry to walk out of the lobby. Mama comes over to me and pulls me off the bench, puts me behind her.

"Sandy is not a freak, Mama!"

"And what about you, Helen? What are you doing living in that farkakteh apartment waiting for the big macha goy to show up with a handful of goisha groceries? What kind of food is that? Goyim food! You're Jewish! The kid's Jewish. What are you doing hanging around Catholics and those two phony priests? And you've got that freak kid of yours calling that Catholic woman 'Aunt Gen.' She's got a real aunt standing here and what does she have to say to her – "nothing"!

"What's become of you, Helen? You could have married Izzy. He was crazy about you, but no, you had to go to New York, to Ziegfeld, a big shot meal ticket, but you wound up with another meal ticket, a big macha goy you found in a hotel lobby." Grandmother puts the back of her hand to her forehead, shakes her head. "I'm to blame for taking that hat check girl job at the Winter Garden. Yeah, I had a fling with Jolie. It was exciting to sneak around with a guy who had his name in lights on Broadway, 'Al Jolson starring in Jolson at the Winter Garden, February 23, 1911.' He called me Sugar and I called him Jolie."

I look at Grandmother's eyes remembering those days. I've never seen her like this before. She looks younger. "Jolie. I thought no one knew, but my mama guessed. The next thing I know Mama sends me to Kentucky to one of the cousins and I wind up coming back with a baby. Mama told everyone it was my sister Dorothy's baby, but no one believed it. You didn't look like any of us, like anyone in the family, and you still don't."

Mama hides her face in her hands, shaking.

"We're taking the train out of here tonight. I've got a bad taste in my mouth. Come on, George, I've had my say and Helen will do what she always does, exactly what she wants. I can't stand one more minute in this place looking at what's become of her and her freak kid."

Mama pulls me behind her, shaking and crying. Grandmother and Grandfather turn to leave. Auntie Ann looks at us and lets the smoke come out of her nose and follows them. There aren't any hugs or kisses this time.

Mama takes my hand. We go over to one of the old dusty, smelly lobby chairs. Mama pulls me into her lap, holds me, kisses me, cries, tells me that she loves me and that nothing Grandmother said was true. I think Mama's right because Grandmother is always making up show business stories.

The sun is going down behind the hotel. I pull on Mama's hand, I want to get home in time to hear the Lone Ranger on the radio. Cousin Richard told me about the Lone Ranger and his horse Silver; hi yo, Silver, away! I love the music, too! So fast, just like a horse galloping. Oh, no. It's Sunday! He's not on! I want to cry, but I won't. What would people think if they see Mama and me both crying and walking to the corner bus stop?

The bench is full of people waiting for the bus, so we have to stand and lean against the comic bookstore window. Maybe they have the new Lone Ranger comic book. "Mama, can I go in the store and see if they have the new Lone Ranger comic book?"

"No, here's the bus. We have to get on. I want to get home before dark."

We try to beat the dark and run the last block to the apartment. Mama pushes the apartment door open. The musty smell is always there. Mama has her keys out to check the mailbox. She closes her eyes and says a little prayer. I know she's afraid there's a bill in there. Her hand shakes when she pulls out the envelopes with her eyes closed. We walk to our apartment door, the second one down the hall on the right. She turns the key. The apartment is dark. She turns on the light, walks to the radio, turns it on to the news, puts the mail down on the table and sits down in the chair by the window. She takes the cigarette package out of her purse, shakes one out, puts it into her mouth, strikes a match on a little book of matches she took from the hotel lobby, holds it to the end of the cigarette, blows smoke out of her nose and mouth, and stares out the window.

"Mama, would you see if the Lone Ranger's on? I don't think it is, but maybe I'm wrong."

Mama's not paying attention to me. All she does is stare out the window, cry and smoke. Grandmother called me a freak. Maybe Mama doesn't want a freak for a daughter. I don't know what to do. I'll try Mama again. "Mama, would you see if the Lone Ranger is on the radio?"

Mama doesn't listen to me, doesn't look at me. All she does is cry and smoke, cry and smoke. Maybe this is what the words to the song "Smoke Gets In Your Eyes" that Aunt Gen taught me to play mean. I'm so sad. I can't stand to see Mama cry. I don't think she'll ever stop. She's crying because I'm a freak and she doesn't want a freak for her daughter.

I go into the bathroom. I know there's poison in the medicine cabinet because there's a dark bottle with skull and crossbones on the label in there. The label spells IODINE. I hope there's enough in the bottle for me to die because I'm a freak and make my pretty Mama cry.

I take the bottle off the shelf in the cabinet, shake the bottle, hold the bottle up to the light to see how much is in it. It's hard to see, the bottle is dark brown and the light isn't very bright, but I can feel liquid inside. I open the bottle, put my finger over the opening, turn the bottle upside down on my finger, right it, put my finger in my mouth, lick and suck to try to get as much liquid as I can off my finger.

The taste is bitter and ugly, and nothing is happening to me. I'll try again, this time with more liquid on my finger. I'm interrupted when the door flies open. "Sandy!" Mama screams, "What are you doing?" She grabs me and the bottle, turns the water on in the sink, pours the liquid out and holds my hand under the stream of water. "What are you doing, my God, what are you doing?"

CHAPTER 8

"Keep Going, Miss Stacey"

May 1950
16 years old

"Always remember you are first and foremost ladies and conduct
yourselves appropriately in any and all circumstances."

~ Mrs. McBride

Oh, look, the mirror can see all of me! Sixteen! Graduating tomorrow!
Mrs. McBride is going to meet with Eva Lee and me this morning
for our pre-graduation talk in the library. So strange to think we won't be
having anymore tea times after today in this beautiful room.

"Girls, I am very proud of you! You are excellent students and just as, if
not more, important, you have grown into lovely and accomplished young
ladies. Your next step is college."

"Eva Lee, due to your family circumstance, you will probably attend
Los Angeles City College. Suzanne, due to your father's connections, you
will most probably attend USC. You both can step forward into your future
schools with confidence. You are well prepared with all the tools you need to
further your education and live full and rewarding lives, to achieve anything
you desire. You have studied French with Mademoiselle L'enhart; ballet with
Ms. Leporska; voice, diction and elocution with Mrs. Gallantine; etiquette

and social graces with Ms. Flaum. You are experienced in attending military balls, promenades, recitals four times a year and in making entrances."

I smile to myself. I also studied making exits with my Grandmother and Grandfather, Mr. and Mrs. Levy.

"Always remember you are first and foremost ladies and conduct yourselves appropriately in any and all circumstances. You are now excused to spend the rest of the day preparing for tomorrow's activities."

I go into the entry to see the mirror one more time. I feel so important; Mrs. McBride's words have my mind spinning. I can see myself on the USC campus. The other students will look at me and wonder exactly who I am as they can tell by my bearing that I am someone important. Maybe word has gotten around that my father is there lecturing on geology, physics and chemistry. He is also President of the Engineer's Club of Los Angeles and that is prestigious. That means I am well-bred, of good stock, and disproves all of Grandmother's words that day in the hotel lobby. Mama's right; I shouldn't let Grandmother's words stay in my head. She always makes up stories to suit her mood and the story she told about Mama being the love-child of her and Al Jolson is not to be believed. If Mama is their love child, what does that make me, a love grandchild of their union? Just because Mama doesn't look like any of her family and because Mama loves to sing and dance and is so good doesn't prove anything. Grandmother is telling a disgraceful story for some reason. I wonder why? Maybe someday I'll find out.

I blow a kiss to the mirror and she smiles back at me. I can tell she is pleased with the young lady I have become. I'm not sad at our parting as I will come back often to show her how I'm getting along and tell her what I am doing. I will never have to hide anymore. She will always be able to see all of me and we will both be so happy!

Graduation day is beautiful – sunshine and flowers. We hold our diplomas in our hands and say good-bye to the beautiful grounds, our school, our teachers, Mrs. McBride and each other. Everything is so sad and so happy.

Mama gives me a big hug and kiss. Daddy shakes my hand and his jeweled Masonic ring presses into my hand. We get into Daddy's car and head back to the apartment. Mama was hoping we could go to a nice restaurant and have a celebratory dinner, but Daddy has to leave right away for an important appointment.

There is something different in the way Daddy leaves this time. Nothing you can see, or feel, or touch, or smell, but something, something so strong, a presence that seems to crush against Mama and me. We look at each other. There is sadness in Mama's eyes as Daddy's car drives away. I don't want to go into the apartment. After all the beauty and thrill of the day, I don't want to face the ugliness and despair of that hallway, the awful gritty sound of the key turning in the door, the musty smell that no amount of carpet sweeping or throw rugs over the holes can disguise, but I don't have a choice.

Mama and I go in, put our things on the couch, and Mama turns on the radio to a music station, but the radio music only makes things worse. Mama doesn't make her music anymore; she hasn't sung her songs in the longest time. There aren't any bananas on the kitchen table, there aren't any more parties at Aunt Gen's since the war ended, no more visits to Cantor's Delicatessen with Grandmother and Grandfather singing "Bye, Bye Blackbird" — just the silence of the apartment with the impersonal, empty-sounding radio noise. All the joy and confidence of the day begins to drain through me like ice water filling my shoes.

Mama doesn't sing me to sleep anymore. Suddenly, I realize I'm all grown up and I don't want to be.

I'm excited! The dime store manager said I have the job! I'm 16. I have a work permit. Mrs. McBride's voice is in my head. I can accomplish anything I desire. I have the right tools to step forward into a full and rewarding life and this is the start, this is my first step. I am going to be the best worker Mr. Conrad has ever had! I am going to clean this store better than any store has ever been cleaned and sell more than he or anyone else has ever sold.

The dime store is on Adams Boulevard within walking distance of the apartment. Mama will walk me to work every morning, bring me lunch, and then walk me home at the end of the day. I am getting paid! I am very excited!

…I can't do this. I don't know how to clean. I've never seen anyone clean anything. I don't know when anyone cleaned the school. Every morning, it looked clean and beautiful. I know Mrs. McBride couldn't have stayed up all night to clean. She must have had a night staff who came to clean when I was asleep. I never saw Mama clean either. She would push the carpet cleaner over the holes in the carpet back and forth, back and forth, but they never looked any cleaner.

Mr. Conrad should have a staff to clean the store after he closes. I can't do it. I don't want to do it. There are dead flies around the store and in the windows — I can't sweep them up into the dustpan. I tried once, but I could feel their bodies shivering through the handle of the broom. I felt faint, I got sick and when I ran into the bathroom, the smell in there was hideous and he said I had to clean in there as well. I can't do this. I won't do this. I'll get my money at the end of the week and tell Mr. Conrad I quit. This is not the kind of job for a lady and as Mrs. McBride told me, "First and foremost, I am a lady!"

"Suzanne, come back here. I have your money."

"Yes, Mr. Conrad."

"First, I want to show you something at my desk. I'd like you to start learning some of the paperwork that is involved in running a store." Oh, no; I don't want to learn any paperwork. I'm quitting, but I want my money, so I won't say anything until it's in my hands.

"What do you want to show me, Mr. Conrad?"

"Come over here, you can't see from there. Here, look at this sheet!"

I lean over the desk. "Come a little closer. You can't understand the numbers from there." I lean over closer and he purposely brushes his arm inappropriately against me. I jump back. "Oh, I'm sorry, Suzanne. Excuse me. Just take a look at these numbers."

"I don't want to look at any numbers, Mr. Conrad. Please give me my money. My mother is waiting for me at the door."

"Oh yes, Suzanne. Umm, there isn't any reason to mention anything to your mother. Here's your money, I'll see you tomorrow."

I take my money: "No, I won't be coming back tomorrow. This is not a job for a lady and I am a lady. Good-bye, Mr. Conrad." Grandmother's loud voice is in my head: "Never let them get you down, kid. A little wave, head high, and its Blackbird, Bye, Bye!" I want to do a little dance step as I walk out the door, but my legs and feet won't cooperate, but I can give Mr. Conrad my best "head high and blackbird wave" and take Mama by the arm so we can walk away together in our best silk underwear walk.

I love my job! I love the lab! I get to work Monday, Wednesday and Friday afternoons from 2 p.m. to 6 p.m. at Cedars of Lebanon Hospital at Sunset and Vermont. I am an assistant lab technician. I get to wear a white uniform and sharpen needles and wash slides. I am sharpening the most and best needles the lab has ever seen and cleaning slides better than anyone else has ever cleaned them. I even get to bring the pathologist his lunch. He doesn't have lunch until mid-afternoon. I bring his lunch to him from the cafeteria and then, according to instructions from the head lab technician, Eleanor, knock firmly on the door three times. I then place the bag directly on the floor under the doorknob. If I don't place the bag in the exact place under the doorknob, he will not take the bag. I have never seen him in all the weeks I have been working, but I know he must be in there because the bag is gone when I take a peek before I leave for my break.

I love lab work. Eleanor lets me look into her microscope and the microbes and cells are amazing as they come to life before my eyes! And I love Zeranda, the only technician who can make the frogs pee on the slide for the pregnancy tests. Zeranda puts a frog on the slide, rubs it's back and croons "Pee Pee for Zeranda, little frog, make a pretty pee pee." And the frog pees! Zeranda is so funny and so good at her job.

"Suzanne, look at this clipping from the newspaper. It's an announcement from the Los Angeles Light Opera Association that auditions are being held at The Biltmore Hotel next week for singers. They need singers for the first show of their season, "Song of Norway". Why don't you try out? You're always singing around the lab and you have a pretty voice. It might be good for you to try.

"One more thing, Suzanne: Get your eyes checked. We haven't been able to use any of the needles you sharpened. They haven't any points. They're all slanted. You probably have an astigmatism. You should get that checked."

Oh, no! There are so many girls here in The Biltmore Hotel lobby. "Mama, I don't want to go in. Look at the line of singers and look at how they're dressed! I can't go in. They'll laugh at me." I look down at my shoes, the saddle oxfords I wore at school and my navy blue skirt and white blouse. I don't fit in, but we haven't had a chance to go shopping for clothes. So far, I haven't needed anything different. My saddle oxfords, blue skirt and white blouse are fine for every day at Los Angeles City College and at the hospital I wear a white uniform they issued to me to work in the laboratory. I look ridiculous here with these glamourous girls auditioning. I can't go in.

"Come on, Sandy. We're here now. Let's see how this all works. Why not give it a try? Let's get in line."

"Name and phone number!"

Name? Oh, my, what name should I use?

"Sandy, put Suzanne down – Suzanne Stacey."

"Excuse me, are you auditioning?"

"No, I'm here with my daughter."

"Then you'll have to wait over there against the wall. This is only for singers who are auditioning." My hand shakes so hard I can hardly write.

"Photo and resume."

Oh, no. "I don't have a photo or resume." My voice quivers and my mouth is so dry I can hardly get my lips off my teeth.

"No photo or resume? How did you hear about this audition?"

"My friend at the hospital lab where I work showed me the notice in the newspaper."

"All right, I have your name and phone number. Go over there against the wall and we'll call you when your group goes in. Have your music ready."

Oh, no; I don't have any music! Oh, dear, everyone else has music in their hands. What will I do? My head aches, my heart pounds so hard I know everyone can hear and I'm getting sick to my stomach. I want to leave, but Mama would be disappointed. She's so excited and happy, but I don't belong here. I'm not prepared. They're going to laugh at me. I see some of the other girls already looking at me, giggling with their hands over their mouths and smirking. This is awful! I don't belong here. I don't belong anywhere. My mouth is dry — I can't swallow — I need water. Mrs. McBride and Mama say never to use a public drinking fountain, but I'm going to have to take a chance of getting germs and do it this one time.

The theatre auditorium is huge and black. I can't see anything, just the outline of seats and some men sitting in them right in the middle. There are four of us girls lined up against the dark wall of the theatre waiting our turn to go onto the stage and sing. The girl before me walks up onto the stage. I've never seen such shiny, black shoes with such high heels. When she walks, they clack against the wood stage. I wonder how she walks in them without falling? She smiles. She's beautiful! Her long, flowing blonde, wavy hair is pulled back from her face with sparkling jeweled combs. Her earrings are long, shimmering and dazzling. I wonder if they're diamonds. She has on a clinging black suit with a cream-colored blouse. She gives her music to the pianist and puts her shiny, black purse that matches her shoes down on a chair by the piano. She isn't shaking! She walks to the middle of the stage in calm, measured steps, like a queen. She looks across the lights and slowly smiles. "My name is Lillian La Bonte and I am going to sing 'Romance' from The 'Desert Song'." Her lush, smooth speaking voice reaches out into the darkness right to the men in the middle.

"Just eight bars, please, Miss La Bonte," a disembodied voice says from the dark auditorium.

"Yes, sir." She nods to the pianist with a tiny wink. He smiles at her and starts to play. Maybe they know each other. Oh, he is just like Aunt Gen and Miss La Bonte's a wonderful singer! Her voice soars and rings out over the front of the stage, filling the auditorium with effortless, bell-tinkling high notes. Oh, no! I've got to run away! I hate her! I can't go on after her! Her eight bars come to an end with a grand flourish of piano chords and high notes. I'm sick. Going to faint.

"Miss La Bonte. We see you sang with us last season. Thank you for auditioning for us again this year."

"Thank you for the opportunity, gentlemen."

She turns and clack, clack, clack, walks back to the piano smiling and giving a little wink to the pianist in her shiny, black, high-heeled shoes. The pianist stands up and shakes her hand as he gives her back her music and hands her the shiny black purse. She smiles her dazzling smile at him and the tiny wink dances out of her eye again. He smiles, nods and turns back to sit back down at the piano.

I am frozen from head to toe. I can't do this. My body seizes. I can't move my hands or feet. My stomach is in my throat, my tongue is stuck to the roof of my mouth, my lips stuck to my teeth. "Miss Stacey, please, you're next.

"My name is Suzanne Stacey." I copy the beautiful girl before me.

"I'm sorry, we can't hear you. Please project."

I can't get my lips off my teeth! I can't get my tongue off the roof of my mouth! I don't know what to do. I can hear eyerolls from the dark.

"Eight bars, please, Miss Stacey!"

The pianist gives me a funny look. "Where's your music?"

"I don't have any." Barely a whisper. His eyes look at me. I hear more eyerolls from the dark. I've got to do something, say something. "Do you know "Makin' Whoopee?"

The pianist eyes are wide. "Makin' Whoopee? Do you know what key?"

I do know the key. Aunt Gen taught me the keys to the songs and I do know the key and I know how to sing the song! Grandmother's voice yells in my ear: "Don't let them get to you kid. You're Jolie's grandkid. Give them a little wave, head high, a little dance step and sing out, kid, sing out! They ain't heard nothin' yet!" Grandmother's right. I'm not going to let these people get to me. I'm Jolie's grandchild; the show must go on. I take a deep breath, look at the pianist like the other girl did, and tell him my key is C. He nods to me and plays a couple of big C chords and here I go. I put my hand against my stomach, take a breath and —

"Another bride, another groom, another funny honeymoon
  "Another season, another reason for makin' whoopee!"

"Keep going, Miss Stacey," the eyerolls call.

"A lot of shoes, a lot of rice, the groom is nervous,

He answers twice, it's really killin',
that he's so willin' for makin' whoopee!

"Thank you, Miss Stacey. Please come down here. Next, please!"

Oh, dear. I hope I haven't done anything wrong. It's dark, I can barely see, but – "Miss Stacey, my name is Ernest Taylor. I am the founder and head of the Los Angeles Civic Light Opera. I'd like to ask you a few questions. Let's sit over there out of the way."

I follow him across the aisle to the back row of the theatre. "I'm curious to know why you chose 'Makin' Whoopee' for your audition."

"It's my favorite song, Mr. Taylor. My mother was a Ziegfeld Follies girl and she also worked with Eddie Cantor in his show, "Makin' Whoopee". She always sang me to sleep with that song when I was little, but she doesn't sing it to me anymore."

"Very interesting, Miss Stacey. I'd like to meet her."

"Oh, she's right outside, Mr. Taylor."

"I didn't mean right now, but sometime later. Did you give your name and phone number to the man out front?"

"Yes, Mr. Taylor."

"Thank you for auditioning for us today. It was good to meet you."

"Thank you, Mr. Taylor, for giving me the opportunity." I copy what Miss La Bonte said.

"One more thing, Suzanne. How old are you?

"Sixteen."

Mr. Taylor smiles at me, reaches out and takes my hand in both of his and gives my hand a big, enthusiastic shake. I wonder why he did that?

I find Mama standing outside in the big room. She looks at me as though she is reading words off my face. "What happened, Sandy?"

"Well, I don't think I did very well, but I did the best I could. I acted like a lady. I sang "Makin' Whoopee."

Mama grabs me, her eyes tearing, glued on me. She's holding her breath.

"Yes, yes, go on."

"Well, after I sang my eight bars of 'Makin' Whoopee,' Mr. Taylor, he's the head of the organization, called me down into the theatre to talk to me. He asked me why I chose "Makin' Whoopee" to sing and I told him it was because you were in the Ziegfeld Follies and worked with Eddy Cantor and you sang me to sleep every night with that song. He said he would like to meet you."

The tears in Mama's eyes spill over her cheeks and she doesn't bother to wipe them away. She just grabs me in the biggest hug she's ever given me. I hug her back for the longest time, then I take her hand and we walk through the lobby of the hotel, head high and a silk underwear walk that would make Mr. Ziegfeld jump to his feet and shout "Bravo!" I give a little wave: "Bye, Bye Blackbird," Mr. Conrad!

Thank you, Mama; thank you, Grandmother! Thank you, Jolie! Thank you, Mrs. McBride! Whatever happens now who knows, but the one thing Mama and I do know is we are stepping into the future prepared with all the tools we need to live full and rewarding lives, to achieve anything we desire. Yes, indeed, Mrs. McBride; yes, indeed!

CHAPTER 9

Eight Weeks' Work!

June 1950
16 years old

"The moving finger writes; and having writ, moves on,
nor all your piety nor wit shall lure it back to cancel half
a line, nor all your tears wash out a word of it."

~ Omar Khayyam

"The job, I got the job, I got the phone call! Rehearsals start next week and I get paid for rehearsals! Oh, Mama, we're going to be all right!"

"We have to tell Gen! She's been praying for you and so have Father Conway and Father Bajagalupe."

"Aunt Gen, Father Conway, Father Bajagalupe! I got the job!"

Aunt Gen lets out the biggest sigh I've ever heard. She must have been holding her breath for at least two weeks and now Father Conway and Father Bajagalupe are crossing themselves, closing their eyes and praying, giving thanks to God for this amazing turn of events for Mama and me.

"Come on, everyone! Let's have some coffee!" We follow Aunt Gen into the kitchen. Mama squeezes my hand, still crying. Aunt Gen pours coffee out of the blue-speckled coffee pot she keeps on the kitchen stove. "Sandy, tell us what happened!"

"Well, the phone rang and a woman from the Los Angeles Civic Light Opera told me I've been selected to be in the chorus of the first show of their season, "Song of Norway". Rehearsals start next week and I get paid for rehearsals! The show opens in Los Angeles for two weeks, goes to San Francisco for two weeks, a week in Portland, a week in Seattle and then home! That's eight weeks' work! I can't believe it! I was so awful at the audition, I didn't know what to do, I just answered an ad in the paper that my friend at work showed me. I didn't have a picture or resume or music, or anything, but I did the best I could singing Mama's "Makin' Whoopee" song. The pianist didn't know it too well, but he played a C chord to get me started and I got to sing a whole chorus. Mr. Taylor, he's the head of everything, heard me and talked to me afterwards and he wants to meet Mama and now I'm hired!" More hugs and kisses all over again…

Dear Cousin Richard,

I'm writing you from San Francisco! I would have written sooner, but I didn't have a chance. I got a job singing with the Los Angeles Civic Light Opera! Unbelievable! I'm in the chorus of the show "Song of Norway" by Robert Wright and George Forrest. It's a miracle I'm making money. My job's at the dime store and the hospital didn't work out and I didn't know what to do. I want to work, but I'm not trained for anything. Getting this job singing is a miracle, and it pays much better than either of the first two jobs, but I don't know if I'll be able to keep doing this. I don't fit in. None of the chorus members like me. They don't speak to me. They don't want me around them. I'm too young. It's like it was at school. I was too young to play with any of the other girls so I sat on a bench at recess and watched them play. This is the first time in my life I haven't been with Mama or Mrs. McBride and I don't like it.

One of the women in the show is my chaperone, so she has to speak to me, but she can't wait to drop me off at the hotel after the show is over and get back to her friends, who all go to the bar across the street from the theatre. It's called the Curtain Call and everyone goes there but me — because of my age, I'm not allowed. It's painful to hear them laughing and singing and have to walk away with Allegra to go to the hotel and stay in my room all alone. I hate the smell of the hotel and my room. It's musty and lonesome. I can't sleep. I didn't bring anything to read. The other night, during the show, one of the chorus boys touched me inappropriately as we ran off stage and I panicked and ran as fast as I could to the girls' dressing room. He and some of the other boys standing there laughed at me. I don't think being in the theatre is going to work for me. I don't know how I'm going to tell Mama because I'm making good money and Mama is so proud and happy, but I don't see how I can stay in this job. I don't have any voice training and I need training. I try to learn from the other women singers, but they aren't interested in telling me how they have been trained.

And then Mama came to see me last weekend and I was embarrassed. The chorus people were giving us funny looks when they saw her waiting for me at the backstage door. The stage manager was nice and stopped to say hello to her, but he was the only one. Well, there are only four more weeks to go and then I'll be home!

Now, after all my complaining, I want to tell you some good things. I'm the happiest when I am in rehearsals and performing on stage. The stars, Jean Fenn, John Tyler and Robert Rounsfeld, are marvelous! When they sing the opening trio, my whole being melts into the music. Helena Bliss is fabulous as the Contessa and her big song "At the Opera" is amazing, beautiful and funny! When I'm able to take lessons, I want to learn that song. I'll write again as soon as I can.

All my love,
Sandy

"Suzanne, wait a minute!" Oh, dear; the stage manager is calling me. I hope I haven't done anything wrong. "Mr. Taylor wants to see you." Oh, no; what have I done?

Mr. Taylor gets up from behind his desk and comes over to shake my hand. "Come in, Suzanne, sit down. I just want to thank you for all your work and participation in this show this year. I understand you did very well and I look forward to you joining us again next year. I want you to know that I hired you at an early age, as I did the same a few years back with another 16-year-old girl because I had a feeling that after getting training with our organization, she would become a headliner and she did. Her name is Mitzi Gaynor. I see the same raw talent in you that I did in her."

"Oh, thank you, Mr. Taylor, for giving me this opportunity. I'm also looking forward to next year." My stomach is grumbling, making me feel uncomfortable as though it knows I'm lying, but actually, I'm not. I'm looking forward to next year not because I'm going to come back here, but because I'm going to ask Aunt Gen, Father Bajagalupe and Father Conway to pray that I find a husband who will take care of Mama and me.

I hope I'm making the right decision. I don't know. What I do know is that I am breaking Mama's heart and disappointing Mr. Taylor, but what if he's wrong? What if I don't have any raw talent? But maybe he's right. He's giving me a chance for a career, to make money, make life better for both myself and Mama, but I'm so unhappy, but what if I'm unhappy with a life with a husband and children? Maybe that life won't help Mama or me, either.

I don't know, but my mind and heart tells me the theatre is not for me; it is mean, no one likes me and I'm so alone. I'm so scared of being alone. If I get a husband and children, I'll never be alone again, but still – oh, I don't know.

I'm scared to try for a husband and children, but I'm more scared to try for a career. I'll cross my fingers, trust my mind and heart, and ask Father Conway and Father Bajagalupe when they pray to add to their prayers to find a husband for Mama and me. I wonder if and when the time will come, I'll know.

CHAPTER 10

Wedding Bells!

September 12, 1952
9:00 a.m.
18 years old

"Flickering lights, countless slivers of rainbows
bathe the inside of my eyes"

~ Sandy

Mama leans on the ironing board. I hear her sobs. She trembles and cries! Oh, no – her dress! She's burned a hole in the front of her mother-of-the-bride dress she's pressing for my wedding tonight. Her dress is navy blue satin, with a sleek wrap-around skirt ending with a large flat bow on one hip. She must have been saving all last year to get this for my wedding night, but I can't get married tonight. I thought getting married would help both of us, but now I don't know. Can I call Sam and tell him I can't marry him tonight? I can't leave Mama alone. What will she do? Who will take care of her?

Mama says she's talked to Daddy and he's supposed to come to my wedding tonight, but who knows? I hope so.

I love Daddy so much and want him to love me. I think children's hearts are made with special little places in them for a mother's and father's love.

The mother's love place in my heart is filled with Mama's love, but the father's love place in my heart is still empty and waiting. I don't know why. I did everything I could to make Daddy love me. I made straight A's in school. I sat so still when he came to the apartment to sleep on the couch; I never disturbed him. I only sat and watched his pretty Masonic ring go up and down on his chest when he snored.

I did upset him one time, though, I remember. His hair was so pretty and red, full of curls that looked like little springs. I wanted to touch one and pull to see if the curl would snap back onto his head. Once when he was sleeping, I took Mama's hair brush and tip-toed to the couch to put her hair brush against the very tip end of a curl so I could brush and make that curl spring and sparkle, but he felt it, woke up, yelled at me and threw the brush across the room so hard it made a little hole in the wall before dropping to the floor. Then, Daddy sat up, put his head in his hands and covered his hair. I was scared. I shouldn't have touched the tip of his curl with the brush. Maybe that's why Daddy doesn't love me. I don't know. If he doesn't come to my wedding to walk me down the aisle, I'll walk down the aisle with Mama the way it's always been, just the two of us.

Grandmother, Grandfather and Auntie Ann, of course, won't be here. They are too busy getting on trains back and forth, back and forth across the country, stopping for dinners in their favorite restaurant, Galatoire's, on Bourbon St. in New Orleans. I guess they don't want to be around Mama or me, but Mama loves them so much that when she gets a letter from them, she presses the paper to her lips and shuts her eyes like she's praying. She doesn't open it for the longest time, then she presses it against her heart as though she wants her heart to read it first and then, and only then, does she sit down and carefully open the envelope with the little kitchen knife and begins to read and cry.

My heart aches for Mama, but I can't stay in this apartment one more day. Sometimes, when I walk in through the front door of the apartment building, I begin to shake. I don't want to come in here. I want to live in a real house, a house with bedrooms, with a bed that doesn't come out of the wall. The mean lady that was here when I was a little girl has been gone a long time. I wonder what happened to her. I wonder if she had any children. I wonder if she had a husband who loved her and took care of her. But I can't think about her now. I have to get a life started for Mama and me. Maybe she could live with us? I owe her so much. I have to pay her back, but can this kind of debt be repaid? What does a child owe a parent? What does a parent owe a child? I don't have an answer. I have to think. Wait a minute: Mama's smart and pretty. She could go back to New York, find Grandmother, Grandfather and Auntie Ann. Maybe Mama could even find a husband for herself; maybe Izzy's still available? Grandmother said that day in the Harvey Hotel that Izzy was crazy about Mama. Who knows, miracles happen. Look at how I found Sam, in a kiddie school of all things, Meglin Kiddies on Venice Boulevard near Western Avenue. Aunt Gen found the school advertised in the paper and gave Mama the address. The Meglin Kiddies, founded by Ethel Meglin. Shirley Temple and Margaret O'Brien are two of her famous kiddies.

So, Mama and I took the bus and found the address and went inside and met the singing teacher, Gordon Johnson. He's singing at my wedding tonight. He introduced me to Sam. Sam's sister, Francine, is one of the dance teachers and she is getting married next month. Sam has a good voice and Francine wants him to sing for her wedding, so she arranged for him to take singing lessons from Mr. Johnson and that's how we met.

I liked Sam from the start. He's good looking, tall, with broad shoulders and he's a good singer. He's 10 years older than me and I like that. He's been in the Navy, graduated from USC, has a job at a corporation in Montebello, has a car and lives with his mother and father in Whittier. Sam liked me from the start, too. I was only 16, but he didn't care. He asked me out to dinner at the Steak 'N Stein restaurant in Whittier. I didn't think Mama would let me go, but she did, and she went with us so the date was all right and she came along with us on every other date until I turned 18. Sam didn't mind. Sam and Mama liked to smoke together after dinner. They liked each other and Aunt Gen liked Sam, even though she had hoped I would marry her next-to-youngest son, Harry John, but he married Donna, so that was that. All the sons, except for baby Mike, are married. Now, it's my turn.

We had an evening wedding in a small church in Whittier. Daddy walked me down the aisle. I wore a knee-length white lace gown with a little collar and covered lace buttons all down the front of the bodice. My shoes were white pumps. I had a little lace cap with a short veil and carried a bouquet of white roses. Sam's sister, Francine, was my attendant and she wore a yellow cotton dress. There were candles all around the altar. Sam's singing teacher sang a beautiful wedding hymn, composed by his friend, Nicholas Brodsky, "Be My Love." It was so pretty, so very, very pretty. We honeymooned in Las Vegas for the weekend. I had never been there, so I was excited to see all the lights and the opulent casinos.

We have a lovely little apartment over a retired couple's garage in Whittier. The retired couple is so nice and so happy to have newlyweds living above them. Sam's Aunt Myrtle moved into a retirement villa a few months before we married and had stored all her furniture. She gave us her beautiful furniture. All the wood is maple and the upholstery on the overstuffed couch and chair is a rose and daffodil green leaf print against a white lattice looking material: so cheery and comfortable.

Myrtle is very nice and loves to knit. I like to watch her fingers hold the knitting needles and see the yarn go over and under the needle to form a stitch. She is making herself a beautiful shawl and says she will teach me to knit and crochet when I come to visit her.

I will be happy to do that as I am so unhappy being married. I am overwhelmed with loneliness sitting day after day in our little apartment with nothing to do except dust our pretty furniture. I can't believe I want my old life back again. I can't believe I miss the apartment, the little mouse. I miss Mama so much. I miss Aunt Gen and her piano so much. I miss Father Conway and Father Bajagalupe and I can't believe I actually miss Grandmother, Grandfather and Auntie Ann. What's wrong with me?

This is the second month of being married. I didn't know being married would be like this, being left alone all day. Sam goes to work every morning and doesn't come home until around 6:00 or 7:00 at night. He brings dinner home with him, usually something from the nearby Chinese restaurant. He sits in the pretty overstuffed chair after dinner and reads until bedtime. He brought me some books from his parent's house to read and that helps a little, but not enough.

On Sundays, Sam's parents invite us to their house in La Habra for Sunday dinner. The house is very cute and his mother is a good cook and sets a pretty table. His father smokes little Bull Durham cigarettes that remind me of Pop Foglesong. After dinner, we play a card game called Pinochle. I have never played any games, so Sam's father taught me.

I like going out there, but his parents don't like me. I feel bad about that. I don't know why they don't like me. I always look nice and I have very good manners. If they had a staircase, I could walk down and make a nice entrance, but they don't. If I knew how to cook, I would make something to bring to their Sunday dinners, but I don't. I wonder if Sam's Aunt Myrtle could help me learn. Oh, yes; Sam has another aunt, Aunt Ann, and she knows how to cook. When I next see her, I will ask her to show me how to do it. That's a good idea.

I think things will be better for me when I learn how to cook. Sam can bring home groceries from the market and Aunt Ann will give me one of her cookbooks. Myrtle will teach me how to knit. That will help, but it still won't be any company for me. I need a human being in my life, someone to talk to and with, someone to do things. A baby! That's what I need! I need a baby!

Eleven Months Later

It's dark. I'm so scared. I want Mama. I need Mama. I can't do this. I feel the wetness on my legs. I'm going to get the seat of the car wet. I hope I don't ruin our car seat. Sam doesn't notice. He's concentrating on getting me to the hospital. The baby's coming, at least that is what I read: "When your water breaks, you must go to the hospital because your baby is going to be born." That's what the book said, but it doesn't say how it is going to get out of you. I've seen babies. They are big. How does it all happen? I'm so scared. I want Mama.

A boy: 10:00 in the morning, the sun shines through the delivery room windows, shines on my son, shines on the dark brown curls covering his entire head and his big wide-open eyes are hazel. He looks like a Botticelli painting. My son. I'll never be alone again.

Two Years Later

A girl! 6:35 p.m. The doctor is holding her up. The sun's last rays shine through the delivery room window on the red hair that crowns her head. Big blue-green eyes gaze at me. She's so alert, so pretty! She isn't crying, just looking around at everything. The doctor gives her to me. She's trying to find her tiny fist and get it into her mouth. She must be hungry. I hold her close to me and she nuzzles, trying to find something to eat — another miracle.

My days are full now. I was right. I'm not lonely anymore with nothing to do. Sam comes home earlier from work now after stopping at the market. for diapers and baby powder and little moist wipes and diapers, diapers and diapers. Oh, my; I didn't know how many diapers little babies, and not so little babies, use. We don't have a washing machine, so I am washing diapers in the bathtub. Thankfully, the retired couple is letting us use their clothes lines in the backyard to dry the diapers. We are going to have to find another place to live. It's so hard carrying baskets of diapers up and down stairs every day. I can't believe I'm saying this: "I want another baby!"

One Year Later

Almost midnight. Another girl. She looks like the Gerber baby on the labels of the Gerber baby food, golden-brown hair, big blue-sky eyes, so very beautiful. I thought two babies were enough, that with two I had nothing more to wish for, but I was wrong. God knew better than I did.

18 Years Later – April 1970
Placentia, California

Change is difficult, wanted and unwanted change – children are born, grandparents die, twists and turns, ups and downs, rollercoaster rides to the moon and stars and then the stomach-lurching, churning, swaying, tumbling from one side to another as you plummet back to earth and your husband doesn't like you anymore and you take the first desperate, frightening steps on the yellow-brick road to see the Wizard, to an uncharted, unknowable destiny.

"Opprobrious — public disgrace — public shame!" Mrs. McBride would swoon or faint if she heard of one of her girls becoming divorced. Oh, no! Ladies did not, could not, become divorcees! The shame! I will not, cannot let that happen. A separation might be tolerable, less disgraceful and shameful. I don't know. I don't know what to do. This can't be happening. I can't think about what's happening. We have three children. I have to take care of them. I must fold the clothes I left on my son, Steve's, bed. Maybe my daughters Kim and Lori could help fold. Maybe I should ask Steve to help, but folding clothes isn't boy's work; it's girl's work.

There are so many clothes. They're piled up to the ceiling. I can't fold them all. I can't, I can't, I can't do it! I don't know how. I wasn't prepared for this! I don't know what to do. I don't know how to clean a house; I don't know where to start cleaning. There are three bathrooms; two upstairs, one downstairs. Do I start cleaning the sink first, or the bathtub, or the shower? I don't know how to wash the clothes, turn on the machine, the dryer — how to market, to cook, to drive, don't have a car. Don't know how to do anything but sing and I don't really know how to do that either, never studied, just a few lessons with my husband's singing teacher before we got married. What is going to happen to me, the children, Mama?

Flickering lights, countless slivers of rainbow bathe the inside of my eyes, my temples explode, what's happening to me, where am I? Where am I?

CHAPTER 11

Therapy Time

Still April, 1970

"I don't know how to do anything but sing."

~ Sandy

O h! *This place is so pretty, look at the pretty stairs, the pretty rooms, pretty flowers on the table! I have a pretty room with a bed by the window. The bedspread isn't pink and ruffly, but the bed is very neat. There's another bed in the room. Who sleeps there?*

Look at this big room. Oh, how wonderful! There's my big round mirror with the gold frame hanging on the wall — hello, mirror, how did you know I was here, how did you find me? You must have followed me from school! You can see all of me! Does Mrs. McBride know you're here? Did you tell her you were coming? I hope you did or she will be so worried about you. Can you stay here with me or do you have to go back to the school? I hope you can stay. Do you remember how little I was the first day I met you? You couldn't see me and I could only look up and see Mama in your frame, but somehow you knew I was there holding her hand and I knew you were going to wait for me to grow up so we could see each other and talk. Remember? That was such a long time ago.

Oh, my goodness; look over there in the corner of the room — there's the big, black grand piano from the hotel! The piano must have followed me, too!

How wonderful, the mirror followed me and the piano followed me. They must like me or they wouldn't have followed me so far to be with me now. Oh, dear; I don't want to disappoint the piano, but I don't think I can play on her. I don't have my music. I think I can remember my cross-hand piece, "Sleepy Lagoon," but I'm not sure and I don't want to try it in front of the people, even though Grandmother says children are allowed to play on hotel lobby pianos. When Mama brings my music, I can play for the guests this afternoon. I think they will like "Sleepy Lagoon" and like how I play it because I cross my left hand over my right and that's fancy. I know Mama can't come today, but she'll be here tomorrow. She says if I like this place, I can stay here. I like it!

"Good morning, Mrs. Raymond. I'm Dr. Gold; nice to meet you. You came to us yesterday. You were quite upset. Your mother's attorney admitted you. He told us you had a breakdown, that you were unstable, violent, a danger to yourself and others. We gave you a mild sedative on admission to keep you calm until we can evaluate your condition."

"How can he say that? He's lying. He hardly knows me. Why is he telling you my name is Raymond, my mother's maiden name, not my real married name?"

"Please stay calm, Mrs. Raymond. I need to talk to you to understand why you are here. If you're unable to talk to me today, we will give you more sedation and postpone today's session until tomorrow."

"Dr. Gold. I'm not unstable, violent, or a threat to myself or anyone else. I'm confused and upset right now and understandably so. The attorney is not a proper gentleman. He didn't stand up when my mother and I came into his office. We should have immediately turned around and left, but we didn't know where to go and we needed an attorney. My cousin in New Jersey, who is an attorney, recommended him. He was my cousin's classmate in college. I want to call my cousin now. Something is very, very wrong. Why is this attorney using my mother's maiden name? Why was he with me? Why is he telling lies about me?"

"I understand he is handling your divorce, Mrs. Raymond?"

"Divorce! No, no! I am not getting a divorce! Ladies do not get divorces! Opprobrious! I will never get a divorce! No! No! No!"

"Again, Mrs. Raymond: Please calm down. We will discuss that at a later time. Right now, I need you to tell me what has been going on that is causing you distress."

"Dr. Gold, I'm not sure I should be telling you about personal problems."

"It's all right, Mrs. Raymond. I'm a doctor. I am here to help you, but I can only do that if you tell me what is causing you distress."

"Dr. Gold, it is nice of you to want to help me, but I'm not comfortable divulging personal information. A lady's personal life is something she does not discuss with strangers."

"Mrs. Raymond, to repeat, I'm your doctor and you are in a facility that helps people with their personal problems. That is my job, that is what I'm here for, and I want to listen to everything you have to say."

"My husband doesn't like me anymore. I'm not a good wife. I thought I would be a good wife as I have had the proper training at my private school, Monticello School for Girls. Our principal, Mrs. McBride, taught us how to act properly with properly trained men and I thought my husband had been properly trained, so I thought I would be a very good wife. I can come down a staircase properly, one hand gracefully resting on the banister, one foot, toe pointed, sliding onto the first step, followed by the other foot in the same position. 'Your posture must be regal, head up, eyes looking at your guests waiting for you at the foot of the stairs and you must smile your prettiest smile because your future might depend on the way you enter a room.' I do that very nicely. I thought my husband and his parents would like that. I thought I would be an asset to him and his mother and father, but they didn't seem to think coming down a staircase was important. Maybe that's because they don't have stairs in their house."

"I see. Go on."

"Well, my problems with marriage began right after we came back from our honeymoon. I had just turned 18. We had a darling little apartment and then my husband went to work the next morning. He told me he didn't like to eat breakfast at home. He liked to have breakfast at a little restaurant on the way to his work. I told him, as I didn't know how to cook, that I thought that was a good idea. After he left, I looked in the little cupboard in the kitchen and found some cereal and then looked in the refrigerator and found some milk, so I had cereal and milk for breakfast. My husband's mother and father had stocked the cupboards with food we would need to get started while we were on our honeymoon so that was good. There was a coffee pot, but I didn't know how to make coffee, so I just had another glass of milk. I didn't know what to do. I was all alone.

"There weren't any books in the apartment or a radio, so I decided to unpack our clothes and hang them in the closet. My husband's mother and father had also brought clothes hangers for us so that was good. I finished hanging up the clothes, then took a little nap, took a little walk and finally the hours passed and my husband came home.

"I was so glad to see him, but he wasn't glad to see that I didn't have dinner waiting for him. I thought we would be going out to dinner. How could he think I could have a dinner waiting for him? I don't know how to cook. I told him that before we got married and there wasn't anything to cook in the apartment anyway. He said I should have gone to the market to get something to cook for dinner, but I didn't know I was supposed to do that and I didn't know where the market was or how I was to get there anyway.

"I didn't know how to drive, but that didn't make a difference as there wasn't a car for me and still isn't. My husband hadn't ordered one. I thought he knew ladies do not drive and I would need a chauffeur. What if a lady is driving and the car breaks down? How does a lady fix it? Ladies need a chauffeur because chauffeurs know where places are. They would know where a market is. I'd never been to a market. I told my husband before we were married that I didn't know how to cook, but I didn't think that mattered as he was a cook in the Navy and loved being in the kitchen cooking all sorts of wonderful things.

"I didn't learn how to do that at my school. Mrs. McBride, our principal at the private girl's school I attended, never allowed us girls near the kitchen. 'It is too dangerous. There are pots of boiling water in a kitchen that can spill on you, sharp knives that can cut you, fire on the stove that can burn you.' No, a lady must never go near a kitchen. Her job is to sit properly in the library, back straight not touching the back of the chair, make polite conversation and ring a little bell so the maid can bring in tea on a beautiful silver tray, in a beautiful China teapot with beautiful China cups and saucers and beautiful little water cress sandwiches. 'A lady does not go to a public market! It isn't proper!'"

"Yes, Mrs. Raymond, go on."

"When we had children, we got a big house. I have three wonderful children, a boy named Steve, a girl named Kimberly and a girl named Lori. Our house has five bedrooms. I don't know how to clean it – I don't know where to start. I don't know where to get the equipment necessary to clean this big house or how to use the equipment. There are three bathrooms! Should I start cleaning the one downstairs or the one in the master bedroom, or the one between my children's bedrooms? Am I supposed to clean the sink first, then the bathtub, then the shower, and then, heaven forbid, the unmentionable? I don't know where to start and I don't want to start! It isn't right!

"And there is so much laundry. What am I supposed to put in the washing machine first? What goes in the dryer and then where do I put the clothes that come out of the dryer all dry? Where do I put the clothes that are supposed to be ironed? My husband told me I was supposed to wash and iron his white shirts for his work. He said he had to have a clean shirt every day. That makes five shirts. How am I supposed to do that?

"He said I needed to starch the collar. I don't know what starch is! Mrs. McBride didn't teach us about starch, but I saw my Aunt Gen on washday boiling a liquid she said was starch in a big pot on the kitchen stove. One of her sons would dip the shirts in it. The liquid was boiling! That's dangerous! It is too dangerous to be in a kitchen with a boiling liquid. I will never do that. Never! And then Sam said I would have to use bleach on his collars. What is bleach and why do you put it on shirt collars? Mrs. McBride never taught us about bleach. She didn't teach us about ironing. If she had thought we were going to have to iron, she would have warned us not to get near an iron. 'They are very hot, very dangerous.' If you leave one on an ironing board, they can burn your house down. And how do you open an ironing board without pinching your fingers? I tried once and caught my finger in the metal parts and it collapsed on me. Ironing boards are dangerous. Mrs. McBride did not train her girls to be cleaning people, or washing, drying, ironing, starching, bleaching, marketing, driving people! These are not ladies' jobs!

"And I don't know where to put all the dry, laundered clothes. I put them on my son Steve's bed and started folding and making stacks, two stacks for my daughters, one stack for my son, one stack for myself, and one stack for my husband, but my husband doesn't want to stay in the house with us anymore, so I guess I don't have to make a stack of his clothes, but where should I put the clothes he didn't take with him?

"I don't know what to do! I left a huge pile of clothes on my son Steve's bed that's so high they reach the ceiling. I forgot how to fold them or where to put them. Steve is my son. He has the 'bonus room' off our master bedroom.

We gave that to him when Mama came to live with us. I don't know why they call it a bonus room. The advertisement when we bought the house called it a 'bonus room.' I'm not sure what that means, but that's what they call it. I think you get a 'bonus' for free when you buy your house. That's why they call it a bonus room. My mouth is dry, Dr. Gold. I've been talking too much. I'm going to drink some water out of this glass that's by my chair. Is that all right?"

"Yes, Mrs. Raymond. Take a drink and then go on."

"Well, Mama's employment agency business went out of business. Her partner was angry with her. He locked her out of her office by changing the locks after she went home. Mama had to move in with us. What else could she do?"

"Go on."

"I thought that arrangement would be helpful and fun to have Mama with us. She's such a good cook and she loves cooking. I thought she and my husband would have fun cooking up great dinners, smoking together after dinner and Mama could help me with the house and kids, but she really didn't know too much about a house or raising children either. Mrs. McBride raised us girls in our beautiful school, but all Mama had was a little tiny one-room apartment with a kitchen and a bathroom. Mama had a carpet sweeper and she would push the carpet sweeper over and over the carpet. I was only with her a few weekends a month.

"My house doesn't have a carpet and I don't have a carpet sweeper. I have a vacuum, but I'm afraid to touch it. I don't know how to run the machine. I don't know how! Mrs. McBride didn't teach us! I'm afraid to turn the little switch on because my husband turned the switch on one day and the vacuum got away from him and ran into the wall and made a hole. He was very angry. He made another hole in the wall with his fist above the hole the vacuum made. The vacuum has an engine that is very loud. I'm afraid to try and push it. I don't know how! It looks quite dangerous with all its brushes spinning around and it's very heavy, it might pull me right across the room! Mrs. McBride didn't tell us about machines for the house."

"Tell me more about Mrs. McBride, Mrs. Raymond."

"Mrs. McBride was our principle and ran a beautiful school for young ladies. She always wore long pink soft gowns that came to her ankles and a beautiful pink jacket with long sleeves. She always had a white lace hanky tucked into one of the jacket sleeves and the lace spilled out over her hands and danced around her fingers. I loved to watch the lace dance around her fingers. Her hair was silvery blonde and she made it into a bun at the back of her neck. She always smelled of gardenias and her eyes were bright blue and you could see tiny bits of powder on her cheeks. She taught us to be ladies who would have a staff when we had a home.

"I'm not supposed to be living this way. I'm a lady! I'm supposed to have a staff to run the house and help with the children, but my husband says we can't afford a staff. He didn't tell me that before we got married. I thought houses came with a staff when you bought the house. I didn't know you had to find a staff. I just didn't know! My husband told me I was supposed to be the staff, do the marketing, cooking, cleaning, washing, drying, ironing, bleaching, driving. The children can't help. They're not supposed to help! They're only supposed to study like I did! I need a library room for them where we can have tea, but maybe that wouldn't be good for my son. I don't know. I'm not a good mother! I don't know what to do with a boy. I don't know how! How am I supposed to know?"

"Go on."

"I don't know how to do anything but sing and I don't know how to do that properly. I need proper training. I've never studied how to sing. I did get a job, a long time ago, when I was 16. They paid me real money, eight weeks' work singing on a real stage in a real theatre, but the chorus people didn't like me and when we traveled, I had to stay alone in an awful smelly, cold hotel room all by myself in the dark every night, all alone, because I was too young to stay with the chorus people and go to the bar they liked to go to after the show. I was so afraid and lonesome and I cried so much. I wanted Mama. I wanted her with me to sing me to sleep.

"I couldn't sleep in the hotel room bed. It wasn't pink and it had an awful smell and the blanket scratched and the sheets and pillowcase were itchy, they weren't silk and ironed like they were in my school. I wanted to sleep on Mama's arm like I did when I was little. I couldn't sleep in that hotel bed so I went into the closet and made a pillow out of my coat and put my sweater over my head to keep warm and slept there. I was used to being in a closet. In the apartment where I lived when I was a little girl, I used to hide in the closet. The closet in the hotel was warmer than the room so that was good because I didn't know how to make the heat come on in the room.

"I didn't want to ask my chaperone, Allegra – isn't that the prettiest name? – how to make the heat come on because she didn't want to come into my hotel room and visit. She wasn't happy about having to walk me back to the hotel. When we got there and walked up the stairs to my room, she just opened the door for me and said, 'Good night,' and hurried back to sing at the Curtain Call, the bar across the street from the theatre. I was too young to go to the Curtain Call after the show, but I wanted to; I wanted to sing some more. Isn't that funny? We had just finished singing a two and a half hour show, but the chorus people and I wanted to sing more in the bar. I love to sing. I could sing you 'Makin' Whoopee!' My mama used to sing that to me when I was little and had to hide in the closet."

"Thank you, Mrs. Raymond, perhaps on my next visit. Right now, I'd like to know why you had to hide in the closet when you were a child."

"The apartment didn't allow children or pets! If anyone heard or saw me, we would have to move and where would we go? Sometimes, I would be so afraid the other tenants would hear me and report me I would go into the closet and hold my breath as long as I could and then I would take Mama's coat off the hanger and put it over my head so I could breathe into that. The walls in the apartment were so thin. If the neighbors heard me breathe, they would tell the mean lady that there was a child in the building and then it would be my fault if Mama and I had to leave. Where would we go? How would Daddy find us?

"Mama found me a pretty school. I couldn't go to a regular school. I was too young. I was only four, but Mrs. McBride liked me and I went to live with her. I loved it there! It was so pretty!"

"All right, Mrs. Raymond; our time is up. Thank you for taking the time to speak with me, but I must leave now. You will benefit from the medication I am going to prescribe for you. It will help you feel more comfortable and help you adjust to your new circumstances. At that time, you will be discharged."

"Discharged? But I can't be discharged! Where will I go? You will have to call my mother!"

"Your mother will be notified. Don't worry. We will take care of you while you are here and after you leave, we will refer you to a doctor who will help you with your new situation. Now, enjoy the rest of your day with us. Our day nurse, Elba, will be helping you."

"But, Dr. Gold, there is something more I want to tell you. It's very important!"

"I'm sorry, Mrs. Raymond, but I really must go. Our time is up. We will talk more next week."

"But Dr. Gold, I, I think it's very important."

"Have a good day, Mrs. Raymond. We'll see each other next week."

CHAPTER 12

Second Therapy Session

July 1970

"Kid, kid, listen to me. You Depression kids are tough –
the toughest of the tough. You can't be stopped! You got
Jolie's blood in you. They ain't seen nothin' yet!"

~ Grandmother

I want to tell Dr. Gold something important today. I want to tell Dr. Gold about a recurring dream that I think is important. I'm standing at the top of two parallel lines that are gradually coming together at the bottom, like a painting showing perspective. I'm very young. A big black bowling ball is rolling down the middle of the lines toward white bowling pins. The parallel lines are coming together, making the space between the lines smaller and smaller. They begin to squeeze the ball! I scream, "Stop the ball! Someone stop the ball!" The ball is being squeezed to death by the lines. My head throbs. The ball is my head! I wake up sweating and screaming, my hands holding both sides of my head, my heart pounding.

I had the dream again last night. I need to make it stop! I don't see anyone else in my dream, but someone is there – maybe the paperboy who delivered newspapers to the apartment before I moved to Monticello. He must have been a naughty boy because once I was standing alone in the outside hallway of the apartment and my Daddy and Mama came running after him and chased the boy out the back door. He was fast so Daddy didn't catch him. Daddy was the maddest I'd ever seen him and I was scared. Mama said Daddy wasn't mad at me, but at the paperboy because he touched me. I don't remember that at all. But I also don't remember how I got into the hallway. There was a lot of commotion that something bad happened to me, but I don't remember anything like that. We got a new paperboy after that and I got to go to Monticello School for Girls. I want to ask Dr. Gold about that dream.

"Good morning, Mrs. Raymond. Sorry to keep you waiting. How are you feeling today?"

"Fine, Dr. Gold, thank you, but I need to speak with you about– "

"I'm glad to hear you're feeling fine. How would you like to go home at the end of the week?"

"What? I don't think that will be possible! You see, my house is being sold, I can't return there. Mama's trying to make arrangements for me and the children to find another place. I don't think she'll be able to do that so quickly."

"Mrs. Raymond, understand this is not an extended care facility. You are now stable. You're on the proper medication to help you function more comfortably. We'll have prescriptions ready for you to fill upon discharge. Your mother will be staying with you to help you get settled and help with the children. You will need to arrange follow-up care with your own private doctor for weekly therapy sessions. You're ready for discharge."

"Again, Dr., I can't get discharged until I talk to Mama. I don't know where we're going. I've always wanted to live with my Aunt Gen Foglesong; she had a big wonderful house and six sons! Can you imagine that? I loved her house and all her boys. I wanted to marry all of them. Aunt Gen loved me, too. She always told me she prayed to God to have a little girl and then

I came into her life. She wanted me! I loved everything about her and her boys and the house. Did I tell you about wash day?"

"No, go on."

"Every Saturday was wash day. All the Foglesong boys went to Catholic school and had to have a clean, starched, white shirt every day. That was five shirts a boy times six. Thirty shirts a week! The oldest boys would string up clothes lines on two sides of the dining room and each boy had an assigned station. The oldest, Ed, ran the Singer sewing machine with the foot pedal and he did repairs on the shirts with the sewing machine and then he sewed on missing and loose buttons by hand. Aunt Gen made starch in a great big kettle on the stove – it smelled so good – Bill would dip one shirt at a time in it. Erny ran the washing machine while Bob ironed. Then Harry John took the ironed shirts and hung them on the clotheslines in the dining room. They looked like soldiers all stiff and white, smelling so good of starch and sunshine, ready to march off to school. Such a happy house, the house smelled so good, so clean and fresh on washday, so much laughter, good, hearty, musical laughter. Nothing's as wonderful to my ears as the sound of Foglesong laughter and then there was the blue-speckled coffee pot perking on the stove, another wonderful smell…yes, that's where I want to go when I leave here, to Aunt Gen's house, but she isn't, you know, there anymore. Pop died of a heart attack one day.

"There was a wake. Pop was laid out in the dining room in a coffin, all dressed up in a suit and tie. Bob had put a pouch of Bull Durham in his shirt pocket with the tab hanging over the edge just the way, you know, Pop always did. Aunt Gen was sitting in her chair by Pop mending socks. I liked to watch her pull a sock over her worn wooden egg and begin mending with her darning needle and thread, in, out, clicking, sliding with each stitch. The daughter-in-laws stayed busy in the kitchen keeping food on the dining room table, keeping clean dishes available. Father Conway and Father Bajagalupe were praying and eating, and I was playing "Smoke Gets in Your

Eyes" for Pop. I always smell little white beans and ham cooking when I play that song. I expected Pop to sit up in his coffin and yell at me, 'Play it again, Sandy, with more feeling this time!' Mama and I were happy and sad all at the same time. It felt so good to be in the Foglesong house. My school was beautiful, but I missed the laughter and homey smells at Aunt Gen's. They asked me how I knew, my true love was true…"

"Go on."

"Mrs. McBride had a hearty laugh, but it wasn't the same as the Foglesong laugh. Nothing is. The smells at the school were different. No smell of ham hocks or little white beans or Bull Durham or whiskey. Mrs. McBride smelled of powder and flowers, especially her little white lace hanky, tucked into her sleeve with the lace spilling over her wrist, so pretty, especially when she gestured with her hand and arm and the lace danced around her fingers. But there wasn't any chatter in the school, no outbursts of joy, excitement or even anger, just lovely polite, calm, gentleness."

"You must have hated to leave."

"Oh, yes! When I left the school, there was nothing but rudeness: chaos, roughness, ugliness, cars, buses, clanking, honking – putrid fumes, shoving, yelling. I hated it! I wanted to get married and live in a house like Aunt Gen. I wanted to have six sons like she did, but after I got married, I changed my mind. I wanted three children, the three children I have, my son, Steve, and daughters, Kim and Lori. Dr. Gold, did I tell you what they intend to do with their futures?"

"No, go on."

"Kim wants to be an actress and Steve wants to go into law enforcement, become a sheriff. My youngest, Lori, wants to marry and have a family. They are all determined to realize their goals. I won't be surprised if they succeed."

"Dr. Gold, is there any way possible you could arrange for me to stay here one more week? I don't think I'll be able to handle everything after I leave. I don't even know where I'm going."

"Mrs. Raymond, I'm sorry, but your time here is over. You cannot stay. Your mother will be here later today to arrange your discharge. Make an appointment with a therapist. The front desk will give you referrals. You will need weekly sessions for awhile. Be sure to fill your prescriptions today. Good-bye, good luck!"

"Mrs. Raymond, do you need any help getting ready for your discharge this afternoon?"

"No, thank you, Elba. I really hate to leave. It's so pretty here and everyone has been so nice. I don't know where I'm going."

I wonder if I should wait in my room for Mama or in the foyer?? No one's told me and I hate to ask. I'm afraid I'll sound unwell. As much as I hate to leave here, I miss Mama, the children and Aunt Gen. Oh, how I wish we could go and live with her. There's so much laughter in her house, and I love Father Conway and Father Bajagalupe. Maybe he could teach me some more Italian songs. I wish I were seven years old again and the war was on. I miss all the boys, the service men and the parties. Why did the war have to go away?

"Mrs. Raymond! Your mother is here waiting out at the front desk. Should I have her come to your room?"

"Oh, no, Elba. That's all right. I'll come to her."

"Let me take your bag."

"Oh, if you don't mind, I'd like to carry it. I don't want Mama to think I'm not well."

"Whatever you like, Mrs. Raymond. Everyone here wishes you well, vaya con Dios. God be with you!"

"Thank you, Elba. Please thank everyone here for me. Everyone has been so wonderful."

"Mama!"

"Sandy!"

"Oh, Mama, you look so pretty! I love that navy blue skirt and cream-colored blouse on you."

"You look great! You look so rested!"

We kiss and hug each other; her Tabu perfume smells so good. Maybe Elba's words are right, maybe God will be with me. I don't know.

"Sandy, I found us a house in Downey. I've made arrangements with a realtor so we can stay there until it sells. It's been vacant for some time and had been vandalized so the owners are glad to have a family stay there temporarily. It's small, two bedrooms, den, but it has a lovely pool. It's in a good school district for the kids. Don't worry about the rent; I can take care of that. The best thing about it is it's not far from Gen. She and Bill are living together in an apartment they found near Downey Hospital."

"Oh, Mama, that's so great!"

Two Weeks Later

Oh, no; he's looking through the living room window. He sees me. Oh, dear; I don't want to be impolite. He did win the case against Mama's business partner and he took it pro bono. That was good of him. I should open the door and see what he wants. Maybe he has another check for Mama. That would be a nice surprise for her when she comes home tonight, or maybe he has some more important papers for her to sign. It must be something important or he wouldn't have driven all this way out here to Downey from Los Angeles. The least I can do is have him come in and wait for her, offer him a cup of coffee or a glass of water. I just wish I didn't have this uncomfortable tingling on the back of my neck. I take a deep breath and open the door…

A blow from a hand, hard and swift across the front of my neck; I fall to the floor choking, unable to scream as my thumbs are twisted, pulled, excruciating pain. I hear his voice: "That's the end of piano and singing. Let's see what you do now."

Five Hours Later

"Where am I?" The bright lights are hurting my eyes.

"Mrs. Raymond. You're in the emergency room at Downey Community Hospital. The doctor will be right in."

"Mrs. Raymond, I'm Doctor Richards. Don't try to talk. You have an injury to your vocal chords and your thumbs are dislocated. We'll take X-rays to confirm the dislocation and rule out any fractures. I've left a message for Dr. Brody, our hand specialist, to come in and take a look. He'll take over your treatment. You'll also need to see a specialist regarding your vocal chords. You'll spend the night here in the hospital. Your mother is in the waiting room and will stay with you."

"Kid, Kid."

Grandmother! How did she find me here in the Emergency Room? She's in Florida! Oh, no, she's going to start yelling! She wants me to play the piano for the hotel guests, but I can't. Something's wrong with my thumbs. They don't work! They hurt and I don't have my music! I want to tell her, but something's wrong with my voice. I can't speak. Oh, no! What's happening?

"Kid, Kid! Listen to me and listen good! You're a fighter! You Depression kids are tough – the toughest of the tough! You can't be stopped! Nothin' stops you! You fought to be born and you're gonna fight now! Lay low, get your strength back then come out swingin' and singin'! Not that fancy, schmancy opera, light opera stuff! Forget that mishegas school! You got Jolie's blood in you! They ain't seen nothin' yet!"

PART II

THE MOUNTAIN YEARS
1970-1980

Dedicated to Chub

"Once you have tasted the back country, you will forever
walk with your eyes turned toward the mountains for there
you have been and there you will always long to be."

~ Paraphrased from Leonardo Da Vinci

CHAPTER 13

Convict Lake

Two months later
September 1970
High Sierras, California

"Sometimes, you come face to face with your definition of a man; not your mother's, not your religion's, not your culture's: yours, just yours."

~ Unknown

It's hot and still. I squint into the shimmering heat of the noon sun, my hands try to shade my eyes, but I'm awkward. My thumbs aren't completely healed, but I can see that he's big – very big, a mountain of a man, fitting right in with the mountain peaks surrounding the lake. I see his horse moving toward me. He sits back in his saddle relaxed, no hurry in him. He gets closer. I hear the clip-clop of his horse's hooves on the trail and see his worn, dusty boots resting casually in his stirrups. He's close enough now that I can see the part of his face that shows from under his straw, sweat-stained cowboy hat. His face is as worn and creased as his clothes. All my fantasies from watching John Wayne Westerns, James Arness in Gunsmoke, Hoss Cartwright in Bonanza, come to life in front of me. Unbelievable! He rides up to me.

"Mornin'." He touches his big hand to the brim of his cowboy hat.

"Good morning." I put my hands down and try to quickly pull my shirt sleeves over my hands to cover the look of my thumbs. Now that he's close, I can see he's not very good looking. He's worn and rough. There's no softness in him, except for his eyes and smile. His eyes are an amazing contradiction to his face; soft, bright sparkling blue like Daddy's and his smile is like the Pillsbury Doughboy in the commercials.

"This yer first time ta the lake?"

"Oh, no, I've been here before, almost every summer since I married. My husband, his parents and grandparents make this their annual vacation spot. I won't be surprised if my children will bring their children up here some day." I talk too fast, give away my nervousness, but I don't want this cowboy to know I'm here alone. Actually, I'm not really alone. Mama can fly up here in a couple of hours. She can get a plane out of LAX.

"Where's yer husband?"

"Oh, he's at work. I needed to get away for a few days. I need a little rest and relaxation and this is certainly the perfect spot." Oh, dear; here I go again talking too fast. I hope he can't tell I'm lying, but actually I'm not. I do have a husband, even though he isn't living with me, and he probably is at work and I am here recuperating, but I don't want him to know the reason. I don't want anyone to know.

"Why don't cha' come over ta the barn an' sit a spell? Ol' Greydog's ready ta get his saddle off an' I'm ready for a smoke an' toddy. Better fer ya to get in the shade, ya look red. The sun's hotter here than yer used ta."

I see the Bull Durham in his shirt pocket with the tab hanging over the edge just like Pop. I mustn't start crying! I don't want to show there's anything wrong, but I am starting to feel strange. What's wrong with me? The horse and cowboy are going in and out of focus as though someone's playing with the zoom lens on a camera.

He swings out of his saddle, walks toward me. My knees start to buckle. He catches me. I'm so embarrassed!

"Whoa there, L'il Darlin', I gotcha. Ya shouldn't be out here without a hat on. Sun'll get ya at 7,000 feet. Probably need some water, I don't see ya carryin' any. Let's git over in the shade in front of the barn."

He holds his reins in one hand and me in the other. The horse walks behind us, the dog in front of us. He's so tall my head comes to just above his waist, and his arm is big and powerful around my shoulders. He smells of Bull Durham, like Pop Foglesong, leather and horse smells – surprisingly soothing and calming. I want to bury my head in his sun-warmed leather vest, wallow in the feeling of comfort and safety. He helps me into a camp chair in the shade of the barn, gets a bottle of water from his cooler, takes the lid off and holds it out to me, "Jest take little sips. Ta much'll make ya'll sick."

Oh, no. I can't take the bottle of water from him. He'll see my thumbs.

"Come on, take it. It's jest water."

"Thank you, I know. I just feel a little shaky. Would you mind putting the bottle in the holder in the arm of the camp chair? It will be easier for me to handle. I'm embarrassed, I don't know why this all happened."

"Purty common 'round here. City folks come up not used ta the elevation an' sun. Altitude sickness gets 'em. Ya can die from it so ye'd better take it easy fer a few days. Stick aroun' the barn, store an' restaurant. Did'ja have breakfast?"

"Breakfast?" A switch in my mind clicks to "off." "I can't remember."

He looks down at me, staring, questioning, "That ain't good. I'll git Greydog unsaddled an' as soon as ya feel up ta it we'll walk over ta the restaurant. Ya'll like it! Ted an' Sally have the best food in the Sierras. People come from all over ta eat here. Hard ta get a reservation on the weekend, but we don' have ta think about that. We'll go in the back an' get ya somethin' in yer stomach."

He turns away from me to tend to his horse and I see a big gun stuck in the waistband of his jeans. My breath catches in my throat as I watch hypnotized by the big gun moving in rhythm with his huge body. "Ok, L'il Darlin'. I'll just tie Ol' Greydog ta the rail an' we can walk over ta the restaurant."

"Thanks so much, but I've got food up at my cabin. I'd rather go up there and have that. It won't keep another day and then I think I'll rest a little. I don't want to get that altitude sickness you told me about."

"Ok, Poco an' me'll walk ya up ta yer cabin. Ya still don't look very steady ta me. If ya feel better later, come on back ta the barn an' ya can meet some'a the others that work aroun' here. We have dinner back a' the restaurant aroun' 4:00 or 5:00 at the latest then head back ta the barn, sit aroun' an' do some storyin' till bedtime. It'll be nice for ya to get acquainted."

"Thank you, that sounds nice. I'd like to meet your friends. It would be nice to have some company." Walking up the trail, I'm impressed again by his size. He must be around 6'3" or 6'4" and he must weigh, well, let's see, maybe 300 to 350 pounds.

"Here we are, right ta your door. Ya gotta good spot here, right near the barn."

"I'm glad. Oh, I'm sorry. I haven't introduced myself. I'm Sandy Raymond."

"Sandy Raymond." He paused, trying it out in his mouth.

"Would'cha mind if I just kept callin' ya L'il Darlin'? I'm used ta it already."

"No, no, that's quite all right. I like it. And you?"

"Chub. Nickname. I was big all my life. Never been called anything else – an' this here's Poco, best trail dog in the Sierras, Australian Shepherd, big for his breed!"

I wonder why Chub didn't give me his last name. Oh, well; he'll probably tell me later as I get to know him. "Chub, I'm glad you think I have a good cabin. Mama made the reservation and we weren't sure which location would be best. We drove up to Bishop last night and stayed in a motel down there and came up here this morning so I haven't tried out the cabin yet."

This time I tried out the sound of his name, "Chub." Yes, it feels right in my mouth. "I will come down to the barn a bit later."

"Ok, L'il Darlin'. Don' forgit ta eat somethin' an' drink water! That's really important up here an' don' wait ta long ta come down. Gits dark pretty quick. Ya have a flashlight?"

"No. I didn't think about that."

"No problem. I git one in my truck ya can use. I'll give it ta ya when ya come down ta the barn. See ya soon."

I'm glad he and Poco are going so I can relax, stop putting on an act that everything is all right in my life and I'm just getting away for a few days. I'm tired. I just want to lie down. I'll call Mama when I go out later to let her know how I'm getting along. She's so worried. I'm not sure if I should tell her I've made friends with a giant cowboy, his dog and his gun and he's going to let me borrow his flashlight. I can't help but smile to myself. I wonder if the attorney will meet Chub? Oh, my, I want to see the expression on his face. What a nice thought. I'm too tired to fuss with food right now. I'll eat later. Right now I just want to sleep and a dream slips into my mind…

…*I'm sitting in front of the barn. Chub's up at the restaurant having lunch. I've borrowed his gun. It rests in my lap. The attorney is due at noon, high noon. I watch the hands on the big barn clock and hear ticking; tick, tock, tick, tock, then music: "Do not forsake me, oh my darlin'."*

I check the chamber on the gun. I like to do that, roll the chamber around with my thumb and count the bullets, five bullets; one empty chamber in case he drops his gun and the hammer drives the firing pin into a bullet and boom! Ok, one more spin to count them to be sure I have five! The attorney said I'd never be able to do that! I smile to myself. He was wrong. I look at my watch.

Well, well, here's his car, light blue, dirty from the drive, right on time. The barn clock strikes twelve – twelve gun shots sound through the roof of the barn, twelve holes mark the time. The attorney gets out of his car, looks around. He doesn't recognize me slouched in the camp chair, my cowboy hat pulled down close to my eyes. He starts to walk toward me. I want him to take twelve steps: one, two, three, four, five - come on, faster - six, seven, eight, nine, ten, eleven - come on, come on, one more, take one more and I won't even have to get up to shoot you! Here it comes, step number twelve! Boom! Bullet number one right through his right shoulder!

He falls in the dirt in front of me. He doesn't know what happened. I see bewilderment in his eyes. Good! I want him to know how pain and confusion feel. Not to know what's happening to him. I want him to see me, to know who is killing him. I stand up, walk over to him, kick dirt onto his writhing body and into his stinking face. I'd kick his glasses off, but I want him to see me good and clear. I want him to know for sure it's me!

"Sandy, my God, what are you doing?"

"Killing you slowly. How's that for a surprise?"

"No, no, I'm sorry. I'm so sorry, forgive me, don't kill me!"

I laugh and scream, "Beg me! I want to hear you beg!"

"I'm begging, don't kill me!"

"Not good enough," I scream at him again and shoot him through the left shoulder. Bullet number two! He screams! "Beg again, with more feeling." I scream into his face while I shoot him in his right leg. Bullet number three!

"How do you feel now, you slimy bastard? I have two more bullets. Where do you want them?"

"Don't shoot, for God's sake, stop shooting!" His cries bounce off the mountain peaks.

I can't resist a bullet in his left leg, bullet number four! This is fun! Think I'll sing him a little song. Thought I'd never be able to sing again, didn't you? Listen up! You damaged my vocal chords so it's not as good as before, but good enough to give you a little serenade compliments of Grandmother and Grandfather!

> *"Pack up all your cares and woe,*
> *here you go, dyin' slow,*

Bye, bye blackbird."

And now, the grand finale, bullet number five right between your legs, but I'm in the mood for another song, so you'll have to wait 'til I finish! This one's gonna be compliments of Jolie:

> *"Toot, toot, tootsie, good-bye!*
> *Toot, toot, tootsie, don't cry!*
> *The choo-choo train that takes me*
> *Away from you no words can tell how sad it makes me,*
> *I'll kill you, tootsie and then,*
> *Do it over again,*
> *Watch for the mail, I'll never fail,*
> *If you don't get a letter then you'll know I'm in jail.*
> *So come on, toot, toot, tootsie good-bye,*
> *Toot, toot tootsie, don't cry!"*
> *BANG!! YEE HAW!!!*

BANG! BANG! BANG! The door bursts open! Chub's giant body fills the doorway.

"What's goin' on? My God, L'il Darlin', are ya all right? Sounds like some-one's gettin' killed up here! I can hear ya yellin' down at the barn!"

"Oh, Chub,I was having a dream!" I'm shaking, sitting up on the bed.

Chub moves closer and puts his big arm around me. I smell Greydog, Poco, Bull Durham, hay, horse, and leather vest again. I want to crawl inside him and never come out. He holds me tight, not saying anything. I could stay this way forever, but he turns me toward him.

"Come on. I'm gonna open that picnic basket of yers an' get ya somethin' ta eat an' some water. You're dehydrated. That'll cause some pretty weird dreams. Let's get over ta the table an' have a look at whatcha got."

He looks in the picnic basket. I feel so stupid, embarrassed, inadequate. What was I thinking? That's the problem; I wasn't thinking, I'm never thinking. I just stumble from one catastrophe to the next and now I've literally stumbled into this giant man's arms and here he is trying to help me. Who is he anyway? What's his last name? Should I trust him? Oh, how I want to trust him, but I must be careful with him and he should be careful with me. I'm a jinx. Anyone who comes in contact with me is destroyed. I've destroyed my life, Mama's, the children's. I'm dead, but I don't know how to stop living.

"L'il Darlin'." His warm, soothing, Southern-sounding voice pulls me out of my morbid thoughts. "I've gone through yer basket. Ya did a nice job packin'. How'd ya like to join the pack station an' become a packer?"

"What?" I gasp, shake my head, look at him in total confusion and then see the twinkle in his eyes. "Oh, you're teasing me; you caught me." I have to laugh a little.

"Good, that's what I want ta do; catch ya an' make ya laugh. Ya look like ya could use a laugh. Ya're a lot prettier when ya laugh. Ya outta laugh more; it'll make ya look an' feel better."

Oh, my goodness, I did laugh. I haven't laughed at all these past months. I used to laugh and sing a lot, but now it's a strange sensation. He's right; I feel better and I hope I look better. I haven't given my looks much thought these past months.

"Tell ya what, L'il Darlin'; I know ya want ta eat alone so I'll leave ya be fer a while, then come on down ta the barn an' I'll see if I can git a few more laughs outta ya."

"Oh, thank you so much, Chub, especially for the laugh. I do feel better. It's been such a long time since I've laughed I've almost forgotten how to do it. I'd like to laugh again. I'll be down in a bit."

What's wrong with me? One minute I want to die and the next minute I want to live and laugh. I turn away from him so he won't see my thumbs and put my face in my hands.

"Hey, turn around, look at me. Git yer head under some water. No more nappin' an' don' wait ta long ta come down ta the barn. Ya ain't used ta the dark up here, no streetlights, only flashlights, an' the dark comes quick an' cools off quick so be shur ta bring a sweater or jacket or somethin'. Want me and Poco to come back an' walk ya down to the barn?"

"Oh, no, I'm fine now, really and thanks again." I do want to go down to the barn and sit close to him and inhale those aromas. They're so comforting. I wonder what his friends are like. How funny that he thought I did a good job packing the basket and would make a good mule packer. I must tell him Mama packed the basket, not me. He was only teasing, but now he's got me thinking. I wonder if I could actually do that. I'm not even sure what a mule packer does. I need a job. I wonder how much it pays.

Oh, my; stop this, Sandy! You're going to have to make up your mind. Do you want to stop living or do you want to become a mule packer? You've never been around a horse or mule. You're scared of heights. For heaven's sake, look how tall these mountains are. Look at the trail winding up that mountain disappearing into the sky. You'd better do as Chub says and get your head under some water. There is no way you could ever work in a pack station.

CHAPTER 14

Friends

Still August 1970

"A glance passes between Chub and Floyd, a glance so
ominous and cold it reminds me of Dante's Inferno, where
the last level of hell is ice cold instead of hot."

~ L'il Darlin'

I walk down to the barn trying to rid myself of my dream. Mama's sliced
turkey with lettuce and tomato sandwich was good and I drank one
of the bottles of water she packed for me. I see Chub in front of the barn
talking to another big cowboy. They're looking at a saddle hanging over a
rail. I don't want to interrupt, but Poco hears my footsteps crunching rocks
on the path, looks up and gives a little bark.

"Hey, L'il Darlin', glad ya came down. This here's Floyd."

I smile up at a man a little taller than Chub, broader of shoulder, powerful arms, powerful legs spread wide, scuffed boots caked with dirt planted
solidly, immoveable. He looks down at me, touches his big hand to the brim
of his worn cowboy hat, gives me a nod, but says nothing, doesn't reach out
his hand. His presence is so powerful he makes me feel breathless without
saying a word, without a touch. His brown eyes give off black-brown shards.
I feel my breath leave my body as I look up at him and feel his power. Unsure

of myself, uncomfortable in his presence, I retreat rapidly into my Mrs. McBride self: "How do you do?" I smile my best entering-the-room smile. I would graciously offer my hand, but I don't want either Chub or him to see my thumbs. What did I think this powerful man was going to do anyway, take my hand and kiss it? He's very good looking, but his eyes cause a chill to run through me.

Chub walks over to the saddle on the rail. "Floyd, take a look at this saddle." Floyd turns away from me to Chub and walks over to the rail.

Floyd doesn't have a gun stuck in the back of his jeans. Why is that scaring me more than if he did? What is inside him that makes me wonder again what I am doing here, hundreds of miles away from anything familiar, with two big cowboy strangers, one carrying a gun, the other so strong and powerful, with hands so big a gun must be unnecessary. He looks as though he just pinches people's heads off rather than shoot them.

Chub and Floyd bend over the saddle and run their hands over the leather as they talk. Chub glances up at the sun, turns to Floyd.

"Will's bringin' a party down, should be here in 'bout an hour. Grab a camp chair, sit a spell. If I twist yer arm, how about a' toddy?"

I sit in my camp chair and look down the road that comes from Highway 395 right here to the front of the barn.

"Spectin' someone, L'il Darlin'?"

"No, no–"

"If ya got someone comin', ya should let me an' Floyd know. We'd like ta meet yer friend."

A glance passes between Chub and Floyd, a glance so ominous and cold that it reminds me of Dante's inferno, where the last level in hell is ice cold instead of hot. I feel a chill up and down my spine.

At that same exact moment in Bishop, 65 miles south of Convict Lake, motel room #5, an ordinary-looking, balding man bends over a grey leather traveling bag. He wears a grey suit, white shirt, grey paisley print tie, polished grey shoes. A burning chill in his spine causes him to straighten up, look around the motel room with colorless, glassy, dead-looking grey eyes behind rimless glasses for the cause. He sees nothing, hears nothing, rubs his arms to get rid of the chilling sensation and returns to his unpacking.

He shakes out new blue jeans, a new cowboy shirt and hangs them in the closet. He needs socks, a cowboy hat and boots, but he can get them tomorrow at one of the many Western stores in town. He smiles thinking she is such easy prey, so deliciously naïve. She won't expect him to follow her up here. He has the element of surprise. He rubs his soft, milk-white manicured hands together and runs his pale, smooth tongue over his color-less lips, enjoying the sensation.

Back at the lake in front of the barn, I continue to protest. "No, Chub, no! really, I'm not expecting anyone." My stomach quivers, turns over. I press my hands over the quivering to keep my stomach still. I don't want Chub or Floyd to see the panic that is rising inside me. I want to tell them someone is chasing me, someone who must be crazy to do what he did, but I can't tell them. I can never tell them. I can't tell anyone. My body trembles, my shoulders hunch beneath my ears, my hands come up and cover my mouth; I can't tell. I shut my eyes.

When I open them, I see Floyd in his camp chair on one side of me calmly reach into his shirt pocket for a flat can, take a pinch of dark matter, put the stuff inside his mouth in front of his lower teeth. I have no idea what he's doing, but whatever the idea is, he's much practiced.

Chub is stretched out in his camp chair on the other side of me. He takes a worn pouch of Bull Durham out of his shirt pocket and some little thin brown papers, creases the paper, shakes the tobacco from his pouch into the crease, touches his tongue to the paper, strikes a match against the sole of his boot, holds the flame to his little roll and cups his hand around the flame as a shelter from the wind. He leans back, blows three smoke rings into the air, and squints against the smoke. The cowboys' relaxation is catching; my hunched shoulders soften, my clenched hands open, slip from my mouth, slide into my lap. The smell of tobacco reminds me of Pop Foglesong and the smell of hay, leather, man and horse soothes and comforts me. I feel completely safe between these two big cowboys.

It's a wonderful feeling – a new feeling that I have never felt before. I only remember scared feelings when I was little, especially when Mama and I were walking those two long dark blocks in the middle of the street to our apartment after the movie, her right hand clenched into a fist with the apartment key sticking out between her fingers, smoking cigarettes so she could burn the bad men who were hiding in the bushes of the houses when they ran out to get us. I never saw or heard any bad men, but sometimes Mama would hear a noise and she would grab me and we would start running as fast as we could toward the apartment. I was so scared I could feel my heart pounding in my chest. I held on to her left hand so tight. We needed a big man with us to fight and kill the bad men but we didn't have a big man. We were always alone, always alone and frightened.

I wish we would have had Chub and Floyd with us then. If only we could have known them back then. A smile pulls at my lips and I feel myself slip gently into a warm, happy, peaceful sleep, the first in, I can't even remember how long…

Chub shakes my shoulder – "Wake up, L'il Darlin."

"Where am I? What time is it?" My heart pounds.

"Yer at the barn. Ya fell asleep. Gittin' time fer supper."

"Where's Mama? I've got to call Mama."

"There's a phone at the store. Ya can call her from there after ya git somethin' to eat."

"No, no! I have to call now. She'll worry!"

"Then ya better git a move on. They don' hold dinner."

"Where's Floyd?"

"Went down to Bishop."

"Oh…"

"Hello, Mama?…"

"Yes, it's good to hear you, too. How are the kids?"

"Thank God. Yes, everything's good for me too. I've made friends with two big cowboys; one has a dog, Poco. He's an Australian Shepherd. I've never seen this kind of dog. They're cattle dogs. They help on the trail and round up cattle. They have different colored eyes, one blue, one brown. Chub tells me he's big for his breed. Chub tells me not to pet him, he bites, just let him come to me first. …

"Yes, I'll be careful, Mama. Chub is nice, makes me laugh, talks about me becoming a 'packer' up here. I don't know what I could do.

"It's a nickname, Mama. Chub says he's been called that since he was a kid because of his size. No, I don't know his last name, yet. …

"Mama, he's just kidding. He thought I'd packed the picnic basket you packed for me. He said I did such a good job packing, maybe I'd like to become a mule packer…

"…I know, I know! It's a joke! I'll tell him I didn't pack it, that you did. Maybe he'll offer you the job instead of me…

"…Don't get mad, Mama. It's a joke, but it helps me. I haven't laughed or had anything to laugh about in so long…

"…No, I haven't told him. Oh, Mama, he's waving at me. The dinner bell's ringing and they don't hold dinner. I'll call tomorrow. I love you, tell the kids I miss them and love them."

"…Mama, I can't talk any longer. Ralph doesn't hold dinner. I have to go. I'll call you tomorrow. I love you."

"I'm coming, Chub, I'm coming!" The smells from the kitchen are glorious! I'm glad I accepted Chub's invitation to eat dinner at the restaurant tonight. My dream has upset me. I don't want to be alone. I'll take my chances on eating with people. I hope no one notices how awkward I am holding my utensils. I didn't realize how hungry I am. Come to think of it, this seems like the first time I've been hungry in ever so long. We walk into a big employee dining room behind the restaurant. Beautiful, large, wood-paneled walls, big wood-burning fireplace and windows all around frame the lake where the late afternoon sun is starting to set, sending sprinkles of sapphires and diamond glitter on the edges of the crests of the little lapping waves.

Good, no one is paying attention to me. They're hunched over their plates, noisily shoving food into their mouths. Mrs. McBride would gasp and tell me to turn and run. I have to look away. There are only men here and some of them are licking their fingers and knives. Oh, no! How awful! Where are the women? Maybe they eat separately. I don't think I should be here. "Come on, L'il Darlin.' Grab one'a them plates, a knife an' fork, an' start loadin' up. Ralph'll be closin' the kitchen. He don' wait! Come on, come on, grab somethin'! Here comes Ralph with the dish cart."

Chub moves down the line of food trays, grabs giant spoonfuls of something that looks like a meat stew with potatoes and carrots. The next group of trays has salad makings in them with different kinds of dressings in little cups. Next come mashed potatoes and brown gravy and last in line are a big bowl of chocolate chip cookies and three different pies. One looks like a dark berry pie, one apple and one lemon meringue. There are big carafes of coffee with smaller pitchers of milk and bowls of sugar. Chub slaps the food onto his plate. I follow him, awkwardly grasping my spoon but I manage to get a few dabs of the stew and potatoes. For a huge man, Chub makes some quick moves to get to a place at the long table. He doesn't wait for me to sit down; he's already eating and I'm standing waiting for him to stop and help me get seated.

He looks up at me: "Put yer stuff down an' grab a chair. Ralph'll be closin' purty quick now." He's back eating again. I resist the impulse to put my plate, fork and knife down on the table, walk out of there, call Mama and tell her to pick me up tomorrow. I'll go to the police. I should have gone to the police when it happened. This is not the place for a lady. However, right now I need to be sensible and eat.

I put my plate, fork and knife on the table, pull out my chair, sit as gracefully as I can under the circumstances and begin to arrange my fork and knife properly: fork on the left side of the plate, knife on the right, blade turned inward toward the plate and look for a napkin. Oh, no; paper napkins in a holder in the middle of the table! I shudder with the thought that Mrs. McBride can see me as I try to pull a paper napkin out of the holder. Mrs. McBride declared paper napkins "barbaric."

Chub finishes by mopping up his plate with a piece of white bread, and gulps down the last of his coffee. "Hurry up, L'il Darlin'. Here comes Ralph with the dish cart."

"Chub, I can't hurry. I can't eat fast. I'm doing my best to sit here calmly and quietly. You go ahead to the barn; I'll meet you there when I'm through."

Chub listens to me carefully, his blue eyes intent. He stares at me as though I have the words written on my face. He nods, walks over to Ralph. They talk and nod. He comes back,

"Take yer time, L'il Darlin'. See ya at the barn."

Ralph makes the rounds of the tables, gathers dirty dishes on his cart. He pushes his cart past me, comes back and wipes his hands on his soiled apron, "Hi, there."

"Hello, Ralph. Chub told me your name."

"Mind if I sit down?"

"That would be nice." I'm lying. I want to eat alone, but I don't want to be rude. Maybe he won't stay long. I hope he can't read my mind. I'd better smile again and make some conversation. "My name is Sandy. I appreciate you letting me take my time with dinner. I hope it's not interfering with your work."

"No problem, Sandy. It's nice to meet you and sneak a chance to sit down. I can't take long, but you take your time. I'll work around you."

"Thank you, Ralph. Would it be possible, and I hope I'm not asking too much, but could you bring me some Chamomile tea and a teaspoon?" Ralph's brown eyes go wide with surprise behind his black framed glasses. Oh, dear; I shouldn't have asked.

"Um, Sandy, let me check in the kitchen. We don't get too many calls for that fancy tea and teaspoons. If there isn't any, could you make do with Lipton and a regular spoon? "

"Oh, yes, Ralph. I'm sorry to be a nuisance."

"No problem. I'll be right back."

The tea is hot and comforting. I almost feel like myself sitting here quietly, calmly, while I stir some milk into my tea, even if it is in a coffee mug, but that's all right. I'm just grateful to Ralph that he found a teabag. The amazing view out the window is even more beautiful with the sunset making everything look magical. The sky is brushed with colors of pink and gold, reminding me of the beauty of Monet's painting, "San Giorgio Maggiore at Dusk". Mrs. McBride had that painting in the entry hall of the school. I loved looking at the water; it looked as though the blue water in the painting was moving just like the vibrant blue water of Convict Lake in front of me now.

As I watch the lake waters, dryness and thirst consume me – a dryness and thirst the tea cannot quench. My lips feel swollen and dry. My eyelids are sandpaper. I want to crash through the window, jump headfirst with all my clothes on into the water – let it gush over me, wash the past months away – but I can't. I can do nothing but sit here, my hands wrapped around the cup's warmth. I need this comfort in my life right now. I should stay here.

I feel safe here with Chub and Floyd, and I'll meet Bobby soon. But who are they and why does Chub remind me of Daddy?

As if on cue, Chub's presence fills the doorway. "Through eatin', L'il Darlin'?"

"Yes, thank you, Chub."

"Let's get on ta the barn, then. Time for another smoke an' toddy, tellin' some windys an' storyin' before we all turn in."

"I'd like that very much, Chub. I really would. Thank you." My fingers don't want to put my cup down. Chub leans over, gently takes it from my hand and puts it on the table. "I got some coffee in a thermos in the barn if ya want more, but we gotta leave the restaurant's cup here." The gentleness of his big hand touching mine reminds me of wanting to feel Daddy's hand on mine. I look up at big, rough Chub, and see Daddy, protector, white knight. Softness and tenderness well up from my heart into my throat.

CHAPTER 15

Suzy Horse

Later That Night

"I want to hold on to Suzy horse forever, but I feel her
step back, look at me, make that soft little sound again,
her breath blowing through her nose and lips.

I drop my arms from her neck."

~ L'il Darlin'

Cold and dark with a million diamond stars shining in a black velvet sky – so close I want to reach up and touch them as Chub and Poco walk me back to the cabin. It was so comforting to listen to Chub's friends and some of the employees from the restaurant sit around and tell their stories, telling about dogs they have loved, horses they have ridden, last year's rodeo champions, who they think will be this year's, talking about a man named Tom, a "helluva" mule trainer and rider. A mule saved Tom's life and ever since he's spent his life in gratitude and love, training mules. It's such a beautiful story. I hope one day I will meet him. It is such a blessing for me to hear these stories. No one is talking about me and all the mistakes I've made, what I didn't do, what I should have done, how I am ruining Mama and the kids' lives and my own. I feel so beaten down, so hopeless, but up here, no one knows me, no one seems interested - maybe Chub, but maybe not. His whole life seems to be the mountains, his horse, Greydog, and his dog, Poco.

Then there is Will: Will is only 15 and a half, but Chub tells me Ted, the owner of the resort, hired him on anyway because the young man was anxious to go to work. He'll be 16 soon enough; he's big for his age. It seems as though packers are all big men. Maybe you have to be big to pack the mules. I think Chub was kidding this afternoon talking about me becoming a packer – we're almost at the cabin. I feel Poco push against my hand. "Chub, look! Poco's put his head under my hand like he wants me to pet him. Would that be all right?"

"Yep, I see 'im. He's tryin' ta make up ta ya. He's gittin' used to ya. Give 'em a little pet, but remember the cowboy rule: Never touch another man's hat, horse, dog or wife – in that order."

I have to smile at his list of priorities. "I'll remember, Chub."

Oh, my; Poco's head feels so soft, furry and warm. I've never had a dog. Daddy had two hunting dogs, a black and white setter named Vicki and a reddish-liver spotted short-haired pointer named Barney, but he didn't bring them around very much so I didn't get to know them. I like Poco. He's giving me a lick; how nice.

"Ok, L'il Darlin'. Here ya are. Poco an' me are campin' in my ol' pickup down there at the barn. If ya need somethin', call out. We can hear ya. Don' try ta walk down, the trail's rough an' it's dark, hard ta see even with the flashlight. Still have it, don' cha?"

"Oh, yes, Chub."

"Good! There ain't no electricity in these cabins. Now, don' call out less ya need somethin'. Voices carry far up here, 'specially at night. Don' do any dreamin' an' yellin'. Ya'll have the whole resort runnin' up here."

"No, Chub, I think I'm tired enough to go to sleep without dreaming. Thanks again to you and Poco for keeping me company. I really appreciate it."

"Ya want me ta go inside with ya an' check aroun'? I hope ya closed yer window tight ta keep the varmints out."

"Varmints! Oh, no! I didn't know there were varmints up here. Oh, yes, Chub, please go in and check and please don't mind my clothes scattered around."

Chub takes his flashlight and goes in with Poco. I hope Poco will chase any varmints out. Oh, dear; what have I gotten myself into? Chub walks out of the cabin and shuts the door behind him. "All clear, L'il Darlin'. Nothin's aroun', prob'ly all scattered when they smelled Poco. G'night. See ya in the mornin."

I smile up at him, shaken but trying to hold my head high, reach for the doorknob, give a twist and walk inside the cabin to utter darkness, complete blackness, blacker than anything I've ever experienced and smells I've never smelled before. I start to panic, but I'm too embarrassed to turn around and call Chub and Poco back. My feet won't move anyway. They're cemented to the floor. I close my eyes, try to focus my mind to banish my fear, pretend the awful smells are the good smells of Bull Durham, leather, horse and dog. Slowly open my eyes and oh, no, it's still black, deep black, blackness even blacker than when I first stepped in. What am I going to do? The only thing I can do is reach out and try to find a wall. I remember the position of the bed from this afternoon. The bed should be straight in front of me.

Now, with the bed in front of me, the wall should be at my left side. When I find the wall, I'll hold my fingers against the wood and slowly walk my fingers along the roughness until I get to the bed. My body shakes as l feel night creep into me right through the cabin walls. I reach out sideways; my outstretched arms and fingers touch air. I take three careful steps to my side, still feeling nothing but air. One more try, three more careful steps and my fingers touch rough wood – the wall! Slowly, carefully, I walk my fingers along the wall and walk straight ahead to the bed. My knees bump against the mattress. A tiny sliver of moonlight coming through the little window ahead is giving some relief. I peer through the blackness and barely make out Chub's flashlight on the bed. I don't want to be a baby, but I don't like this. I don't like being alone, don't like the dark. I lean over the mattress and feel for Chub's flashlight on the bed. Yes, here it is! Now to figure out how to turn it on. Oh, good; I feel a button. I push down and a beam of light shines across the mattress, but that's all. Why on earth did I think the flashlight was going to light up the whole room? It's going to take forever for me to find my clothes and get ready for bed. I wonder what would happen if I just went to bed without washing my face, brushing my teeth, putting on my pajamas. I'll just take my shoes and socks off and sleep in my clothes. I don't want to sound rude, even to myself, but I don't think anyone around here would notice if I slept in my clothes.

I use my fingertips to pull the bedspread back, shuddering as I think of varmints running over it, shudder again as I try to find the top sheet. There isn't any, just a scratchy blanket with an odd musty smell. I've got to keep it away from my face – and the bottom sheet is scratchy, too. Nothing feels or smells pretty like my pink pretty bed and sheets at Mrs. McBride's. Our sheets were always ironed and smelled of gardenias. I wish I had Aunt Gen's rosary. Where did those precious, smooth, round beads and silver chain go? I can't remember. Why can't I remember? I can remember Aunt Gen's parties, Pop Foglesong and my beautiful Mama singing and dancing in front of all the service men in a conga line. I can still hear Pop yell, "Hit it, Gen!" and Aunt Gen raise her hands in the air and her long beautiful fingers come down to touch the black and white piano keys in chords that shook the big upright grand piano. I can remember Father Bajagalupe and Father Conway help me say my President Roosevelt speech, but I can't remember where I put my rosary.

I want to be seven years old and sip tea with Mrs. McBride in the library at Monticello, instead of here in this cold, dark cabin in this uncomfortable bed, Chub's flashlight clutched in my hands for dear life. I want to let go of the cold knot in my stomach, let go of the tears flooding my eyes to remind me there is no home, no apartment, Aunt Gen and Pop, their house, the parties, my pink fluffy, pretty gardenia bed, the school, Mrs. McBride all gone, all dead. The knot in my stomach churns and lurches from side to side. I double over, retch with grief. I must stop feeling sorry for myself; accept the fact that they are in heaven and learn to live with it. I wonder if they look down on us and shed tears over our earthly despair. I hope they don't. I hope they rest in peace, their life struggles over. They shouldn't have to continue to worry and struggle over our mistakes. It's up to me to make the best I can out of this frightful set of circumstances I've brought upon myself, Mama and the kids.

Now, I'm here with two big, dangerous, powerful men – strangers, untrained in the ways of civilized living, but I'm not living a civilized life. I'm running from a crazy person and keeping company with two unknown cowboys who seem to be trying to help me and I still don't know why.

I'm not making it easy for them by not telling them why or who I'm running from, but they probably have made assumptions. What do most women run from, a bad husband or boyfriend? That makes sense, but that's not what I'm running from. It's no use. I can't sleep. My brain is a kaleidoscope: Each time I turn over, I see bits and pieces of me making bizarre pictures at the end of the tube. My hands and arms ache from clutching Chub's flashlight. How could I have fallen asleep? I can't see my watch. How much time has passed?

Oh, no! What's that, thunder? Oh, no! It's an earthquake! The flashlight hits the floor, rolls under the bed, but I left the flashlight's light on so I can see it, but it's out of reach. What's that sound? Oh, knocks on the door.

"L'il Darlin'" – Thank God! Chub's voice!

"Yes, yes, Chub. I'm here, I'm here."

"Poco an' me thought ya might wanna see the horses runnin' ta the barn. It's a purty sight this early in the mornin'. Ya probably heard 'em runnin' already. Git dressed. We'll wait fer ya out here."

"Oh, Chub, I'm dressed. Just wait a minute for me. I'm having trouble finding everything. It's hard to see in here. I thought that noise was an earthquake. I dropped the flashlight under the bed and I can't get it, but I left the light on so I can see it."

"No, that warn't no earthquake, just horses runnin' ta the barn for their breakfast. Don't rush. If ya miss 'em this mornin', ya'll see 'em tomorrow."

"No, no, I'm coming. I want to see them this morning!"

I give Chub my flashlight to put in his jacket pocket. The walk from the cabin to the barn is breathtaking – thin, clear, sweet air, sunlight beginning to touch the trees making shattered little rainbows. Morning's opening up all around us in the grey dawn. Chub carefully takes my hand and a shock goes through me. It's the day the war was over. Daddy's holding my hand for the first time in my life. I feel the pressure of his Masonic ring making white spots on the side of my hand as we follow Mama, Grandma, Grandpa, Auntie Ann and all the people and service men down the street singing "You're A Grand Old Flag." The memory staggers me and I fall over my shoe. Chub balances me and looks down. "All right, L'il Darlin'?"

"I don't know, Chub. I don't know anything anymore." I want to cry, but I don't want to cry here in front of him and Poco. As if he can read my mind, Chub leans down, kisses the top of my head.

"Don't cry, L'il Darlin'. Don' be afraid. Yer safe up here. Yer with ol' Chub now. Ya got me an' Floyd an' tonight yer gonna meet Bobby. We rode trail together an' trail dust is thicker'n blood. Whatever's happen' ta ya is gonna get fixed. It'll help if we know somethin' about who yer afraid of, who yer watchin' fer comin' down the road, or who ya was yellin' at in your dream, but even if ya don' tell us, we're pretty good guessers, we been around, we can handle it. All ya gotta do is let us.

He talks as we walk. Poco runs ahead of us, but I can't answer. There's tightness in my throat. All I can do is listen, stare down, watch my shoes lift dust from the trail in little poufs.

"Look there, L'il Darlin'!"

"Oh, Chub, horses! They're beautiful. I want to hurry down to see them closer!"

"No, walk slow. Rushin' at 'em ain't no good. Walk slow, right up front to 'em. Don' come from the side, that makes 'em anxious. They're flight fear animals. They'll run."

I listen to Chub, but I'm distracted by one horse, a little like the color of my hair, that's looking right at me, ears straight up. "Chub, I want to see that reddish-colored one up close. It keeps looking at me."

"Shore, come on, we'll walk down to her. She is kinda like the color of yer hair, call that a sorrel, the white down her nose is called a snip an' blaze an' she's got two white socks on her hind legs. She's good lookin', all right. She's a quarter horse."

"Chub, her ears are still straight up, is that good?"

"Yep. She's lookin' atcha'. Horses use a silent language. Ya can tell a lot from a twitch of their ears, change in the slope of their shoulders, shifts of their hips. It's their way'a talkin' ta each other, sends ripples a messages ta the herd. I'd say Suzy likes ya."

"Suzy, is that her name?"

"Yep, we call her Suzy horse 'cause we got a Suzy mule in the string. They'll be comin' down later."

"Oh, Chub, my given name is Suzanne. My Daddy hated the nickname Suzy so he nicknamed me Sandy. Do you think it's possible that Suzy already knows me because we share the same name?"

"Anything's possible, L'il Darlin', 'specially up here in these mountains. Ya stick aroun' an' yer gonna see an' do things ya never thought possible."

As Chub talks, Suzy horse and I walk toward each other, the other horses slowly move out of our way. She stands right next to me and a big wet sigh mists over me. She hangs her head down next to my neck. I bury my face in her big muscular neck and then the sobs and tears come so hard they roll over my cheeks into my ears and mouth. I hang on to her for dear life. She makes soft little horse noises and nuzzles against me. My chest can't contain my heart; it's beating so hard I'm afraid it will split my chest open. My breath gets deeper and I feel her breath against me. I'm drawn to her like a magnet. I'm in heaven, miles from where I know I should be, hugging a big red horse and crying my heart out.

"Looks like ya got yourself a horse, L'il Darlin', if ya decide ta stay here."

"Oh, Chub," I gulp with sobs, my head still buried against Suzy's neck, "I want to stay. Do you think I could learn to be a packer, really? Could you teach me?"

"Let's talk about that after breakfast. Ralph's ringin' the breakfast bell. Let's not be late this time."

"But I don't want to leave Suzy."

"Suit yourself, but I'm gonna go up git me some coffee an' breakfast. Seems like ya charmed Ralph last night so he'll probably save ya somethin'. Take yer time with Suzy. See ya when I see ya."

I want to hold on to Suzy forever, but I feel her step back, look at me, make that soft little sound again, her breath blowing through her nose and lips. I drop my arms from her neck. I go to her one more time to kiss her neck. "Wish me luck, Suzy. If Chub says so, I'll sign on. I'll call Mama and the kids. We'll work something out."

Suzy nods her head. I blow her a kiss and turn to head up to the restaurant and then I feel her follow me. I stop and feel her warm breath on the back of my neck. Ripples run through every nerve and fiber of my being. I shake; my cloak of shame slips from my shoulders as though I'm starting a new life. Could that be possible? Could this really be the start of a new life – and you and Chub are going to be the ones to show me how to live it?

CHAPTER 16

The Bathtub

"I wonder how Chub and the rest of them bathe."

~ L'il Darlin'

"Oh, dear, I'm late; there aren't very many people in the room. Oh, Ralph, I'm so sorry. Please forgive me."

"No problem, Sandy, I've got scrambled eggs, bacon and coffee put aside for you." He smiles at me.

"Thanks so much. Again, I'm so sorry I'm late and worse, I'm in a hurry."

"Oh, I hoped we might have a chance for some talk after you're through eating."

"Oh, dear, I wish we could, but I have to get right back to the barn and talk business with Chub. I'd like to sign on at the pack station – be a packer, if he'll take me on and teach me. I don't know anything about it, but I can learn, at least I hope I can learn."

"I bet you can. I know I can't. I'm scared of horses, mules and heights. So, you've been around horses and mules before?"

"Oh, no, Ralph, the only horses I've been around are in the movies. These are my first real horses and I love them, especially that reddish one named Suzy horse. I want to learn to ride her if Chub will teach me."

Ralph brings me my breakfast. I start to talk and eat at the same time without a care if I have a linen napkin or my silverware is in the right place.

"Ralph, thanks so much for keeping my breakfast warm and please forgive me for rushing away, but I want to talk to Chub and see if he really thinks I can do this job. He's probably kidding, but I must find out."

"Sandy, wait up, just one minute!" Ralph sits down opposite me, takes his glasses off and wipes them on the bottom of his apron.

"What is it, Ralph?" I'm a little annoyed. I want to get back to Suzy horse and Chub, but without his glasses on, Ralph's brown eyes look deep into mine with such intent, sadness and yearning to speak to me I put my fork down.

He puts his glasses back on. "Sandy, if you do sign on at the pack station, you're going to need a place to bathe. There's a public shower down at the campgrounds but it isn't very good and it doesn't work half the time. I've got the only cabin with a tub and believe me, a good hot soak after you've been on the trail is mighty nice at the end of the day. If you want, you can use my place. I'll have hot water, towels and Dove soap ready for you. I like Dove soap. Is that good for you?"

A public shower at the campgrounds! Oh, no! I can't use a public shower in a campground! Mrs. McBride wouldn't approve! I just can't do it! I didn't think about bathing facilities up here…

"Oh, yes, yes, yes, Ralph! I'd be so happy to use the bathtub in your cabin."

I'm amazed as I look into his eyes. Here is a near stranger offering me the use of his cabin and bath. "Oh, Ralph, how kind. I never thought about bathing facilities. Thank you so very much and yes, yes, yes, I do like Dove soap, too. I love Dove soap!" I reach up and give him a kiss on the cheek. He's startled but pleased. I hope I didn't do anything wrong. He's a nice man and offering his tub is so very nice. I do need a bath today. It's been two days now since I've been here. I wonder how Chub and the rest of them bathe.

"Ralph, could I take you up on your offer a little later today? Chub said we are going into Bishop to meet one of his friends and I would like to freshen up."

"How about 3:30 this afternoon? I'll have everything ready for you. Just go on over to the cabin. It's open. No one bothers to lock doors around here. Just get your bath and leave. I guess you won't be in for dinner tonight then."

"No, but I'll come by and thank you after my bath." I reach up and give him another kiss. I'm so touched tears come to my eyes. Such kindness from a man I barely know. My throat tightens with a little muffled sob as I see the smile shining on Ralph's face before it could reach his eyes.

"Chub, where's Suzy horse?"

"Up the trail, L'il Darlin'. She's out on a day ride. Be back later."

"Oh, Chub, I want to be here when she comes back. Do you know what time she'll be back because I'm going to take a bath at Ralph's cabin at 3:30 p.m. before we go down to Bishop? Is that a good time? He said he'd have hot water, soap and towels ready for me. Isn't that nice? But I don't want to miss Suzy. And how will we have dinner and still see your friend?"

Chub's eyes are wide. "Ya say Ralph offered ya his tub an' is gonna have hot water, soap an' towels ready for ya? Damn! I never heard a' that happen' before, but then ya never happened before. L'il Darlin', if ya decide to stay here, looks like yer gonna work in real good."

CHAPTER 17

Back of the Chutes

"Rodeo smells, very different from barn smells – rodeo
grounds ringed by purple shadowed mountains, rough
tough men, massive black, bucking bulls."

~ L'il Darlin'

Chub's driving his old pickup down 395. Poco's curled up on the floor by my feet, a cozy feeling. We're all going into Bishop to meet Chub's friend at the rodeo grounds. I've never been to a rodeo before and can't even imagine what a rodeo's like. I'll probably find out before long. I wonder what Suzy horse is doing right now and the other pack station's horses and mules.

This is a different world, a world void of my problems. That world doesn't exist anymore. I haven't even taken the medication the doctor gave me before I came up here. I haven't needed any. I'm feeling fine. I can't believe I'm saying this. I'm feeling fine! For the first time in my life, I feel safe. I was scared hiding in the closet in the apartment, scared on those dark walks home from the movies with pretty Mama making a fist with the apartment key sticking out between her fingers to fight off bad men. Now, I'm with big men who can fight off bad men without any keys between their fingers.

"Chub, we haven't had our talk about me working at the pack station. Do you really think it's possible? I'm a quick learner. I have a good memory and I love Suzy horse. I'll do anything I can to stay near her. Just show me what to do."

"We're almost at the rodeo, L'il Darlin'. We'll talk later. Hang on, the road's a little rough here, we're goin' back of the chutes."

"Good grief, Chub, what is that over there?"

"That's a bull." A huge dark shadow against the twilight sky is lumbering toward the rail of the fence.

"Chub, stop the truck! I want out. I want to see the bull!"

"Ok, but don't start wavin' your arms or git too close."

"I'll stay back. I just want to see the bull. I've never seen anything like that. It's gigantic!"

"All right, git out. I'll park over there. Just stay back and stay still around 'im."

The bull and I look at each other. He's enormous – a black, hulking body, horns, wet nose. I feel waves of energy coming from him. Chub's walking toward me.

"That's Slingshot yer lookin' at; one a' Andy Jauregui's best buckin' bulls. He went un-rode for six or eight years, can't quite remember exactly. Bob Maynard was the first one ta ride him in 1950 at Devonshire Downs in Los Angeles, then the next time he got rode was Maynard again in '58 at the Cow Palace in San Francisco."

"How much does he weigh?" I can't keep my eyes off him.

"Oh, maybe 1,300 pounds give or take. He's a black Angus."

"Oh, my!"

"Come on, L'il Darlin', there's Bobby goin' over to his pickup. Let's say hello."

"All right, but can we come back and tell Slingshot good-bye before we leave?"

"No problem."

The arena lights are spilling out over the corrals and parking area, making it easy to see Chub's friend, Bobby. I like what I see, a tall man, not quite as tall as Chub, broad muscular shoulders, powerful arms and hands. His cowboy hat is pushed back a little, showing a tanned, handsome face and his smile is making his dark blue eyes light up.

"I'm Bobby," he nods and holds out his hand to me.

"I'm Sandy," I smile, reluctant to take his hand and show my thumbs but I can't be impolite. I take a breath, reach out, my shirt slides back from my hands and my thumbs show. There's nothing I can do but take his big hand. It's rough and strong. He leans on the fender of his pickup; one leg rests on the running board. He reaches into the front seat, grabs a paper sack, pulls out a bottle, twists off the lid and hands it to Chub. Chub puts it to his mouth, leans his head back and takes a long drink, wipes the mouth of the bottle off with the heel of his hand and gives it back to Bobby. Bobby brings it up to his mouth, leans back, takes a long drink, wipes the top of the bottle off with the heel of his hand and offers it to me. I'm not sure what to do; I've never had whiskey before and I do need a glass.

Bobby asks, "Whatcha lookin' for?"

"A glass?" I'm so embarrassed I'm whispering.

He laughs. "Ain't no glasses out here, jest the bottle," still offering it to me. I'm so uncomfortable, not sure what to do. I don't want to be rude. I'm not even sure I can hold the bottle, but I do; I show my thumbs again and raise it to my mouth. I don't tip my head back, just shut my eyes, touch my lips to the top of the bottle and taste the wet on the glass lip. Oh, my, I like the wet, hot taste.

"Thank you, Bobby." I hand the bottle back to him.

His eyes smile at me, such nice eyes. He doesn't take the bottle. "Take another taste, ya hardly got any. Let me ask ya somethin'. I see ya messed up yer thumbs. Ya don' look like it, but I'm gonna ask anyhow; ya a roper?"

"Oh, my goodness; no! I had an accident and dislocated my thumbs a few weeks ago. They're just about healed; they should be all healed in another few weeks."

Oh, Mrs. McBride! What am I doing here drinking whiskey out of a bottle with these two men? You would be fainting. Mama would be fainting. I'm not sure about Grandmother. I'd better go back home tomorrow. I must be crazy thinking about working at a pack station. What am I turning into? This isn't the way I was brought up. There isn't anything lady-like about this whole situation. These are not Mrs. McBride-trained men and yet I feel good and safe with them. What's wrong with me?

While I'm doing all this thinking, Chub and Bobby finish the bottle, wipe their mouths on their shirt sleeves. "L'il Darlin', we'd better let Bobby git back to work. He's pickin' up buckin' horses."

"Oh, my, that sounds exciting although I'm not sure what that is, but I'd like to see you do that."

"Ya'll like watchin' him, L'il Darlin'. The bare back riders an' the saddle bronc riders voted Bobby to be their pick-up man in the 1964 World Finals. That says a lot."

"Can we see him tonight?"

"Not tonight, maybe tomorrow. The rodeo'll be here over the weekend. We'd better start back ta the lake and grab a hamburger on the way for some dinner, unless Ralph has put somethin' away for ya. It seems L'il Darlin' here's cast a spell on ol' Ralph, Bobby – charmed him right out of his bathtub, soap an' towels."

"That right?" Bobby's eyes narrow a bit as he looks down at me. I look down and feel myself blushing, glad it's dark so no one can see. What's wrong with me? I clear my throat to speak as properly as I can.

"Yes, Ralph has been very kind. I'm quite grateful to him for helping me because Mrs. McBride taught us never to use public facilities – no public drinking fountains, no public libraries and certainly never a public shower!"

A glance passes between Chub and Bobby. I actually stammer, trying to hold on to my proper Mrs. McBride self, but feel silly, realizing how futile and inappropriate it is in these surroundings, but I must say something. "It was so good meeting you, Bobby. I do hope we can come back tomorrow night." I reach for his hand, not thinking about my thumbs. I want to touch him again.

My mind is spinning on the walk back through the parking lot to Chub's pickup. The place is full of rodeo smells, very different from barn smells – rodeo grounds ringed by purple shadowed mountains, tough rough men, massive black bucking bulls. And back at the lake a red horse nuzzling, breathing on the back of my neck, old pickup trucks, and a blue- and brown-eyed dog: It's not the world I was brought up in, but it's a world I'm starting to love and Bobby is now a part of it. Oh, Mrs. McBride, Mama – don't look! Please, don't take them away from me.

"Whatcha thinkin' bout, L'il Darlin'?"

I don't want Chub to know what I'm really thinking about but I have to tell him something.

"Chub, Bobby asked me the strangest question. He asked me if I was a roper? What's a roper?"

Chub smiles down at me. "Let's get goin' in the truck an' I'll tell ya."

Neither Chub nor I notice a dirty light blue city car parked in a dark corner of the parking lot.

CHAPTER 18

The Note!

My second week at Convict Lake and first pack station job

"Don't scream, L'il Darlin'! Ya'll have the whole place come runnin.'"

~ Chub

"Oh, Chub, I love this!" We're sitting in the camp chairs in front of the barn. I've just finished shoveling up from the horses and mules, so proud to see how clean the front of the barn looks. This is my first pack station job – keeping our barn area clean and as fly controlled as possible. I'm not officially signed on as yet; this is my trial period.

"Chub, I don't want to think about the end of the season, I don't want this to ever end. I dread the thought of going back to the city. This is another world for me up here, safe, beautiful, everything I love. I used to say that about singing, but the stage and singing is all pretend. This is nature, real, spectacular, beyond my dreams, beyond anything I have read or seen in books, the comforting smells, feel of the air, it's wonderful! I never want to leave. I wonder if I could persuade Mama and the kids to come up here and stay with me forever. I miss them so much. I just wonder."

"L'il Darlin', as much as ya love it here at the lake an' the barn, it's the back country, back a' the lake, thousands a' feet higher than all this that gits into yer mind, yer blood an' soul. Once yer in the back country, yer whole self changes, yer different, yer never the same again."

"Oh, Chub, make next week come fast."

"Don't wish away yer life, L'il Darlin', treasure each day. Most people ain't smart enough ta know when they're well off, always wishin', wantin' somethin' else, hurryin' toward the end a' the trail, 'stead a' takin' time ta look down, see the flowers an' rose hip berries under their horse's feet, see the sides of the mountains in front of their noses, there are fossils in the rock, ya can reach out an' feel 'em under yer fingertips. Enjoy yer today, L'il Darlin'. Next week'll come when it comes…"

We're around in back of the barn so no one can see us. I don't think the other employees of the resort or the owners or the tourists want to watch me try to get on a horse. I'm sure they think that anyone wanting to work at a pack station has been riding since birth. I'm probably the only one in the history of all the pack stations that has never seen a horse or mule in real life.

"Stand still, Suzy. I'm going to try and get on you." I'm so excited standing right by Suzy horse in my new boots from the camp store. Real riding boots! Oh, my, this is too much!

"Will, get roun' the other side." Chub squints against the sun. "I'll push L'il Darlin' on the count a' three – ok, put yer left foot in the stirrup, that's it, whoa – keep yer balance, grab the saddle horn with yer left hand, back of the saddle with yer right, bounce a little on the count of one, two, an' when I say three give a big bounce an' throw yer right leg over top of Suzy to the other side. Ready? Ok, here goes – one, two, threeeeee."

I'm frozen with my left foot in the stirrup, trying to balance on one leg, falling backwards. My foot comes out of the stirrup. Chub catches me. I've turned to lead. I'm dead weight; my body refuses to leave the ground.

"Ok – let's try it again. Ready?" I can barely nod my head. Chub tries to help me lift my left foot into the stirrup again but I'm in a panic. I'm afraid if I put my foot in the stirrup, Suzy will be tired of waiting and go off at a run and drag me to my death with my foot stuck in there. My new life is over before my new life even begins.

"Thanks, Will, we'll try tomorra'. Unsaddle Suzy. Let's have lunch! L'il Darlin', this is all new ta ya. Ya need to get confidence in yerself an' yer horse. That takes awhile, but we don' have a while. We gotta git our year's worth a income in aroun' ten weeks. Yer doin' a great job keepin' the front a' the barn clean, that keeps the flies down an I'll getcha started rubbin' down the horses an' mules at the end a' the day. We give 'em a rub with cool salt water. They love that cool salt water a' the end a' the day, an' ya have a piece a' apple an' a carrot in yer pocket ta give em' an' they'll love ya even more an' look forward ta that every evenin'. Jest think, if us people kept a piece a' apple an' a carrot in our pockets fer people we meet, we'd be lovin' each other all the time."

"Chub, I don't think I can do that. I'd better just stick to shoveling manure. I can do that, no pressure, no one is waiting in the wings ready to take my job away from me and I feel so good and happy when I see it all clean and pretty. And speaking of pretty, that's such a pretty horse you brought up yesterday, but how come all you're doing is sitting there looking at the horse?"

"I ain't just looking at 'em L'il Darlin', I'm studyin' 'em. That's whatcha gotta do when ya add a new horse ta the string; ya gotta study 'em. Grab a camp chair an' pull next to me an' I'll show ya what I mean. Horses an' people have routines, tend ta do the same thing every day. Ya got ta study yer horse, see what it likes ta do. Ya can't out-muscle a horse; they're too big an' too strong. Ya got ta learn ta work with 'em not agin' 'em. Be good if people took time to do that with each other, 'specially a man who's got himself a new woman. He'd be smart ta study her fer a week or so 'fore he starts messin' with her. Now gettin' back to ya shovelin' manure, if ya wanna start drawin' wages, L'il Darlin', ya'll have to do more than shovelin' an' do it pretty quick, so think about it."

"Chub, I want to stay here. It's so beautiful and I feel so good, but I miss Mama and the kids."

"Ok. Poco an' me are goin' up to the store. Need anythin'?"

"No, thank you, Chub." So, this is it. Either I pull myself together or I'll have to go back to the city, the attorney and the police. I've got to think this through carefully. If I stay here, I'll be safe, able to earn money and it's only for a few more weeks. I'll get confidence in Suzy horse. I know she likes me and doesn't want to hurt me. If it weren't safe to get on her, Chub wouldn't let me. I'll try one more time, but if I can't I'll be forced to quit, go back and deal with the situation myself. No! I can't – I'm more afraid of the attorney than the horses, mules, bulls and heights all put together! Maybe Mama and the kids can at least come up here to visit if they don't want to stay.

"L'il Darlin', picked up a note for ya from the store. No one knows how long it's been sittin' there or who left it."

I take the note from Chub and read. "Oh, my God!" The typed note falls from my fingers. I can't breathe. I freeze. I can't sit here. I wrench myself out of the camp chair, run to the barn, bury my face in the darkest corner. I feel my body shut down, I lose balance, grab one of the saddle mounts, hang on for dear life, feel Poco and Chub come up behind me. Chub pries my hands off the mount, and turns me toward him. "Hang on to me, L'il Darlin. It's easier on yer hands an' thumbs." I bury my head in the warmth and smell of his leather vest. Chub holds me. "No one's gonna hurt ya, L'il Darlin', not while I'm alive. Let's git back out front a' the barn. No good ta hide."

Panic shreds me to bits and pieces – the attorney's here! How did he get here? How does he know I'm here? Where is he staying? What does he want from me? What did I do? I fall into my camp chair. Chub leans over me. "Now, ye're gonna have to tell me what's goin' on."

A knot in my stomach climbs into my throat. I choke. I can't speak. I shake my head at him. Chub finds the water bottle I dropped under my camp chair, hands it to me. "Sip some water. Don't talk. Let me guess. I'm a purty good guesser. Ya gotta friend ya don't want to have. He's caused ya a lotta hurt. Maybe he needs some hurtin' himself. Now, let's see what he has ta say in his note."

Chub leans down and picks up the note I dropped along with my water bottle. He holds the paper to get more light from the fading sun. "Sandy, miss you. Hope you're having a nice vacation. Regards to your friends."

"Oh, my God, Chub, he's here – watching me – where is he?" I want to run, but my feet won't move. My legs are numb from my knees down. Chub reaches into his jacket pocket. I hear Suzy nicker.

"I'm coming Suzy, I'm coming."

I feel myself slip into a kind of daze. Chub holds his bottle of Jim Beam in front of me. I push it away. Poco pushes against my hand and gives it a lick.

"Come on, take a sip. It'll help. That's it. We gotta talk. This guy's got me an' my friends involved. We wanna know who he is, what he looks like an' why he's after ya. "

"I can't tell. I don't know. I can't tell!"

"What does he look like?"

"Nothing, he looks like nothing!" Suddenly, a vision of the attorney's pale, grey face flashes in front of me and a scream starts in the bottom of my stomach, rises into my throat, starts to slide out of my mouth, but Chub sees it coming and puts his hand over my mouth. "Don't scream, L'il Darlin'. Ya'll have the whole place come runnin'. Let's get inta the camper…ok, yer with me now, don' do any screamin'!" Poco pushes against my hand and gives it another lick.

My body's limp. I give up. I'm so tired, not the kind of tired that you fix by sleeping, a tired-of-life tired, tired of trying to live as though nothing's happened tired. The attorney's after me and I don't know why. Chub helps me sit on the sofa bed. I can't stop shaking. He sits next to me, holds me with both his big arms around me. My head falls against his vest again; my tears soak the front. He doesn't mind. He holds me, strokes my hair, tells me I'm brave and strong, pats my shoulder.

"No, I'm not brave and strong. I ran. I'm running now. I'm a coward, and now look at what I've done, got you and your friends involved. I'm so sorry, so very, very, sorry and so scared."

I sink against him; fall apart in a soft, sweet cushion of safety, leather, Bull Durham, hay and horse smells. I curl into the warm circle of his arms, fall into a deep, peaceful sleep of one who has been lost and searching and finally found home, and the next thing I know shafts of soft grey light are coming through the window of the pickup, reflecting on Chub's sleeping face.

Oh, no! Oh, no! Oh, Mrs. McBride! I've slept all night in Chub's lap! He's been sitting here holding me in his arms all night. Poco's sleeping on my feet. I'm ruined! My reputation is ruined! No decent woman sleeps all night with a man – not her husband – holding her. I've sinned against you, Mrs. McBride, against everything you taught me in my upbringing!

"L'il Darlin," Chub stirs, gently shakes me. "Time ta git up. Poco an' me'll git ya back ta yer cabin so's ya can wash up an' we can git breakfast. We missed dinner last night an' I'm hungry."

"Chub, forgive me." I look up into his eyes. "I didn't mean to fall asleep in your camper. This is so awful! I'm so sorry. I've ruined your reputation." He looks down at me; a smile shoots from his eyes, then disappears. "L'il Darlin', there's nothin' wrong with ya havin' a good cry an' a good sleep. Now let's git ya up ta yer cabin. I'm gonna lock yer cabin door an' leave Poco inside with ya while I go down to the store ta make a few phone calls. Don't open the door fer no one but me. Anyone Poco don't know, he'll tear 'em apart. After I make my calls, I'll come up an' git ya an' Poco an' we'll all have breakfast. I'm shore hungry."

"Will, glad I caught ya."

"Hey, missed ya at dinner last night. Everything all right? Where's Poco?"

"Left 'im with the new gal at her cabin. She's spooked up here by herself. I'm gonna make a couple of calls, then git her an' Poco an' we'll have breakfast. I'm hungry, missin' dinner last night. Will, I'm gonna need ya ta cover the barn fer me when Floyd and Bobby get here. Gonna go up ta the Queen, check things out 'fore we git busy the last coupl'a weeks. I'll give ya the dates later."

"Ok. Don't worry about nothin'. I'll take good care'a everything."

"Thanks. Right now, I'm goin' up to the store, call Mike, he'll probably be in the office this early goin' over the books. The Forest Service shore should be glad they got 'em. Not many big, smart, guys wanna be rangers anymore."

Chub leans back in one of the old camp store chairs he's pulled over to the wall phone, drops in his coins. "Mike, wanna check in. Goin' up ta the Queen next week fer four or five days. Will's coverin' the pack station. There's gonna be four a' us, Bobby, Floyd, me an' the new gal. Wanna get her goin' on the trail so she'll be able to handle some of the overload next coupla' weeks, an' Mike – spread the word, 'specially at the campground, we could use a little last-minute payin' business. Have a look fer an ordinary lookin' city guy, middle age, attorney type. See if ya can sell him a trail ride up ta see the back country. He'd shore be welcome an' give 'em a' nice discount, an' if ya git 'em give 'em Martin horse ta ride."

Chub ends the call, puts the receiver back on the hook, lounges back in his chair. His big body settles; his big tobacco stained fingers reach into his shirt pocket for his Bull Durham. He rolls himself a smoke, blows a few smoke rings against the wall, watches them change shape, heaves himself out of the chair, stands up, leans against the wood paneled wall, blows a few more smoke rings into the air, takes the receiver off the hook, drops in more coin and dials. His head turned to the wall, his voice deliberate and soft: "Bobby, get a'hold a Floyd. Need ya guys by next week. Goin' up ta the Queen fer a few days."

He hangs up. His big body lumbers to the front door, down the stairs. He throws the remains of his Bull Durham into the dirt, stops, looks down at the tiny bit of brown paper and slowly, methodically grinds the remains into nothingness with the heel of his big boot. He reaches behind him in his waistband, his fingers wrap around the handle of his 45, the gun as much a part of him as his hand. He pulls the gun from his jeans, takes a red bandana kerchief out of his pocket and carefully wipes the gun clean. His thumb kicks open the cylinder. He sees five bullets and one empty chamber. He reaches into his shirt pocket for his spare bullet, thumbs the bullet into the gun; six bullets, fully loaded. He smiles. He reaches back, slides the gun back under his waistband, and gives it another pat. He smiles again. Everything is in order; plans are made. Of course, there's always the unexpected, but you deal with that when it happens.

He stretches, walks over to a nearby tree, leans back bear-like against the trunk, scratches up and down, side to side, yawns, checks his watch. He'd better git on up to L'il Darlin' an' Poco. He leans back, pats his stomach with both hands. He's mighty hungry. Doin' all that thinkin' makes a feller hungry fer some biscuits and gravy!

CHAPTER 19

On the Trail

"Ya just might make yerself some extra money croonin'."

~ Chub

The air is sweet and clear, the mountains majestic, the morning sun adding fresh beauty every hour to an atmosphere of absolute purity: overpowering, breathtaking, beyond imagination. We're a week early – and I don't want to think about why, but it has to be because of the attorney's note, because the attorney's followed me, because the attorney's here. I think Chub, Cowboy Bobby and Floyd want the attorney to follow me on this trip, follow me into the back country. How strange to think of Bobby now as Cowboy Bobby, but Chub told me that's his nickname; that's what everybody calls him. Chub said he used to be called Preacher Bob a long time ago, but he isn't called that anymore. I'm glad; it doesn't suit him. Cowboy Bobby suits him now, especially because we're actually on the trail going into the back country. I only want to think about the beauty of this trip, but that's not possible. There's an ominous threat in the air that's hard to ignore no matter how hard I try to only think of the miracle happening at this very moment. I'm on Suzy horse, on the trail with Poco trotting beside me wearing the leather boots Chub made for him this morning. His feet are tender so Chub made these tie-on dog boots out of scrap leather from the barn.

It's funny to see Poco get his boots on. He lies down on his back, all four feet straight in the air so Chub can tie them on. After a few moments, he stands up and starts taking steps with his feet way up high in the air until he gets used to the feel of the boots and then he's off! He's the best trail dog in the world and the only one up here in the Sierras with specially made and fitted real leather boots.

We enter a canyon where it seems the sun has been a magician turning the canyon walls into orange and pink candy stripes. So beautiful, it's another world! The beauty crowds out every bad thing that's happened to me these past months. I'm with Chub, Floyd, Cowboy Bobby, Suzy horse, Poco, the mountains, the lake, the air, the sun, a crystal stream splashing and stumbling into a waterfall, and imprints of sea lilies against glistening rock! My mind is silent; my breath in gasps, my heart skips beats, my body tingles, my eyes cannot believe!

Chub is on Greydog in the lead with Poco now, Cowboy Bobby's behind me on Cotton, Floyd's behind him on Kip, leading two mules named, #23 and Little Bit. We're going to make camp above Lake Mildred – elevation 9,700 feet, depth 45 feet, near the entrance to an abandoned mine, The Calcite Queen. We're going to stay four or five days. I can't believe I'm doing this! I didn't know this world existed! If only Mama and the kids were here.

I do have one little concern, though, nagging at me. I don't think I've had the proper amount of riding lessons. Chub and Cowboy Bobby just pushed me on Suzy this morning: "Put a leg on each side, yer mind in the middle, hold the reins in both hands, hang on to the saddle horn an' don't look down over the side, keep yer face to the mountain." That was it! That was my riding lesson. I think there should be more to it, but Chub said no, that's everything I'll ever need; I believe him, I believe his friends, and that is so strange because I barely know them and they barely know me. I wonder what the part of them that doesn't show is like. I wonder if they wonder the same about me, but I shouldn't be thinking about that now. Chub said to keep my mind in the middle and I know he was referring to riding Suzy on this trail, not mind-wandering.

I must concentrate; focus on what I'm doing. Let's see, what else did Chub tell me regarding this trail ride? Oh, yes; when we come to the narrow part of the trail, I'm to turn my face to the mountain wall, start singing and don't look back. I'm to face the mountain wall until we get to top! "But Chub, I can't sing anymore! It isn't any good."

"Well, L'il Darlin', let's let Suzy, #23, L'il Bit, Cotton, Kip, an' Greydog be the judge a' that. Horses, mules an' cattle all like the sound a human voices; helps 'em keep track a' where the humans are, settles 'em. Keeps cattle calm all night on a drive. You know, a croonin' cowboy draws extra wages keepin' cattle from stampedin' an' the bosses from losin' all their money. Ya just might make yerself some extra money croonin.'"

"Really, Chub, really?"

We stop to give the horses and mules a rest before we start up the next leg of the trail, the part that Chub tells me gets narrow, but Chub says not to worry. The animals have been up and down this trail for years. I do feel quite comfortable on Suzy. She looks back at me every so often to see how I'm doing and I reach over and pat her neck, rub and ruffle the base of her mane, as Chub told me to do to let her know I'm ok. She nickers at me and gives her head a little shake so I know she understands.

I read a book last night that I found in the lobby of the resort about the horse being considered among humanity's most revered and sacred companions across many civilizations because they carry us physically and spiritually into uncharted territory. This comes to life for me this morning as Suzy carries me thousands of feet up this mountain into my uncharted territory. My Suzy horse is my companion, my friend who will take me to beauty I didn't know exists. I must let the past go, wait calmly, patiently and optimistically for the future, stay in the present with Suzy, but it seems I can't. I remember when Mrs. McBride told us, "Men should not be allowed in the company of women until they have been properly trained in civilized behavior."

Mrs. McBride was right. If I had listened to her, I would never have allowed the attorney in the house. The assault would never have happened. The assault was and is entirely my fault and in some ways, perhaps I still haven't learned my lesson. Where am I now? I'm going into the back country with three untrained in civilized behavior, cowboys with guns prepared to make the attorney disappear from my life. Now, my common sense tells me these cowboys are to be feared, but I don't fear them; they are my protectors. Because of the cowboys, I feel free to let my emotions thrill, be astounded by the grandeur of nature, feel free to sing songs when one of the purposes of this trip is…stop! I must stop thinking about that! I must stop thinking of the past! I must only think of the present. To survive, I must stay in the present!

The sun overhead is hot. I let go of one of my reins to unbutton a couple of the top buttons of my blouse, pull it down a little off my shoulders. My cheeks, neck and shoulders feel the sun's rays touch and stroke my skin, then the sun goes back to its real work, transforming mountain walls into flaming ruby and gold candles.

A cool breeze shakes me out of my reverie. I feel the air get thinner and the trail start to cling to the edge of this dizzying cliff, start to push toward the sky. I feel Suzy engage her hind end, reach out with her front legs, start up the steep part of the trail. I pull my blouse up, button the buttons and give all my attention to these new sensations. Chub looks back, gives me a smile and thumbs up, our pre-arranged signal to remind me to turn my face to the mountain wall and start a little song. Oh, no; I know I promised. I mustn't be rude, but singing doesn't seem right, but I'll sing a very short song that Daddy told me he sang to his two horses, Babe and Jerry, when he was growing up. Daddy told me he was born in Kentucky and his daddy bred horses.

"Old faithful, we've rode the range together.
Old faithful, in every kind of weather.
You can hear the coyotes howl to the moon above,
Carry me back to the one I love.
Hurry up old fellow 'cause we gotta get home tonight."

Chub looks back, grins, makes a little circle in the sky to sing it again and when I finish and look back, to my utter surprise and delight, I see the mules' long, tall ears are forward. Chub says that means they like my singing. They're waiting to pick up the sound of my voice again! And then I see Kip, Cotton, Greydog's and Suzy's ears are forward! Of all the singing I have done in the past, of all the applause, none has meant as much to me as the applause given me by mules – #23, L'il Bit and the horses, Kip, Cotton, Greydog and Suzy. I'll sing one more little song for them that Mama used to sing to me. She didn't have horses, but she had songs!

"Tough guy, Levi, that's my name,
I'm a Yiddish cowboy.
I don't care for tommy hawks or ki, ki, Indians,
blooey, blooey, blooey, blooey!
I'm a regular tough guy, Bill, I'll shoot until I die.
I'll marry a squaw, I'll make a war.
I'm a real tough guy, Blooey!"

A few more songs and we're safe! The scary part of the trail is behind us. The trail widens. I sit back in my saddle and breathe a huge sigh of relief, as though I've been holding my breath for hours. Against the material of my shirt, I feel my heart beat. I let go of my right hand rein to cross my fingers for thanks and luck. I want to knock on wood, but there isn't any so I make a fist and tap the side of my head like Grandmother and Grandfather used to do in their vaudeville song and dance to get a laugh.

Chub twists in his saddle, looks back at me, yells over the wind and his shoulder. "Open your eyes, L'il Darlin, quit daydreamin', look over there, there's yer meadow!" I jerk my body erect, turn my head, open my eyes and there is the meadow, beyond beautiful! There's the stream again, tumbling and splashing into another waterfall, green grass, bright little blue, red and yellow flowers, a perfect place to stop and have lunch, but I know we can't; we're still about two hours from Lake Mildred. We'll just eat out of our saddlebags as we ride.

I twist around and let go of my right rein again to grab my sandwich out of my saddlebag. My hand is clumsy getting the sandwich out of the plastic bag. Suzy looks back at my activity; I pat the side of her neck for reassurance and then I'm startled when I feel her head suddenly rise in the air, see her ears move forward. I see Greydog's head go up, his ears move forward. What are they doing? I'm not singing. They're looking at something. I follow their eyes and see a tiny spot of flickering light flash for a second against the mountain ahead of us.

"What's that, Chub?"

"Not shore, but that flash a'light could be from the sun hittin' binoculars. Maybe yer friend got up here ahead of us, waitin' fer us at the Queen." My sandwich drops in the dirt, my body freezes, turns to ice. The muscles in my thighs twitch and a chill possesses my body as though someone has just stepped on my grave. I feel the attorney here, the attorney's here! I hear Cowboy Bobby ride up next to Chub, but I stay quiet.

"Whatcha think?"

"I'm thinkin' we might'a run inta' a l'il luck. Save us some time if he ain't too far away."

"That so? I'll tell Floyd. Yer right, if he ain't too far off maybe we kin' git L'il Darlin's business outta the way 'fore dinner. Nice ta eat jest kickin' back. Did'ja ask her ta do some readin' after dinner?"

"Nah, gonna wait 'til we take care a' her business an' make camp. She's spooked right now."

"I bet she'll unspook when she gets ta Lake Mildred."

"Hard ta' tell, Bobby, hard ta' tell."

"L'il Darlin'," Chub twists his big body around, leans over his shoulder and yells, "we're 'bout an hour an' half from Mildred, three hours from that flickerin' l'il light we saw. Nothin' ta worry 'bout, nothin's gonna bother ya. If yer friend's up here, we'll take care a 'im. Ya got the best cowboys money can buy with ya an' we g'arantee we won't charge extra if ya put a smile on yer face an' start enjoyin' yerself."

Chub turns back, makes a clicking sound with his tongue, nudges Greydog with the heels of his boots and we're off!

CHAPTER 20

The Back Country!

Day 1

"Once you have tasted the back country, you will forever
walk with your eyes turned toward the mountains, for there
you have been and there you will always long to be."

~ Paraphrased from Leonardo Da Vinci

Lake Mildred! I see Lake Mildred! How can anything be so beautiful? Sapphire-blue waters, little lapping diamond-edged waves. We're getting closer and closer and closer and oh, no! Greydog walks in! Poco's by him splashing in with his leather boots. Now Suzy walks in! We're going into the lake. Oh, no! We're going into the water! Chub didn't tell me. I don't know what to do. Chub looks back, grins – "Enjoy yerself, L'il Darlin', Suzy'll take care a' ya!"

My head and stomach reel; water splashes the soles of my boots! Oh, no, how deep is it? Chub didn't tell me, why didn't he tell me? Oh, no! Suzy's swimming! Her feet aren't touching the bottom! I hold my breath in a panic until suddenly I feel a rocking, suspended, gentle forward motion. Suzy and the water hold me in an embrace I have no wish to break. Suzy turns to me, nickers and I feel myself start to breathe again and for a mystical, magical moment of time I feel the flow of the lake, my breath and heartbeat all in cadence. I read in a brochure at the store: "The mountain lake is the Earths eye; looking into the beholder measures the depth of his own nature." And here I am looking into this mountain lake, the Earth's eye, as I swim with Suzy in the midst of creation. I close my eyes, grab the saddle horn to keep my balance as I'm lifted, transported on a swimming Suzy carrying me away from my disgrace, connecting me with an unscarred soul. Can this be the Buddhist Nirvana, the place of no voices, an inner silence transforming my life, a place where I can forgive myself, a place where I feel only my heart, not my head and the animals who once lived only in my fantasy, real beneath my legs and hands?

Suzy's hooves touch ground and the spell is broken. I open my eyes. Chub's ahead of me, Greydog and Poco are shaking sun-caught sparkling water drops into the air. I look back to reassure myself of my senses and, sure enough, the horses and mules are still there and Cowboy Bobby and Floyd smile at me, making a "good job" sign with their fingers. I feel so happy, so proud! Only moments in time, but a time I'll remember for the rest of my life.

We're at the camp site. Poco's on his back again, four feet straight up in the air. He waits for Chub to take off his shredded, torn-to-pieces boots. Chub's made him new ones from scraps of leather he brought up from the barn for the trip back. Cowboy Bobby and Floyd unpack the mules, set up two little pup tents, organize the gear. Cowboy Bobby digs a hole for Chub's Dutch oven and famous peach cobbler, loads the hole with coal and gets a fire started.

I watch from my camp chair, sore from the unaccustomed six and a half hour horse ride. Cowboy Bobby tells me I'd better keep moving so I don't get stiff. Keep moving, keep moving, that's all I've been doing for months now, moving, running, moving, running, first alone, now with three cowboys, but no matter how fast I run, I can't escape from myself, my thoughts. Here I go again, swirling around in a circle of useless thoughts. My mind is a broken tape recorder constantly playing over and over again the same words, same thoughts: "It's my fault, all my fault." I don't deserve help. I can't bring these cowboys into the horrible mess I've made. I've got to go back to the police, report the attorney, live with the disgrace – the cloak of shame I put on myself and my family.

A sticky wave of memories begins to spin in my mind, the same memories, over and over again. We should have left the office when Mama and I walked into the attorney's office and he didn't stand up. When he didn't stand up, I should have known. Mrs. McBride taught me the importance of a man showing respect to a woman by standing when she enters a room. Mama and I should have turned around and walked away, but we needed a lawyer and thought he was the one our Cousin David, who is an attorney in New York, had recommended. When the attorney told us he was not the attorney Cousin David recommended, but his replacement, we should have left. But left to where? Where would we have gone? We didn't know another attorney. We needed an attorney willing to take Mama's case pro bono.

Cousin David told Mama she had a good case because Mama's business partner locked her out of her employment agency without notice. Mama's agency was successful, the best in Downey, but business had slowed down due to the economy and one day Mama went to work to find the locks changed. She was locked out, all her files, equipment locked up, her company car gone. Mama called cousin David in New York to ask him what she should do and cousin David told Mama he would look up his law school chum who was practicing in Los Angeles. He told her he would ask his chum to help Mama, take her case pro bono as a favor to him. The memory causes my heart to start beating so hard I'm sure the cowboys can hear. Will this ever stop?

"Chub, did we make this trip early because of the attorney's note?"

"Yep."

"Do you think he's followed us up here?"

"Hard to tell."

"What will you, Cowboy Bobby and Floyd do if he has?"

"Scare 'im off, L'il Darlin, don't worry about that. Ya gotta start thinkin' about where ya want to throw yer sleepin' bag now." His voice, his question, brings me back to the present. "I don't know. Where are you, Cowboy Bobby and Floyd going to throw yours?"

"I'm puttin' my bag in that pup tent up there. Bobby's gonna take his bag above us a'ways behind those rocks. Floyd's gonna take his bag back down the trail behind those rocks."

"But Chub, if you're going to be sleeping in a pup tent and Cowboy Bobby and Floyd are going to be sleeping behind rocks, how will they be able to tell if the attorney's coming?"

"Oh, we'll all know, L'il Darlin'. I tol' Will to put any attorney type who wants ta come up here on Martin. Martin horse and Kip horse are in love. They been separated a day now. If Martin comes up the trail, he'll sense Kip up here, start nickerin' an' snortin' an' Kip'll start nickerin' an' snortin' back, an' that'll git Cotton goin'. With the three of 'em nickerin' an' snortin', Suzy an' Greydog join in, the mules'll start hee-haawin, settin' Poco ta barkin' an' Martin could just git so agitated he might throw his rider. Now that'd be ok – save us some work.

"Won't find a body in these canyons 'til spring, maybe never. But if Martin don't throw 'em, Floyd's gonna let the attorney git by 'em, let 'im into camp, then we got 'im. Floyd, Bobby and me'll close in, scare 'em so bad he'll git outta here an' never come back. Then we can git to the other part of our business up here. That answer your question, L'il Darlin'?"

The easy way Chub is talking makes a chill strike me from head to toe, my insides spin, my heart tries to jump out of my chest – "Chub, I want to go back. I can't do this. It's not right. I should go to the police."

Chub settles the bulk of his big body down in his camp chair, takes his hat off, runs his hand over the top of his bald head, scratches a little down by his neck back of his ear, puts his hat back on, takes his pouch of Bull

Durham out of his shirt pocket, builds himself a smoke, reaches around in his big jacket pocket, pulls out his Jim Beam bottle, puts it down beside his camp chair, stretches his legs toward the Dutch oven peach cobbler, blows smoke rings, watches them disappear in the air. "Can't go back now, L'il Darlin'. I tol' ya, we got business up here besides yer friend. Me an' the boys are goin' up to the Queen tomorrow. Gonna stake a claim."

"A claim? The Queen?"

"Queen's a calcite crystal mine up here, belonged to Ol' Henry. Died up here last summer, found his body right near the mouth a' the main shaft. Probably died a' heart attack. By the time we got word at the barn, got up here ta pack 'im out, he was stiff as a board. Will had a helluva time tyin' him on Bridger. Trail's too narrow. Had to put 'im end to end, legs stickin' out each side a Bridger's neck, head huggin' his tail."

"Oh, my God, Chub! That's so awful!" I look into Chub's eyes, wait to see sadness, some kind of emotion, but there was nothing, just his mouth blowing smoke rings, as though he was telling me what we're going to have for dinner. Another chill strikes me. Who is he? Who are the others? What are their secrets? I swallow, try to get a voice: "Did he have any family?" I really don't care. I'm just trying to bring some civilized normalcy into this situation, but it's no use. Panic starts to overtake me. I've run from one life-threatening situation into another. Here I am thousands of feet up a mountain with no chaperone, three big cowboys, two with guns, one who doesn't need a gun because he just pinches people's heads off rather than shoot them. That frightens me more than if he had a gun. What have I done?

I feel Poco nuzzle my hand. I rub my finger on his nose. He snuggles against my leg. I pet him, rub his head, get comfort from him, and forget Chub's warning: "Never touch another man's hat, horse, dog or wife in that order." I'd better stop petting him.

"L'il Darlin'. Don' worry. We'll getcha back ta the lake in four days or so an' then ya do what ya have ta do, but right now let's git dinner – easier to eat while it's still daylight. Gits dark early up here."

His voice calms me. My heart slows down, breathing comes easier, my voice returns. "Chub, thank you, Cowboy Bobby and Floyd for bringing me up here. It's the only chance I'll ever have to see this back country, swim on Suzy across the river and sleep out under moon and stars. These are dreams I haven't even dreamed of coming true, but I can't keep running from the attorney; I see that now. When we get back, I'll go back to the city and press charges."

Chub, Jim Beam bottle in hand, heaves himself out of his camp chair, pinches the remains of his smoke in his big fingers and throws it into the little fire around the peach cobbler. His eyes reach out over the little, licking flames, out over the mountains. What's he thinking? Maybe he's happy to hear I want to leave to go back to the city. I shouldn't have run in the first place and now I'm bait, a lure, dangling on the edge of a mountain, waiting for the attorney to bite like a trout and be pulled from the city sewer water to his doom.

"Come on, L'il Darlin', Bobby an' Floyd are puttin' on the steaks. Taste better when they're hot 'stead a' cold. I'll git the salad an' biscuits. Bring yer chair over. I got a favor to ask ya after dinner. We'll talk about yer plans ta go ta the city tomorra' after we get back from stakin' our claim at the Queen. Bobby an' Floyd don' mind if ya wanna put yer claim in, too. There's plenty a'room in ol' Jim Beam's bottle."

Me, stake a claim? Oh, my goodness. This is like "Treasure of the Sierra Madre". Maybe that's what has happened. I'm in a movie. This isn't real – Poco nuzzling my hand, swimming across the lake with Suzy, Ralph's bathtub, Dove soap, Cowboy Bobby, Floyd, Chub, the attorney. The only thing that's real is the ache in my legs, the ache in my thumbs, the ache in my throat, the ache in my heart. Those aches tell me it's real, its happening. Please God,

Mrs. McBride, Mama, Grandmother, watch over me. Keep me safe until I get off this mountain, back to the city, to the police.

Chub has the fire going in the pit. He puts ingredients together in a bowl, stirs, pours everything into the Dutch oven, takes some hot coals from the fire with long tongs and puts them around the lid of the Dutch oven's raised edge, like a ceremony. With that done, he gets the steaks, potatoes and fresh salad out of the cooler. My watering mouth betrays any thoughts of leaving.

The air is cool, beautiful. I still smell the green grass and flowers from the meadow below and now the scent of peach cobbler begins to permeate the air. Certainly, this is the aroma of heaven. Swedenborg, Helen Keller's favorite philosopher, says heaven smells like freshly baked bread, but that's because he's never been up here in the back country to smell Chub's peach cobbler. I know Mama's angry with me because she's worried, but I just couldn't help but want to come up here to this back country Chub's been telling me about and he's right, it's beyond anything I have read, anything I ever imagined. The pure atmosphere carries my vision to and over the purple mountains and my eyes reach out further and further until they lose themselves against the blue sky. It's unbelievable!

The two little pup tents are set up close to the fire pit. Poco and I walk over to look more closely at them. One has our gear in it and the other is empty. I wonder if that's mine. Poco sniffs each one. I put my head inside the empty one and pull out quickly. Ooh – I don't like the smell and there aren't any windows. I want to see the moon and stars in the back country sky. Chub tells me they are amazing, but I can't see anything from inside the tent. This is my first night up here – I want to sleep under the moon and stars!

"Chub, Chub!"

"Yep, L'il Darlin'?"

"Chub, I don't want to sleep in the tent. Would it be all right to put my sleeping bag outside so I can see the moon and stars and feel the air?"

"Well, let's give that some thought."

"Of course, I don't want any bugs to crawl on me. Are there any bugs or snakes up here? I didn't think about that."

"There ain't any snakes at this altitude, least I never seen one, but there may be some bugs. Let's see if there's some rough rope on one of the saddle bags. Go ahead an' throw yer bag down where ya want."

I grab my sleeping bag and lay it out flat in the middle of the clearing.

"Bobby, check an' see if we got some a'that rough rope with us an' grab a groun' sheet fer under L'il Darlin's sleepin' bag while yer at it."

Chub, Floyd, Poco and I watch Cowboy Bobby stretch a rough, fuzzy rope in a big circle around my sleeping bag, cowboy roper style. He ties the ends together with a cowboy flourish, jumps up, takes his hat off and makes it circle over his head! I applaud.

"There ya go, L'il Darlin. Bobby's got the groun' sheet under yer sleeping bag an' the rough rope 'roun' yer sleepin' bag. Nothin's gonna go over that rope!"

At that instant, Poco steps right over the rope, goes over, lies down on my bag and looks at us. Oh, how funny! We laugh.

"Well, L'il Darlin', I didn't say it would keep Poco out an' he's made it clear he's gonna be yer one an' only sleepin' companion."

"Oh, Chub." Tears are in my eyes; my worry over these men fades and gratitude takes its place. "This is all so beautiful. I can never thank you or Floyd or Cowboy Bobby or Poco enough. How can I repay you?"

"Well, there are a couple of things. First, let us take care of ya, the second I'll tell ya after dinner."

Chub has the steak frying in a giant frying pan, two feet across, handle three feet long. He says it comes from a Russian troller. The potatoes are baking in a coal-lined hole Floyd dug in the side of the little hill, and there are biscuits, salad and Chub's famous peach cobbler: marvelous! Maybe I'm wrong, but these can't be bad men. Bad men can't cook like this. I help out by doing the dishes, all but the frying pan which takes special care. It must be wiped out with a piece of paper towel; never use soap, never! That is a rule!

Chub, Floyd and Cowboy Bobby stretch out in their camp chairs around the fire pit: Copenhagen, Bull Durham, Jim Beam at the ready. "Now, L'il Darlin', I tol' ya I'd tell ya the second thing ya can do for us after dinner." Chub's big hands pull open a couple of snap buttons midway on his shirt, reach inside, pull out a worn, frayed, fragile paperback book, hands it to me: "Guns of the Timberlands" by Louis L'Amour. "We ain't had a lot of schoolin', so it'd be a real treat if ya'd read to us." A wisp of a glance goes between Chub, Floyd and Cowboy Bobby.

"Of course!" A tender-hearted ball rolls from my heart to my throat, threatening to overwhelm me. These big, rough, tough men can't read! They want me to read them a Louis L'Amour story, a bedtime story! I am so wrong about them, so very, very wrong.

Cowboy Bobby and Floyd light the lanterns. Cowboy Bobby twists open the Jim Beam bottle. Floyd puts Copenhagen in his mouth in front of his lower teeth. Chub rolls himself a smoke and blows his smoke rings. All is ready.

I carefully open the little book. I hope my voice holds out. I glance up from the book to see how Cowboy Bobby, Floyd and Chub are enjoying my reading, but they're not looking at me. They've moved their chairs back from the fire, looking over the flames out of the corners of their eyes. "Should I stop?"

"No, L'il Darlin'. Keep readin', we're listenin'. Can't see out there in the dark so good if we're starin' in the fire. "

"All right," but I'm not all right. I'm anxious. I put the attorney out of my mind over dinner. Everything was so peaceful, the smell of peach cobbler, the sound of the horses crunching grain in their nose bags, snorting, the stream splashing, but now darkness has fallen. Chub, Cowboy Bobby and Floyd are watching out of the corners of their eyes for signs of the attorney.

My hands shake as I hold the book. I put the book in my lap to steady it and continue to read.

CHAPTER 21

A Snake, a Snake!

"Just act like nothin' happened, L'il Darlin', an'
they will, too. That's the cowboy way."

~ Chub

I scrunch way down in my sleeping bag, cover my eyes, try not to remember the bedtime story and try to sleep, but the moon is so bright it hurts my eyes. Poco's been asleep in my bag. I wanted him to stay in my bag with me as my one and only bed partner, but he didn't want to. Maybe it feels too crowded. Now that I'm inside the sleeping bag he warmed for me, he's curled up outside lying beside me to keep me warm. He's such a good dog. Oh, my goodness, this is exciting to sleep like this with my arms around him.

Even with Poco to hang on to and the cowboys close, it's kind of scary. I'm not comfortable wearing all my clothes and boots, but Chub says that's the best way to sleep up here. He also told me not to zip my sleeping bag…

…Oh, no! I have to go to the bathroom! How am I going to manage this? Where did I put Chub's flashlight? Oh, good, here it is. I can feel it on the inside of the bag. I'll just carefully wiggle out of the side of the bag. Goodness, my clothes keep bunching under me with every move. This is so uncomfortable. I'll try to push the top of the bag behind me so I can get my legs out one at a time, but I still have cramps in my legs from the ride today. I need to set my feet down flat and fast! I don't want to scream with the pain. I don't want to wake everyone up. I need to stand up, but first I have to push Poco out of the way. He's heavier than I thought.

Chub's right about keeping my boots on and not zipping the bag. It's a lot easier when you have to get up. I'm going to try not to wake Poco. He's actually snoring! Now, where should I go? I'm afraid to be walking around by myself, but Chub said the animals would wake everybody if the attorney comes and I have to go to the bathroom and I don't want to wake Chub, Floyd or Cowboy Bobby to come with me. I don't want to get too close to the tents or my sleeping bag. That wouldn't be proper. I need to find a big rock. I shine my flashlight and see one just a few more steps ahead of me. Everything's so pretty in the moonlight. I almost don't need the flashlight, but I know it's better to have it.

I can see the stream! I can see the stars' reflections moving around in the water, the moon sprinkling patterns through the leaves, the light bouncing off the black water making thin little silver boats. So beautiful, so very beautiful! I'm lost in the beauty as I unzip my jeans and pull them down with my underpants to my ankles, reaching out to balance on the rock, when something ice cold, slimy wet pushes against my nakedness!

"A snake! A snake!" I scream, lose my balance, jeans and underwear tangle around my legs, trip me. I fall on my face, scratch my cheek on the pebbles on the ground! Am I bitten? I keep screaming. The horses whinny, the mules hee-haaw, the cowboys come running. Chub grabs me: "Are ya all right?"

"No! Chub! There's a snake! Did it bite me!?" Chub has me upright in his arms, shines his flashlight, checks me and the ground around me.

"Yer all right, L'il Darlin', just a scratch on yer face. Ain't no snakes up here."

"But Chub," I'm breathless, pant, shake in fear, "something wet and slimy and ice cold pushed up against my back when I started to go to the bathroom. Find it! Shoot it!"

"There's nothin' here, L'il Darlin'. Bobby an' Floyd are lookin', too. From the way I saw Poco pass me in a belly-to-the-ground dead run back to camp, I bet it was Poco's nose. He cold-nosed ya, tryin' ta make sure ya was all right."

"But Chub, he was sleeping when I got out of the sleeping bag."

"Well, he musta got up when he saw ya leave an' foller'd ya. He's lookin' out fer ya, L'il Darlin'! Come on, pull yer pants up an' let's get back to camp an' settle down. Mornin'll be comin' pretty quick."

"Chub, I'm so stupid! I'm so embarrassed, humiliated! How can I ever face Floyd and Cowboy Bobby in the morning?"

"Just act like nothin' happened, L'il Darlin', an' they will, too. That's the cowboy way."

I get back into my sleeping bag and pray Poco will come back to me. I scared him so bad. I hope he knows the cowboy way and forgives me. I look up at the stars and the black wall of the mountain, close my eyes and try to go back to sleep, but sleep won't come, only thoughts. How did this all happen? I hear Poco coming toward me. "Oh, Poco, I'm so sorry I screamed and frightened you. Forgive me. I love you. Don't ever leave me again." Poco curls beside me. I put my arms around him, hold him close, he licks my cheek and I go back to my thoughts. *I shouldn't be here. I should be in a city – maybe London – married to a diplomat, living in a lovely home, with a staff, a chauffeur, cook, gardener, spending my leisure time reading the classics, Dostoyevsky, Tolstoy, sipping tea from little English china teacups in the library with my children after they come home from school, sleeping in a pink ruffly bed with ironed silk sheets and pillowcases. Instead, I'm lying all alone in a sleeping bag with all my clothes and new wet boots on, thousands of feet up a mountain, fleeing from the devil, with three rough cowboys standing guard, ready to kill him. My entire body begins to shake.*

"Suzanne, you are a frightened grown woman now, but you were a four-year-old frightened little girl when you came to me. You rarely spoke and when you did it was just a whisper. Try to remember."

It's Mrs. McBride's voice. How did she find me? Oh, no; I don't want her to see me like this.

"It's all right, my dear. I'm only here tonight to help you sleep. Do you remember the first night you slept at the school? You were frightened then and didn't think you should have been there. But you were safe with me and you are safe now. Just close your eyes and remember when you were a little girl."

My eyes close and I remember the big Greyhound Bus Mama and I took to meet Daddy in California. Mama and I sat on the long back seat of the bus. Mama made my hair in curls. I had a black dress with little yellow and red flowers all over it and a pretty white collar. There was a little pearl button that held the collar together. I liked to touch that button, so smooth in my fingers. Mama took my hand away when she saw me touch it. She was afraid I'd pull it off and then my dress would be ruined and I wouldn't look pretty when we met Daddy at the bus station in California. It was very important for me to look pretty so I sat as quietly as I could and tried not to touch the button.

"You were the most quiet child I ever had in the school."

I had to be quiet on the bus or the bus driver would have made Mama and me get off and then we would have been lost. No one would be able to find us. No one would know where to look. Who would look for us?

"I was beginning to wonder if physically there was something restricting your speech?"

No, Mrs. McBride, not then. I could speak, but I was afraid. I spoke in my mind. I wasn't supposed to be there. If anyone heard me, they would make Mama and me get out of the apartment and we'd be lost. No one would be able to find us. No one would know where to look. Who would look for us?

The memory brings tears to my eyes, my heart pounds like a thousand drums beating. Mrs. McBride, do you remember when you called Eva Lee and me into the dining room the day we were leaving the school? You told Eva Lee she would go to Los Angeles City College because of her financial situation, and I would go to USC because my father taught physics and geology there. I was afraid then because you didn't know Daddy didn't live with us. That was Mama's and my secret. Where did he live? Where did he go when he left us that day? Did he turn into someone else? Had he been disguised as a husband, a father and a professor? Was Mama disguised as a wife and a Mama? You didn't know Mama was a Ziegfeld girl when she was young, that she sang and danced at Aunt Gen's parties and I was disguised as a proper young lady, but I wasn't proper at Aunt Gen's parties. You didn't know I stood by Aunt Gen at the piano singing all the war songs, clapping for Mama as she led the Conga line of soldiers, sailors and Marines in and out of the kitchen.

Mrs. McBride, were you disguised, too? Was your disguise your pale blonde hair, streaked with silver, pulled back into a bun at the nape of your neck, your pink full-length dresses, jackets and your pink shoes? Were you so used to disguising yourself to us girls that in the end you disguised yourself to yourself? I never saw you leave the school. I never saw you with any friends. Your whole life was lived inside the school. The school was a cocoon you spun for yourself. You hid inside the school. What secrets were you hiding? Were you hiding a secret like me, like Mama, like Daddy? Were we all pretending? Mabel, our cook in her white uniform; was she pretending to be a cook? We girls curtsying and speaking French at the recitals; were we pretending to be proper young ladies? Was everything pretend? Perhaps it wasn't a school for young ladies after all, only a pretend school with everyone pretending to be something they weren't.

The smell of fresh coffee, trout and thin-sliced potatoes sizzling in the giant frying pan rouses me, makes my mouth water. Poco and I get up and start toward the campfire. Floyd and Cowboy Bobby look comfortable sitting in the morning sun, watching the coffee water get hot. They look up at me as I walk to the campfire, nod – no words, just a little crinkle shows around their eyes. I nod and smile at them, take a mug of coffee from Chub. Chub's right. It's best to pretend nothing happened. Poco knows that's the cowboy way, too.

CHAPTER 22

The Cloud

Day 2
The Back Country

"We staked our claim! Time for a toddy!"

~ Chub

"L'il Darlin', after breakfast we're gonna ride up to the Queen, look aroun', stake a claim."

"Stake a claim? This is so exciting, like in a movie. Why are you doing that?"

"'Cause we want ta. Never can tell. Might find some good calcite up there. Maybe find a few pieces purty enough fer ya to make inta earrin's fer yer Mama an' girls."

Chub's eyes are the clearest blue this morning, full of sparkles. He can't be a bad person. Maybe I just don't understand him – the way he has lived. He said we'll go back down to Convict Lake in a few days, more or less, depending. I'm not sure depending on what, but whatever the day, when I get back to the city, I'll go to the police. Today, I'm going to stake a claim with these cowboys and look for some pretty calcite for Mama, Lori and Kim. I'll never have this chance again.

"Please God, Mama, Grandma, Mrs. McBride, just let me enjoy these few days up here."

"L'il Darlin', let's git ya on Suzy. No more pushin'. Bobby's got 'er saddled, ya grab 'er reins an' lead 'er over ta that big rock. She knows what's comin'. Get 'er on over. I'll come with ya one more time, then ya wanna be on yer own. Now, stand on that rock, it'll help, hold the reins in yer left hand, grab the saddle horn, git that left foot in the stirrup. Put yer right hand on the back of the saddle, get yer balance an' swing yer right leg over, 'cause I won't leave ya here by yerself an' we wanna git our names in the bottle 'fore anyone else gits the idea."

"All right. Just stand by Suzy so she doesn't run off with me hanging."

"Ok."

I'm sprawled on my belly over the saddle, but I'm on top! Suzy's steady. I push myself upright using the saddle horn. I sit up, but my foot came out of my stirrup and my other foot isn't in either. Chub helps me get my feet in the stirrups.

"Ok, yer good, L'il Darlin'. Foller me over ta the other horses. Suzy knows where ta go. Ya did good, yer gettin' confidence. Trust Suzy, that's important. Trust an' respect her. If ya don' she'll never be any good to ya. Come on, let's find some crystal up at the mine purty enough fer yer Mama an' girls."

"Oh, Chub, thanks so much."

"Don' thank me yet. Haven't seen the mine this year, might not git anythin'. Ol' Henry was a good man, but purty worthless at minin'. Thought he could get crystals outta the shaft jest shovin' sticks a' dynamite in it. Blew up everythin', damn near himself, splintered an' cracked all the crystals. Stuff's useless. Used to be used for bomb sights durin' the war, then camera lenses, lotta stuff, but now it's all messed up. Ok, let's git goin', see what we can find."

Floyd and Cowboy Bobby are ahead of us. The day is beautiful: blue skies, sunshine, sandwiches, fruit and chocolate cake from the restaurant in our packs, water in my thermos, Chub, Floyd and Cowboy Bobby nipping at their whiskey bottles from time to time. I treasure every moment, every little detail. Everything makes me want to cry. I don't know why. Blurring tears well up as I watch Cowboy Bobby take the stub of a pencil and a piece of paper, lean on Floyd's back and slowly and carefully mark an "X." *Oh, my, Mrs. McBride! He can't write his name; this big, strong, tough man has to labor over making his mark.* I can't believe it! Floyd is doing well on Cowboy Bobby's back, signing his name. Chub, too, is doing well signing his name leaning on Cowboy Bobby. I lean on Chub. I do well; my thumbs are healing. Names and mark written, Chub stuffs the paper in the Jim Beam bottle, sticks it in the dirt at the mouth of the mine. That's it. We staked our claim! Time for a toddy!

The horses are standing a little way from the mouth of the mine, ropes from their Bosals looped around and over some big rocks. Chub walks over to Greydog's saddle bag, pulls out his Jim Beam, twists off the lid, throws his head back, gulps a drink. Cowboy Bobby and Floyd look for a flat rock to sit on, get out their Copenhagen, wait for Chub to pass the bottle. I look at a silky, blue sky hung with huge, fluffy white mounds of mouth-watering whipped cream-meringue clouds, one so low I want to stick my finger in to get a taste.

"Suzanne. That is not polite."

My hand jerks back to my chest. Mrs. McBride's voice is coming from the cloud – the cloud turns into her face, her white cloud hair piled high on her head!

"Suzanne, you know that is very bad manners."

"Yes, Mrs. McBride. I'm so sorry. I don't know what came over me."

"Perhaps, my dear, it is the company you're keeping. Your new friends have not yet acquired skills necessary for interacting with ladies. Perhaps you could help them with their manners at table, their grammar and penmanship."

Oh, I'm so embarrassed. Mrs. McBride has been watching us stake our claim. "Umm, Mrs. McBride, I've been meaning to introduce them to you, but I haven't had a chance."

"My dear. They need no introduction. You are in a difficult situation and you are reaching out to men who have the desire and skills to help you. However, you must remember to maintain the propriety and decorum you have been taught. You are a lady no matter where you are or with whom you associate."

"I know, Mrs. McBride, I know."

"L'il Darlin', looks like yer doin' a lot a cloud watchin', daydreamin' over there. Come on over here, have a little toddy. We're celebratin' stakin' our claim."

"Oh, thank you, Chub. You're right. I was lost in a cloud daydream. I'll be right there, but I'll pass on the offer of a toddy."

"Suit yerself." Chub turns back to Cowboy Bobby and Floyd and shrugs his giant shoulders. His shrugs fascinate me. They seem out of place in a man his size. Cowboy Bobby lifts the Jim Beam bottle in a toast to me. "Yer not the Lone Ranger, L'il Darlin'. I remember watchin' clouds with my mama when I was a kid. We'd lay out on the grass back'a the house watchin' clouds turn into all kindsa shapes: people's faces, animals, things. We'd play a guessin' game, try'n figger out what them cloud picher's was." Cowboy Bobby's eyes squinch and turn up to the sky.

My newly christened boots crunch over the calcite, chip small pieces off the edge of the crystals. The crystals are so pretty. Some of them show bits of color where the sun hits them. There are so many – so many different shapes. I think it's going to be impossible to find any two that might become earrings for Mama, Lori and Kim. But earrings would be so beautiful if by some miracle four small matching pieces would appear on the surface of the layers of broken pieces. Maybe I'd have more luck looking nearer the mouth of the mine. I squint against the glare of the sun on the ocean of broken calcite. How awful for Ol' Henry to put dynamite into the mine. How could Ol' Henry think that the explosion would send useable chunks of calcite out of the mine? What was he thinking?

"L'il Darlin', come over here! Poco's sniffed out some purty calcite."

"Are you kidding me? How could Poco find anything I could use?"

"I don' know, but he shore did."

I crunch over and to my surprise, here's some pretty pieces small enough for Ted to make into earrings. "Oh, Chub, how wonderful! There are even more than I thought – there's enough to make a pair for Sally. That would be a good thank you for all the lunches she's made us."

"Don't ferget yerself, L'il Darlin'. Ya could wear 'em an' they'd be a good advertisement fer somethin' ta do on a pack trip, hunt for crystals for jewelry." Cowboy Bobby, Chub and Floyd are quiet, staring at the rock formations around the mouth of the Queen. I wonder what they're thinking. It's hard for me to imagine these rough men as little boys with mamas.

A slanting sun tilts toward the mountain ahead of her. Time to start back to camp, but I don't want to go. I turn Suzy around for one last look to say good-bye to the Queen, the bottle of names, cast-off pieces of crystals and Ol' Henry's spirit in case it's still in the mine shaft when suddenly, the setting sun hits the Queen's mountain and I'm blinded by an explosion of light, sending showers of glitter and sparkle into the air – thousands, millions of glittering diamonds. I'm stunned, not daring to move.

"Chub, what am I seeing?"

"Yer seein' the full glory a' the Queen, L'il Darlin'. Not too many people see this. Ya gotta be jest at the right time, in the right place ta catch the sun turn all the broken, cast-off pieces a crystal into diamonds. Let's sit here a little. Floyd an' Bobby are goin' on ta camp, gettin' thing's ready fer dinner an' some more storyin', but we're gonna wait jest a little bit more. I wancha ta see the rest of the show."

"The rest of the show?"

A shadow starting at the base of the Queen's mountain starts to spread, creep up the side slowly, slowly, slowly, covering rocks, closing the mouth of the Queen's shaft, creeping upward until only the glittering peak is left at the very tip-top, looking like the most beautiful star ever seen at the top of a Christmas tree. The shadow pauses for a moment as though it knows we're watching and gives us just a little more time to gasp, gape and remember. Then, it closes over the peak, glitter and diamonds gone, spell broken. Greydog and Suzy toss their heads make their little horse noises. They're tired of waiting.

"Come on, L'il Darlin', I'm hungry an' Bobby an' Floyd won't wait dinner."

The horses turn.

It's fried chicken, roasted ears of corn on the cob, salad, hot buttered biscuits and Chub's peach cobbler with vanilla ice cream on top. It's all so wonderful, so good, so breathtakingly beautiful with a round-up of stars dancing above us ringing the still full moon, its light so bright we can almost do without the lanterns. Whiskey, Copenhagen, Bull Durham, sharpened knife and fully loaded guns at the ready, the Louis L'Amour book, "Guns of the Timberlands" in my hands, I'm ready for tonight's story'in.

Poco's bark, the whinny of the horses, the hee-hawing of the mules, bark, stops my reading. Chub, Floyd and Cowboy Bobby are on their feet, guns and knife drawn, peering into the darkness. I'm shaking, drop the book, hide my face in my hands.

"Hello, the camp! Chub, we're comin' in. Put yer guns away."

"Leonard? Whatcha doin' out here this time a' night?"

"Me an' Bill got called out this mornin'. Some hiker reported seeing a guy hurt up here. We been lookin' up this trail at the Queen, behind the Queen almost to Dorothy, but nothin'."

"Well, stay the night. We got leftover fried chicken, corn on the cob, biscuits, Sally's apple pie. Beats those p'nut butter sandwiches I bet yer carryin'. An' if we twist Bobby's arm, he'll break out another bottle a' Jim Beam."

"You ol' son of a buck! Ya shore know how ta get ta a couple'a fellas, right, Bill?"

"I'm already off my horse an' droolin'. Hey, how'd ya git that purty gal ta come up here with ya bad boys an' read ya a bedtime story?"

"Charm an' good looks, Leonard, somethin' ya an' Bill still waitin' ta git."

My goodness, my audience is growing by leaps and bounds, two more horses, two more cowboys. Of course, all the best seats are taken, but the newcomers are making do on their bed rolls, leaning against their saddles. The Jim Beam's passing around. I pick up the book; back to the story. I start to read and blink as a flicker of light behind the cowboys' heads flashes in the ink-black darkness. Poco raises his head, ears alert. What's he seeing?

"Chub, quick! I saw a flash of light overhead on the mountain behind you. It's the attorney. It must be the attorney. He's at the Queen! He's hiding in the mine! He's taunting us!"

"Yep, we saw Poco spot somethin'. Yer attorney got himself a good spot to spend the night, warm, dry and probably got his belly full. He won't bother us tonight. Too many of us. He's not a fool. Go ahead and read the rest a' the story, L'il Darlin."

My hands and arms shake. I steady the book on my lap. I don't trust my voice, but I'll read all night if I have to. I won't be able to sleep tonight and I don't want anyone else sleeping either.

CHAPTER 23

To Keep the Rangeland Straight

Late Afternoon
Day 3

"We're cowboys an' men an' yer our Queen, our Calcite Queen."

~ Cowboy Bobby

W e said good-bye to Leonard and Bill at first light when they resumed their search and then headed back up to spend the day at the Queen. The day has been long and hot, but Chub, Cowboy Bobby and Floyd wanted to do an independent search of the interior of the mine and the surrounding area for signs of the attorney. They found nothing. Sally's lunch eaten, the cowboys leaned back against some shady rocks. Chub starts to roll a smoke and have a toddy. Floyd, Copenhagen tin in his hand, leans against his rock and joins him. I find a shady flat rock and look up at the clouds. I smile at a little fat, white dumpling of a cloud that seems as though it has been following me all day.

Cowboy Bobby's coming toward me. He doesn't walk; he moves like he's still riding Cotton. "L'il Darlin', I'm wantin' ta thank ya fer last night's storyin'. I really like hearin' ya read all them words, makes me feel like I'm right there in the book. Ya read real good."

"Thank you. It's fun reading to you, Chub and Floyd. Oh, yes, and last night there were Leonard and Bill. You're good listeners."

"Yep, we like listenin'. I know ya thought we wasn't listen', but we was. We was listen' an' watchin'. That's why we was sittin' back a'ways not lookin' in the campfire. Can't see good in the dark if yer lookin' in the campfire."

"I understand. Your eyes need time to adjust between light and dark."

"Yep, an' ya ain't got time when somebody's after ya." Cowboy Bobby squats down in front of me. It seems as though he has something to say. I'm surprised. He hasn't talked that much to me. "L'il Darlin', I know yer scairt an' ya just ain't scairt a' that guy, yer scairt a' Floyd an' me an' Chub. Ya only let Poco aroun' ya."

"Oh, I'm so sorry. I don't mean to be rude. I just don't know you gentlemen very well, yet."

"Well, I'm gonna fix that. No good ya not knowin' who to be scairt of. Now Chub's always polite 'round women, an' Floyd an' me, we're ok, kinda rough sometimes, but never aroun' women. My Pa taught me to respect women. Pa an' me treated Ma like a queen."

"Hey, Bobby, if yer gonna be talkin' ya better git some talkin' juice. Time fer a toddy!"

"Well, Chub, ya jest twisted my arm." Cowboy Bobby gets up and goes over to Chub. Chub wipes the mouth of the Jim Beam bottle with his hand, holds it up to Cowboy Bobby. Cowboy Bobby puts it up to his mouth, puts his head back, takes a big gulp, licks his lips, wipes his mouth on his sleeve. Mrs. McBride, please don't look!

"Now, L'il Darlin', gonna tell ya a story."

"Well, git with it. I ain't gonna sit here all rest a' the day."

Cowboy Bobby turns, eyes narrow, snake eyes, stares at Floyd, his voice low, teeth clenched. The air turns heavy. "I git all day if I want, Floyd." Seconds pass: one, two, three.

"Have another toddy, boys." Chub passes the bottle. They take drinks from the bottle. Cowboy Bobby settles himself on the ground in front of me.

"L'il Darlin', I was jest a poor ol' country boy, 'bout 16, 17 years, workin' on a neighbor's cattle ranch. One day, this purty gal come up to me all smilin' and sashayin' aroun'."

"Come on, Bob, don't be tellin' a windy. Why would a purty gal come roun' you like that?" Cowboy Bobby's doing his snake eye look again, stares at Floyd, makes his voice low, bites his teeth together, talks slow: "Don't know, Floyd, but she did." More seconds pass: one, two and three. I hold my breath not knowing what to expect. But there was nothing.

"She talked ta me real purty. Talked me into goin' ta one a' them outdoor movies. I tol' her I didn' have no money an' she said that's ok, she had money. She took me ta the movies, bought me a hot dog with mustard, a beer – paid fer everythin'. Next day, Pa heard me tellin' my brother 'bout it. I thought it was real swell, her payin' for everythin'. Pa grabbed holt a' me, took me out back a' the barn. He was madder than a wet hornet. He leaned into me nose to nose, his voice low and growly: 'Never, an' I mean never, let me hear ya lettin' a woman pay yer way. Big as ya are I'll take my belt an' whoop ya 'til ya can't sit a horse for a month.' His hands were fists. I was scairt! I ain't never saw Pa like that. He kept starin' me in the eyes. Then he shook his hands loose, took a step back, reached 'round to his back pocket, pulled out his wallet. His hands was shakin', but he got holt a' piece of folded paper, pulled it out real careful as he could what with shakin' an' all. 'It's time I give ya this.' His voice was gravely: 'Time you read it.'

"The sun was boilin' down on me. I wanted to get in the shade, but Pa made me keep standin' right there. 'Read them words!' Sweat was stingin' my eyes. I couldn't make out the letters. 'Read 'em!'

"I cain't read good, but Pa didn't care. I did the best I could, readin', sweatin' like a runaway horse, 'til I git the last word said. Then Pa reached his hand ta me, looked me in the eye: 'Son, never, an' I mean never, forget them words.'"

"That's quite a story, Bobby. Yer Pa's a good man." Chub reaches down to pet Poco.

"Yep." Cowboy Bobby stands up, reaches behind him for his back jeans pocket. His arm makes a semi-circle in the air. Floyd and Chub watch him like hawks.

"I'll be. He's goin' for the paper."

"That's right, Floyd. Kept it all these years!"

A strange sensation floods the air. A wind comes out of nowhere, flutters the yellow edges of the folded paper Cowboy Bobby pulls carefully from his wallet, and then moves on. For some reason, I glance at my watch. Oh, no – the second hand isn't moving. It must be broken.

"Ya fixin' to read that?

"Nope, Floyd. I'm fixin' ta give' it ta L'il Darlin'. She's good readin' words.'

Floyd spits a stream of Copenhagen into the dirt. "Good."

"L'il Darlin'." Cowboy Bobby reaches his hand out to me. "I'd thank ya ta read this."

"Wait a minute, L'il Darlin'."

Chub reaches in his shirt pocket, finds the little string and tag on his Bull Durham pouch. Floyd gets his Copenhagen tin open for another pinch. I carefully take the paper from Cowboy Bobby and drop it as I feel a faint pulsing in my hand. Cowboy Bobby's quick to catch it.

"I'm so sorry. I'm so sorry."

"That's ok, L'il Darlin', I git it, but ya gotta be careful, it's purty old." He gives it to me again. This time, I'm prepared and the paper is quiet. It must have been that sudden little wind.

I carefully open the folds of the paper, smooth it out on my leg. The print is smudged with big fingerprints, but I can make out the words. I take a sip of water from my bottle, clear my throat, ready to read, when the wind comes up again fluttering the paper in my hand. I hold it still. The wind passes.

I look out at my audience to be sure I have their attention. Three big cowboys, one Australian Blue Merle Shepherd dog, one blue eye, one brown; four pair of eyes all look at me waiting. The butterflies in my stomach wake up, start to flutter.

What's the matter with me? I'm not on stage about to start a concert, but my body doesn't seem to know that. I'm having stage fright. What is going on?

I start some deep diaphragmatic singing breaths; try to calm my now fluttering in time with the wind heart. "Gentlemen, I'm ready to begin."

Code of the Cow Country

It don't take such a lot o'laws
To keep the rangeland straight
Nor books to write 'em in,
'Cause there are only six or eight.
The first one is the welcome sign,
Written deep in Western hearts
My camp is yours and yours is mine
In all cow country parts.
Treat with respect all womankind,
Same as you would your sister.
Care for neighbors' strays you find,
And don't call cowboys "Mister."
Shut the pasture gates when passin' through
An' takin' all in all,
Be just as rough as pleases you,
But never mean nor small.

I pause in my reading. The wind's on the paper again. I try to hold steady, look up to check my audience when butterflies in my stomach swarm into my throat. What's happening? Everything changes before my eyes. Cowboy Bobby's 16 years old, sitting straight and tall as he must have those many years ago, his eyes focused on me and the yellow-edged paper.

Sixteen-year-old Floyd's hunched over, cleaning the dirt from under his fingernails with his pocket knife.

Chubs' full round 16-year-old face, eyes squinting against the smoke of his Bull Durham, leans forward in his camp chair, elbows on his knees. While he smokes, he reaches down to pet a little brown-eye, blue-eye pup, Poco, curled between his boots.

I fight for control, for breath; violin strings pull tight in my chest, the bow scrapes over them. Breathe, Sandy, breathe, look away, stop looking at the men turned boys, Poco turned pup. Go back to the fluttering paper, breathe, breathe. Control your voice, stop looking, start reading.

Talk straight, shoot straight
Never break your work to man nor boss
Plumb always kill a rattlesnake
Don't ride a sore-back hoss.
It don't take law nor pedigree
To live the best you can
These few is all it takes
To be a cowboy an' a man!

The words hang in the air, waiting for the wind to carry them away. I stare at the paper afraid to look up at the 16-year-old cowboys and Poco pup.

"Thank ya, L'il Darlin."

Cowboy Bobby's grown-up voice is in my ears. It's safe to look. He stands up and reaches for the now steady paper in my hand, and his arm makes that semi-circle again as he puts his father's bequest back in his wallet.

"Thank ya, L'il Darlin'. I wancha ta see that Chub, Floyd, an' me, we gotta code. We're cowboys an' men an' yer our Queen, our Calcite Queen, an' here's a purty piece I found for ya."

Cowboy Bobby presses a piece of calcite in my hand. I curl my fingers around the treasure, glad to feel the rough edges against my flesh. I look at my watch again and the second hand is moving. The watch is not broken, it's real, I'm real, Cowboy Bobby, Floyd, Chub and Poco; we're all real. It's not a dream. I have this piece of calcite pinching the flesh of my hand to prove it.

CHAPTER 24

September 1970

Day 4

"There are no short cuts to life.
Every day, to the end of our days,
Life is a lesson often imperfectly learned."

~ Unknown

My body, curled tight inside my sleeping bag, sobs without restraint, suffering the anguish of a million nightmares that have collected inside me these past months, nightmares suddenly releasing like an avalanche of mountain rocks. I feel myself falling with the rocks, dust and dirt filling my mouth and eyes. I squeeze my eyes shut in terror!

"Wake up, L'il Darlin'! Open yer eyes!"

I don't want to wake up. I want to stay inside my sleeping bag with my eyes shut and cry and cry and cry. Poco pushes his head against my shoulder, pushes the sleeping bag aside so he can lick the tears on my cheek. A big hand reaches down and shakes me. I have to look up. Chub is standing over me coffee cup in one hand, a big finger on the other hand pointing at purple mountain peaks silhouetted against a clear, blue sky.

"Hardly anybody gits ta see a sight like this, L'il Darlin', an it'll be gone fast so take a look!"

I open my squeezed shut eyes and look up. I don't want to be rude. Chub and his cowboy friends have taken time from their life to bring me up here to see the wonders of the back country. It's wrong of me to stay in my sleeping bag all day.

"Come on, L'il Darlin, keep yer eyes open. It'll be over in a minute an' I wancha ta see it an' remember it the rest of yer life."

My eyes open wide with his words. "Oh, Chub! It's beautiful! Red, yellow, pink, lavender arrows of sunlight are shooting over the purple mountain peaks. As I look, the clear blue of the sky, the arrows of color and the color of the mountains begin to fade and disappear, never again to be seen on this earth in just the same way. It's hard to wrap my brain around all of this. Chub was right; the spectacular sky didn't last longer than a minute and I will remember it for the rest of my life. I'm grateful to Chub and Poco for waking me to see the beauty. I need beauty like this to help erase the attorney from my life forever. I wonder if that will ever happen.

"L'il Darlin', Bobby an' I are gonna take a last look around the high country lakes fer the attorney. Floyd's gonna stay with ya. I'll tell him yer awake now an' he'll be startin' breakfast purty quick, so git yeself up, git yer head under some water, run yer fingers through that purty red hair an' have a cup a' coffee an' breakfast with him."

Now, sleeping in your clothes and boots makes getting up and getting ready for the day a quick job. I get out of my sleeping bag, stand up, brush off the front and back of my jeans and that's it. Poco and I walk down to the stream, I wash my face, run my fingers through my hair, rinse my mouth and I'm ready. I'll brush my teeth after breakfast. I walk toward the smell of coffee, bacon, pancakes and see Floyd stirring the pancake batter.

"Mornin', I'll have yer pancakes ready in a couple a' minutes. Ya want maple syrup?"

"No thank you, Floyd. I prefer butter if that isn't inconvenient."

"No way. I got if soft fer ya in case ya wanted it. How about some bacon? There's trout from last night's fishin' I can fry up fer ya and fried potatoes."

I smell and hear the bacon sizzling; my mouth waters. Floyd flips a light brown pancake over on the griddle. Oh, me; oh, my! I've never thought too much about a heaven, but now I hope heaven has campfires and big cowboys to make coffee, sizzling bacon, trout, fried eggs and fried potatoes every morning. As Eliza Doolittle says in My Fair Lady, "Wouldn't that be loverly."

Breakfast eaten, dishes set aside 'til later, Floyd gets his can of Copenhagen out of his pocket and takes a pinch to put in his mouth in front of his lower teeth.

"L'il Darlin', mind if I sit a spell with ya?" Floyd pulls a camp chair around and sits down in front of me.

"As ya know, Chub an' Bobby are scoutin' roun' the high lakes jest doin' another check fer the attorney before Chub starts stirrin' up his peach cobbler for dinner tonight. L'il Darlin', I'm glad ya read Bobby's 'Code a' the Cow Country' to us yesterday. Now ya know we got rules 'bout how ta act with people an roun' ladies an' I'm glad Bobby gave ya a piece of calcite to remember what ya read. Hang on to it. Ya never can tell, it might bring ya luck.

"I know, Floyd, I'm hanging on to it. I have it right here in my pocket. I can never thank all of you enough."

Floyd's elbows are on his knees leaning his big body toward me, eyes looking straight into mine. I've never been around people like this, simple, direct, uncomplicated. They say what they want to say, no hidden agendas that I can tell. It's nice to sit a spell with Floyd.

Floyd settles in his camp chair, takes his Copenhagen can out of his shirt pocket, pulls off the lid, reaches in with his thumb, first and second fingers, pulls out a pinch, puts it in his mouth in front of his lower teeth, settles it down with his tongue, stretches out his long legs in front of him and gives a sigh. "Ya feelin' ok?"

"Oh, yes." I'm not lying. My thumbs and voice are better each day, but I have to admit, inside me I'm upside down with conflict. How do the cowboys do it? None of them seem angst ridden about anything. They seem to take one day at a time, one problem at a time, either solve it or forget it with a shrug of their big shoulders. I've read the book "Atlas Shrugged". I'd like to write a book called Cowboys Shrug.

"I'm glad ya ain't so scairt anymore. Ya know yer ok with me, Bobby an' Chub. We ain't gonna let nothin' happen to ya."

"I know, Floyd. I can never thank you enough." It's nice talking with Floyd and this is probably the only time I'll ever get. I'm not going to let this chance go by. I want to know about him and his friends.

"Floyd, how did you meet Cowboy Bobby and Chub?"

"Met 'em at a rodeo in Prescott, Arizona 'bout 30 years ago. Bobby was bull doggin', ropin', doin' the pick-ups. I was bull doggin' an' ridin' saddle broncs."

"What's bull dogging?"

"That's where ya ride up 'long side of a steer, jump off yer horse, throw the steer down as fast as ya can. The winner's the one who has the best time."

"The best time?

"The fastest time. Fastest time gets the money."

"So that's how you, Cowboy Bobby and Chub earn your money. The rodeo is your job."

"Yep, part of it. We pick up odd jobs here an' there."

"What event does Chub ride in?"

"Chub's too big to ride in events. He's behind the chutes, part of the three-man team who do the wild horse race. Chub's the 'mugger', ears 'em down. Takes a powerful, strong man to grab the horse's ears, jerk their head down an' hold 'em still so the other two can saddle an' ride."

"Good heavens, Floyd. That sounds dangerous and hurtful to the animals."

"More dangerous an' hurtful for the cowboys. The stock is prime, best in the country. They're kept that way. They're worth big money to the owners. Same as horse racin'. My family's got racehorses. Always thought they got better care than us kids." His brown eyes twinkle, making little gold specks sparkle in them at his joke.

"I'm sure that's not true, Floyd."

"Think so. They're seven of us, one sister and five brothers an' we wasn't winnin' any money fer 'em".

"My goodness, that's a big family."

"Yep."

"Floyd, I'm going to change the subject. Chub told me the lakes up here in the back country all have girls' names. I know a little about Convict Lake, which, before it was renamed Convict Lake, the Paiute Indians called Lake Wit-sa-nap. Do you known anything about its legend?"

"Nope."

"Neither do I. I wonder if Chub knows."

"Hard ta tell." Floyd gets up, moves his chair into the shade, stretches his long legs out again.

"Can you tell me anything about the names of the lakes around here all being the names of girls?"

"Not much. All I know is some cowboy's supposed to've named 'em after his girlfriends."

"Do you know any of the names?"

"I know 'Mildred'. That's the lake we crossed comin' up here an' we usually fish 'Edith' or 'Dorothy'. They're the ones above us. That's where Bobby an' Chub are this mornin'. Let's see, I think 'Dorothy' is the highest or maybe that's Bunny – 10,950 elevation. Can't remember the others, but Chub most likely knows.

"Maybe these gals were aroun' here 'cause of the Gold Rush back in 1849. There's a town not too far from here called Bodie. Some prospectors found gold in the mountains aroun' there an' a town started with prospectors and saloons. Attracted a lotta people hopin' to make a fortune. Ask Chub; if he knows, he'll tell ya."

"I wonder how those girls felt having a lake named after them."

"Hard ta tell."

"I think I'd like to have a lake named after me. Oh, my goodness, I'm beginning to feel like the creature, Androgynous, I read about when I was a little girl in Mrs. McBride's library. Have you heard of him?"

"Nope."

"It's a Greek legend. I'd like to tell it to you. It's short; it won't take long."

"Ok." Floyd reaches in his shirt pocket, gets his can of Copenhagen, opens it, takes a pinch and puts it down behind his lower lip in front of his teeth.

"Ready, L'il Darlin'."

"Androgynous is a four-legged, four-armed creature who tried to scale heaven to challenge the Greek Gods himself. Zeus thwarted the threat by splitting this strange creature in two, thus creating man and woman as they are today. Plato, in his Symposium, described the results and I'll tell you the rest. It's short."

"Ok."

"After the division, the two parts of man, each desiring his other half, came together longing to grow into one. Each one of us when separated, having one side only, like a flat fish, is but the indenture of a man, and he is always looking for his other half. And when one of them meets the actual other half of himself the pair are lost in an amazement of love and friendship and intimacy, and one will not be out of the other's sight."

"Floyd, could it be I was once a part of these mountains, lakes and then was split in half, one part sent to Mrs. McBride's school carrying the indenture of a mountain life and I have always been looking for the other half of myself? Now I've found it here in the mountains, in the back country and

I'm lost in an amazement of love, friendship and beauty and do not want to let that love, friendship and beauty out of my sight."

"Hard ta tell, hard ta tell."

FOUR HOURS LATER

I sit back in my camp chair, staring at the sky, thinking about my conversation with Floyd and Androgynous when I hear Chub's voice.

"Hello, the camp! Chub an' Bobby, we're comin' in. Wanna git the peach cobbler goin' 'fore we lose light."

"Hear ya. Come on."

Chub washes up and starts mixing the peach cobbler. Cowboy Bobby's tending to the horses, getting them watered, fed, rubbed down, hooves checked for stones and little rocks, backs checked under their saddle blankets for rough spots, sores, bag balm rubbed on any abrasions. The rule is the horses are taken care of first before the riders sit down to have coffee, hot toddies, Bull Durham or Copenhagen.

"Everythin' clear up there?"

"Yep. Nothin' ta see. If he's up there, he found a good spot to hide."

I put my fingers against my temples, lean down and put my elbows on my knees. My shoulders sag as the death of hope and optimism sweeps over me. Now, what are we doing to do? How long are the cowboys going to keep looking for him? If they found him today, it would be all over now. He'd be gone, never to be found until spring or possibly never. The mountains and canyons would swallow him up, one less madman to terrorize and stalk the earth.

"L'il Darlin', yer lookin' sad. No need. Floyd, Bobby an' me'll handle the attorney. We wantcha ta enjoy the back country. Not too many people ever git to see it. Now Bobby tol' ya his Code a' the Country an' I gotta a code I'm gonna tell ya.

Chub sits down in front of me, takes both my hands, and looks me straight in the eye. "Sit tall in yer saddle, keep yer head up high, keep yer eye where the trail meets the sky. Live like ya ain't afraid ta die. Jist enjoy the ride." His bright blue, sincere eyes look deep into mine.

"Thank you, Chub, I'll try, I'll really try."

CHAPTER 25

The Reverie

September 1970
Evening of Day 5

"I want to be held close, kissed and remembered."

~ L'il Darlin'

P oco and I curl against each other ready to sleep, my body tired but not my mind. My mind whirls with thoughts of the back-country lakes named after the cowboy's girlfriends – Lake Edith, Constance, Mildred, Dorothy, Bunny, Genevieve.

Chub told me last night around the campfire that gold was discovered at Sutter's Mill in the western Sierra foothills in 1849. I wonder who those girls were, where they came from. I guess from everywhere and nowhere. I've got to stop thinking. Poco is already snoring and I'm scrunched down as far as I can get in my sleeping bag, the stars and moon so bright they hurt my eyes, and then my mind slips into a trance-like dream.

I'm at the foot of a mountain twisting the tube of a sparkling, jeweled kaleidoscope aimed at a small shoddy building. I peer inside, down the shimmering tube to see spinning red, green, blue, pink, purple dots slide into my vision. The dots become dancing girls swirling their colored silk petticoats high in the air, their black lace-stocking legs kicking high, doing cartwheels, splits. They scream with excitement to Jacque Offenbach's "Can Can" music from the piano, form a line swirling, kicking, screaming to come one by one to the front of the stage; Mildred in red, Constance in green, Edith in blue, Bunny in pink, Dorothy in purple doing acrobatic solos to the screams and yells of the gun-shooting, rough, hard-bitten cowboys, desperate gamblers, unshaved gold miners, sourdoughs, their picks and shovels propped against bullet-pocked walls.

The sparkling, jeweled kaleidoscope twists and turns to the sight and sound of a battered, old brown upright piano ravaged by bullet holes and a pretty saloon girl in a low-cut emerald green satin dress trimmed with black lace, curls of red streaked with gold piled high on her head, tiny wisps of tendrils caress the back of her alabaster neck, diamond earrings dangle from her shell-pink ears – long, strong, graceful fingers and red painted fingernails fly over the broken, yellowed piano keys. She doesn't look at music, she plays by ear. Her right foot presses a broken foot pedal against a rotting, battered floor. A wave of hot air, thick with the smell of cigars, Bull Durham and the sour odor of bad whiskey attacks the nostrils. It's a saloon in Bodie, California – June 21, 1849. Where did these dream people come from? Everywhere and nowhere.

A big cowboy comes over to the piano, puts his giant hand on the girl's shoulder. She looks up at him with incredible, turquoise eyes. He signals her with his blue eyes to come with him to the bar for a drink. She raises both hands high, brings them down on the piano keys to do three, four-octave arpeggios from the lowest bass to the highest treble in a big flourish, then gracefully pushes back from the piano. They walk to the bar and their blue and turquoise eyes meet; they drink and their eyes meet again. They leave through the swinging barroom doors.

The sparkling jeweled kaleidoscope twists and turns as the girl rides double in his saddle in front of him on his white horse. He leans down, pushes her red-gold tendrils to one side of her neck, puts his lips against her neck, tastes the twilight dew of her alabaster skin, and pulls her close against his body. She leans back, presses against his big chest.

A full moon shines on Lake Genevieve's water, causing millions of glittering diamonds to rise to the surface. The blue-eyed cowboy and the turquoise eyed girl sit together on his bed roll at the edge of the lake. The girl's mind spills tinkling piano keys into her emerald-green satin lap, her fingers play on the keys as he looks down at her and softly joins her melody, singing "You Are My Sunshine."

The lake's diamond-tipped waves rise and fall to the melody. Turquoise tears dot her emerald satin lap as she softly sings back to him, "You'll never know, dear, how much I love you, please don't take my sunshine away." He lifts the girl's face to his, kisses the words from her mouth. She whispers deep into his mouth: "Please don't take my sunshine away."

"Never, Genevieve, never." Their hands entwine, his hands are callused, hard and warm and when he touches her his touch makes her want to sing. Their next kisses are harder against their mouths, their bodies press close, and their eyes close thinking separate thoughts except for one that co-incided and took their breaths away. The sparkling, jeweled kaleidoscope twists and turns to black. The dream ends.

Poco and I stir against the red and yellow light streaking the bright mountain blue sky. I hold Poco tight in my arms, the dream still swirling in my mind. I want to be held close and kissed. I want Chub to name a lake after me, Lake L'il Darlin'. I want to be remembered.

CHAPTER 26

The Campfire

Evening of Day 6

"L'il Darlin', there's nothin' like a dyin' campfire to make
ya think about life. Ya start out a l'il spark, flare up for a
while, then yer fire goes out an' ya turn ta ashes."

~ Chub

I sit in my camp chair, tired but not sleepy, unwanted memories coming
to me in little bits like a patchwork quilt, filling my mind with shadows,
weird witch shadows out of the darkness. Story time's over. Floyd and Cowboy
Bobby have turned in, Poco's dozing on my feet keeping them warm, and
Chub's dozing beside me in his camp chair. A soft wind moves through the
fluttering dying campfire, the coals burn low in the fire pit, casting shadows
on his face, and overhead the stars and moon look down to say good-night.
And then Grandmother's voice, the voice I thought I left behind in the city,
her same voice over all these years.

"*You weren't wanted, weren't wanted, weren't wanted.*"

I know Grandmother, I know. I put my head in my hands. I know.

"*Your father hated you. You never saw him again after graduation day.
You looked and looked and looked, but now he was hiding.*"

Chub stirs in his camp chair.

"Crying and cursing were your lullabies."

Chub wakes, reaches for my hand.

"L'il Darlin'? L'il Darlin'?"

"Yes, Chub, I'm here."

Chub takes my head. "Ya all right? Yer hand is cold."

"I'm all right, Chub. You must have been dreaming. I'm good!"

"I know yer good, L'il Darlin'. You're very good."

I wish Chub hadn't been sleeping. I wish he could have heard the voice and know how much I want to be wanted.

"Shore you're not cold? You're shiverin'!"

"No, I'm all right."

Chub gets up, adds some wood to the campfire, walks around it to his pack, pulls out his big, down jacket, puts it on, takes a bottle of whiskey out of the pocket. How strange. If he thought I was cold, why is he putting his jacket on? He comes back, settles in his camp chair, and takes a drink from the bottle. He reaches into his shirt pocket for his Bull Durham. His big fingers shake the tobacco carefully into the little crease he's made in the thin, brown paper and he makes a roll, touches his tongue to the paper, likes the taste of the tobacco, lights it, blows on the end to make the glow bright, sending little sparks of fire into the night.

"L'il Darlin', there's nothin' like a dyin' campfire ta make ya think about life. Ya start out a little spark, flare up for awhile, then yer fire goes out an' ya turn ta ashes."

"Oh, Chub, don't say that. It makes me sad." He doesn't answer me, just sits, looking into the dying coals, smoking, taking another swallow from the Jim Beam bottle, lost in thought. Finally, he pulls himself out of his camp chair, stands, turns to me, and shrugs out of his jacket.

"Here, L'il Darlin'. He leans over me, puts his big jacket around my shoulders, helps me get my arms into the sleeves. "Put this on. I got it nice an' warm for ya." He takes his time to get the zipper in place, zips it up to my chin, so tender and caring, tears come to my eyes. I don't want to move or breathe, just sit swaddled in his jacket, the warmth, the man smell.

"There ya are, L'il Darlin', snug an' warm."

He sits back down, throws the last of his smoke into the fire. "Now it's gonna be better if ya start tellin' me at the start if yer cold, or want or need somethin', easier than me tryin' ta guess. That wastes time an' wastin' time is wastin' money. We got short seasons up here. Gotta make money in the days we got left. We can't use up time thinkin' about stuff that's happened or gonna happen. Up here, we gotta keep our minds on what's happenin' now. If ya love yer horse, mule, dog, friends, ya gotta love 'em enough ta watch out for 'em, day and night. Ya can't be mind wanderin'. As purty as it is up here, it's dangerous. Ya gotta be thinkin' an' lookin' all the time. Ya gotta be lookin' out the corners a' yer eyes, that's the first an' best way to see things movin', 'specially after the sun goes down an' the glare is gone. That's when everythin's still an' things kinda stand out; anythin movin' is easier to see, an' sound carries better."

He shifts his weight in his chair, leans over to me, elbows on his knees, eyes intense. "L'il Darlin'. I been studyin' the fix yer in, causin' ya all the trouble. Ya know, it's easy to fix up here, an' ya know I'm usin' ya as bait right now, but if that don't work, the boys an' me'll get 'em in the city. Ya don' gotta worry."

He sits back in his camp chair, another swallow of whiskey, lets his big body relax. "Now, I don' know if ya been doin' any more thinkin' 'bout hookin' up with the pack station. I think ya'll make a helluva packer, the first woman packer up in these parts. I'm purty good at sizin' up people. Got to be to live this long. Ya did a great job handlin' the trail, singin', keepin' calm, lettin' Suzy swim ya across the lake. But if ya don' want ta pack, Sally'll take ya on at the restaurant. Helps ta have a purty red-haired, blue-eyed gal greetin' the customers. Help's hard ta get up here. Most hires are drifters, drunks, end a' their luck, no families, no futures, but they all got a helluva lotta past."

He leans into me again, eyes fixed on mine. "L'il Darlin', growin' up the way I did, I ain't got a lotta words, an' no real purty ones. I gotta tell things straight out, make the words I got do. I want ya to stay with the pack station, with me. I been alone all my life, time to think about partnerin' with someone. Nothin's better than two, a man an' woman who walk, talk, an' ride together. When they walk right, talk right, ride right, no way's too long, no nights too dark."

"Chub, those are beautiful words."

Chub takes my hand, "I tol' you what I want. Now, think about what ya want, L'il Darlin'. Let me know soon's ya know."

"Chub, I have been thinking every day and night since I got up to the lake. It's so beautiful. In the city, I'm running from a madman. Up here, with you, Poco, Cowboy Bobby and Floyd, I'm safe, but I know I can't stay here forever. I have my family – Mama, my son and daughters. I know these are short seasons. You have to close the barn and leave before the snows come and I have to leave, go back to the city, tend to my family, go to the police, and straighten out my life."

"I been winterin' in Lucerne Valley with my cousin, Juanita, an' her vet son, Leroy, helpin' on their ranch, but this winter I'll stay in the city with ya, if ya want, get ya straightened out."

"Chub, that would be wonderful, but wouldn't your family object?"

"Not after they meet ya. You drive south with me an' Poco, we'll swing by their place. They'll be right happy to see me with a nice, purty gal with schoolin' like ya. Juanita'll make ya some homemade bread an' fresh churned butter. Nothin' better than her cookin'. Then, I'll drive ya on home an' meet yer kin."

Chub smiles, holds my hand in both of his big hands.

"L'il Darlin', if ya want, I'll do whatever it takes ta keep ya with me. I'm old enough ta be your father an' got some health problems, but if ya throw in with me, I'll see to it ya'll never be hurt again."

How can I make a life with him? He's rough, unschooled, ekes out an existence as a mule packer a few weeks each summer. I wonder what other jobs he does to make a living. He's everything Mama abhors. He's everything that Mrs. McBride warned us girls to stay away from. Yet, I feel drawn to him, happy and safe when I am with him, sad and afraid when I'm not.

"Chub, my singing career is over, the attorney saw that to that, but you showed me up here I can sing a little on the trail. Maybe Will could bring his banjo on pack trips and we could sing around the campfire. We could advertise, maybe get more trips for next season. I don't know, but Chub there is something, one very, very important thing, something that will make or break my decision."

Waves of concern wash over Chub's face, his eyes narrow, look at me. He lets go of my hand. He sits back in the camp chair, knuckles white in the dying fire light. His body stiffens as though preparing for a blow.

"L'il Darlin', tell me."

"Chub, I never want Poco to cold-nose me again. I want you to build me a padded commode that I can put in those bushes over there."

His sigh of relief echoes off the mountain, his eyes light up the dark and he grabs both my hands. "I'll build it, L'il Darlin', I'll build it!"

There are no dawns like the ones that come to the back country mountains – no colors, no pastels, no atmosphere with the clarity. The sky is pale, red arrows of sun open up the morning to the blue and gold of the sky, shadows flee and everything sings in the crystal morning air.

"Well, I'll be damned! Look at those two! Holdin' hands! Looks like they been sleepin' all night in their chairs. L'il Darlin's got Chub's jacket on, got Poco sleepin' on her feet. Never saw anythin' like this before! Should we wake 'em?"

"Hell, yes; it's his turn to make the coffee!"

CHAPTER 27

Jack's Place

September 1970
Day 6

"I'm especially glad this morning that the two of them finally decided
on Jack's as they have boycotted almost every other restaurant
or diner along 395 on the way up from Yucaipa to Convict."

~ L'il Darlin'

I duck my head back inside my sleeping bag, so cuddly and warm inside I
don't want to ever have to crawl out. I feel Poco outside my bag pressed
tight against me.

"Come on, Poco, rise and shine, we're burnin' daylight." I know we're
really not as the sun isn't even up, but I just like to say the words the way
Rowdy does on the TV show Rawhide. I push on Poco, but he doesn't move.
I'll just have to stretch out and get my head out of the bag. Outside is dark
and quiet, too dark to see my watch and I don't hear Cowboy Bobby or Chub
stirring. Floyd headed back to his place in Washington, I think, yesterday
in his rig, but Cowboy Bobby's waiting with us today, tailing us in his rig in
case we have any trouble on the drive down. I'll learn to drive Chub's pickup
next season if things work out.

Yes, this season is over. We can't stretch any more days out of late autumn.
Chub said it was early for frost, but I see spots of white glittering on the

mule packs. The air has a bite. How fast that happened. Yesterday, the sun was warm and fragrant with the smells of wildflowers, the sky cloudless, but today, I smell only the cold and feel winter in the air against my skin. Time to head back down to the lake, gather the gear, load Chub's pickup and start the trek down 395 to Redlands, Yucaipa and Downey.

It's only going to take about two hours to get our gear in the truck. Ted and Sally, the owners of the resort, will do the final shutdown of the barn with their teen-age twins, Jan and Josh, and take the string of horses and mules back to Bishop. They'll keep the restaurant open another month so they have time to close the pack station, boat and fishing concession. The restaurant and concessions don't stay open in the winter – too dangerous, too much snow and cold.

Cowboy Bobby'll take Cotton and Greydog in Chub's old horse trailer down to Cowboy Bobby's ranch in Calimesa just next to Yucaipa. Poco's now under the dash in the front of our truck. I'm going to have to keep my feet out of Poco's way as we drive, but he's used to dodging feet, having ridden many a mile this way.

After a long discussion, Chub and Cowboy Bobby decide to stop at Jack's Place in Bishop for breakfast a few hours down from Convict Lake. I'm especially glad this morning that the two of them finally decided on Jack's as they have boycotted almost every other restaurant or diner along 395 on the way up from Yucaipa to Convict. I can't believe how they boycott all these places. They're not cowboys, they're restaurant critics; a waitress gives them a cold look, she takes too long to take their order, the eggs and coffee are cold, and that's it – they walk out and don't come back, but so far, thank heavens, Jack's has passed the test. Mazel Tov! We can eat!

Jack's Restaurant and Bakery is a tradition – a must-stop in Bishop, with trophy trout lining the walls celebrating the Eastern Sierras' fishing tradition. The restaurant has been here over 70 years. The aroma of pancakes, their advertised mouth-watering bacon sizzling on the grill and fresh coffee make my stomach start to rumble.

The waitress sees us and is coming over as we sit down at the counter. I look at her chipped, partially broken badge hanging at an angle from her faded, pink uniform pocket. I think her name is "Marge" even though the badge only shows "M-a-r-g." Marge looks as old as the restaurant. Her hair's a faded grey with a few leftover blonde strands. She's used way too much hair spray and her hair's sprayed back flat against her head. Her earrings don't look as though she bought them; they must be a present. They're too dainty and dangling for her with tiny gold hearts dancing inside hoops. I bet a former boyfriend gave them to her. She doesn't look as though she has a boyfriend now.

She's carrying a full, steaming glass coffee pot. I see swollen blue veins on the back of her hand like a relief map of a meandering river and red knuckles on her swollen, creased fingers. Pain lines frame her eyes, but she smiles as she turns slightly away from us to try to hide the absence of a tooth at the side of her smile. Even though her shoulders are stooped, she pours our coffee with a swift, practiced motion. It's clear from her manner she's known Chub and Cowboy Bobby for a long time and knows they're good tippers.

I haven't known them a long time, but I, too, noticed right away they are good tippers. If their food is good and they have good service, they reach into their jeans and pull out a wadded, crumpled dollar bill to send back to the cook and give one to the waitress. Mon Dieu! Mrs. McBride! Chub and Cowboy Bobby are Beau Gestes! From their looks, one might not think so, but from their actions, it is clear they have graceful and magnanimous manners. However, I know they aren't aware of their wonderful gestures; they're too practical. Chub tells me, "When you think about it, you can't buy much in a store with a dollar, but a dollar tip to the cook when he cooks you a good steak, you can pretty well guess he appreciates it and won't spit on yer steak next time ya come in."

Jack's is full of cowboys and flat-landers traveling up and down 395. The parking lot has space for ours and some other horse trailers. Cowboy Bobby's already taken Cotton and Greydog out of the horse trailer to stretch their legs and filled their buckets with water so they can get a drink while we're eating. Poco's on his own to run around and get a drink out of his bowl. I love watching the horses and Poco get their exercise and love smelling their warm animal smells mixed with the delicious smells of the food from the diner.

We sit at the counter on brown, leather-like stools that turn easily. Chub says this place has been around for more years then he can remember and he can remember a lot. I'm ordering their bacon well done and soft scrambled eggs, a toasted English muffin and fresh-squeezed orange juice. Chub orders bacon and eggs, sunny side up along with their famous biscuits and gravy. Cowboy Bobby is a biscuit and gravy man, too. He's always joking with his bride-to-be Diane, saying he wouldn't marry any gal if he knew how to make biscuits. Diane doesn't think that's funny.

Marge has our food in front of us in an acceptable amount of time and we're eating. She refills our coffee cups for the second time. I'm beginning to understand why cowboys don't care about the proper, civilized way to dine. They're always in a hurry, going from rodeo to rodeo to place entry fees, taking care of their horses. Cowboy Bobby says whenever you stop your truck, for whatever reason, for every 15 minutes you stop, you lose a half hour on the road. If you stop for 30 minutes, you lose an hour and so forth, ergo one has to eat rapidly or use the facilities in a hurry so you don't lose road time. But this morning I have requested extra time as I need to talk to Chub. My future hangs in the balance. I shouldn't have let the attorney in the house. I shouldn't have gone to the mountains, but that's useless thinking. I'd better focus on getting a job. Chub says he has an idea. We finish breakfast and he's sitting back getting ready to build his smoke. Marge is at the ready to top off our coffee cups, but we shake our heads. Chub wants to talk and he doesn't want his coffee to get cold.

"L'il Darlin', when we get back to Redlands, I'm gonna talk to my sister, Louise. She's takin' care of Ma's house now. Ma lived across the street from the high school an' turned her little house into a candy store. Louise ain't interested in running it, so she wants to rent it. Louise an' me don' get along too good so's I doubt she'll rent to me, but maybe after she meets ya an' thinks yer with me, she'll feel ok about it. Maybe she'll think ya'll teach me how to behave better."

"Chub, I think you behave nicely. Why does she think you need to learn anything?"

"Well, maybe it's some my fault. A while ago when Greydog an' me come out of the mountains, we woke up in Redlands with nothin' ta do." Marge stops again with a fresh pot of steaming coffee. It smells so good, but Chub shakes his head. He's telling a story and his coffee will get cold. Chub's having fun. His blue eyes are all sparkles remembering and I'm glad we're having this time. Trying to talk in the truck is impossible. Our truck and all the others on the highway make so much noise we can't hear each other. Chub breaks a piece of his bacon in half, wraps it in a napkin and puts it in his pocket for Poco. He never leaves an eating place without breaking a piece of something for Poco.

"Come on, Chub, get with it. I ain't gonna sit here all day."

"I'm talkin' ta L'il Darlin', Bob. Ya don' like it, sit in the truck with Poco or git in yer own rig an' head out."

"Maybe I'll do that or maybe I'll jest sit here an' have another cup a' coffee. I ain't decided." Marge overhears and comes over with her fresh pot of steaming coffee. Cowboy Bobby pushes his cup toward her, she refills and he takes a careful sip, settles back and gets his Copenhagen out of his shirt pocket.

"Oh, dear, Chub, I hope I'm not causing trouble."

"No way, L'il Darlin'. Cowboy Bobby jest likes ta have fun agitatin'."

"Oh."

"As I was sayin'. Greydog an' me didn't have nothin' ta do that day, so's I thought we outta visit my sister, Louise. I been gone most a' the year, so's I thought that'd be nice. I saddled up Greydog an' we started down the shoulder of the road to Louise's place up the mountain. Weather was good, we was enjoyin', I was nippin' on my bottle of Jim Beam.

"We got to 'er driveway an' there was a bunch a cars sittin' there. I wondered what was goin' on, so's Greydog an' me rode up to 'er front door ta take a look. I was ta lazy ta get off Greydog, find a place ta tie him up an' walk ta the door, so's I decided jest ta ride up, push the door open an' ride ol' Greydog inta the house. Didn't mean ta kick the door so hard getting' it open, but there we were, Greydog an' me in the front parlor an' there was Louise with her lady friends holdin' little plates on their laps an' fancy cups with their little fingers stickin' out, talkin' away a mile a minute.

"Oh, no, Chub!"

"I was polite, L'il Darlin', took my hat off, said, 'Good mornin', ladies', nodded my head, toasted 'em with my bottle of Jim Beam when all hell broke loose. You'd think I was Jesse James fixin' to rob 'em. They was runaways, jumpin' up, spill'n stuff, smashin' the little plates an' cups on the floor, pushin' each other outta the way ta git out the slidin' glass back doors ta the garden, then bawlin' an' runnin' like a herd a' stampede'n wild cattle fer their cars an' Louise's two fancy cats was spreadin' their claws on the way ta the window, clawin', grabbin', shreddin' the drapes, slashin' strips in 'em getting ta the ceilin'! Well, I jest sat there, pushin' back my hat, nippin' at my Jim Beam. Greydog was lookin' wide-eyed at all the commotion. 'What's that all about, Louise? Ain't they never seen a cowboy on a horse before?'

"'Not in my parlor, you bastard!' She was madder than a wet hen, screamin', picken' up some a' the fancy little pillows on her couch, throwin' 'em hard as she could at Greydog an' me.

"Now, there was no need fer her to use language like that an' Greydog an' me was getting tired dodgin' those fancy pillows, so I figgered it was time ta git. We started back out the front door an' I was still polite, tipped my hat again, said thanks for the visit an' asked if she had any leftover sandwiches I could take. Now, that war' a mistake. She grabbed some sandwiches off the floor an' started throwin' em at me, screaming words that I won't say in front of ya, L'il Darlin'. Greydog's head was dodgin', eyes rollin', snortin' an' I wasn't feel'n good 'bout the way things was goin'. I don' like talkin' with a high-strung woman like that, so's I give ol' Greydog a kick an' backed 'em out the front door, tipped my hat, said 'Thanks for the visit. See ya next year!'

"Before I know'd it, here come the empty sandwich platter through the air, comin' right at me an' Greydog, an' her screamin' that I'd better never come back. She don' ever wanna see me again, never! A' course, that war a couple a' years ago, so's maybe she's over all that now. She's always been kinda high strung so ya can't tell."

"Oh, Chub, you shouldn't have done such a thing. Why did you do it?" I was doing my best not to laugh at Chub and his description of the incident, but it was hard. He was looking so sincerely innocent.

"Well, maybe I shouldna' done it, but I thought it was kinda funny lookin' at a room full'a snobby women thinkin' they was mighty important in their fancy hats, holdin' little teacups with their little fingers stickin' out in the air. Didn't look so important when they started jumpin' aroun' like they was barefoot on a hill a'uh, pardon me sayin' this, L'il Darlin'— hot manure, breakin' cups, screamin', stampedin'."

"Chub!" I'm trying again not to smile or laugh, but look serious and sincere. "I don't know if enough time has passed for Louise to forgive you. You embarrassed her terribly in front of her friends."

"Well, all we can do is try'er out when we get to Redlands." Cowboy Bobby interrupts Chub. "Ya know, ya ain't the only one with a story. I got one I wanna tell ta L'il Darlin'."

Chub pushes his coffee over to the back edge of the counter. "Ready fer coffee now, Marge." She comes over for a third refill. Cowboy Bobby pushes his cowboy hat back a little from his forehead, takes a careful sip of coffee. Chub starts to build another smoke and I stand up for a minute to stretch my legs. Cowboy Bobby waits for me to sit down and begins.

"One Saturday night when I was stayin' in Pedley with Red an' Sue, I was feelin' kinda frisky an' decided to take Cotton out for a ride. We was goin' down the side of the road an' I saw a big neon sign, 'The Long Branch Bar.' I was thirsty an' decided to ride Cotton through those swingin' doors right up to the bar an' git me a beer. I looked over Cotton's head an' tol' the bartender I wanted a beer. I'll tell ya what, that bartender's eyes got big as headlights starin' at me an' Cotton. The people at the bar took off out the back an' then some toughs came over an' one threw a beer bottle an' hit Cotton. Now, that's one thing ya don' wanna do to a cowboy's horse. I jumped off Cotton, picked my rope off'a my saddle an' smashed it into that guy's face. Now, a 30-foot rope has about 10 coils in it. It's better than a quirt or a stick. I kept hittin' those two toughs with it, 'specially the one that threw the bottle at Cotton. 'Don't ya ever throw nothin' at my horse!'

"Don' know why the bartender didn't call the cops, but I'm glad. I wanted to end the whole thing. I was still thirsty an' hadn't gotten my beer. Anyway, the toughs decided to leave an' the bar was empty. 'Where the hell's my beer?' The bartender got me my bottle, I tossed my coin down, got back on Cotton an' went out the swinging door again. The bartender was yellin, 'You bastard, don't ya or yer horse ever come in here again.'

'Why would I? Yer service is lousy.' So, that's my story an' now we better get movin.'"

Chub starts to roll another smoke before we get in the truck to head back down the highway. Cowboy Bobby checks his watch and shakes his head. Greydog and Cotton are back in their horse trailers. They're easy to load after all these years. Poco is in the front under the dash again. Chub leans over and gives him his piece of bacon. Chub turns the key in the ignition and we sit there letting the engine warm up. Cowboy Bobby checks his watch, shakes his head again and gets in his rig. I pull down the visor to check to see if I have any food on my face. Good, there's only a little crumb on my cheek. I brush it away.

Engine warmed, Chub pushes the floor pedal with his left boot, shifts the gear stick into first gear. I watch as I don't know how to drive his truck and I must learn if I'm going to stay with these cowboys. I'm going to have to contribute, "pull my weight," as I hear them say. I turn my head around to say good-bye to Jack's Place when a tiny flash of light bounces off the visor mirror and makes me blink. I put my hand over my eyes.

"What's a' matter, L'il Darlin'? See something?"

"Just a little flash of light from the sun. Let's go."

"Give me a second. Need to talk to Bobby before we start."

Chub walks back to Bobby's rig. I watch as he leans in the window. "Bob, keep a lookout. The attorney's 'round here somewhere. L'il Darlin' spotted a flash a' light in the mirror, thinks it's from the sun. I'm not gonna tell her different, but the sun ain't at the right angle fer that. It's the attorney with those binoculars."

"Gotcha!"

Chub gets back in the driver's seat. "Ok, L'il Darlin', all set; let's go!"

CHAPTER 28

The House Where it Happened

Two weeks later
Downey, California
October, 1970, 7 p.m.

"Ya know, we're all heroes an' villains different times a' our lives,
but ya did 'em both in one night. Never seen that before."

~ Chub

Mama and the kids are out for dinner and a movie. Poco's in the pickup parked across the street in the mall. Chub and I are in the kitchen. Chub has a plan to get the attorney to come out here to the house where it happened so he can see the attorney, see who he'll be looking for.

Nothing's been right since we left the mountains. Mama isn't happy with Chub. He doesn't look right in the city. He doesn't fit in, too big, too rough; if only she would see him through my eyes. He's here to help us get rid of the attorney. It would have been easier in the mountains, but now it has to be done here in the city.

"What if he doesn't call?"

"He'll call." Chub takes his time, rolls his Bull Durham, licks the paper, lights it, blows it into life and smoke rings. His eyes squint against the smoke.

"How can you be so sure?"

"L'il Darlin', let ol' Chub handle this." He stretches out in the kitchen chair out of sight of the window. I look at my watch: almost eight o'clock.

"Chub, he's not going to call."

"He'll call." He blows a smoke ring, watches the shape change in the air.

"What will we do if he doesn't?"

"He'll call."

RING!

"Oh, my God, it's him! It's him! What'll I do?"

"Answer it!"

"I can't." My body seizes.

RING!

"Pick it up! Pick it up!" He pinches his smoke out. I can't move.

He grabs the phone, shoves it against my ear. "Say 'hello'!"

"Hello? Yes, it's me. No, just me. Mama and the kids are at the movies… All right."

"He's coming! He's coming!"

Chub slams the receiver back on the cradle. He pulls me out of the kitchen chair, walks me into the living room, sits me on the couch, goes over to his big down jacket, the one that gave me such warmth and comfort in the mountains, takes a bottle of Jim Beam from the pocket, twists the lid, raises it to his mouth, tips his head back, swallows, swallows, swallows, wipes his mouth on his shirt sleeve.

"What are we going to do?"

"Wait."

"I can't."

"Ya got to. Ya gotta tell me this is him. Answer the door. Open it wide. The porch light's on, say his name. I gotta see 'im in the light, see who I'm lookin' fer, then get outta my way. I'll take it from there. Ya gotta do this, I need yer help."

That mantle clock is so attractive. I think they call it a carriage clock. Funny I never noticed this clock. The previous owners must have left it behind, I wonder why? It's about to strike nine. Tick, tock, tick, tock. "Do not forsake me, L'il Darlin…"

We hear a car approaching, see headlights turn into the driveway. Oh, my God! The dirty blue car! It's him, but it's too soon. He must have been calling from the mall across the street, not from Los Angeles. My body starts to shake. Chub grabs me, shoves me in front of him, walks me to the door; one body — two heads — four arms — four legs. "And the two shall become one, 'til death do they part."

KNOCKING! Three more steps to the door. One, two, threeee! "Toot toot, Tootsie, good-bye!"

Chub reaches over me for the doorknob, one big hand turns the knob, yanks the door open wide — the smell of night blooming jasmine — his face, his face! Screams rise in my throat. Chub pushes me out of the way, I stumble against a table. Chub's huge body fills the doorway, gorilla shoulders hunch, gorilla arms bulge, gorilla fists against thighs. The attorney's already pale face drains the last ounce of color, deathly white – running feet, car door slamming, tires screeching.

"He's getting away! Bring him back in! Shoot him!" I run around the living room looking for Chub's gun. "Don't let him get away! Kill him! Kill him!" Blood pulses in my throat. Chub grabs me, pushes me down on the couch, leans over me. "He won't get away. He won't bother ya, yer Mama or the kids again."

"He will! You've got to kill him!" I pound Chub with my fists, look at him with my eyes blue slits. "If you won't, I will!"

Oh, no! What have I turned into? I'm going to be sick. I run to the bathroom, go to my knees on the bathroom rug, bend forward, put my face down on the cool, white bathroom tile, smell the remnants of disinfectant, gag. My mind spins, sees headlines: "Two Fugitives Wanted for Murder in California, L'il Darlin' and Chub!" No more a lady, no more no more. "Good-bye lady, good-bye lady, good-bye lady, it's time to say good-bye!"

Chub grabs the phone, dials. "Bobby, hook up with Floyd. Gonna take ya guys out to a steak dinner tomorrow night, usual place."

In the bathroom, my head pounds, a pulsing, booming ache. He got away. The monster got away. He's a monster! I'm a monster! My body shivers. I hold myself to keep from shaking apart.

Chub knocks. "I'm comin' in."

I'm not answering, I don't care if he comes in or not, I don't care about anything anymore. It's over. There's no use. He got away and I've turned into a killer.

"Come on, get up!" He reaches down to help me. "I don't want yer Mama or kids to see ya like this. Wash yer face, comb yer hair. Leave a note. We're goin' out for coffee."

He's right. I can't let Mama or the kids see me like this. I'm afraid to look at myself in the mirror. I'm Dr. Jekyll turned into Mr. Hyde. Mr. Hyde waiting, wanting to kill the attorney, shoot him in the stomach, watch the blood pour out of him like it poured out of me.

"Come on, L'il Darlin', git with it. Where's yer comb, yer purse?"

"On the chair in the kitchen."

"I'll git it. Start washin' yer face."

The phone rings. I drop the comb in the sink. It's him again. It's got to be him. Panic pumps into my system. Chub calls me. "L'il Darlin, ya gotta take this."

"No, no, no, no!"

"Come on. It ain't him. It's some guy, Grady."

Grady? My brain isn't functioning. Chub's fooling me. Why would he do that?

Chub comes toward me, phone receiver on the table. "L'il Darlin', ya gotta talk ta this guy."

I'm underwater walking toward the phone, my arms and legs sweep against the tide, grab a seaweed-dripping receiver.

"Hello?"

"Suzanne, I didn't know you were back. I'm trying to get your Mom. It's Grady! I need help! The ambulance just took Debbie to emergency. She's hemorrhaging. I need to be with her. Can you and your friend come over right away and stay with the twins, they're boys, until they get Debbie settled? I'll be back as soon as I can."

"Twin boys? I don't know, Grady." I lean over, put my free hand on my diaphragm, deep breathing.

"Please, Suzanne. I've called Debbie's folks, but they're three hours away. I need someone now. Please!" Grady chokes up.

Chub shrugs into his big jacket, holds my purse in his hand, my sweater over his arm. "Grady, I have to leave a note for Mama and the kids. We'll be there in about thirty minutes, less if possible."

"I'll have everything ready for you."

"Fill me in on who this is, what's it all about, while I drive." Chub turns the key in the ignition, starts warming up the pickup.

"Chub, I worked awhile in Downey Hospital. Mama got me the job in admitting. I was working there when this all happened to me with the attorney. I worked with Debbie in admitting. She married Grady, he worked in emergency."

"Come in, come in! Debbie's in the emergency room! They're giving her transfusions."

Grady's face is white. There's a baby boy in each of his arms, one in a blue blanket, one in green.

"What happened?"

Chub takes off his jacket, throws it on a chair. "Give 'im to me." He reaches his big arms out to Grady, gets a baby in each arm. "Git to yer wife; give us a call when ya know somethin.'"

The babies start to cry with the change of arms. Chub shifts them around. He's so big, they're so tiny, just six weeks old. Their eyes open, stare at Chub, cry louder, try to find their fists. "Get goin'. We'll handle everythin.'"

"Debbie's pumped milk. It's in the fridge. They're hungry. They haven't finished eating. Three seconds in the microwave," he yells as he runs out the door, jacket in hand.

"L'il Darlin', I know yer upset, but there ain't no time fer that now. These babies gotta eat. Take the green one while I get myself in the recliner with the blue one. Start warmin' the milk."

"Ok, Chub. I'm going to put the milk in the microwave for one minute instead of three seconds." Three seconds, that couldn't be right. Grady couldn't have been thinking right. Chub's in the recliner. I give him back the green one, both babies sucking their fists. "Chub! Did you feel that?"

"Feel what?" A rumble, shaking, cupboard doors rattle, start to swing open.

"An earthquake!"

Chub lurches out of the recliner. "Git in the doorway!" The building sways, dishes fall out of the cupboards, break on the counters and floors. "Git in the doorway!" Chub yells as the babies scream.

I try to hold on to the kitchen counter, stumble my way toward the doorway. Chub's behind me with the twins somehow walking in a kind of rhythm with the bucking floor. He presses me against the door jam, shields me and the screaming babies. And then everything stops, silence, until frightened voices and anxious knocks come to the door. "Are you all right in there?"

Chub yells, "Git back inside. There'll be after shocks. We're good." Another round of shaking, rumbling, rattling, phone ringing. "Don' answer."

"I have to. It'll be Grady." I sway toward the phone.

"Yes, yes, Grady we're all right." I hang onto the end table. "5.6 – oh, God! How is Debbie? How are you?" The phone goes dead.

Night blooming jasmine fills the air. Everyone must have a bush in their yard. The air is cool. I'm glad Chub thought to bring my sweater. He puts the key in the ignition, starts the pickup, lets the engine start to warm up. Poco lies on my feet under the dash looking very glad to see us.

"L'il Darlin', this was a damn rough night." He reaches for the key again, turns the ignition off. "I'm gonna build a smoke, wanna talk to ya before I getcha back to yer place. The ritual rolling finished, he sits back, blows a smoke ring, watches it touch the windshield, change shape, float away. He stares at the disappearing smoke ring. "I know ya wanna kill the bastard, but that ain't good. Ya gotta think about yer Mama an' the kids. They need ya. They don't need to be visitin' ya in jail an' I don't wanna visit ya there either. I got nobody in my life, but ya an' I don't wanna lose ya." Chub turns his big body around to face me.

"Ya ain't a bad person wantin' ta get my gun an' shoot the bastard. Ya ain't a villain, yer a woman who got hurt bad. Ya got every right to wanna kill the guy that done it. But look: Ya took care of two tiny baby boys tonight, got 'em fed, burped, changed diapers all in the middle of an earthquake. That ain't a villain, that's a hero!" He turns back to the windshield, pauses, smokes, eyes look far away. "Ya know, we're all heroes an' villains different times a' our lives, but ya did it all in one night. Never saw that before. That's purty damn good!" He rolls the truck window down, pinches out his smoke, flips it in the street, reaches for the key in the ignition and turns. The engine catches.

"Let's get back to yer place. I'm ready for a toddy, maybe two." The engine rumbles, we move. I lean back in the seat exhausted. I can't go on anymore. I'm done, there's nothing left, but Chub's words echo in my brain; "heroes, villains"? I wonder, are we all really heroes and villains at different times of our lives? Who knows? But I do know this: He's right. It's damn hard to do all in one night! There's just enough energy in me to reach over, touch Chub's arm. "Thank you, Chub, thank you."

CHAPTER 29

Terror on the Switchback

June 1971

"My fingernails dig deep and white into the flesh of my hand now
flecked with traces of blood, my palm squeezing a fistful of buttons."

~ L'il Darlin'

W e're gathered in front of the barn ready for the first trip of this, my second season, 10 of us. Socrates said, "There are no ordinary moments. Everything is a miracle. Pay attention!" Ever since coming to the mountains, every moment has been a miracle for me – falling in love with the back country, the three big cowboys, Poco, Suzy horse, the mules – and the biggest miracle of all: the attorney is now out of my life! I don't know what happened to him. I'll probably never know. Chub told me a few days before we left for the mountains that I don't have to think about him anymore. "He's gone, L'il Darlin'. It's over." Then he turned and walked away from me and from the way he turned and walked, I knew not to ask any questions.

And now here I am now with a group, ready to ride the trail up to the back country with honeymooners Mike and Cindy. They met here at the lake. Mike's a young, strong, big guy with the Mammoth Forest Service. Mammoth Mike's his nickname because of his size and job location, a nice play on words. He and Chub are close. Chub calls him "his son." Cindy, petite and slender, works as a maid here at the resort. They are so in love they shine.

Cowboy Bobby has a wife, too, Diane, and we all love her. How could anyone not? Smart, kind, gracious, exquisitely groomed; no cowboy hat to disturb her lush mane of shiny black hair rolled into a royal upsweep at the back of her head and, wonder of wonders, she has a full make-up kit with her. I haven't seen make-up since I joined the pack station – bag balm and sunscreen are my face cream, Blistex my lipstick, mosquito spray my perfume. Mama and my girls can't believe what has happened to me. I'm a far cry from my make-up kit, hair extensions, and false eyelash singing years.

Chub calls. "We're burnin' daylight; move 'em out!" A cloudless, heart-breaking robin-egg-blue sky above us, a lemon-yellow sun, the comforting, rhythmic clip clop, clip clop of horses' hooves making little whirls of dust as their noses snort frosty morning air: We're moving out! Cindy's first-time-on-the-trail A-rab is full of energy, prancing and tossing her head. A-rab, as Chub calls him, is not Chub's choice. He's not a fan of those blankety-blank Arabs, no way, no how, but Cindy loves her and this is her honeymoon.

Bill and Red trailered up their own horses, Fancy and Geronmino. Cowboy Bobby trailered up Diane's horse, Gru, for her and an extra for me, Nobody's Darlin'. Nobody's Darlin' is from his Pa's ranch as it was thought best to give Bill's wife, Dorothy, first-time trail rider, my Suzy horse. Chub on Greydog and Poco, in his leather dog boots, are in the lead and next are the honeymooners; Mammoth Mike on Pancho, leading four mules and little Cindy on her A-rab. Bill's on his horse, Fancy, and Cowboy Bobby's on Cotton bringing up the rear. That's an important position as the caboose rider sees the entire string ahead of him and spots any potential trouble, slipping saddles or packs on the mules and riders, campers on foot walking down from the back country toward our string with loose wind-breakers flapping in the wind spooking our string of riders and mules.

Zig-zag, upward-angled, winding narrow trails called "switchbacks," 50 to 60 feet long, 30 inches wide, carved parallel into the mountainside are taking us up 3,500 feet to our destination – a falling-down, makeshift structure nicknamed Chub's Hilton above Lake Mildred at the foot of the Queen, the calcite mine. A beautiful morning, so clear you can see forever and that's what Nobody's Darlin' is doing. An hour on the trail and I'm still uneasy on her. She's doing something Suzy never does, nor any of the other trail horses. Instead of turning the corner at the end of each switchback following the horse ahead of her, she walks right to the edge of the switchback, a 300-foot drop, stops dead still, leans over the edge, scans the mountains below, ahead, above us, sweeps her head up and down, side to side. I turn and yell back to Cowboy Bobby. "What's she doing?"

"Doin' her job, lookin' for cattle. Pa's got a longhorn cattle ranch. She's good, won't jump, don't worry – well, 'less ya see 'er put 'er hoof ta 'er head."

"Ha, ha! Not funny, Bobby." But I do have to admit to a little smile. The big ball of lemon-yellow sun's climbing and I pull my shirt off my shoulders to take advantage of its warmth. The wind starts to whip up and I have to hold my hat down, though Diane's elegant, shiny upsweep roll remains royal, not one hair out of place. I can't help but stare. We've just rounded the third switchback; Chub, Poco, Mike and his mules and bride Cindy are directly above us. The ride continues to the usual trail sounds, the clip clop of the horses' hooves, squeaks of creaking saddles, an occasional cough, and then, behind me, Cowboy Bobby's off Cotton, inching, stomach sucked in flat as a fried egg, between the mountain, me and Nobody's Darlin', shoving Cotton's reins into my left hand, twisting his head over his left shoulder and looking up, eyes glued on Cindy and A-rab above us, his back plastered against the mountain, skinnying between the mountain, Gru and Diane in front of me, angling toward the inches of space in front of them. What's he doing? What's he seeing? I follow his eyes. Oh, no! A-rab's gathering herself, bunching, bowing; she's going to buck and throw Cindy! No, no! Not here, not here!

Cowboy Bobby's hips twist. He jams his left side into the mountain, eyes locked on A-rab, feet moving in counterpoint to A-rab's, Fred Astaire to Ginger Rogers. Cowboy Bobby, barely able to read or write, signing his name with X's, doing split-second mental calculations, aerodynamics, concomitant with A-rab, the wind and the mountain.

Cindy's airborne for seconds then slams into the mountain dirt, body sliding, falling rocks going over the cliff into silence hundreds of feet below. The only constant, the implacable mountain and Cowboy Bobby throwing himself face forward into the stone face, arms and toes braced against its side, pushing up making space beneath his body, calculating the exact second Cindy will slide feet first into and under him, pressing her hard against the mountain, a Stone Age embrace, a dance of death and A-rab looks down in an equine haughty apotheosis of relief.

Cowboy Bobby steadies Cindy, turns her around underneath him so she can begin climbing back up the mountain, her feet on his powerful shoulders, her clawed hands try for rock, gravel, anything to hold, help her up. Husband Mike's above, lying under his horse, stretching arms over the edge, waiting to grab her, pull her up the last few feet, as she gains a little, backslides a little with Cowboy Bobby below pushing her one leg at a time, pushing, pushing not against the mountain but with it.

I'm frozen, hypnotized at the scene, until rocks begin tumbling in front of me and Nobody's Darlin'. Then, a heart-stopping sight: in front of me, Diane's horse, Gru, whinnies, rears up into the air, back legs pirouetting, twirling, front legs high in the air over the edge of the cliff, swinging toward me to find footing back on the trail facing me! L'il Darlin' and Nobody's Darlin' are face to face, nose to nose with Diane and Gru. Gru and Nobody's Darlin' stare wide-eyed at each other. I stare wide-eyed into Diane's face stark white beneath her make-up; her brown eyes and my blue eyes look at each other so wide they're ready to fall out of our heads, unbelieving, our mouths gaping, chins on our chests, frozen, a Fredric Remington bronze – a Frederic Remington painting he would have to name "Terror on the Switchback!"

Cowboy Bobby's head twists over his left shoulder away from Cindy's back, still pushing her legs to keep her from slipping, yelling at Diane against the wind: "Turn his head back the other way, away from the mountain. Do it, Diane, do it!"

Diane and I look at each other in horror. Gru will have his feet airborne over the edge again. I can't look! I squeeze my eyes shut. I need to pray. Where is Aunt Gen's rosary? My shirt buttons! I grab for them in the bunched, scrunched folds of my pulled-down shirt, find one, hang on to it for dear life, pulling it off my shirt. "Hail Mary, full of grace, the Lord is with thee" — frantic fumbling and pulling for another — "Blessed art thou amongst women and blessed is the fruit of thy womb, Jesus." Ripping my shirt for another — "Holy Mary, mother of God, pray for us sinners now and at the hour of our death!" My shirt's torn wide open and I don't care! I open my eyes. Facing me is the most beautiful sight I have ever seen in my life: Gru's rump and switching tail, Diane's royal, lustrous black upsweep, still every hair in place, staring me in the face. My fingernails dig deep and white into the flesh of my hand now flecked with traces of blood, palm squeezing a fistful of buttons. I wipe tears from my cheeks with my fist and hear Cindy's victory cry "I need a drink!" echo atop A-rab once more from one mountain peak to another to fade into the canyons.

"Amen!" I have no voice, only a dry whisper.

"Amen?" No! "L'chaim!" Grandmother's voice resonates off the mountain. "What are you doing with those mashugana Catholic prayers? You're Jolie's granddaughter! You were born a Jew, you'll die a Jew!"

I drop my reins and throw my hands up in the air in surrender, my voice still a dry whisper. "Yes, Grandmother, you're right – I was born a Jew and I will die a Jew, but not today, Grandmother, not today!"

CHAPTER 30

Champagne and Mules

Five hours or so later

"I wonder if champagne can be packed up on the mules
without the altitude causing it to explode?"

~ L'il Darlin'

W e're carefully, very carefully, breathing again, trying not to think
about Cowboy Bobby and Cindy clinging to the mountain, Diane's
horse Gru rearing, front legs hovering in the air over the edge of the cliff,
back legs twirling, pirouetting on the shale trail, trying to find footing facing
the wrong way. My body shudders with the memory, but shudders or not,
we must keep going. This trail is like life. Once you set foot on it, you have
to keep going forward to stay alive, no matter what happens.

To think the scariest part of the trail is still ahead of us, the part where
the trail clings to the edge of a dizzying steep cliff then narrows to about 25
inches, one side going straight down hundreds, maybe a thousand, of feet
and the other side scraping the mules' saddle bags against the mountain.
This is my cue to sing, but my body won't cooperate. I can't take a deep
breath; my heart can't find its normal rhythm. We approach the final curve.
I hear the mules' saddle bags scrape, scrape, scrape. I try to take a singing
breath, but it's no use. I try to calm myself, turn my head to the mountain,

remember the brochures in the restaurant tell about this mountain range and the scratches left by the long-ago glaciers that helped create these Sierras. I want to lose myself looking at the mountainside shining so brightly from the polish left by the ice's passage that the light seems to come from inside the earth itself. I want to keep my mind thinking of the woolly mammoths and wolves that once stalked these mountain sides and, as John Muir said, "the tender snow-flowers noiselessly falling through unnumbered centuries."

The horses and mules are waiting for me to sing. I see their ears, one forward, the other backward. They're waiting for the sound of my voice. They know the routine and it's now or never and it better be now. Here I go:

"Oh, give me a home, where the buffalos roam,
Where the deer and the antelope play,
Where seldom is heard a discouraging word,
And the skies are not cloudy all day."

My voice is soft and shaky. Even when I'm not scared to death, it's hard to sing at this altitude, but I can't stop now. I hope the others will join in on the chorus.

"Home, home on the range,
Where the deer and the antelope play,
Where seldom is heard,
A discouraging word
And the skies are not cloudy all day."

Well, I have a little more voice and, lo and behold, I actually remember another verse.

"Where the air is so pure,
And the wind is so free,

The breezes so balmy and bright.
That I would not exchange, my home on the range
For all of the cities so bright."

I hear Cowboy Bobby's voice behind me start to join in singing la, la, la because he doesn't know the words and then Diane's in front of me singing some shaky la, la, las, but she's doing the best she can and now the others are starting to join in. I even hear Chub start to join in on the chorus.

"Home, home on the range,
Where the deer and the antelope play,
Where seldom is heard,
A discouraging word,
And the skies are not cloudy all day."

And then I hear Bobby sing out behind me, "'Cause what can an antelope say?" Oh, my, Bobby's making a joke! He's sure happy and happy he should be: He saved Cindy, Diane and Gru, Nobody's Darlin' and me all at the same time, and now he's got everyone laughing. Well done, Bobby, well done!

Everyone's laughing and singing now and we do two more verses with their choruses. The horses and mules applaud with their ears twitching and moving forward and backward, and I consider that a standing ovation and of all the standing ovations I've ever had, this is the one most full of meaning, most amazing, most life affirming.

I drop my right rein, put my hand over my heart in grateful prayers, this time in both Catholic and Jewish to appease Grandmother and cover all bases, and I feel my heart find its rhythm beating in sync to the cadence of the horses and mules. Encouraged – euphoric – I raise my hand and call out, "One more time! One more time!"

Our chorus of horses nickering and mules braying and human voices singing loud and clear on the trail is evidence of our victory over fear! The horses and mules are striding out with long legs and that makes me think they're happy. I'll have to ask Cowboy Bobby when we get to the top if that's true or not. Even if it isn't, I like to think it's true because that makes me feel happy and I start riding tall in my saddle, smiling, and hanging on to the saddle horn with fewer white knuckles than I had before.

The trail is inches wider now, the steep climb over. In less than an hour, the horses will have their hooves in Lake Mildred's sapphire waters. We'll feel the amazing, magical sensation of being lifted on our swimming horses, transported, floating in the current, rocked like babies in the water's arms until hooves touch bottom again and a million sparkling, sun-filled rainbow rain drops from shaking horses, mules and Poco fill the air.

The noon sun is high and bright above us, watching the activity of setting up camp. Poco's dog boots are off. Cowboy Bobby digs a hole for Chub's peach cobbler then gets a little campfire going.

"Chub, do we need a campfire so early?"

"You bet we do, L'il Darlin'. We had a scare this mornin'. We need some calmin'. When you're nervous in a strange place, there's nothin' like bein' by a little campfire, smellin' the smoke, hearin' the wood cracklin', feelin' yer hands git warm to help ya calm down, feel comfortable – like yer home." Chub is right. Bill, Dorothy, Red and Sue are coming over to stand by the fire, putting their hands out over the little flames even though the weather is warm. Diane and Cindy join them. Cowboy Bobby gets the rest of the camp chairs off the mules so everyone can sit down. Chub makes coffee in the speckled blue coffee pot just like Aunt Gen Foglesong used to do, so calming, and the aroma does remind me of home, cozy and safe.

Bill and Dorothy decide to ride up to Lake Edith for some fishing even though it's noon, early for the trout to be biting, but you never can tell. I think they just feel like doing something more than sitting around talking. However, Diane and I have no desire to get back on our horses now or possibly ever. We're still in a state of shock. Just about five hours ago, we were on the brink of death, frozen in our saddles, staring into each other's eyes, unbelieving, struck dumb, until Cowboy Bobby's yells at Diane roused her to pull with all her might and strength on a protesting Gru's reins, to get his head turned back, to turn him back over the cliff's edge, his back feet pirouetting, twirling, front feet pawing the air, trying to find footing again on the trail facing forward.

I recall Cowboy Bobby telling me, as he took the reins from my hand after getting Cindy back up the mountain and Gru facing forward again, not to get off my horse when we got to camp until he helped me. I was so scared I couldn't answer him, but my mind was talking inside my head telling him not to worry because I wouldn't be able to get off Nobody's Darlin' then or possibly ever. My leg muscles wouldn't stop cramping from the stress in my calves, clutching Nobody's Darlin's sides in an effort to keep my balance, but now as Diane and I are off our horses and sitting in our camp chairs around the campfire, we begin taking deep breaths of fresh mountain air as though we're taking drinks of cold, clear water. We reach out to touch each other with all the fingers on both hands crossed and try to stop shaking, try to feel brave. Diane takes a sip of her red wine and I sip my stream water. A pale Cindy comes over to join us with her bottle of Stolichnaya. We lift our glasses to her bottle in silence and unable to speak, toast with our eyes.

Over by the horses and mules, Mammoth Mike, with emotion bigger than himself, thanks Cowboy Bobby for the millionth time for saving Cindy. Chub is stirring his peach cobbler, nipping out of his Jim Beam bottle. Oh, my goodness, did I see him pour Jim Beam into the cobbler? Oh, dear! Oh, no! I hope no one else sees that.

Bill and Dorothy are back from fishing, proudly showing off their string of trout. We'll put their trout, wrapped in newspaper, into the pile of ice and snow banked up against the mountain side to keep for breakfast tomorrow, but right now it's time for lunch, another feast basket full of Sally's fabulous assortment from the restaurant: roasted prime rib rubbed with sage, fennel and garlic, basil-roasted chicken stuffed with rice and wild mushrooms, herb-crusted trout, garnishes of julienne carrots, French-imported cheese, crackers, celery stuffed with peanut butter, homemade chocolate devil-food cupcakes filled with soft, creamy chocolate and rum centers. Wonderful food, companionship, fresh air, comforting song of horses and mules chomping rolled barley in their nose bags, Poco warm against my side.

Cindy's asleep in her camp chair, cheeks flushed from her Stolichnaya but still pale around her eyes. Diane, Red and Sue want to get oriented, check out the territory and take a walk downstream. I unpack my satchel, get our Louis L'Amour book, Treasure Mountain, at the ready in case there's a need, but I think with this big group and what happened this morning, everyone would rather sit around the campfire talking and listening to our real life story rather than the book's. Cowboy Bobby's tending the horses and mules, waves to Red, Sue and Diane as they go by…

"…All right, Diane, I know somethin's wrong. What is it?"

I'm going through Chub's pack, making sure his insulin is where he can reach it easily and I hear Cowboy Bobby and Diane talking from their little pup tent; strange how sound carries up here. They have such a little tent I don't know how they're going to manage. They can't stand up in there. The only thing they can do is crawl in and out and back in again to get into their sleeping bags. How is Diane going to get dressed and put on her make-up?

"Nothing's wrong, Bobby, nothing's wrong."

"Suit yourself. I'm gonna see if I can twist Chub's arm an' have a toddy." Cowboy Bobby's head, elbows and arms, new straw cowboy hat in hand, belly crawls halfway out of the tent.

"Don't go, Bobby. I'll tell you. I just feel so stupid." He stops crawling forward, reverses his long body back into the tent. It's fascinating to watch the procedure. I shouldn't stay here listening, it's not polite, but I wonder what is wrong with Diane? She was fine when she left with Red and Sue.

"Red thought he saw the horses on the other side of the stream heading back to the lake. Sue and I wanted to help catch them, turn them around. I thought I could jump the stream. I didn't realize it was so wide. I jumped, slipped, hit a rock and cut my knee."

"Ok, let's take a look. Damn! That could use a couple of stitches. No problem. Chub'll stitch it with his string an' horse needle."

"No, no, Bobby! Don't tell Chub! I don't want him to stitch it. This is a terrible way to start our vacation. I shouldn't have come. I shouldn't be here. Chub must hate me. First, I couldn't control Gru, almost got Sandy and me killed along with Gru and your Dad's horse and now I've cut my knee. I should go home before I do anything else. "

"Hell, don't feel bad an' believe me, Chub don't hate ya. He's right fond'a ya. If he weren't, ya wouldn't be here. He's the kind of guy if he likes ya, he'll go to hell an' back for ya an' if he don't an' sees ya layin' in the gutter, he'll step right over ya an' keep goin'. Now, I'll tell ya a little secret. He loves gooseberry pie. Ya make him one of those when we get back an' ya got a friend for life."

"But Bobby, Chub has diabetes. He can't eat anything sweet."

"Oh, he'll tell ya he saw his doctor an' he ain't got it no more an' bring ya a couple a' cans of gooseberries ta get started. Come on, smile! Chub'll tell ya he won't charge ya anymore if ya start havin' a good time."

My goodness. I didn't know this about Chub. Oh, dear, Diane's crying. She'd better stop before she ruins her make-up.

"Come on, Diane. Don't start cryin'. Chub'll hear ya an' come on over. Soon's he sees that cut he'll be headin' straight fer his string an' horse needle an' while he's stichin' he'll tell ya the story what happened ta Freckles Brown at the National Finals in '58, after one a' the bulls hit 'im in the back with his horns an' hooked him. I'll tell ya what, that was one mean bull. Ol' Freckles was the first cowboy ever ta ride that son of a buck. Hell, when ya git hit an' hooked with that bull's horns in ya, ya got some hurt' put on ya. Now, stop cryin' an' I'll get some'a that apricot brandy from my pack an' some tape an' pull that cut together. Then we'll get out by the campfire. It's almost time for dinner."

"Thanks, Bobby. While you're out there, ask Sandy to crawl on in here and keep me company."

Another feast! I'm still full from lunch. I've got to stop eating like this, but I know it's tradition to go all out on the first day and night in camp. I try not to react poorly to not having tables for this group and consequently, no tablecloths; however, Sally did supply linen napkins, thank heaven and Mrs. McBride. Without tables, it's impossible to place the cutlery in the proper position and there isn't any place to put glasses, but I mustn't act like a poor sport and remember I'm lucky to be alive, so here we go again: rib eye steaks grilled over the open fire, potatoes baked in the rock coal-lined oven dug into the ground next to the peach cobbler, stuffed with butter, sour cream, chives, corn in their husks, slathered with seasoned butter, wrapped in aluminum foil, steamed tender in the campfire, the famous peach cobbler, flavored with Jim Beam due to this morning's circumstance, then smothered in rum-flavored heavy cream.

I try to eat slowly, balance my plate in my lap, cut my steak properly, fork in left hand, knife in my right, but I'm coming to realize that — along with Diane, Cindy, Sue and Dorothy — attempts at civilized dining are futile. The cowboys make an easier time of it, spearing their steak with their pocket knives in their left fists like they're driving spikes into the plates. The fancy steak knives from the restaurant don't suit them. Their pocket knives are razor sharp and the forks they've speared their steaks with to keep the steaks steady on their plates so they can saw off a piece of meat with their right hand work very well. Then without taking their left hand fork and transferring it to their right hand, they just pull out their forks, turn their left fist over, palm up and shovel the steak into their mouths.

I watch and think about talking to Chub tomorrow to see about the idea of being the first pack station in this area to offer gourmet pack trips, dining on a banquet-size folding table with candles and flowers. I wonder if champagne can be packed up on the mules without the altitude causing it to explode and sending a spooked mule string and rider over the edge of the cliff. Champagne would give a marvelous romantic flair to the trip, along with white tablecloths, linen napkins. I think a folding banquet table would pack nicely on the mules. I'll see what Chub thinks. I wonder if I could talk Chub and Cowboy Bobby into using steak knives instead of their pocket knives, but I must admit the pocket knife does give a certain je ne sais quoi quality to the scene. Well, I'll see. I'd better stop daydreaming, or maybe it should be called evening dreaming, and pay attention to what's going on. Of course, after-dinner aperitifs will be passed around: Jim Beam, Stolichnaya vodka, apricot brandy, scotch…

The sun begins to slip behind the mountain, shadows dance against the mountainside, the air cools, down jackets are on, lantern's lit. Cowboy Bobby stokes the fire while everyone gets settled for storyin'. Chub sits back in his camp chair, long legs stretched out toward the campfire to begin the ritual. His big fingers push around in his shirt pocket to grab his Bull Durham pouch and papers and takes his time pulling at the string of the pouch. His ritual rolling of his smoke begins. His eyes are bright with anticipation of the first taste of tobacco entering his mouth and nose. He takes a swallow of Jim Beam, looks up, blows a smoke ring, squints against the smoke, blows two more ritual smoke rings, sighs, closes his eyes, and runs his tongue over his lips. He smiles to himself, slowly beginning to enjoy his tobacco and whiskey.

After dinner, everyone waits and watches; even the breeze seems to stop in deference to his ritual. He leans back, blows one, two, three more smoke rings into the still air to hang there while his eyes, full of memory, watch the breeze begin to move again in front of him softly dancing the smoke rings away toward the mountain. He moves a little in his camp chair, finds just the right feel for his body, coughs into the crook of his elbow and takes another deep drag on his Bull Durham, another swallow from his bottle. The bright, full moon gazes down in interest. Apparently, the setting sun did some whispering before slipping below the mountain.

"Yes, siree!" Chub is ready to start story'in. "Ol' Bob was voted ta pick up in the '64 National Finals Rodeo in Los Angeles and ya shore can see why." Chub leans back in his camp chair, head nods while he talks. "He saw that goofy son-of-a-buck A-rab gatherin' an' humpin', went into action, gettin' in the right place at the right time. Figgered out where Cindy was headin' an' caught her underneath him slick as a whistle. Got 'er turned 'round on a dime with seven cents change. Got 'er goin' up hill 'fore ya could blink an eye."

Chub pauses for another big swallow of Jim Beam, drags more on his Bull Durham then pinches what's left between his big fingers and tosses it into the campfire.

"Yes, sir! I'll say it again, Ol' Bob's voted pick-man in the '64 National Finals Rodeo in Los Angeles, an' he's a helluva bull rider an' roper to boot." Now, leaning forward in his camp chair, elbows on his knees, he gets confidential: "One rodeo, Jim Stone an' me saw he gotta thumb tore off an' we was out in the arena lookin' everywhere for it 'til Ol' Bob started yellin' an' wavin' the hand with his thumb hangin' in the air by a slice'a skin. I coulda' sewed it up right there, but the rodeo Doc come over an' did the job. Yep, we're shore lucky to have him with us today. Right, Cindy?"

Cindy runs over to Cowboy Bobby, he leans down, she stands on tiptoe trying to get her arms around his neck to give him a big hug and kiss, then raises her Stolichnaya bottle to him, "Here's to Cowboy Bobby!" Bottles up! Cheers ring out! Bottles clink! Cowboy Bobby stands tall and his big, calloused, roper hand with its scarred thumb reaches up, raising his hat high above his head, makes a full circle in the air, bends from the waist and makes the biggest, best, rodeo cowboy bow this side of the Mississippi! More cheers, more clinking apricot brandy, Stolichnaya, whiskey, scotch, more hugging, kissing. The horses and mules take a few moments from snorting around in the dirt trying to find some dropped bits of rolled barley to stare at us.

Poco's gone up to get my sleeping bag warm for me. I don't think I'll be reading Louis L'Amour tonight. I'm ready to turn in, watch the moon and stars have a turn at putting on their show. I'm body-aching, mind-weary tired. I want to go up, step over the fuzzy rope, get to Poco, and have him snuggle against me. I need to hold my head between my hands, press my fingers against my temples, rub little circles to see if I can chase the headache away that has been flitting around my brain since morning. I look up at the moon and stars, hold Poco tight against me. A flash of light in the sky catches my attention. A falling star! It's coming right toward us! Poco, look! I put both my hands over my heart to hold it in place, cold air blows through my hair and somehow, Mama's voice from heaven comes to me in a song I can't exactly remember, but it's about catching a falling star and putting it in your pocket to save for a rainy day.

Oh, Mama, I miss you so. Please forgive me for coming here and staying, but I feel so good and safe when I'm with the cowboys and so scared and lost when I'm not. You know I've promised that I'll be able to make it up to you somehow, someday, someway.

"Mike, better rouse Cindy. Start packin', smell a storm comin', could be a toad strangler, don't wanna get caught on a wet trail or in that damn crossin.'" Chub's head is down, shaking from side to side, staring at the dirt, remembering. "Just can't forget it, Mike. Jeff found 'em downstream, Rocky twisted around a rock, Ol' Pink a few miles further hung up in them trees, had to pull him out with a wench. Turrible! Damn fine horse! Damn, damn fine horse!" Mike knows the story, most everyone does, but Chub isn't talking to Mike anymore, he's talking to himself. "Damn fool, Rocky! He'd been warned. Everybody know'd that's a bad crossin'. Looks easy 'til the rain comes an' it turns killer." Chub's head is down again, his big hand wipes streaks off his cheeks.

Everyone's in action clearing camp. Diane's knee is better, but I hope she goes to the doctor when she gets to Yucaipa. Cindy's recovered from her scare. Poco's got his dog boots on for the return, staying close to me. Horses, mules, humans all good to go. Chub rides over to me, squints into the cloudy sky, sniffs the air again.

"L'il Darlin'. Let's ride up ta the Queen, get some more purty calcite fer yer mama an' yer girls. We got time an' we might not be gettin' up here again fer a while.

"Red, head 'em out. Bobby take the rear. L'il Darlin' an' me are goin' up ta the Queen. Red, don' let any fool packers get above ya. Make 'em step below. They git above ya, kick rocks down, spook the animals an' ya got a helluva lot a' trouble ya don't want. Storm won't hit fer another five or six hours or so. We'll be caught up with ya by then and past the crossing."

We wave, blow kisses, call out empty rituals of promises never to lose track of each other, have another reunion up here next year and all the next years, but the scare we had on the trail coming up here last week is still reeling in our minds. We know, really know now how fragile life is, how it can be snatched away in seconds even with the best pick-up cowboy in the country at your side. I look around for Poco. "Look Chub, he's already headed up to the Queen. How does he know that's where we want to go?

"He's a helluva trail dog, L'il Darlin'. He knows, he always knows."

Our gourmet pack trips are successful. Tables and chairs, white tablecloths, flowers on the table, wine glasses, Wrangler Will and his banjo and me with my songs and sing-a-longs are a good attraction. Everything is good, except Chub's health has begun to fail and my, Cowboy Bobby's, Floyd's, Will's, Greydog's and Poco's hearts have begun to break apart, a little piece at a time every hour, every minute, every day.

CHAPTER 31

I've Never Held a Gun

"I promised him I would, but I don't think I can."

~ L'il Darlin'

"**L**ook at the lunch Sally packed. Brian, you've won her heart in a big hurry! You've only been here a week and you've got Sally and all the gals around the restaurant, store and lake all a-flutter!"

"It's not easy being me, Suzanne. There's a lot of pressure to keep up the public persona. I'm glad we're finally up here in the back country so I can relax."

"That is if the women or paparazzi haven't followed us up here!"

"Don't even joke about that!" Brian rolls his eyes and puts the back of his hand to his forehead in his theatrical way.

"Ok, Mr. Show Biz! Oh, Brian, I'm so happy you're with us. Who would have thought 20 years ago when we first met at Melodyland Theater we would wind up together in the back country of the High Sierras? What were the chances of that – zero? No, less than zero, minus zero, not even possible, but here we are."

"Hey, Brian. Need some help gittin' the tents up. Ya gotta couple a' minutes?"

"Be right with you, Chub. Suzanne and I were just indulging in some retrospection."

"Oh. Well, take yer time, jest so's we get 'em up before it starts ta get dark. Gets dark early back here, an' purty sudden."

"Brian, you go ahead and help Chub with the tents. I'll unpack the lunch." I'm happy the sun is hot and high over the Queen, the sky cloudless and blue.

"Hey, Brian, Chub! If you're done with the tents, come over here and see what Sally packed us!"

"Damn! Brian, ya'd better stay with us! Sally's never gone to this much work for anybody long as I remember!" Chub moves things around in the basket – I look over his shoulder – "Oh, Chub, let me see! Oh, my, look at this! Chub smiles and moves out of my way, goes over to his camp chair to roll a smoke.

"She's wrapped two bottles of wine!" I'm glad Chub said it was all right to pack wine up here. And look at all these slices of prime rib, a bag of sourdough rolls from Mammoth Bakery, a big bag of arugula, buffalo mozzarella, capers, heirloom tomatoes! I bet they're from that farm south of us. Sliced purple onions, feta and oh, my, crystal wine glasses wrapped in white linen napkins from the restaurant.

Chub leans back in his camp chair, smiles and blows smoke rings. "I'm glad #23 didn't know what he was packin'! He might'a spooked himself right off the trail! Hey, did she put my favorite red velvet chocolate cake an' carton a' milk in there! Ya an' Brian can have the wine, I'm stickin' to Jim Beam an' milk."

"Yes, she put in red velvet chocolate cake and milk. I'll go put that in the stream so it'll stay cold. Brian, it gets cold up here at night; take a couple of mule blankets to put over your sleeping bag. You'll need them around 3:00 or 4:00 in the morning, even sleeping with your clothes and boots on. "

"Thanks for the tip!"

"Ok – you and Chub finish up with what you need to do while I get lunch together. Doing ok, Chub?"

"Just fine, L'il Darlin', just fine. Glad ta have Brian with us. He's a top hand. Let's git with that lunch!"

Chub pats his stomach with both hands. "That's it! I'm done! Couldn't eat another bite if someone had a gun to my head! I'm gonna rest a little. Leave ya two to finish things up."

"Good plan, Chub. I'll follow L'il Darlin's orders."

Chub rests in his tent. Lunch is put away. We're sitting in the old camp chairs by the fire pit. Brian's laying out wood for tonight's campfire. Poco curls up at my feet.

"Brian, bless you for making this trip. You've been so good to Chub, making him steps so he can get in and out of the camper more easily, fixing him pancakes over the campfire, learning to make his peach cobbler to carry on the tradition, making him laugh with show biz stories of us at Melodyland and Las Vegas. There's no way to repay you."

"You're right, Suzanne. There isn't any way to repay things done amongst friends. They're priceless, time is priceless. All we can do is soldier through life the best we can. I've heard somewhere, what we do for ourselves dies with us and what we do for others lives on, at least I hope so."

"Brian, that's beautiful and you live that thought. I remember what you did for the two elderly ladies who lived up the hill from you, visiting them in the afternoons, bringing them your warm home-baked cookies, making them laugh with all your carrying on."

"They were good friends to me, Suzanne. I enjoyed every minute with them and I'm enjoying every minute on this trip with you and Chub."

"I know and you know how much I thank you and love you." My eyes are wet. I shake my head. "Brian, who could have imagined this turn of events? Chub! My hero! Someone as big and strong as rawhide and steel and the mountains, big as the law in Oklahoma, the bounty wanna-bes. How can he be dying from tiny rogue cells in his body! 'Myelocytic leukemia!' That's what the doctors call it. A slow-moving leukemia complicated by his diabetes. He gave me a new life and I want to do the same for him but this is beyond me. He's in remission right now. The doctors say there's nothing to be done, just live life until the day he wakes up and can't saddle his horse. That will be the beginning of the end. When that happens, come back into City of Hope.'"

"Myelocytic leukemia? I've never heard of it."

"I know, neither had I. I can't believe there's nothing that can be done. Somehow, I keep thinking that if I keep doing everything calmly, you know optimistically, handle the transport to City of Hope, his injections, dressing the open wound on his foot, those cells will realize no one's paying attention to them and go away. Chub's planning ahead, figuring out our next move, thinking about his dream of going to Alaska. He's got a friend at a resort up there that runs a pack station. Chub thinks we can get hired on. His friend in Redlands, Rich, is a mechanic, so when we get back down there in a couple of weeks, he'll take the truck in to Rich, get it ready for the drive up the Alaskan highway. I don't think this is a viable plan, but I'm going along with it. It's important that he's got a plan, something to think about but I couldn't work as a packer in Alaska!"

"I don't know, Suzanne, '*there are strange things done in the midnight sun*.' There might be something you could do. You're pretty much free to do as you like right now."

"Yes, I'm free – a double-edged sword and word. You know Janice Joplin's lyric, 'Freedom's just another word for nothin's left to lose.' And there's Sarah Teasdale's poem, 'Only the lonely are free.' I don't want to be free, Brian. I don't want to have nothing left to lose, to be lonely. Steve, Lori and Kim are situated now. Mama's gone. I feel lonely and free and I don't like the feeling. I want to be connected, to be held in a man's arms and never let go, to live here in these mountains, season after season with Chub at my side, Poco at my feet. I never thought or considered a man as big as Chub could get sick – maybe a cold, but nothing he couldn't shrug off, the way he's always shrugging those big shoulders of his. I tell him someday I'm going to write a story about him and call it 'Big Cowboy Shrugs' or something like that."

"Tell me more about him and if your book turns into a movie, I want to play his part."

I know Brian's teasing, or maybe not, and my mind sifts through memories. "When I first met Chub, I was in such a frantic state; all I saw was a powerful giant of a man and his two friends, all ready and willing to help me. I was being stalked by a crazy man."

"A crazy stalker! Suzanne, you never told me about that."

"Another time, Brian. Chub and his two friends turned out to be angels from heaven, not pretty angels but beautiful in my eyes. I wished that had been true of mama's eyes. To her, Chub and his friends were bad men. She was horrified at their sight and horrified that I brought him into our home, our lives. I couldn't explain to her or the kids. Today, I feel so guilty for doing that, but at the time, I believed it was the only thing I could do to protect us."

"I'll wait until another time to ask all about that. Right now, I want to ask if you have a plan as to how you're going to manage without Chub when mule-packing is over?"

"I don't have plans. I don't know where to start. I've lost contact with everyone since I've been up here, but most of my friends are singing friends. Professional singing and playing the piano is out of the question forever, the crazy man saw to that, but I don't want to talk about all that now. I want to think about something happy. First of all, I'm staggered and thrilled that Chub has welcomed you like his long-lost son. I can't believe it; I doubt anyone could believe it."

Brian leans forward, looks into my eyes. "Suzanne, there's something else you want to tell me. I see it in your eyes."

"Yes, Brian, there's something else so heavy on my heart that much of the time I can't even breathe. I need to tell you before Chub gets up. I told you the doctors told him a day would come when he doesn't have the strength to saddle his horse and that will be the day we must go back into City of Hope, so –" I start to choke.

"Take a good singing breath. That's better."

"As we walked out of the doctor's office, heading for the truck that day, Chub spotted a bench on the grass under a tree. We sat down and Chub took my hand. I couldn't imagine what he was going to tell me and of all things that flashed into my mind, I wasn't prepared for his words. He asked me to promise that when 'that day' comes, instead of driving back to City of Hope, he wants us to go into the back country."

My voice falters again. I put my head down, look into my lap.

"Go ahead."

"Brian, Chub wants me to shoot him, kill him, at the entrance of the Queen. He doesn't want to die in the hospital hooked up to machines. I promised him I would, but Brian, I don't think I can. I've never even held a gun." My hands start to tremble.

Brian takes my hands. "I don't think you can either. Now, here's a promise I want you to give me: You call me when that time comes and I'll be the one to drive you, Chub and Poco up to Convict, saddle the horses and we'll come up here to the back country, to the Queen, and I'll take it from there."

Sounds from the tent interrupt us. Poco gets up to go over to Chub.

"Hey, you two, you look pretty serious. Whatcha talkin' about?"

"Talkin' about you, Chub. Have a good nap?"

"Yep."

Brian gets up, lays out more wood for the fire.

Chub sits in his camp chair, Bull Durham and Jim Beam at the ready.

"Any of Sally's chocolate cake left, L'il Darlin?"

CHAPTER 32

You Don't Want a Fur Coat!

"There's no business like show business."

~ "Annie Get Your Gun," Irving Berlin

"**S**o, Brian, got any winterin' plans down there in Hollywood?"

The wistful sound in Chub's voice breaks my heart. "Winterin' plans." There won't be any winterin' plans for him. His time is near; he can feel it, I can feel it, so can Brian. The three of us are playing out a charade, acting as though this is just another trip into the back country, but we know it isn't. Chub tries to be strong, but the look in his eyes tells the story. His giant hands shake, hardly able to hold the reins at times. This is our last trip up here. Brian's never seen the back country before and Chub wanted to show the beauty to him. So strange, a man like Chub has taken to Brian as though Brian was his son, Brian, show business personified and Chub, gun-toting, macho cowboy personified.

I try to focus on the immediate job, getting Chub's favorite chocolate cake and milk for him. A little thing, but now at the end, that's what life's all about, little things: tick, tock, do not forsake me, oh my darlin', "winterin' plans." Oh, Brian, answer him quick, make the clock stop ticking, the music stop playing. I need to hear your voice, quick!

"My agent's supposed to be lining up some things, but you never know. You can't count on anything in this business, even after you've got the job.

I've missed a couple of good opportunities. It's such a miserable business. I should have done like you and Suzanne, got myself up here, become a packer, be one with nature, but the acting bug bit me bad years ago and I've never recovered."

I scold a little in mock jest to keep him talking, "Brian! Don't say that. Look at the good runs you had doubling for James Garner in those TV shows Rockford Files and Maverick."

"True, but they didn't last as long as the run we both had at Melodyland, Carousel and Circle Star Theatre's; six seasons, over 40 Broadway musicals, movie stars playing the leads, L'il Darlin' and me with resident principal white contracts. L'il Darlin' making big bucks understudying everybody – a photographic memory, everybody nervous that she was going to mug them in the parking lot and go on stage for them and then, just for fun, she'd flirt with the Vegas gangsters."

Chub's eyes are wide, his head a little to one side, looking at me. Good. Brian has him caught up in his story. We have to keep talking.

"Brian! That's not true! Chub, that's not true!" I put on a big show of protest as Chub's eyes light up. We have his attention. "Brian, I wasn't flirting, you know that. I was just in the bar one night after the show showing George and Sammy one of Tammy Grime's fur coats. I didn't know they were going to send gangsters to the back of the theatre with a limo trunk full of fur coats for me!"

"Whoa, there! Ya never told me that story, L'il Darlin'. Brian, I'd like ta hear more of that. Sounds like this might call fer a toddy an' smoke." Brian and I grin at each other. Chub settles back in his camp chair, his body relaxing, his hands steady taking the worn Bull Durham pouch out of his shirt pocket and building his smoke, complete with smoke rings. The Jim Beam bottle already by his camp chair is lifted into his lap, cap twisted off, and his head goes back, he takes a swallow, leans back and blows another smoke ring. "Go ahead, Brian."

Oh, my, Brian is going to have to give his all to the tale. I lean over to give Chub a little kiss on his cheek, cold.

"Wait a minute, Brian." Chub's big down jacket is next to the picnic basket. I'm going to get it, put it on, get it warm for him the way he did for me so long ago. I take a little longer than necessary to be sure I've got the jacket warm enough.

"Here, Chub, lean forward, let me help you. Remember when you first did this for me the first time?" I put it over his big shoulders so he can shrug into the arms.

"Thank ya, L'il Darlin'. I remember." The look in his eyes weighs hard on me. I turn to Brian, swallow tears. "Now, Brian, start the story." Chub stares at the sky. "We got a couple more hours before the sun hits the Queen."

"Uh, oh, Brian, we'll tell you about that after you tell your story, but I warn you, you're going to be upstaged when it happens. Better get started!"

Brian gets up theatrically in front of Chub and gives a Shakespearean bow. I call out, "Let the show begin!"

In lieu of a musical fanfare, Brian's fist goes up to his mouth and he does a big theatrical cough.

"Chub, a moment to set the stage as I take you back to yesteryear." He waves his arms, turns around, his back toward Chub, more arm waving to pantomime the backward passing of time, then completes his turn stage front to Chub.

"The year: the fall of 1963, third season of a fantastically successful run at Melodyland, spirits high amongst the producers and investors. Your L'il Darlin' and I trodding the boards together for three years. I thought I had her pretty well figured out, but the scare she gave me one night was one I could never have imagined, the worst of my life, and not to boast, I've had more than my share! But back to L'il Darlin', a natural on stage, a director's dream, dependable as a Swiss train, bright, never missing a cue, a show, an innocence about her that charmed the audience, directors, the investors, but one dark, moonlit night in the back alley of the theatre, that innocence almost got the two of us killed!"

"Brian! You exaggerate! You make it sound worse than it was."

"Now, L'il Darlin', let Brian go on. This story calls for another toddy." Chub's eyes are wide. He's got a tight hold on his Jim Beam bottle as he brings it to his mouth for a big gulp. Brian is a good storyteller

"'Worse than it was'! Ye gads, my child!" I have never seen as big an eye roll as Brian is giving at this moment.

"Go on, Brian!"

"Well, Chub, your L'il Darlin' and I were doing the show "Unsinkable Molly Brown" starring the one and only Tammy Grimes with Bruce Yarnell, her co-star. Tammy was a loose canon, difficult to say the least. Ah ha! A job for L'il Darlin' if there ever was one. Director Jim Thimar sends out the call for L'il Darlin' to the rescue: understudy Tammy, stay with her in her dressing room, keep her focused, happy and on time.

"'Oh, my, stay with Tammy in her dressing room! How fun!'" That's L'il Darlin', always happy and excited to do whatever is called for.

"Now, while L'il Darlin' is doing her job with Tammy, she sees Tammy's dressing room is full of fabulous fur coats. L'il Darlin' is wide-eyed as an owl at midnight. Tammy gets a big kick out of L'il Darlin', tells her to try on the fur coats, borrow one if she wants. They belong to her, so she can lend one to her. L'il Darlin' is having the best time wearing one after another in the bar after the show each night to show George and Sammy, the bartenders."

Brian is in his element, playing me sashaying, posing, batting his eyes, showing off the coats to George and Sammy in the bar. Chub is wide-eyed again, laughing, slapping his knees. Brian's doing my voice: "'Oh, George, you should see all the fur coats Tammy has in her dressing room. She's letting me wear them around the theatre. Oh, how I wish I had one.'"

Now Brian's imitating George's gangster style, talking out of the side of his mouth softly. "'Suzanne, too much of a crowd in here tonight to be talking about Tammy's coats. Let's talk tomorrow. Tonight, just sit here, look pretty in the coat, talk about the show to the customers and let them buy you a drink. Order a straight shot and water back. I'll give you tea. Don't let anyone around your drink. Nurse it. I'll be watching. Enjoy yourself. You look great. Fur becomes you! You're good for business.'"

Brian's back to narrator voice. "So L'il Darlin's happy and comfortable, petting her fur, sipping her shot of tea, chatting it up with everyone, everybody's darling. Sammy's paying attention to L'il Darlin', keeping tabs on her shot glass of tea."

"The next night, after the show, we're in our dressing rooms taking off our make-up when the voice of Denny, our stage manager, comes over the intercom."

Brian's doing Denny's voice now: "'Attention backstage, Suzanne Raymond is wanted at the backstage door.'"

Chub's having the best time, nipping at his Jim Beam, smoking his Bull Durham, loving Brian's impersonations.

"I'm almost finished taking off my make-up, getting changed to my street clothes, mildly curious as to who wants your L'il Darlin' at the backstage door and I glance at my watch. L'il Darlin' always knocks on my dressing room door when she's ready to go into the bar together after the show. She doesn't think it's proper for a lady to walk into a bar unescorted, but there isn't any knock. Where is L'il Darlin'? She should have knocked by now. I better go out back to the stage door and see what's going on. I open the stage door and freeze!" Brian strikes a big theatrical freeze pose. "I can't believe my eyes!"

Chub's eyes are wider than ever in anticipation.

"Your L'il Darlin' is draped in a full-length white mink coat, posing, prancing up and down in front of two snake-eyed, cool-as-ice gangsters, stopping to turn herself around so she can see the back of the coat in the limo's side mirror." Now, Brian is doing a truly wonderful impersonation of me squirming and squinting into the limo mirror with the gangsters shining their flashlights, helping me see.

Chub's body is tense, leaning forward, so caught up in the story he looks ready to take on the two gangsters. "'Oh, Brian!' Little Miss Fur Coat squeals in excitement as she sees me in the limo mirror, thanks to her lighting boys, Lefty and Scarface. 'Isn't this gorgeous? It's real mink and look' – she holds her arm up to me to illustrate – 'If you blow on the fur, you can tell – if the fur goes this way or that – whether it's male or female.' She gently blows against the fur. 'I think this is a male fur, but I'm not sure. I think the female fur has more fur in it or maybe the other way around, but it's hard to see. It's so dark.' Lefty and Scarface jump to attention, aiming their flashlights on her arm." Brian's puckering and blowing, swishing his arm this way and that. A perfect imitation.

"'And look, Brian, there are more furs in the trunk.' So, on cue now, Lefty and Scarface shine their lights on the furs in the trunk. It's unreal — L'il Darlin's climbing head-first into the limo's trunk going through the furs as though she's shopping at Bergdorf's in New York, instead of the trunk of a gangster's black limo in a pitch black alley with two blood-curdling gangsters as her salespeople."

Chub is so caught up in the story he puts down his Jim Beam bottle, his hands turning into flexing white-knuckled fists.

Brian's speaking in my voice: "'Look, Brian! These gentlemen told me George and Sammy told me to pick out whatever coat I wanted as a gift from them. Isn't that nice?'"

Brian's narrator voice: "My mind spins. I need to get L'il Darlin's head out of the limo's trunk before they shove her in the trunk, close it, shoot me and drive off with her! I quickly go into my Maverick persona, big smile, a little cocky – not too cocky, just enough. I square my shoulders, do a theatrical cough, drop my voice an octave: 'Suzanne, enough shopping! I came out here to tell you you're wanted on stage, now! We have to run over that last scene, sharpen it up for tomorrow night's show.' I narrow my eyes a little to Lefty, hoping I look tough –not too tough, just enough. I'll tell George and Sammy you boys stopped by with the furs."

"'Oh!' L'il Darlin's pulled her head out of the trunk looking at me. 'Brian, I just need a few more minutes. I want to try on this gorgeous brown one. Look, it has a stand-up collar; that's so special, I think! What do you think?'

I grabbed L'il Darlin' so fast and hard she knew I meant business, pulled her out of the trunk, pushed her through the backstage door, into the hall, into the first door we came to, which turned out to be the men's room, but I didn't care. I pushed her up against the wall so I had her full attention. 'What the hell do you think you're doing? You could have gotten us both killed out there!'"

L'il Darlin's eyes were wide and scared. 'Brian, I'm so sorry. I just thought it was so nice of George and Sammy to want me to have a fur coat and they didn't have time to shop so they asked their friends to come by in their limo to show me some.'

"I was shaking from fear and anger. 'Suzanne, I can't talk to you right now. We're going to go into the bar and you're going to tell your buddies, Sammy and George you changed your mind. You don't want a fur coat! Understand me? Repeat after me! Your don't want a fur coat, never, ever! You're allergic to fur! If you wear one, you will die! And that is not so far from the truth. Now, you'd better start praying that this will be the end of it.'"

"I push L'il Darlin' in front of me into the bar. 'George, a double shot of whiskey for me and the usual for Suzanne. We're going to take that back table over there. We need some privacy.' I'm surprised my voice is still down an octave. I'm going to have to use this if I get a tough guy part. George gives us a nod. I square my shoulders, liking the feel. Our drinks arrive. I toss mine down in one gulp, slamming the shot glass against the table. Yeah, I'm getting the tough guy part down. I lean into her across the table, still an octave low.

'Now, Suzanne, I'm going to tell you what happens to girls who accept fur coats from gangsters, and it's not a pretty story!' Curtain down! The end!"

Brian whirls around and does a big theatrical bow, blowing me a kiss.

I lead the applause. Chub unclenches his fists, puts the Jim Beam bottle down and joins me. Poco starts barking his bravos! Brian gives his best bows. I stand shouting more bravos. Chub grabs my hand hard. Brian walks over to us. Chub reaches out to him. Brian leans over to take his hand.

"Thanks fer takin' care of my L'il Darlin' 'til she found me." His eyes are wet. I turn away. I don't want to cry. Chub motions me to lean down, so he can give me a hug and kiss.

"Yer my life, L'il Darlin'. Before ya came, I was wanderin' 'round these mountains, rootless as a tumbleweed – Greydog, Jim Beam an' the man-in-the-moon my only friends, then ya showed up, gave me somethin' to live fer, a purty red-haired, blue-eyed gal to rescue. Not many ol' cowboys get that chance!"

The Queen didn't disappoint. She never does when the slanting sun starts to slip behind the mountains, turning the mountain into a diamond-glinted monument of light reflecting the millions of scattered pieces of calcite clinging to her side. Brian is stunned by the beauty and afterglow, the pinkish re-illumination of brilliant lights of staggering splendor.

We sit in the camp chairs, Poco at my feet. I've never heard Chub talk about the man-in-the-moon before, but I look up and sure enough, there he is, the man-in-the moon looking down at us as we sit watching the soft wind flutter the dying campfire – listening, sifting the night sounds with our ears, the gurgling of the stream, the snorting horses and mules looking for bits of rolled oats fallen from their nose bags.

Thoughts fill my heart with rocks as big as the Queen's mountain. Chub takes my hand, his fingers barely able to grip mine. I'm sick with sorrow, as though all of life is learning to say good-bye. If you're lucky, you get a chance to start over, but that can't happen for me, not for this mountain life. Without Chub, my mountain life will exist only in my memory.

CHAPTER 33

Climb Every Mountain

"I'm not leaving my make-up kit!"

~ Brian

"**B**rian, are you sure you can do this?"

"Suzanne, we don't have a choice. Besides, how many times have we done "Sound of Music"? I've climbed the Alps at least a dozen times these past seasons. Don't laugh."

Brian's walking out, back down to the lake to get help. Chub's too weak to leave his tent, too big for Brian and me to lift him onto Greydog and ride the six hours down the trail.

"Are you ready? What's under your arm? Leave your gear. We'll bring it down with us."

"I'm not leaving my make-up kit, Suzanne!"

"What! You brought your make-up kit here to the mountains, to the back country?"

"You can never tell where or when you might run into an agent, Suzanne, never tell!" Brian strikes his best Mr. Show Biz pose, runs his hand over his gorgeous wavy, mahogany hair, puts both hands on either side of his face, head cocked from one side to the other, looking down right into my face and in his best South Pacific Bloody Mary shtick sings, "You got to have a dream, if you don't have a dream, how ya gonna make a dream come true?"

"Brian, you're impossible and worse, you're making me laugh! I shouldn't be laughing under these circumstances. You would have had me laughing on the Titanic."

"Good! I want to make you and Chub laugh!"

"Well, you've done your job. Now, Eidelweiss yourself down the trail and be careful."

Brian pirouettes, does a few dance steps, whirls around in another big show biz finale pose, blows me a kiss, takes a rib-swelling diaphragmatic breath and in his best baritone lifts his arms and voice to the mountains in an imitation of Mother Superior from "Sound of Music" and sings "Climb every mountain, ford every stream, follow every rainbow, 'til you find your dream!" Poco's by my side watching the scene, barking his bravos! I laugh, blow a kiss, cry, applaud and shout "Bravo," all at the same time. "Mazel Tov!" I shout to the sky, thinking I'm going to beat Grandmother to the punch this time.

Brian begins his trek. Poco and I head back to Chub when all of a sudden, I remember Brian's lunch. Good grief! I forgot to give him his lunch! "Brian! Brian! Come back! Your lunch! I forgot to give you your lunch!"

He hears me and turns. "Bring it to me, Suzanne. I've already made my big exit and I'm not going to repeat it! I'll wait right here!"

"Come on, Poco, let's get Brian's lunch!"

"All right, Brian, here it is." We grab each other, tears well up in my eyes. "Don't cry, Maria! It's going to spoil everything. It's not in the script. You know how it goes. We're all going to get over the Alps and go on to fame and fortune. Now that's in the script and it can't be rewritten."

His words, the memories – my stomach's doing summersaults. Brian takes my head in his hands, tilts it up to his: "Listen carefully. After I send help back up here, I'm going to go back to Hollywood to check my answering machine." He lets go of my head, puts the back of his hand to his forehead, and does a head-shaking sigh. "That's going to take three days at least!" Another pose, another theatrical run of his hands again through that gorgeous hair. "Seriously, when you and Chub get settled into City of Hope, call me and I'll cancel everything, come right over and stay with you and Chub until – for God's sake, smile, Suzanne, smile. That's the medicine we all need right now, especially Chub."

"I know. I'm trying, but this whole thing, it can't be real, can't be happening!"

"It's real. Keep your wits about you. I've checked the horses, there's plenty of grain. There's plenty of Sally's lunch left. Chub's got another bottle of Jim Beam in his saddle bag and there's all that gorgeous water in the stream. Poco's with you. You'll be fine 'til help gets here tomorrow afternoon. Keep it together. The show must go on!"

"I know, I know." I stand on my tip-toes, reach up to kiss him. Nothing is left to say or do except, "Thank you, take care, I love you."

I shade my eyes with my hand against a bright lemon yellow sun, watch Brian get smaller and smaller, and then disappear around the bend of the trail. I'm in a kind of daze. Any minute now Brian's going to change his mind, come back around that curve in the trail, grab me in his arms and point me toward the audience, hold my hand and together we start taking bows — first to one side, then the other, then the front, then the back, used to taking bows on the circle stage of theatre-in-the round.

My mind plays tricks on me. I hear cheers and bravos. We've done it! Our director, Jim Thimar, tells us if we don't have the 3,500-capacity theatre-goers on their feet at the end of the show we haven't done our job. Well, tonight we did our job; the audience is giving us a standing ovation! Harve Presnell, Gogi Grant, and "Show Boat", one of our first productions in the first season of the new theatre, Melodyland. The first theatre-in-the-round in Orange County – 3,500 seats, huge, beautiful – selling out every night. Brian and I are part of the 12-resident company of singers and dancers, but we have "white contracts," we're resident principals, co-starring with the big stars the theatre brings in for the season.

Brian and I are a team, partners because we have the Jean Harlow "It" look, but we know our place. We're here to support and enhance the super-stars not quite comfortable in their first circle-stage appearances. Movies and television are their forte, not running up and down in the dark of the long aisles of the theatre, dodging moving scenery, doing quick changes at the top of the aisles in little curtained spaces, working with their backs to two thirds of the audience at all times.

Brian and I are their caretakers, their understudies, making good money even if some of the duties are mundane: running to the drug store for cough drops for Betty Grable because her husband, Harry James, forgot to put them in her make-up kit. Me watching Tammy Grimes' dressing room door a half-hour before curtain so she can romance co-star Bruce Yarnell because she believes he will be weakened, enabling her to out-sing him in their show, "Unsinkable Molly Brown".

The show biz stories multiply season after season with Brian and me trodding the boards, playing so many parts, dancing the only dance we know, the Charleston that Mama taught me and I taught Brian, making it work no matter the show to the despair of the Russian choreographer, ballet diva Zoya La Porska, who tries to teach us the Russian Kazatsky for "Silk Stockings", which still came out the Charleston. Zoya pulled her short shocks of white hair into spiky tufts of despair, groaning as she didn't have a back row on the circle stage to put us in.

We rehearsed one show during the day, played another show at night with producers Lewis and Dare from Las Vegas, smiling and rubbing their hands together as they stood watching from the top of the aisles at the full house audience on their feet, cheering at the end of each show each night, parties after the show with big names from Hollywood screen life, Cary Grant and his curly-haired new wife, Dyan Cannon.

The seasons flew by with Melodyland giving birth to its first child, the Carousel Theatre in Covina, same size, same audience capacity, and then a second child born in San Carlos, the Circle Star, again same size, same audience capacity, English star Georgia Brown and the cast from London flying over to open the first show of the season, "Oliver".

A glorious time: I loved the sound of the orchestra tuning up, the overture, theatre smells, and the parties. Where did it go, leaving me standing in the back country at the top of the trail watching Brian disappear, my only audience 13,000-foot mountains, a dying man and his dog? How could my life end this way? The scene isn't in any script. I try to comfort myself, hug myself, and blink away the tears. Brian's gone. I'm alone, no show, no script, no director, just Poco and me left to watch Chub in the tent.

"Chub, darlin', how about some water? I don't see you carryin' any." I'm smiling and winking at him. "The sun'll get you at 13,000 feet." Chub smiles up at me from his sleeping bag, both of us remembering that first day some years ago, remembering him catching me, his strong arms holding me, the only memory I now want to hold close.

"L'il Darlin', what time is it?"

"Twelve thirty. Do you feel like something to eat?"

"Not yet. Don' know why my stomach's feelin' poorly. That was shore a good lunch Sally fixed up for us. Let's get her somethin' nice when we get back to Redlands. We'll go to the mall, maybe find her a purty necklace."

"That's a good idea. Jewelry's always a good present and Sally can use it. She looks so nice at the front desk of the restaurant handling the reservations."

"L'il Darlin', do me a favor. Bring your camp chair in, sit a spell, sing me that pretty fancy I-talian song I hear you hummin' so much."

"Sure, but Chub, I'm not certain which one you mean. I'm always humming bits and pieces of songs from Aunt Gen's and the theatre."

"Well, I think the song's I-talian. I don' understand whatcha sayin', but the melody's really purty."

"Let me think. Oh, you mean the one from "La Traviata" by Giuseppe Verdi, "Parigi o, caro–"

"Can't tell by that, L'il Darlin'. Just start an' I'll tell ya."

"Ok." I don't want to tell Chub it's a sad song. I don't think I can even get through it, but I'll try. I'll think of something funny so I won't cry. I know, I'll think of Brian this morning with his make-up kit, running his hand over his hair a la Captain Von Trapp. That was so funny. I'm right; he'd be the best one to be with when you hit an iceberg."

Chub holds my hand and shuts his eyes. Poco curls at my feet, calm and restful. I start to sing: "Parigi o caro, noi lasceremo, La vita uniti trascorreremo…"

A terrifying, ungodly scream pierces the air! Poco jumps up and runs into the corner of the tent, shaking. The horses start stamping and whinnying. I grab the arms of my camp chair, white knuckled, song forgotten — "Oh, God, Chub! What is that?"

"Calm down, L'il Darlin', it's a mountain lion. May be miles a'ways the way sound carries up here, but it's hard ta tell. Let's scare him off." Chub's having trouble talking; his breath is labored, he feels around at the side of his sleeping bag. "Here's my gun. It's loaded." He pauses to catch his breath. "Go out front a' the tent, point it up in the air, squeeze the trigger. It's heavy, use both hands." He takes another breath, "All yer doin' is makin' a big noise that'll scare 'em off. Ya know, this is his territory, he was here before us, but we shore don't want him doin' us any hurt." Another breath. "Go on, git out 'n scare him. He might come back an' ya'll have ta shoot again." His talking tires him out, but I have to ask. "Do we have enough bullets?"

"Shells in the saddle bag. Get 'im, reload after yer shot. Mountain lions usually don't take after people – mostly livestock. Ya can do it."

But I don't think I can. My knees are jelly. My legs won't hold me, but Chub can't walk, stand up, isn't strong enough to hold the gun. What if the mountain lion's out there waiting for me and Brian – oh, my God, Brian?

Has the mountain lion trailed him? No! No! I can't think of that. I'm Chub's partner. I've got to keep my wits about me because Chub needs help. I have to get the shells from his saddle bag.

I run, afraid to look around for fear the mountain lion's lurking. I stare at the ground, hold my hands like blinders on each side of my head; if I can't see him, he can't see me. I lift my head to see the saddle bag right behind Sally's basket. Just another few feet – run, run, run!

Got it! The leather's warm from the sun. I grab it, hold it to my chest, bury my head in the leather smell, memories flood for an instant, throw it back down, lean over, yank it open, hands digging, feeling around. There's his insulin, socks, where are the shells? What's this? A box, right by his Jim Beam bottle! Yes, yes, white with a red X on it, pistol and revolver cartridges. Got it, I've got it! Run back to the tent, "Here it is! Chub! Here it is!"

"Calm down, L'il Darlin'. Chances are that ol' mountain lion's miles away by now." His shaking hands take the box. "Yep, that's it, still full, 50 cartridges." I sit down.

"Ok, L'il Darlin', git with it."

I stand in front of the tent in a daze, hold the gun in both hands, point it in the air, close my eyes, try to keep my hands steady, squeeze – BANG! My body jerks backwards, hands and arms shake, I open my eyes, I did it! I did it! The sound of my shot slaps against the mountain, echoing off the peaks into the distance.

Chub crawls to the front of the tent, half in, half out. My heart turns over to see him like this.

"Chub, Chub, I did it! I shot the gun! Did you see me?"

"I saw ya, L'il Darlin'. Gonna have ta start callin' ya Annie Oakley!"

So good to hear him make a little fun. I sit on the ground beside him, we hold each other. I didn't let Chub down. I shot the gun. My mind flashes back to his request a few months ago not to let him die in a hospital bed, his wish to die in his beloved mountains. I couldn't say no. His blue eyes were so desperate, pleading. I told him I would and now I know I can. I shot the gun. I look at the gun in my hand, my fingers in a vise around the handle, my knuckles white. I shot the gun. Realization, implication, sadness and horror wash over me. I want to throw the gun away, throw the gun over the cliff so hard minutes will pass before it reaches the bottom, shatters into a million pieces, never to be found under the winter's ice and snow, but Chub interrupts my thinking, looking straight into my eyes, his voice low. "Give me the gun, L'il Darlin.'"

"Yes, Chub. Are you ready for a little something from Sally's basket? How about a bite of chocolate cake and some milk? Does that sound good?"

He nods. "Think you can run out ta Sally's basket again?" His eyes smile up at me. "Might as well bring the basket in here an' bring yer sleepin' bag, too. Sleep in here tonight. Don't think Poco'll stay out with ya not with the smell of that lion aroun.'" Another breath. "It'll be nice havin' yer company."

"Ok, I'll get Sally's basket and my sleeping bag. Almost time for the Queen's show. I want to see it one more time. After that, show me how to load the gun."

The Queen's show does not disappoint; it never will. The Queen will forever put on her show whether we're here to see it or not, uncaring as to what we humans are enduring. The earth will keep revolving, the sun will keep shining, the moon will keep shining, and the stars will keep their little campfires burning in the sky, no matter our sadness, our grief. Somehow, it doesn't seem right.

The lantern glow fills the tent. Chub takes a few bites of Sally's chocolate cake and sips of milk. He starts to pick up the box of bullets, but his hand shakes. I take the box from him.

"Show me how to reload."

"Let me catch my breath, L'il Darlin.'

"No problem, Chub. We've got all the time we want." He dozes off, his hand on the gun beside him. The activity of the mountain lion and my shooting has worn him out. I'm tired, too, but it doesn't matter, nothing matters anymore. Chub stirs. That's the truth, nothing matters anymore. Horrifying – what was always so very important in the past turns out to be bits of pieces of nothing. "L'il Darlin', let's see those bullets."

I take one cartridge carefully out of the white foam-like holder in the box, hold it in the palm of my hand, and feel the weight. The cartridge looks so harmless, incapable of causing damage, much less killing a human or beast.

Chub gives me the gun. "See that button? Give it a little push, that's right." Pause, breath, pause. "There's the round cylinder. Turn the cartridge with yer thumb, stop at the empty hole, put the bullet in." Pause, breath, pause. "Leave one hole empty. Hold the gun by the handle." Pause, breath, pause.

"Ok, Chub, just check to be sure I did it correctly."

"Give me another minute." Chub closes his eyes again. I put the gun in my lap. It scares me when he goes to sleep like this. Such awful aloneness – memory floods over me. I'm back in the apartment closet smelling Mama's Tabu on her clothes, hiding so no one will see me, hear me breathe. If I breathe, the bad lady will know I'm here. I remember how I couldn't hold my breath any longer. I had to bury my head in my hands, press my head into my lap, into the folds of my dress, smell the soap Mama used to wash my things, take the tiniest breath I could so no one would hear me and make Mama and me leave the apartment. Where would we go? How would Daddy find us? What would happen to us?

Chub stirs. "L'il Darlin', did I ever tell ya how a mountain lion almost got Greydog, me an' Poco?"

"No, Chub." I'm happy he's awake and talking, chasing my memory away. "Tell me."

Chub takes a breath, his eyes distant, remembering. "We was ridin' aroun' the back side a' the lake when one came screamin' outta a tree, tryin' fer Greydog with his mouth, missin', claws slidin' back down Greydog's rump. If ya look, ya can still see the scratch marks." Pause, breath, pause.

"A runaway for Greydog, Poco an' me. Barely got off a shot to scare him away." Chub's breathing's heavy. "Can't ride Greydog under a tree ever since. Poco's scared ta death when he hears that scream. It's a scream ya never ferget, sends ice water up yer spine, makes the hair on the back of yer neck stand up an' crawl."

"Once you hear it, ya never ferget it. A scream like a woman gettin' killed! So many years ago…"

His eyes close, voice drifts off. Poco nuzzles his head under my hand. I pet him, the little bit of white around his muzzle glows in the lantern light. "Don't worry, Poco." I pat the gun in my lap. "I've got the gun. I can use it." My stomach gives a lurch remembering. Chub gave me my mountain life; I can give him his mountain death.

"L'il Darlin'." Chub stirs as though he's reading my mind.

"Yes, Chub."

"I know what I asked ya ta do. Now ya know ya can do it, but this ain't the right time. Ya'd be in a lotta hurt if they found me dead, you bein' the only one here, me too weak ta hold the gun ta my head. They'd be knowin' what happened. Don't want nothin' happen' to ya." Chub's breathing is faint, his hand is cold.

"Let's not think about that now, Chub. Let's rest awhile." My eyes close. I feel myself slip off. I start to dream, and my dream mind takes over to hear —

— *rustling outside the tent, movement. The mountain lion's head pushes through the tent flap, glaring yellow eyes, white fangs, hot musky smell of animal breath. I grab the gun from my lap, point it at the head, squeeze, BANG! A ruby red-pink orchid blossoms between sparkling blue eyes as a smiling Chub looks at me. "Thank ya, L'il Darlin', thank ya."*

"Oh, my God, I killed Chub, I killed Chub!"

Chub pushes himself up from his sleeping bag, stretches his arm out to me. "Give me the gun, now!"

"Yes, Chub, yes!" Now I know I'll keep my promise to Chub when the time comes – can and will! My body's weak. My heart is pounding out of my chest as though it had torn loose inside me and was banging against my ribs like a bird trying to break out of his cage. My ribs hurt, my insides twist, there's sweat on the back of my neck running down between my shoulder blades. I slide from my camp chair to the tent floor. Poco licks tears from my cheeks. I put my arms around him, bury my face against him, hold him, squeeze him, pet him. "I know Poco, I know. I shot the gun." He whimpers into my shoulder, our hearts breaking.

CHAPTER 34

The Last of His Kind

May 1980
City of Hope
Duarte, California

"One day, you'll write his story. I know you. You'll keep your promise."

~ Brian

W here am I? Brian's arm is over mine, my head in his lap. My eyes blink, trying to wake up. I smell the fragrance of his French cologne, feel the soft angora sweater against my cheek. I made that sweater for him during our breaks when we were doing "My Fair Lady". He sat next to me for weeks as I was knitting with the robin egg blue yarn so I could be sure of the fit. The sweater is beautiful, with a cable-stitched collar and sleeves. I had such a crush on him — so handsome, so smart, so caring, so unavailable. I smile to myself. "Brian, are you awake?"

"I am now. Hard to sleep with you squirming around asking questions."

"I'm sorry. I didn't mean to fall asleep in your lap."

"I must admit, it's a first." Brian gives me that look, shrugs his shoulders, makes me smile. "Come on, let's go over to the cafeteria and get some coffee and something to eat."

"Oh, no! I don't want to leave until Chub's out of surgery. What time is it?"

"Noon. He went in around 10:30 am. It'll be another couple of hours. These amputation surgeries take a long time. I talked to the nurse earlier. She's very nice. Her name is Theresa Newman."

"Brian, I don't think they should be doing this surgery, put him through all this, but Chub said he wanted to do it. The doctor told him it was his only chance due to the gangrene in his foot and leg and Chub wanted to take the chance, to live long enough for us to go back to the mountains. You know he wants to die in the mountains. He says he's spent more time in the saddle in the mountains than anywhere else and that's where he wants to die, but — have you checked on Poco?"

"Yes, I talked to him through the truck window as soon as we came in. I'm cautious with him. Chub tells me he bites."

"Oh, yes. He bit the mailman and had to go to the pound for two weeks, but then he helped the police catch a wanted felon who made the mistake of breaking into the house we were renting in Downey, remember? The man ran into our backyard, Poco bit him, he climbed the tree and Poco stood at the foot of the tree barking until the police got there. Of course, Chub had his gun, but he doesn't show it around police."

"Indeed, I remember the Downey house. That's where I first met Chub and your cowboy friends, Bobby and Floyd. How on earth did you get yourself involved with them?"

"It's a long story. Someday I'll tell you."

"That must have been quite a trip yesterday."

"Chub and Poco slept most of the way down, but I didn't have any trouble staying awake, I had so much adrenaline going. I was afraid Chub was going to need insulin. I'm good at giving shots so that didn't concern me. I was just anxious to get Chub help. Sally packed the insulin in an ice bag that I had on the seat between us. Brian, I don't want Chub to die in a hospital. You know my promise to him, to help him die in the mountains at the mouth of the Queen, but I'm afraid he'll die here. I don't know what to do."

"I know. Let's not talk here. Let's go to the cafeteria. We both need something to eat."

"One more minute. I'm not ready. Brian, this is all so awful, so sad, so everything, but City of Hope is so good. Sally called ahead, told them we were coming. They met us at the ambulance entrance with a gurney. Then an orderly had me follow him in the pickup to a motel area here on the grounds — nice room, good shower and the phone in the room is hooked up to the patient's room. You don't have to go through the operator. Just pick up the phone and it rings by the patient's bed. And Brian, there's no charge for anything. Chub pays nothing, absolutely nothing. If I ever get any money, the one place I'm going to donate is City of Hope."

Nurse Theresa Newman interrupts us: "Suzanne, your friend Chub is still in surgery. Why don't you and Brian go into the cafeteria and get something to eat? I'll come and tell you when he's in recovery. Recovery could take five to six hours, so you have plenty of time."

"Thanks, Theresa, but first I want to let Poco out of the truck for a little while."

"Sure, you can put your dog in your room if you'd like and there's also a little park area for him to walk around. You'll see it from the parking lot."

"Thanks so much, but right now Poco is happiest in the truck. It's full of smells he loves."

"All right, just remember we're here to help you. Let me know what you need."

I'm at the cafeteria table, a turkey sandwich and coffee in front of me, my stomach in knots, the smell of the food makes me nauseous. I take a deep breath like a drowning person gulps for air, double over and let the table hold me up.

"This can't be happening." I'm talking to the table. "This has to be a dream. How can real life seem more like a dream than a dream?"

"Sit up, Suzanne, talk to me even if I don't have any answers. What I do know is this is not a dream and you must come to grips with it."

"I know, Brian, but it's three deaths for me. When Chub dies, Daddy dies and L'il Darlin' dies. I'm not sure how to deal with that. I'm not sure how to start over. It's my own fault. Instead of becoming a mule packer those years ago, I should've been in school learning a trade that would give me a living. What do I have to put down on an employment form? Occupation – mule packer and singer? I don't think there are many calls for that. I was wrong to stay in the mountains, earn my money at a pack station; that seemed right at the time, but now that thinking seems foolish. I never thought the pack station would end, that Chub would or could get sick. He's too big, too strong, but I was wrong. I never thought his death was a possibility, that death doesn't respect size or strength. Death's the great equalizer, the long foot of time coming for all of us; good, bad, decent, indecent, man, woman, child."

"You're not thinking straight right now, Suzanne, that's understandable. Given a little time you'll realize how well off you are. You have three great children all willing and capable of helping you."

"Brian, when you help your childen, your children and you are happy, but when your children have to help you, it's embarrassing and sad. I don't want that.

"Well, as Chub says, time will tell and he's right, but right now, you'd better eat that sandwich. Whether you want to or not, I'm going to talk about your future and think about pulling yourself together."

"I know you mean well talking about a future, but I can't think about that now."

"Suzanne," Brian's tone is firm, "I've been preparing this talk for the past few days now, and whether you like it or not, whether you want it or not, I'm going to talk to you and get plans going for you. Chub would want it, you know that. He spent these past years being sure that you lived. That was all he thought about. Don't let his efforts be in vain. Be grateful you're alive because of him, honor him by showing courage in the life you have, the life he gave you. Live it to the fullest. Didn't you and Chub talk about that after I left to walk back to the lake?"

"You mean, before or after the mountain lion?"

"The mountain lion!? Oh, my God! Is there no end to your 'Perils of Pauline' stories? A mountain lion? Well, as much as I want to hear about that and obviously you, Chub and Poco survived, let's put that story on the back burner and focus on a plan for your future. Right now, I'm thinking you might include in that future a book about your time in the mountains."

I hear Brian talking, but I don't know what he's saying. It's just a mumble of sounds and a jumble of facial expressions and gestures. I try not to be rude, but I wish he'd stop. Just let me sit here.

"I can see you're not listening to me or eating. I'll stop talking and get us some more coffee."

"Here, Suzanne, fresh coffee. Sip a little, focus and let's see where you'll go from here." I can see Brian's intent on planning my future. There's no use trying to stop him. I'll cry later when I'm with Poco.

"You're currently running a little candy store in Redlands across the street from the high school, correct?"

"Correct."

"The candy store is open in synch with the high school, which means you should open in a couple of weeks. Correct?"

"Correct."

"Without Chub, who do you have to help you?"

"Lori will do that."

"You told me Chub's sister plans on selling the store. What will you do then?"

"I don't know. I don't want to know." I put my head on the table again; feel the cool, sterile, uncaring plastic on my forehead. Everything in the room is sterile, uncaring. The big, ugly, stark, round, sterile white clock staring down is uncaring, the uncaring hands going round and round and round as they tick-tock Chub's life away.

"Come on, Suzanne, sit up and listen to me! This may be the only chance we have to talk about this. Even if you're not totally focused on what I'm saying, you're going to remember some of it, trust me! This is a bad time for you now, but you'll get through it and you'll learn to live with it. I've said it before up in the mountains, you have more going for you than you think."

Brian is right. I owe him my attention. "Thanks, Brian. I do have a little money saved from some part-time teaching at one of the private schools in Redlands. A friend told me about that job opening and I was hired."

"I didn't know that. What were you teaching?"

"Etiquette and Social Graces, thanks to Mrs. McBride."

"Etiquette and Social Graces! No wonder you've always said you didn't fit in anywhere. Those skills are way out of date, completely antediluvian. Why on earth would your folks send you to a school like that?"

"I don't know, but I'm glad they did. Everything was beautiful. It was my refuge. The beautiful school, the chauffeur, the groundskeeper getting our tennis balls when we missed a shot in our game of lawn tennis – and we missed a lot. Mrs. McBride told us it wasn't proper for young ladies to run after tennis balls, you know, bend over and pick them up. The groundskeeper did that. We curtsied when our teachers came into the room or any adult. Eating was a holy ritual — calm, courteous, interesting, pleasant conversation only, nothing to upset our digestions. I learned everything beautiful, but nothing in the way of negotiating my way through life, being a wife, a mother, getting a career that would support me."

I shouldn't be talking so much, but I can't help it. It's as though someone pulled a plug out of my mouth and the words won't stop pouring out. "Chub's old pickup isn't going to last much longer. I have two pair of jeans, three shirts, some underwear, Chub's big down jacket and I have to start my life over. Chub used to tell me that he and his parents and grandparents had to start their lives over in the Dust Bowl, pile what they had in their old car and head for California, like the movie "The Grapes of Wrath". He said they didn't complain, just gritted their teeth and started out and if they had something to eat, were warm and dry, there was to be no complaining. I never heard Chub complain. I saw his lips get thin sometimes, but he never complained. I shouldn't have come into his life. I caused him so much trouble."

"It wasn't trouble you caused Chub. You gave him something he cherished, a good and lovely woman by his side, a woman who respected him, who looked at him as her hero. As rough as Chub is, there's a sentimental streak in him, a sense of chivalry, to save a pretty woman in distress. Not many men get a chance to be heroes, but you did that for Chub and for me as well — with your fur coat shopping in a back alley. Ha! It was my first, and I hope only, chance to be a hero."

Nurse Theresa comes into the dining room: "Excuse me. Chub is out of recovery. Follow me and we'll meet him in the hall on the way to his room. He's awake." I knock over my coffee, spill the cup on the table. My chair sticks to the floor. I push the table away, Brian dodges the spilling coffee and tipping table, and grabs the table before it goes completely over. I run into the hall.

"Chub, are you all right?" His eyes are half open; he's pale. He tries to say something. I bend over to hear him. His voice is a whisper. "What time is it?"

"It's six o'clock. Are you all right?"

"I don't know."

"Oh, no! He says he doesn't know. Someone do something! Do something!"

Brian puts Vaseline on Chub's nostrils and lips. His breathing is shallow, his eyes open wide. He's crying, "Help, help! I'm in here! Help!"

"What's wrong, Chub, what's wrong? We're all here. Chub, it's me, L'il Darlin'. You're safe. You're with Brian and me. Poco's in the pickup waiting for you. You're safe."

"The fire!"

Now I know. I turn to the doctor and Theresa, who are hurrying in. "Chub's dreaming about the time there was a truck accident. He was asleep in the back when the truck turned over and caught fire. Cowboy Bobby pulled him out before the truck blew up. "Chub, it's a dream. You're here in City of Hope!"

His hand reaches for mine, his eyes are opening, and his voice whispers: "L'il Darlin', ya never finished that purty I-talian song." My heart leaps into my throat. How can he remember? My voice is a gulp. "I'll finish it now, Chub, and in English so you know what it says." My voice is unsteady, tears cloud my eyes. I swallow, try to take a breath. I can't sing. I'll talk the words to him.

"Dearest, we will go to the mountains,"

Chub's eyes dim as if the trail's hard to see.

"We shall spend our life together…"

He presses my hand – no longer a lone man riding in a lonesome country.

"You'll be free of hurt, your health will bloom.
You are sight and life to me and our future will be bright!"

He smiles up at me. His hand relaxes and his eyes close, his breathing shallow. Brian sits in the corner, hands over his eyes. Bobby and Diane walk in, come over to me, touch my shoulder.

Bobby takes in the situation. "It's all right, Chub, I'm here. I'll take care a' L'il Darlin' now. You can let go. It's all right."

Bobby and Diane have their hands on my shoulder. Chub looks up at me. His eyes are fixed, staring. I hear a strange, soft kind of rattling sound from his chest. Brian comes over. The doctor and nurse come in. Brian gently pulls me away from Chub so the doctor can look at him. I stand beside Brian, L'il Darlin' dying along with Chub and her mountain years. Nurse Theresa takes my hand, looks straight into my eyes. "The doctor and I will take care of Chub now. All of you go into the cafeteria, wait for me. I'll see you soon."

In the hall, the big, white, ugly, sterile, uncaring clock on the wall stares down at me.

"Stop staring at me! How dare you be the one to mark Chub's life! You don't care about him. You should be ashamed of yourself! You're cold, lifeless, and indifferent! Do you know he saved my life? He's a caring, loving, warm, courageous man; the clock ticking away his life should be magnificent, made of beautiful wood, with gold numbers and blue eyes that cry sapphire tears for this man, the last of his kind. And there should be an inscription on it by Louis L'Amour."

My hands shake as I look in my purse for my wallet. At last, I open it, take an old folded piece of paper and hand it to Brian. "Brian, read this to the clock so it knows the kind of a man Chub was. I can't do it." Brian clears his throat. I take Bobby's hand and squeeze as hard as I can so I won't dissolve into a heap of grief.

Brian takes my hand, leans down to me. "We'll take his ashes up the trail to the Queen and spread them there. And one day, you'll write his story. I know you: you'll keep your promise."

CHAPTER 35

"Personal Intentions, Please, Not Business Intentions."

May 1980, 2 p.m.

"I need to go back to sleep! I haven't finished my dream!"

~ Suzanne

C hub died two hours ago. Brian is somewhere with the nurse attending to the paperwork. I sit here in the waiting room counting the dots in the ceiling tiles. How am I here, mourning the death of a last-of-his-breed cowboy mountain man, the death of my mountain years? What did I do to myself joining a pack station in the High Sierras?

My body and brain are exhausted. I haven't slept in days, except for little snippets, not real snuggle-in-my-sleeping-bag-with-Poco-curled-beside-me sleep. My eyes ache from the glare of the overhead fluorescent lights. For some reason, I start to think of Mrs. McBride. Sometimes, I'd imagine her finding me in the mountains with the cowboys and I would be humiliated, devastated, embarrassed beyond imaginings. I would stand before her, once her pride, her straight A student now flunking life, a dusty, unkempt mountain mule packer keeping company with three rough, tough cowboys, a bitter disappointment to her, Mama and Daddy. All the money they spent to give me the best education possible, the best start they could in life, all the effort and loving care Mrs. McBride gave me I threw away to live in the back country, sleep with a dog, trade Shakespeare for Louis L'Amour, lawn tennis and ballet for a trail horse named Suzy. I know what drove me to the mountains, but what made me stay?

I fall into a dream-sleep, fragmented thoughts and visions of what a meeting between her and Chub might be. I let the two of them slip into a dark place behind my eyelids and see you, Mrs. McBride, and Chub in the mountains in front of the barn; I see you in your pink jacket, pink ankle-length gown skimming the tops of your pink satin, low-heeled shoes, diamond studs in your ears, mountain sunlight tangled in your impeccably coiffed pale blond hair, lovely pink polished nails, your posture exquisitely regal.

Then I see Chub in his old, worn cowboy shirt, sweat-stained hat, dusty jeans and boots, sitting in his camp chair in front of the barn squinting at you through his Bull Durham smoke and smoke rings, wondering who you are, how you got to the pack station. His bright, blue eyes are wide looking at you. He has never seen anyone like you. A jolt of mountain lightning hits him, heaves him to his feet. He stumbles over Poco, hat flying off in the wind. The mountain gods alert! They know a gentleman does not keep his hat on nor allow his head to be below a lady's when in her presence.

My 10-year-old self comes out of the barn from where I'm hiding in a state of shock. Why are you here? Are you here to take me from the mountains, the cowboys, Poco? I'm frightened, flustered, trying to remember my manners as a proper young lady raised in Monticello School for Girls. I must introduce you and Chub properly, but my mind is blank.

"Chub, may I present, Mrs. McBride?" Oh, no; that's wrong. It's rude. One does not present a lady to the gentlemen.

"Mrs. McBride, may I present, my friend Chub." That's better, I think, or is it? I've never had it straight.

"Mrs. McBride, sit a spell. I'll getcha a camp chair."

"Thank you, Mr. Chub."

The camp chair becomes a throne as you regally take your place.

"Can I getcha some water?"

"No, thank you, refreshments are not necessary. Mr. Chub, as Suzanne's mother and father are unable to be here, I am here as their representative. I intend to speak to you regarding your intentions toward Suzanne."

"Intentions? Well, she's a hell — I mean, a good mule packer, first woman mule packer in these parts, good fer business — purty gal, great guide, takin' people up into the back country, singin' songs fer the people, horses, mules, gettin' 'em over the bad part a' the trail, sellin' pack trips at the Sportsman show for next season. She increased our packin' business big time with her idea a' gourmet pack trips. Yes, sirree! We done real good with her with us!

"Mr. Chub." Mrs. McBride leans regally forward in her camp chair throne, takes a proper diaphragmatic breath, nostrils slightly flaring as she becomes aware of the pungent barn smells contrasting with the delicious restaurant smells. She takes her white lace hanky from the wrist of her pink jacket and dabs at her nose, shaking her head to rid the distraction. "I am interested in your personal intentions, not your business intentions."

Chub leans back in his camp chair, thoughtfully blows colorful Bull Durham smoke rings, watches while they disappear in the air.

"Mr. Chub. Suzanne came to me when she was four years old, a lovely child, very quiet. I love all my girls. They are all my daughters. My love is unconditional. They will continue to be under my care no matter their age or location. I am waiting for you to respond to my last statement regarding your personal intentions toward Suzanne."

Chub blows more thoughtful, colorful smoke rings into the air, watches them change shape in the wind before he speaks, "Mrs. McBride, I love L'il Dar — I mean, Suzanne - an' want to partner with her. No road's too long, no road's too dark when ye're partnerin' with someone ya love."

"*Those are lovely words, Mr. Chub, but evasive. Are you proposing marriage? What means do you have to support her, protect her?*"

"*Two fists, gun anna' dog. Nothin's ever gonna hurt her while I'm alive.*"

"*And after that, Mr. Chub?*" *Mrs. McBride's words hang in the air for a moment before the waning winds of truth cast their breeze and carry them away. She regally rises from her camp chair throne, Mrs. Madie Burmester McBride, the once and future protector of her girls — now women. "I will go now."*

"*No! No! No! Mrs. McBride, wait! Don't go, don't go! I need your permission to stay here!*" *my 10-year-old self cries. "Wait, wait! You didn't discuss your Code of Ethics. You didn't hear Chub's ethics, the Code of the Cow Country. You and he are not that far apart, you're not. Stay just a few more minutes. I heard you cry that night at school, your voice choking as you cried, "Those poor boys, those poor boys!" It was D Day during World War II. My pink ruffly bed was next to yours, only the wall between us. I heard Chub cry at night, my sleeping bag close to his tent. You both cry at injustice. You and he are not that far apart, you're not, you're not! Please give me your permission to stay with him. You don't understand. I can never leave Chub. Never! Don't you see? Why can't you see?"*

My 10-year-old self cries again with sagging shoulders, beaten. No one can understand or see, Chub and Daddy are one! Daddy is hiding inside Chub, a hiding place no one but me can see! I found Daddy, I found him! At last, I found him! Daddy didn't leave me. Daddy's always been with me, inside Chub all along. Can't anyone understand? He never left me, he's been with me all this time.

"*Mrs. McBride, give me your permission to stay in the mountains with Chub, Poco, Cowboy Bobby and Floyd. Please, please, you must, you must! I'm broken. Your permission is the only way I can be made whole again, pick up my sleeping bag and walk.*" *The mountain gods whisper in my ear: "It's no use. Mrs. McBride is gone! She can't hear you."*

A fierce bolt of lightning jolts Chub from his camp chair. A gentleman does not remain seated when a lady leaves the room. Mrs. McBride is gone! The mountain gods voices thunder: "Alea iacta est!" The die is cast, left the hand, rolling has begun, the outcome irrevocable. "No! No!" I cover my eyes! I won't look at the dice, I'm afraid to look!"

Brian gently shakes me. "Suzanne, wake up. You're having a dream."

"No! No! Stop shaking me! I need to go back to sleep! I haven't finished my dream! The dice are still rolling! They haven't stopped! I haven't seen the outcome! I need to see the outcome, see what's ahead. I've got to go back to sleep, my dream isn't over!"

"Suzanne, look at me. I have Chub's things!" Brian holds a nondescript, plastic bag with Chub's belongings in the air in front of me. I make out his belt buckle behind the plastic!

What's that? My eyes try to focus to see behind Chub's belt buckle. Almost hidden in the folds of the plastic, I see the faint sparkle of daddy's Masonic ring!

I grab the arms of my chair to keep from falling into the ceiling. The room spins. I look up and the ceiling spins; the uncaring, sterile clock looks at me. It can't be. Daddy's Masonic ring is in Chub's belongings! I reach for the bag. I need to open it. I want to take Daddy's ring, hold it, feel it, put it on my finger, but the mountain gods scream at me, "Stop! Don't touch it! Don't open it! This is Pandora's box! In the beginning, Pandora's box was a bag!"

I drop the bag in horror, turn and run to the door leading into a hallway. Brian picks up the bag, runs behind me, grabs me, and turns me around in his arms. I hit at him with my fists, unrestrained fear and anger pounding against his chest. "Let me go. Let me go! I've got to get away." The dice are rolling toward me, chasing me!

The floor rises to my face. Everything is mercifully black. Let it stay that way. I don't intend to come back.

CHAPTER 36

47 Years Later

December 31, 2017
8:30 p.m.

"Should auld acquaintance be forgot,
And never brought to mind?
Should auld acquaintance be forgot,
And days of auld lang syne"

"Bobby, I know this is going to sound odd to you, but after all these years, if you know, would you, could you, tell me what happened to the attorney?"

Bobby's in his dark beige corduroy recliner, tipped back with his favorite dark-red electric lap blanket over his legs next to an end table holding a reddish-brown ceramic owl lamp with a tipsy shade. Year after year, this owl has been staring at me with his lamp shade tilted at a lopsided angle, which takes away from the wise look owls are known to have. Next on the table is a cream-colored telephone, a picture of Bobby and Diane at his 45th high school reunion. He looks so happy in his tuxedo, white shirt, black Western tie from Sulfur Spring, Texas tied in a perfect square knot and Diane in a white knit scooped neckline sheath and jacket, with diamond studs in her ears holding three white dangling pearls framing her face. Her lush, black hair is swirled in a chignon, her hand is on his shoulder and her head tilted toward his and his arm is around her slender waist. They are so in love. A just-poured glass of Jim Beam, no ice, at the side of the picture announces the start of the evening. Diane has been gone nine years now. She and Bobby were on a campout with their Camper Club. It was one of the member's birthdays. The party was almost over when Diane told Bobby she didn't feel well. They walked back to their camper. She died in his arms of a heart attack sitting on the edge of their bed, January 2008.

Almost a year later, December 2009, my husband, David, died in my arms at 8:30 in the morning in the doctor's office while waiting to receive his chemotherapy. Now Bobby and I sit here, December 2017, in his and Diane's house, both of us without our beloved partners, waiting for the New Year to begin. I'm in a reflective mood, sorting through my life.

For the most part, I try not to think about the attorney. He's in the long ago part of a past I try to forget. The past I want to remember belongs to memories of the births of my three children, my singing years at the Melodyland Theater, Chub and the back country, my second husband, David, my seven grandchildren, and eight great grandchildren.

Bobby married his first wife, Ann, when they were 18 and I married my first husband, Sam, when I was 18. Bobby has two grown children, four grandchildren – three living generations. I have five living generations counting Auntie Ann, who is 91. With all this wonderfulness, for some inexplicable reason, tonight I am thinking of the attorney and wondering.

My question causes Bobby to look across the room out the picture window that faces a Seventh Day Adventist Church across the street from his house, his eyes narrow with remembering. He and Diane bought this house soon after they married. The original part is adobe, two bedrooms and one bath. They remodeled and added a master bedroom, office and bath. I hope I haven't made a mistake in asking him about the attorney, but it's been so long ago I don't think my question can cause any harm.

Years ago, Chub told me I could stop worrying about the attorney. The way he said it – the way he turned his big body away from me and walked away – told me not to ask any questions then, but now, I'm pretty sure it's all right. Chub has passed. Bobby, Floyd and I are the only ones left from that time to remember.

Bobby goes into the kitchen and pours me a cup of coffee from the pot he just made. I always tell him he makes the best coffee west of the Mississippi. He comes back into the living room, hands me my coffee, settles himself in his recliner and blanket, and reaches for his glass of Jim Beam. He takes a drink, puts it back down, looks at me and says, "Let me tell ya a little story."

I sit down in the 90-year-old overstuffed chair that belonged to his mom, put my feet up on its footstool, run my hand over the textured material on its overstuffed arm that Diane chose to use to recover – a light beige background sprinkled with green leaves, red, yellow and lilac roses – faded, but still beautiful. I'm ready to hear Bobby's story, though now I'm starting to doubt my asking. But Bobby's ready to start and I don't want to be rude. He takes another drink of Jim Beam, coughs into the crook of his arm to clear his throat and begins.

"One Saturday night, Floyd, me an' ol' one-eyed Bill went to a dance at one of the local bars. Ol' one-eyed Bill was a helluva bull rider in his day 'til that freakin' #18 gored 'im in the eye. Turned that eye milk-white blind."

"Oh, my God, Bobby. That's awful. Did they take that bull out of the competition?"

"No! He was a good buckin' bull."

"What was his name?"

"They didn't give bulls names back then. They called 'em by the numbers branded on their hip after they started buckin'. Number 18 was branded #18 because he was the 18th bull branded in Cotton's herd."

"So, it doesn't matter if a bull is dangerous? They just let them stay in the competition?"

"No, every so often ya get a rank one. Number 18 wasn't rank, he bucked with his head up. Just an accident when ol' one-eye Bill got 'is head down over 'im jest as he threw 'is head up an' 'is horn jabbed 'im in the eye. On the other hand, one a' today's bulls is rank, lookin' to hurt ya. He's so stout an' big, riders refuse ta git on 'im. When he hits the groun' an' the rider gits over his head, he throws his head up on purpose an' knocks ya in the face, knocks ya out plumb cold."

"Bobby, why in the world would anyone want to ride a bull?"

"Money, darlin' an' not much sense, I guess, but let me git back to my story." Bobby reaches over, lifts his glass to take a few swallows of Jim Beam, licks his lips, likes the taste, puts his glass back down and begins again.

"So, we was havin' a good time, drinkin' an' dancin' when this young kid comes walkin' through the door. Ya could see right off the kid was trouble, swaggerin' aroun' the room showin' off polished high-heeled boots, big, fake silver-lookin' rodeo belt buckle, checkin' people over with a nasty, smarmy, cocky smile on his face an' zeros in on ol' Bill dancin' with a gal.

"He sashays himself across the dance floor an' jabs ol' Bill with his shoulder. Bill asks the kid what he was doin'. The kid got in his face an' smartmouthed he was watchin' an ol' one-eyed man tryin' to dance with a lady. Bill tol' 'im ta watch somebody else. The kid got in Bill's face again a' tol' 'im 'make me.' Bill stopped dancin', walked the lady back to her table with the kid followin'. He tol' the kid if he wanted to start trouble to take it outside.

"Things happened real fast. The kid stomped on Bill's foot, hit 'im with a fist full a' rolled up quarters that knocked 'im down, started to kick 'im in the ribs when Floyd jumped up, grabbed 'im hard, then I jumped up an' grabbed Floyd. Floyd's a toughie. He likes ta fight – ta hurt. Once he starts, he don' wanna stop. Floyd's got his arms locked aroun' the kid, I got my arms locked aroun' Floyd an' I puts my mouth against his ear. I tol' 'im we better git outta there before they call the cops. I tol' 'im to take the kid outside, throw 'im in the back seat of the pickup.

"We drove to a spot we know'd an' strung that no-good, smart-mouthed coward up by his wrists on a tree branch, just enough to where he could stand on his tiptoes. We tol' im we'd be back in a few hours. By the time we got back, the kid was just about fainted. We cut 'em down, tol 'im never to bother Bill again unless he wanted more 'a the same. Heard later the kid could hardly use his shoulders or arms for a' couple a' weeks. He had it comin' to' im, ol' one-eyed Bill was no match for the kid. If we'd a' had a bull handy, we would'a tied that coward kid on 'im. Let 'im try sittin' on a rank buckin' bull for eight seconds. Let 'im see how tough he is when he gits throwed, gits his head drove in the ground, an' his teeth rattled loose."

Bobby's knuckles are white around his Jim Beam glass. "Now I'm not shore that's what happened to yer attorney, but I betcha dollars to dough-nuts Chub scared him off one way or 'nother so he never bothered ya or yer family again."

"Oh, Bobby, do you think so? Oh, how I hope so! I've always been afraid that he might have done something worse and if he got caught he would be in a lot of trouble, maybe even you and Floyd, maybe even me."

"No darlin', no chance a' that, Chub warn't no dummy. He don' wan' no trouble fer himself er any of us."

"Oh, how I hope you're right. I blame myself. I brought Chub, you and Floyd into my troubles. If anything had happened to the three of you, I'd never forgive myself. Why, oh, why did that all happen? I can't understand the reason for any of it."

"There's a lotta things ya can't figger out a reason fer, darlin'. Ya never git ta understan' everythin' in life so if yer smart, ya decide not ta let the bad stuff keep ya on a bad trail and ya chose a happy trail to ride, enjoyin' yer life an' jest doin' yer best every day."

Of course, Bobby's right and what he says is true. I know I'll never under-stand or figure out everything in this life, but for some reason I decide to let things haunt me – not always, but every so often. Tonight, I've decided to let Bobby's story upset me. My stomach feels queasy, my head pounds, my coffee's cold and my mouth is as dry as though I've been lost in the desert. I want to do something, but I don't know what to do. I settle for taking my cold coffee into the kitchen to warm it in the microwave. Why are the numbers on the microwave's front panel moving, upside down? I close my eyes, blink to make them stop.

Now I don't know which number to push. I just stand there staring.

Bobby's come into the kitchen with his empty Jim Beam glass. "Whatcha doin', darlin'?"

"Warming my coffee."

"Ya gotta put the cup in first. Better let me help ya so's ya don't burn yerself. I shouldn't a tol' ya that story or anythin' else. I don' wantcha' thinkin' Floyd an' me are bad guys, but we jest can't do nothin' when we see bullies poundin' on helpless people, kids, animals or you."

He pours more Jim Beam in his glass, turns, walks back into the living room. The house is chilly. He pulls his electric blanket over his lap up onto his chest. His big fingers feel through the folds to find the control button and push "on." He's warm and we're quiet, having nothing to say.

Now I'm starting to feel cold. I get my sweater from the bedroom and come back into the living room. A New Year is minutes away. The church bell across the street begins to chime.

"Look Bobby, listen, they're singing 'Auld Lang Syne.' Let's go over to the window."

Bobby takes his blanket off, gets up and joins me at the window to listen and watch the Samoan congregation, big, joyous people, colorfully dressed walk out of the church onto the front lawn and form a circle. As they sing, they walk to the center of the lawn holding hands, and then turn under their arms to end up facing outwards with their hands still joined. They start to sing verses I've never heard before:

"We two have paddled in the stream
from morning sun 'til dine,
but seas between us broad have roared since auld lang syne.
We two have run around the slopes and picked the daisies fine,
and wandered many a weary foot since auld lang syne.
So here's a hand, my trusty friend
And give a hand to thine,
And we'll take a right good will draught for auld lang syne."

We two, Bobby and me, have been trusty friends riding around mountain slopes together, even having seas between us. I take his hand. We squeeze our hands together. He leans down, gives my cheek a kiss. My tears wet his lips, trusty friends, sharing violence and struggle, making deep ties holding us together now after so many years.

Bobby's back in his recliner, eyes closed, quiet. He says he doesn't show emotion and he doesn't in the usual way, but I've learned over the years to read the little white throbbing pulse at his temples, the slant of his big shoulders and the little pulse along his jaw line I see beating.

"Bobby, if you could go back in your life, would you change anything?"

"Nope, not a thing. I ain't got no regrets. I did what I wanted ta, enjoyed it an' intend ta enjoy the rest 'a my life. What abou' cha?"

"Oh, Bobby, I'm not like you. I hang on to the bad times, regrets, guilt, shame. I punish myself by staying filled with so much guilt some days I don't want to go on living. I try to come to some peace by thinking that maybe the bad times aren't meant to be changed, that for some inexplicable reason they're necessary to bring about the good, like the song says, 'You can't have one without the other.' Sometimes, I think I would have been better off if the attorney had killed me that day. I shouldn't have been born. I'm a Depression baby; nobody deliberately wanted a baby in those days. I was a mistake. I've always been a mistake. Everything I've ever tried to do has turned out wrong. I've tried to make sense out of it, but I can't."

"Darlin', no use tryin' to make sense outta stuff that ain't got no sense. Why d'ya wanna take the blame fer everything, 'specially fer what the attorney did to ya? Seems ta me ya ain't ta blame; seems ta me the attorney's the one to blame fer that. Yer actin' like ya was in court in front a' judge and jury an' ya wan 'em ta give ya a life sentence over somethin' ya couldn' help. Chub helped ya git rid a' that bad stuff, but seems like ya decided to hang on ta' other leftover bad stuff an' put that bad stuff 'roun' yer neck like a heavy rock necklace.

"Maybe someday, ya'll take it off, maybe not, but yer not thinkin' straight now, Darlin'. Ya only got todays and tomorrows. Yesterdays are gone; ya can't never get 'em back an' fix 'em, but yer tryin' ta live in yesterdays, keep tryin' ta fix 'em, an' ya can't. They're gone forever. All ya got is today an' if yer lucky, a tomorra'. Ain't that enuf for ya?"

"You're right, Bobby, you're right. I'm wearing myself out trying to fix the past, the 'unfixable,' but that's who I am. If I stop, take off the rocks I've put around my neck, who will I find? I'm afraid to find out who I really am."

Bobby gets up from his recliner, walks over to me, and gives me a big hug and kiss on the cheek.

"Let me tell ya who ya'll find when ya take the rock necklace off; ya'll find a beautiful woman, with a beautiful kind heart and soul."

"Oh, Bobby, thank you. I'm not sure that's true, but it's good to hear it and I'll try. I'll try to do as you do, leave the past alone, stop trying to change it, just live and enjoy the day I have and my tomorrows."

"Darlin', I couldn't be happier to hear ya say that an' I know all those ya love are cheerin' up in heaven right now. All they ever been waitin' fer is fer ya to drop the ugly stuff from yesterday an' enjoy the life ya got today so's they can enjoy the life they got up there. I know it ain't easy. It's not easy fer nobody, but ya can do it if ya want to. Holdin' on is hard, but lettin' go is a damn side harder. 'Member when Chub was in the hospital dyin' an' we all was there, you, Diane, an' yer friend, Brian?

"Yes."

"I tol' Chub I'd look out for ya so he could let loose an' let go."

"I remember, Bobby." Tears cloud my eyes.

"Let's see, that was 'bout 35 years ago. That was a promise I made ta Chub an' I been lookin' out fer ya ever since. Ya did good findin' a good husband an' a good partner an' I did good findin' a good wife an' a good partner, but we're alone now an' we been ridin' the trail alone the past 12 years. Might be time ta' think 'bout teamin' up. Ya don' need to go the rest a' the trail alone, less ya wanna. Jest tell me an' I won't bother ya agin."

"Oh, Bobby." The tears clouding my eyes break through, stream over my cheeks, into my ears and mouth. Bobby gets out of his recliner, comes to me, takes my hands, pulls me into the circle of his arms; our bodies press close, our eyes close each of us thinking separate thoughts. The feel of his arms around me make me feel as though I've been lost and searching and finally found my way home.

"I love you, Bobby, but I don't know."

"I know, Darlin', jest think about it. Like the song says, 'If it takes forever, I'll wait fer ya.'"

Pictures of Li'l Darlin's World

Sandy Stacey 3 years old (1937)

Aunt Gen Fogelsong and Mama (1941)

Aunt Gen and the Fogelsong brothers- Michael,
Harry John, Erny, Bob, Ed, Bill (1956)

Cowboy Bobby pick-up man for bronc rider Bill (1966)

Cowboy Bobby riding a bull (1954)

Cowboy Bobby and Floyd at rodeo (1972)

Li'l Darlin' and Cowboy Bobby at Octoberfest (2012)

Lake Dorothy in Eastern High Sierras,10,350 ft.(1978)

Poco near the Calcite Queen mouth, 10,000 ft. (1978)

Son Steve and wife Judy (1998)

Daughter Kim and husband John (2018)

Daughter Lori